STRANDED

STRANDED

A white-knuckle adventure above and below the sea

A novel

BEVERLEY SCHERBERGER

Publisher's Cataloging-In-Publication Data
(Prepared by The Donohue Group, Inc.)

Names: Scherberger, Beverley.
Title: Stranded : a white-knuckle adventure above and below the sea : a novel / Beverley Scherberger.
Description: Second edition. | [Sedona, Arizona] : [Beverley Scherberger], [2017]
Identifiers: ISBN 978-0-9990543-0-7 | ISBN 0-9990543-0-9
Subjects: LCSH: Scuba divers--Fiction. | Castaways--Fiction. | Shipwreck survival--Fiction. | Island animals--Fiction. | Man-woman relationships--Fiction. | LCGFT: Thrillers (Fiction) | Action and adventure fiction.
Classification: LCC PS3619.C44 S77 2017 | DDC 813/.6--dc23

Printed in the United States of America

ACKNOWLEDGMENTS

First and foremost, I want to say a warm "Thank you!" to the Cotacachi Writers Club. The members have been a great source of motivation and support. Our brainstorming sessions never failed to spark a new idea; their suggestions and comments sent me home newly-inspired.

My writer friends Carol Buhler and Don Robertson, both with published books of their own, pushed me in the right direction and many times I benefitted greatly from their wisdom, experience, and expertise. Carol spent many hours showing me the ropes and I hope someday I can pay it forward to another newbie needing help.

A sincere thank you also goes to my sister Judy and my friends and co-workers who, over the years, have urged me to write a book. Their support has been invaluable – as was their eager anticipation of the final product. You are too numerous to mention by name.

Damonza seemed to look into my imagination and brought my vision for the cover to life. Although we're told from the time we're young children not to judge a book by its cover, the jacket images are crucial components of getting the novel off the shelf and into the readers' hands.

It's one person's vision that begins the tale, but it takes an entire team to tell the whole story. My heartfelt thanks goes to everyone who played a part in making *STRANDED* a reality.

Chapter 1

Lissy

My dive buddy and I finned head-first toward the bottom of the sea. I had visited Cozumel, Mexico, several times before and thoroughly enjoyed the drift dives common in this area. We didn't have to monitor the current, navigate back to the boat, or watch for an exit point. Jumping into the water and drifting with the flow allowed us to simply "be" and relax into the whole dive experience.

I knew the captain would observe our bubbles and follow along in the current, ready to motor over and pick us up when we surfaced. He would also be alert and nearby in case of an emergency. It couldn't get any easier.

Of course, I'd heard horror stories of people being left behind following a drift dive, but couldn't imagine how that could easily happen. If there were fourteen divers to begin with the captain just had to count bodies before heading back to shore. Certain that our captain and crew were competent enough to ensure that everyone was present and accounted for, I turned my attention to my new dive partner.

We had met the previous day. Following the morning dives, our group had mingled with the locals at a popular lunch bar. With plenty of tequila and tacos for everyone, we'd made new Mexican friends. We were on vacation! It was the perfect time to let loose.

Across the bar, I noticed a tall, attractive guy staring in my direction. Before making a fool of myself, I turned to my right and glanced around to be sure he wasn't making eyes at someone behind me. *Nope, nobody looking his way.* When I turned back, prepared to practice my rusty flirting skills, there was only an empty space at the bar. Not even a beer bottle to indicate he might return. *Hmpf... Missed my chance.*

A smooth voice, speaking English with a strong Mexican accent, startled me out of my pout. "Hola. You dive weeth these Americanos, no?" I raised my head to see the vision from across the bar standing at my side. Up close, he was even better-looking than I'd thought. A shock of wavy black hair fell into his eyes and as he brushed it back, I appreciated the careless look emphasized by his well-worn T-shirt and snug-fitting jeans. Soft curls brushed his shoulders and he gave his head a sexy toss to throw it off his face. Broad shoulders, olive skin, a square, masculine jaw, and perfect white teeth completed the package. His intimate smile, coupled with intense dark eyes that bored into mine, made me blush. He stood so close his left leg brushed the naked skin of my thigh. I wished I hadn't worn shorts.

"Yes, I'm with the group." Anxious to keep the conversation going, I asked, "Are you? A diver?"

"Sí, I dive weeth mi padre for many years, then mis amigos. I know many very good places to go. Places not for tourists. You would go there weeth me?" I looked up into his bottomless dark eyes and found myself unwilling to say no. But I couldn't just go off with a total stranger. My mind searched frantically for an acceptable way to spend time with this Latin hunk.

I had an idea. "Why don't you dive with our group tomorrow? Maybe the captain would let you select the site and you can show us some of your favorite spots." I smiled back, hoping he'd say yes.

"What ees your boat?" When I told him the name of the dive operation and that our captain's name was Carlos, he nodded. "Sí, es mi amigo. I speak to heem and arrange for special dive weeth your group tomorrow. You weel like thees beauteeful place."

Putting his empty bottle on the bar, he said, "I am Rodrigo. You call me Rigo. And what are you called, beauteeful American chica?"

Again, I blushed. "My name is Alyssa, but my friends call me Lissy."

"I like Leesa more better. That I weel call you. Hasta mañana, Leesa!" I could feel the heat in my face as he walked away, the tight jeans hugging the curve of his ass.

"Oh, my God, Lissy! Who was *that*?" Two of the girls from the dive group descended on me with a barrage of questions. "How did you meet him?" "What's his name?" "Does he have any gorgeous friends?" I explained that he was going to talk to Captain Carlos and see if he could dive with us in the morning. I was hoping to see the beautiful places Rigo had told me about, not to mention the beautiful Rigo himself.

And sure enough, the next morning, he was on the dock talking animatedly with Captain Carlos. The two men pointed seaward and nodded, evidently in agreement. The butterflies in my stomach threatened to come right up my throat as Rigo glanced in my direction and smiled. I nearly melted into a puddle there on the dock, but my friend Joanne grabbed my elbow and kept us both moving.

"Hola, Leesa! Buenos días! We weel dive on a beauteeful place. You weel theenk eet ees perfect." In true Latin fashion, he kissed me on both cheeks, causing my face to flush again. I introduced him to Joanne and he charmed her immediately. "You weel be Cho, pretty amiga of Leesa."

The crew efficiently loaded the scuba tanks onto the boat. Our fourteen divers arrived in various small clusters and eagerly boarded, stowing personal gear under the bench seats. As the boat motored slowly away from the dock, I introduced Rigo to my friends and told them about the non-touristy dive site.

Captain Carlos came up on deck and asked for our attention. "Good morning, divers! Today, thanks to Rigo, you will dive on a very beautiful reef. It's much more secluded and farther away than we usually go – almost two hours – so get comfortable. It's not visited by the dive operations in Cozumel because of the distance so it's pristine." We all grinned and applauded our new friend. "Yay, Rigo!" "We'll buy you all the beer you can drink tonight!"

The captain continued. "You'll have to watch your depth in this location. The bottom slopes to a drop-off that is way too deep for sport diving – over three hundred feet – and the current can be tricky. Try not to get separated from the group. You might see whales or sharks so be sure to take your cameras." We cheered, thrilled about a new adventure.

Everyone chatted enthusiastically for the first hour. Later, lulled by the heat of the sun and the drone of the boat's motor, some napped. At last, Captain Carlos cut the engine and Rigo announced, "We are here! The perfect place for to dive!" We cheered and began donning our gear. When everyone was ready, the captain motioned for us to enter the water. "Please, be careful, watch your depth, and when you surface, I'll come pick you up."

Although I'd noticed a storm brewing in the distance and the dark clouds on the horizon had become even more ominous during the lengthy ride, the sun shone brightly on us as we rolled backwards off the boat. All was calm and serene underwater.

As Rigo and I cruised downward, we saw the others descending around us. The group leveled off above the bottom at a depth of sixty feet and it quickly became apparent that Captain Carlos was right about the tricky current. We zoomed along, alert for humongous rocks jutting up from the sea floor. Many were as large as small houses, but thankfully, the visibility was good so we could avoid them by angling left or right. At this depth, the water filtered out color, leaving the scene various shades of blue-grey. Darker shadows hid entrances to caverns and swim-through arches created by overlapping rocks. Boulders of all sizes and shapes dotted the floor; stands of spiky Elkhorn Coral decorated the areas in between. As we zoomed over the seascape, the rocky floor gave way to a coral reef punctuated by massive rock formations.

The reef was, indeed, pristine and beautiful. I saw no broken coral or dead white branches. Everything was healthy with a wide variety of marine life. Many different types of sponges and coral provided homes for a plethora of fish, but we were moving so quickly it was impossible to take photos. Afraid of slamming into a boulder if I took my eyes off the path ahead, I held the pricey camera close to my body.

Then, suddenly, it seemed as though a giant hand pushed me toward the bottom. The monster current drove us helplessly downward and I could see the other divers reacting as I did, instinctively and futilely kicking upward. We plunged ever deeper, the sea floor ahead sloping sharply into the dark blue abyss.

Frantic, I grabbed Rigo's hand and he pulled me to his side, motioning toward a huge boulder jutting into our path some distance ahead. Instead of angling to go around it, we turned in the water to meet it feet first. I prayed the current would hold us against the rock, preventing further descent. We desperately needed time to think, to plan.

We struck the hard surface and I felt the jolt throughout my entire body, but my knees cushioned the blow. Held there by the same huge hand that had previously been shoving us downward, I watched my friends zoom past and disappear from view. Horrified, I knew I might never see them again.

Clinging to the rock, I knew we had to find a way out of the down-current. The compressed air in our tanks would cause nitrogen narcosis beyond a depth of 130 feet. Symptoms such as feelings of euphoria, impaired decision-making, and diminished motor skills could cause us to disregard the danger and make incorrect choices concerning our safety. Continuing to descend would certainly be fatal.

Rigo and I tried to slow our breathing. We didn't want to run low on air and compound our serious situation. After a short time, using hand signals, he motioned that we should swim to our left. In the distance was another rocky upthrust we could use for refuge. I suddenly understood. If we could swim *across* the current, we might be able to get out of the strongest downward flow and ascend to a safer depth.

My gauge showed eighty-five feet. I pantomimed crawling up the rock, relieved to see Rigo nod in comprehension. We hugged the rocky slope and slowly made our way fifteen feet up the boulder like a couple of oddly-attired and very awkward mountain climbers. Thankfully, the rock wasn't sharp-edged or covered with coral that would cut through our thin dive gloves and shred the knees of our Lycra wetskins. Rough and slightly porous, the surface contained nooks and niches for finger holds and the rock sloped enough that we had no trouble shimmying upward. Our fins prevented us from using our toes to gain further purchase, but the current helped hold us in place.

When the rock narrowed, we stopped and took each other's hand. Our eyes met and we nodded, simultaneously launching ourselves off, kicking hard to the left. We flew through the water and for a while I thought we were going to soar past the next big boulder, but it suddenly loomed large in front of us. We turned and met it feet-first. My gauge read ninety feet.

We rested briefly, shimmied twenty feet to the uppermost portion, and again hurled ourselves into the current. When we finally thudded into the next large rock, my gauge showed ninety-five feet. I looked at my watch to see how long we'd been in the water and found it had been the longest eighteen minutes of my life. Concerned about our depth and bottom time, I checked the laminated NAUI dive chart I wore clipped to my BC. According to the tables, we needed to begin ascending soon or we could end up with the bends. This, too, could be fatal.

We had no choice but to keep moving. This peak was taller than the others and we crawled up to seventy feet before once more taking flight. I thought the flow seemed less powerful and hoped it wasn't just wishful thinking, but when my feet hit the next rock, the impact was much less forceful. I knew we'd reached the outer edge of the current. Almost afraid to check the time, I said a short prayer before raising my wrist.

We'd been underwater for a total of twenty-two minutes and had yet to begin our ascent. The NAUI tables indicated we must hang at fifteen feet for five minutes to offgas enough nitrogen to surface safely. *Would we have enough air?* I reached for Rigo's gauge – only 150psi. Mine read 200. We would normally finish with no less than 500psi in each tank, leaving enough air for the ascent. The good news was that as we ascended, the air would expand. But we needed to start up immediately.

We crept to the pinnacle and took off at a depth of sixty feet. I felt a distinct difference in the force of the down-current and we actually made some slight upward progress. The current lessened more and more as we drifted. No more boulders loomed in front of us and I checked my gauge to find we had ascended to fifty feet. Finally we were heading in the right direction. I pointed upward.

Turning vertical in the water, still holding hands, we worked our way toward the surface. At thirty feet, I checked the time – twenty-five total minutes. I slowed our ascent and held up my wrist. Rigo nodded to indicate he knew we'd have to decompress.

At the appointed depth, we stopped and faced each other. The water seemed choppy and we had difficulty maintaining the fifteen foot depth but it was imperative that we offgas nitrogen before surfacing. Anxious to board the boat, I'd even welcome a bout of seasickness right now. I just wanted *out* of the water.

We tried to relax and breathe normally although we'd both used up precious air fighting the current and I knew Rigo's tank would soon be empty. Time seemed to stop as I watched the second hand creep slowly around the dial. With one full minute remaining, Rigo reached for my octopus – a secondary regulator that can be used to buddy breathe. His tank was empty. Afraid to look and see how much air was in mine, I figured it was irrelevant, anyway. We'd breathe this tank down to nothing and then surface to deal with the consequences.

In short order, we sucked the last bit of air from the tank and kicked slowly upward. As we pulled the regulators out of our mouths and gulped for air, we got another shock. Directly overhead ugly storm clouds hung low and threatening. Wind howled, waves tossed us high in the air and then dunked us in the trough, and rain poured down in sheets. Thunder boomed across the water and lightning flashed repeatedly against the black sky. And the boat was nowhere to be seen.

Shouting to be heard over the tumultuous storm, I yelled, "Where's the boat? He didn't *leave* us here, did he?" Turning in a frantic 360-degree circle, I searched in vain for the vessel. The only time I had any view at all was when the waves carried us to the crest, right before dropping us back into the trough, and all I saw in every direction was miles and miles of rough water.

Rigo cursed Captain Carlos then in his next breath offered a plausible excuse for his absence. "He could not see our bubbles een thees water. Had to save hees boat – thees storm ees un diablo." He held onto my BC and showed me where to hold his; we *had* to stay together. I wondered what had happened to my friends. *Did they survive the down-current or had it swept them to their deaths? Were they frantically searching for the boat at the surface, scared and alone, as we were?*

I suddenly had another frightening thought and yelled over the storm's noise. "Rigo, what do we do about sharks? How do we protect ourselves?" I shuddered at the idea of teeth biting into my legs from below, dragging me under.

His shouted reply surprised me but brought a small measure of comfort. "When beeg storms come, sharks go deep to be safe. There ees no danger." He looked up at the black sky and added, "Not from them."

A sudden strong wave lifted us high and when we dropped again, our tanks crashed into each other. The back of my head slammed hard against the metal valve and I hoped I wasn't bleeding. Even with Rigo's assurance that sharks dove deep during storms, I didn't want to bloody the water. Rubbing the back of my head, I said, "Rigo, let's release our tanks. They're useless now and I just hit my head on the valve." He nodded and I turned in the water. The waves heaved us to and fro and he had trouble undoing the latch securing the tank to my BC. Meanwhile, I held onto him with my left hand and used my right to release the connecting hose in front. We pushed the steel tank away from us, watching it slowly sink and disappear. Then he turned his back to me and I fought to undo his.

When both tanks had dropped out of sight, I reached for my weight belt. Then, I had another idea. I pulled myself close to Rigo and yelled into his ear. "Why don't we free our weights but use the belts to lash ourselves together? Then we won't get separated."

I couldn't believe he could flirt at a time like this, but his reply did make me smile. "You are smart, too, pretty chica. Es un buen idea."

Since we had dumped our tanks, we blew into the manual inflation tube – similar to blowing up a balloon – to inflate our BCs. We wanted to be as buoyant as possible. Then, one at a time, we removed our weights from the belts. The lead sank quickly. I buckled my belt back around my waist, but lengthened it so it was no longer snug. Rigo lengthened his and fed it through mine. In this way, after he'd refastened his belt, we were securely attached without having to physically hold onto each other.

I didn't relish spending much time being tossed about like flotsam on an angry sea, but there was nothing more we could do. Nothing except pray.

Chapter 2

Joanne

I saw Lissy and Rigo enter the water, followed by several others of our group. I was suited up but my dive knife had disappeared and I was loath to go without it, so four of us spent a few minutes searching. Tom gleefully announced, "Found it!" as he pulled it from under one of the bench seats. I buckled it securely to my leg.

Tom, Robbie, Sarah, and I rolled backwards off the boat. Finning toward the bottom, I saw the rest of the troupe ahead and relaxed. Captain Carlos's warning to not get separated from the group had been playing a loop in my head. We stayed close, soaring over the bottom and playing "airplane." Arms outstretched, we flew like small single-engine planes, tilting and turning to avoid the humongous rocks.

Suddenly, the current switched from fun and exhilarating to terrifyingly uncontrollable. Forced downward, I saw the bottom slope sharply away into the depths. We kicked upward to no avail, grabbing hands to stay together. The terror on their faces mirrored my own.

Up ahead, I saw Lissy and Rigo turn to meet a huge pillar feet-first and remain plastered to the rock face. I pointed and the others nodded. We spotted the next enormous boulder and aimed our flight so it was directly in our path. Turning in the water, we thudded hard against the rock, held in place by the forceful current. Hugging the rough surface, we tried to slow our breathing and control the panic.

I'd been diving for several years but had never encountered anything like this. We had to maintain control and think this through or we'd never survive. I quickly took stock of my buddies' strengths and weaknesses. Except for Sarah, we often dove together as a group so I knew them rather well.

Past middle-age, Tom was a veteran diver and very fit and strong; he was our best asset. About six feet tall, he sported broad shoulders and a severe buzz-style to his gun-metal grey hair. A widower, his great personality, quick wit, great smile, kind-heartedness, and wonderful sense of humor often hid behind his military bearing. Retired from the Navy, Tom was well-acquainted with anything to do with the sea and dove as often as possible. I had every confidence he could help save us. But we all had to do our part.

Robbie was older, a retired college professor. He was a less experienced diver but very competent and level-headed, more nerdy than athletic. Kind and compassionate, he'd had a reputation as a demanding but fair teacher and his students had always seemed to enjoy his classes. His intelligence and self-control would also be an advantage. Tall and lean, his wild head of wavy white hair gave him a "nutty professor" look but he had a big heart and I knew he loved the outdoors. He'd only discovered a passion for diving in the last year or so, but had studiously attacked the books and took the underwater exams very seriously. What he lacked in experience, he made up for in book-smarts. Another asset.

Sarah was the least experienced of our group. About thirty-five, she was a slim brunette, her long, dark hair whipping in the current like a flag in a high wind. Relatively new to the sport, she had signed up for this trip as a spontaneous gesture to her commitment to become a more proficient diver. Not at all equipped to handle this type of situation, terror showed plainly in her huge eyes. Bubbles billowed from her regulator. She had to calm down and breathe slower or she'd run out of air far too quickly. I vowed to do my best to help her through this.

Sarah crushed my hand in a vise-like grip. I turned my head to meet her eyes and pointed to her regulator, then fluttered my fingers quickly upward, mimicking her bubbles. Letting the current hold me against the rock, I forced my fingers out of her grasp. I patted my chest to indicate breathing, and then put my arms at my sides, hands waist high. I slowly pushed my palms toward the sea floor, much as I'd seen my yoga instructor do when she wanted us to exhale slowly. I pointed to Sarah to do the same. She nodded. We repeated this movement several times until her eyes lost that crazed, panicky look and the amount of bubbles flowing from her regulator lessened.

I made a circle with the thumb and first finger of my right hand, the universal scuba sign meaning "Are you okay?" She nodded and repeated the okay signal back to me. I turned to Tom and motioned that we should swim to the next big rock.

But instead of pushing off, he gestured upward and began crawling up the rock face. When the peak became too narrow for four of us abreast he stopped and pointed toward the next boulder. I understood that he wanted us to lose some depth before diving back into the current.

Still holding hands, we launched off the pinnacle, kicking as hard as we could to the left. In a short time, we landed on the next rock, working our way *across* the current to escape the worst of the down-flow.

When I saw Tom check his watch and examine his NAUI tables, I knew we might also have another problem. We had to keep moving to try and reach the surface as soon as possible, minimizing our bottom time. He looked up and met my gaze. I could see the worry in his eyes.

We repeated the climb-and-flight-to-the-next-rock routine several times and finally the current lessened. I hoped we'd soon find Lissy and Rigo waiting on the boat. This was one dive I was anxious to end.

As we clung to the last pillar before ascending, Tom showed us his NAUI tables. He pointed out the box that showed we needed to hang at fifteen feet for five minutes to offgas nitrogen before surfacing. We all reached for our gauges: 150psi; 120psi; 100psi; and 60psi. Sarah had, indeed, used up a lot of air in her initial panic.

We hurled ourselves into the much-diminished current and Tom led us upward at a safe rate. As we ascended, I could sense Sarah's building terror – now out of the monster current she was frantic to reach the surface. I held her hand tightly, afraid she'd bolt. Rising faster than her exhaled air bubbles could cause the bends and I wanted to protect her.

At the prescribed fifteen feet, Tom stopped. I gripped both of Sarah's hands and turned to face her. I could see the raw panic in her eyes. She looked upward and yanked one hand free, kicking desperately for the surface. Tom and Robbie both grabbed for her BC. Her flailing fist knocked my mask off and I instinctively let go of her to replace it and clear the water from around my nose. Her other fist hit Tom on the temple and momentarily dazed him. Robbie held Sarah's BC with one hand as he checked her remaining air. At that moment, bubbles stopped flowing from her regulator and her eyes grew even wider – her tank was empty. As I reached toward her with my octopus, she jerked free of Robbie's one-handed grip and bolted for the surface.

I started after her, but Tom grabbed me and vehemently shook his head no. We still had three minutes remaining to offgas and there was nothing we could do for Sarah now that she was at the surface. Nitrogen bubbles in her blood would have expanded and lodged in her system. And, inexperienced diver that she was, she had most likely held her breath during the race to the surface possibly also causing an air embolism.

Looking upward, I could see her lying face down at the surface, eyes open, immobile and tossed by the waves. She was only fifteen feet away and I couldn't help. A nurse by profession, it went against my very being to do nothing, but helping her would put myself at grave risk, too. Tears burned my eyes. *What had happened to the rest of our group? Had the sea claimed more than one life today?*

Robbie pulled his regulator from his mouth to show he was out of air. We checked our gauges and I handed my octopus to Robbie to buddy breathe. Soon, all the tanks would be empty.

The three of us faced each other, held hands, and tried to slow our breathing. It became harder and harder to suck a breath from my tank. Tom was watching, ready with his octopus when we drained the last of the air. He handed it to me for a breath, I handed it to Robbie who then handed it back to Tom. In this way, we finished off the final tank. With no other option remaining, we slowly finned to the surface, exhaling as we went. I hoped we'd off-gassed enough nitrogen to avoid the bends.

The world as we knew it when we'd entered the water earlier no longer existed. Thunder boomed, lightning flashed against the angry purple-black sky, and rain poured down in buckets. Waves carried us high and then dunked us back under water, leaving us spluttering and coughing. Sarah's body had drifted away, buffeted by the storm and the howling wind. We didn't even have a chance to say good-bye.

Terror claimed us once more. The boat was gone and we were alone on a storm-tossed sea. Again, retired Navy man Tom came to our rescue. We released our empty tanks, manually inflated our BCs, and removed the lead from our weight belts. Lashing ourselves together with the nylon belts, we took a small measure of comfort in the physical closeness. There was nothing more we could do. I closed my eyes and spoke to God. I hoped He was listening.

Chapter 3

Lissy

Although the Caribbean water had felt warm when we began the dive, my teeth chattered and the drenching rain driven by the howling wind felt like icy pinpricks on my face. I shivered. Rigo shouted, "You are cold, Leesa, no?" I opened my mouth to reply and choked on saltwater. Coughing and spluttering, I nodded.

He unhooked his weight belt and turned to face me, reconnecting the buckle to keep us together. Wrapping his arms and legs around me, he enveloped my small frame. In any other scenario, I would have objected to this physical closeness with someone I'd known such a short time, but today I huddled against him, welcoming his body heat.

I had no idea how long we bobbed and choked and cursed the wind and pelting rain, but eventually, the storm lessened in intensity. The wind slacked off, the waves lost some of their previous anger, and the thunder and lightning moved away into the distance. We watched the light show from our front row seat and I was amazed that I could appreciate its beauty after nearly drowning in the storm's fury a short time earlier.

As the water calmed, clouds parted to allow the sun to shine once more. At first it felt good and I lifted my face to the heavens. Slowly, my body warmed and soon I could feel my face beginning to heat up. The sun shining down from above and reflecting off the water would burn my fair skin quickly. Rigo had the advantage of an olive complexion and a lifetime spent outdoors in the tropics.

Then, I saw something in the distance. "Rigo, is that land? Or am I hallucinating?" Still lashed together, we turned as one so he could see.

"Sí, Leesa, eet ees land!" We whooped and hollered, hugging each other with relief. Smiling into my eyes, Rigo gently kissed me on the lips. "I want to do that since first minute I see you. Now ees good time."

I smiled and said softly, "Yes, it's a good time."

Unable to swim while buckled together, we undid the nylon belts and fastened them back around our waists. Thankful we still wore our fins, I fell into a steady rhythm beside Rigo. He matched my pace and I was relieved that he wasn't pushing me faster. I was already exhausted.

The current, now our friend, carried us quickly toward the island. Oddly, it increased in strength as we approached land and before long, we could see a kidney-shaped lagoon with a gently sloping, white sand beach, a smallish mountain rising up in the background. The island seemed to welcome us as we rode a wave up onto the sand. We lay there, thankful to be on solid ground once more.

I didn't want to move but the sun was even more intense there than on the water, reflecting off the powdery sand. Rigo helped me to my feet and we staggered into the shade of the trees that ringed the inland edge of the beach. Cool and comfortable, I stretched out on the ground. Rigo rested for a few minutes and then went exploring for fresh drinking water – and perhaps nearby people who might be able to help.

Exhausted, I fell asleep almost immediately – and awoke to bloodcurdling screams only a short while later. I shot up, totally disoriented. About fifty yards from shore, I saw three people frantically swimming toward the beach. Some distance behind them, a large dorsal fin broke the surface of the water.

I ran to the shoreline and screamed for them to hurry; the shark was quickly closing the gap. One man made it to the sand and collapsed. Another man and a woman were trying desperately to reach the beach, but were losing the race. The dorsal fin submerged and my heart sank, expecting the beast to drag one of the people under at any moment.

Suddenly, a huge shark leapt straight up out of the water directly behind the flailing couple. While it was still airborne, a second shark broke the surface, leaping toward the first with its mouth gaping wide. Razor-sharp teeth gleamed wetly in the sunlight before the monstrous mouth snapped shut mere inches from the other animal's side. Both sharks hit the water with a tremendous splash, sending an enormous wave rushing toward shore, carrying the couple far up onto the beach.

I ran toward the newcomers and realized Tom, Robbie, and my dear friend Joanne had survived the down-current, the storm, and the too-close shark attack. Relief swept over me. Knowing Sarah had been with them, I looked around and asked, "Where's Sarah? Wasn't she diving with you guys?"

Joanne burst into tears. Tom hung his head and said, "We stopped at fifteen feet to offgas and she ran out of air. Before we could stop her she bolted for the surface and the storm carried her body away. We never saw her again."

Half afraid of the answer, I asked, "Did any of you see what happened to the rest of the group? Do you know whether they survived the current?" They shook their heads no. The four of us cried, holding each other and mourning the loss of Sarah and the unknown fate of the rest of our friends. Then Joanne looked me in the eye and softly said, "Where's Rigo? He made it, didn't he?"

I nodded. "Yes. He saved my life. He's looking for fresh water." Just then, Rigo bounded out of the trees and stopped short when he saw the group. "I hear screams, Leesa. I theenk you have trouble!" He trotted over and draped his arm around my shoulder.

Smiling into his eyes, I said, "I'm fine, Rigo. You remember Tom, Robbie, and Joanne from the dive boat, don't you?"

He nodded. "Sí, I know you all. Why do you scream?"

I told him about the two huge sharks battling it out in the lagoon and he looked puzzled. "Sharks no act that way. Es strange, for sure." He shook his head. "But I glad they fight each other and not eat our friends." After staring out toward the lagoon for a long moment, he said, "Eef sharks come near, we must be careful een the water, even close to shore." A ripple of fear ran up my spine at the memory of the enormous beasts so close to the island.

We settled into the coolness of the trees and shared our survival stories. At a break in the conversation, Rigo said, "There ees water no too far. We go now?" Feeling rested and lacking containers to carry water, we forced ourselves to our feet. Crusty with dried salt, I wanted nothing more than a freshwater rinse and a salt-free drink.

Walking through the trees, sunlight dappling the path ahead, I wondered what island we'd happened upon. The jungle smelled of rich earth and dampness and vines straggled down from the thick canopy above. Every now and then, a bird call broke the silence, but for the most part, the quiet unnerved me.

Rigo hadn't seen any human inhabitants, but hadn't gone far when he'd heard the screams.

A short walk later, we came to the edge of the stream, a pretty, bubbling brook about six feet across that looked very clean and clear. Shallow water burbled over smooth rocks and wound around a bend a short distance downstream. Tom, Robbie, Joanne, and Rigo walked into the water, allowing the coolness to wash around their ankles. Joanne bent over and threw a handful of water at Robbie and the splash-fight began.

Leaving the excited giggling and splashing behind, I walked unnoticed to the bend, hoping to find a deep pool that would allow me to submerge completely. Saltwater crystals had begun to chafe my skin and make my scalp itch. *Aha!* Exactly what I was searching for: a wide pool edged with rocks and shaded by overhanging branches. With barely a pause at water's edge, I climbed onto the rocks and stepped off, sinking gratefully into the cool, deep water. I felt refreshed almost immediately.

For just a moment it seemed selfish not to call out to my friends, but I decided to keep this delightful treat all to myself for a few more minutes. I luxuriated in dunking my head and scrubbing my scalp; I rinsed my mouth and used my finger to clean my teeth and get rid of the lingering salt taste; and finally, I removed my knife, wetskin, and dive booties. I squeezed and squished them to get all the saltwater out and thought about taking my swimsuit off to do the same with it. But the way the day had gone so far, I'd get caught buck naked by my friends. Best to leave it on.

I threw the knife, wetskin, and booties onto the rocks and floated face-up in the pool. Recalling the terror of being tossed about in an unmerciful sea, I was surprised that I could be so completely relaxed in this small body of water a short while later.

A twig cracked; my friends had found me. I waited a moment for someone to call out and then raised my head at the continued silence. The rocks were empty. I turned in a circle and saw no one. But I could feel eyes on me and the fine hairs on the back of my neck stood up. Gooseflesh tightened the skin of my arms.

"Leesa!" "Lissy!" I heard my friends calling and decided it was time to share. "Over here! Around the bend!" They found me treading water in the center of the pool, a huge smile welcoming them into my new-found watering hole. But my eyes continued to scan the rocks and trees for whoever or whatever was watching.

Everyone joined me in the water and repeated the procedure of rinsing and then removing knives, wetskins, and booties. After the adrenalin-packed, exhausting, and terror-filled day, we needed the emotional release of cavorting like puppies with utter abandon. I soon forgot those few seconds of feeling "not alone" and joined in the fun.

Once we had soaked the salt away, Tom suggested we make camp while we still had plenty of daylight. "We have no supplies whatsoever, so we'll have to improvise. We need a shelter and makeshift beds. And it would be great if we could figure out how to build a fire without matches. Any ideas?"

No one spoke up but I offered to gather firewood, anyway. "If we figure out a way to build a fire, we'll need wood. I'm on it!"

Tom led us to a clearing he'd spotted on the far side. Located about a five-minute walk from the creek and north of the deep pool, it provided height above and a little distance from the stream in case of rain and flooding, but proximity to water for cooking and drinking. And bathing would be south of camp, downstream.

Tom took charge of building the shelter once he and Rigo dragged long poles to the campsite. Joanne offered to collect palm fronds for the roof and bedding and I roamed toward the beach for driftwood and kindling. Tom and Robbie began clearing the area for the shelter and arranged rocks for a potential fire pit. We were nothing if not optimistic.

Soon we had piles of long poles, fronds, firewood, and rocks. At Tom's direction, everyone set about creating a workable campsite. The guys constructed a sloping thatched roof between some trees that would suffice for the night. Tomorrow they would add three sides to make it more weather-proof.

Using flat rocks and dive knives, we dug shallow, people-sized depressions in the ground and then added a thick layer of palm fronds over the soft earth for cushiony beds. As tired as we were, I figured solid rock would feel like heaven, but, hey, I wasn't going to complain about palm fronds! All five of us would share the shelter since there was safety in numbers and we had no idea if we were actually alone on the island. That thought brought to mind my earlier uneasiness, but I didn't want to scare everyone needlessly.

We arranged rocks and large logs around the fire pit for seating and the guys dug a latrine between the trees a short distance away. We didn't want the loo too close to camp, but neither did we want to have to go too far, alone, to take care of business.

Once the work was completed, we sat around the fireless pit. My stomach growled loudly and I wished for a blazing bonfire, burgers, and S'mores – my hunger fed my imagination and made my mouth water. We'd eaten nothing since a light, pre-dive breakfast early this morning and we had absolutely nothing to eat now. It was nearing sunset and with darkness approaching, our plight seemed even more desperate. The only illumination throughout the next eight hours would be moonlight – a pathetic substitute for a blazing fire or powerful flashlight. Rigo felt me slide closer to him on the log and put his arm around my shoulder. "Eet will be okay, Leesa. Eet ees time of full moon. There ees much light tonight. You no worry."

Joanne moaned, "I'm *so* hungry – I may just gnaw on one of these tree branches!"

At that, Rigo jumped up and said, "I come back!" He ran off into the trees, leaving us all wondering what he was up to. In only a few minutes he returned, carrying three large coconuts. After our initial excitement, we realized we had no way to crack the shells open. It would've been funny – five adults sitting and staring at three coconuts as though they would break into a song and dance – if we weren't so desperately hungry.

Tom said, "I have an idea!" and ran over to the pile of scuba equipment we had laid out to dry. BCs, wetskins, masks, snorkels, fins – and dive knives. He selected the biggest and most wicked-looking knife and then scanned the area for a good-sized rock. When he found one he liked, he placed a coconut and the knife on a flat rock and turned to look at the group. "Who wants to hold the knife and the coconut for me?"

I realized he wanted someone to hold the knife point to the coconut while he hammered on the handle with the rock. *Hmmm… Sounds risky.* Rigo volunteered. After positioning the knife on the eye of the shell, we held our breath as Tom brought the rock down. They perfected the positioning of both the knife and the coconut and tried it again. And again. The point finally penetrated the eye far enough that a few drops of coconut water leaked out.

I could see Rigo pondering the situation. Using another, rounder rock, he laid the fruit on its side and pounded all around the center line of the coconut until we heard it crack. Water gushed out. "Yay!" A chorus of shouts praised the guys for their efforts.

Tom handed the two halves to Robbie who pried the meat out of the shell with another knife. Joanne and I crowded round to get a piece of the flavorful meat as the guys went to work on the second coconut. Soon, everyone had eaten a few pieces and the sharp edge of hunger faded away. Rigo cautioned us not to eat too much because raw coconut could cause diarrhea, especially on an empty stomach. Not a pleasant thought, under the circumstances. We voted to save the third one for morning.

Once we'd taken the edge off our hunger, sleep was next on the list. Tom and Robbie settled near the front of our crude shelter. Rigo claimed a spot to my left and Joanne lay down to my right. In less than a minute, Tom and Robbie snored softly. But I was still wondering who or what had been watching us at the pool earlier and wasn't anxious to fall asleep. However, the day's extreme exertion and emotional stress had taken their toll. I'd no sooner placed my head on a cushy pile of palm fronds than my eyes closed and I fell into a deep and dreamless sleep.

Chapter 4

First Full Day on the Island

Lissy

Morning dawned bright and breezy with no hint of the storm that had taken such a toll the day before. Much to my amazement, I'd slept well.

Rigo and Tom had obviously attacked the third coconut and gone searching for more. Remnants of several shells lay broken on the rocks. Sections of another containing fresh coconut meat sprawled invitingly, but as hungry as I was, I wished someone had figured out how to brew a pot of coffee instead.

About that time, Joanne and Robbie strolled into camp from amongst the trees with their arms laden with fruit. "Delicious mangos and papayas for everyone!" Joanne sang out, the sticky juice around her mouth evidence that she hadn't waited. That sounded much more appetizing than another coconut and I eagerly reached for a juicy fruit.

Mangos were on my list of favorites and I quickly devoured one and reached for a second. "You didn't find a coffee stand out there anywhere, did you?" I could only hope. Not at my best in the morning, I growled, "I guess I'll have to learn to eat fruit for breakfast. And lunch. And dinner."

With a smile tugging at the corners of his lips and a devilish sparkle in his eye, Rigo said, "Leesa ees not happy en la mañana. You are better later, no?"

"I am better with a cup of coffee!" I instantly regretted snapping at him and smiled ruefully. "Sorry, Rigo. I'm really not a morning person and without coffee, it'll take a while for me to become my usual cheerful self. Just steer clear for a while. I think I'll go to the pool for a quick dip. Maybe that'll perk me up."

I set off alone for the swimming hole, leaving the others chatting and devouring the rest of the mangos. I wished I had something to throw on over my bathing suit – even a T-shirt would make me feel less exposed. I hated the thought of spiders falling out of the trees and snakes slithering over my bare legs. And my fair skin burned so easily, a cover-up would be extremely useful. I didn't want to wear my wetskin into the pool, figuring we'd probably go exploring later and I wanted it to be dry. Slogging around in wet clothes all day wasn't an appealing prospect, either.

When I stepped up onto the rocks at the edge of the pool, I recalled the broken twig and yesterday's anxiety. Scanning the area, I spotted nothing out of the ordinary. The tranquil pool, the soothing sound of water burbling over the rocks, and light filtering softly through the trees calmed my nerves. Determined to enjoy my morning swim, I bent to remove my dive booties so I'd have dry feet later, too, and left them sitting neatly, side-by-side, on the uppermost rock.

Diving head first into the refreshing water, I surfaced and swam briskly to the far side, then drifted into the center of the pool. Trees shadowed the ripples and a thick curtain of bright green vines hung from the lowest branches, nearly brushing the water's surface and obscuring the tall rock wall behind it. The early morning sun beat down from above, promising a hot day to come. I could feel myself beginning to relax as I floated on my back, the sun warming my face.

I heard splashing from behind the veil of vines and lifted my head to stare hard into the shadows between the folds. Curious, I drifted once again to the far side of the pool, straining to see between the viny ropes. I reached up to part the vines, hoping for a small waterfall. I imagined washing my hair or taking a cooling shower in the falls, but my hand froze in mid-air when a face appeared in the dimness, staring at me out of the dark. I blinked and the image disappeared.

Gasping with fear, my heart pounded wildly and my hands shook. I whirled and swam rapidly back to the rocks. Scrambling out of the pool, I scraped my knees and left bloody smears on the rock as I grabbed for my booties. I wanted to get back to camp as quickly as possible. But once again, my hand froze in mid-air. The booties were now at right angles to each other, one upright and one on its side, about a foot apart. I could picture how I'd left them, standing neatly, side-by-side.

"Who's there? What do you want?" I yelled into the silence. Nothing moved. No one answered. I waited another moment and sat down hard on the rock. With trembling hands, I put the booties on and pushed myself to my feet. With one last look, I jumped off the rock and darted down the trail toward camp. Something moved in the brush and rustled the overhead canopy. It was fast. And it followed me all the way home.

I burst from the trees and stopped at the fire pit, my chest heaving, pale-faced with fright. Everyone whirled as I collapsed onto a log. Rigo trotted over and sat next to me. He took my hand and asked, "Leesa, you are alright? You are una fantasma."

Before I could answer, everyone else crowded around. "Lissy, what happened? Are you okay?" Joanne echoed Rigo's concerns. Pragmatic Tom brought me some coconut water. "Here, drink this. Then tell us what happened. You look scared to death."

I took a sip and launched into the story, beginning with the snapping twig from the day before. Everyone was silent.

Tom spoke first, his voice soft, lacking recrimination. "Why didn't you say something yesterday at the pool?"

"I didn't want to scare everyone if it was nothing. I didn't see anything and only heard the crack of a twig." I hung my head. "I'm sorry. I should've told you."

Robbie was more direct with his question. "Are you sure you saw a face? A *human* face?"

"I think so. It was there and then gone. And it was in the shadows. But I *know* something or someone moved my booties!" I leaned against Rigo when he put his arms around me. And then, with a sinking heart, I whispered, "And it followed me back to camp. It knows we're here."

After a short discussion, we agreed on a few initial rules that could be modified and added to in the future:

No one goes off alone, even to the latrine

Collecting fruit, palm fronds, or firewood is done in pairs — one man, one woman

When leaving camp, you tell the others where you're going and who's going with you

If anyone sees or hears anything unusual, it is shared with the group

No one leaves camp unarmed

We moved the dive knives closer to the fire pit so they'd be convenient if needed. Tom and Rigo collected sturdy sticks of an appropriate thickness and made spears, sharpening one end of each with a knife. Heavier branches were made into clubs and kept near the pit in the daytime, to be moved into the shelter at night. We hoped we'd never need to use any of the weapons, but wanted to be prepared, just in case.

Although eager to explore the island, we placed more importance on making weapons and adding three walls to our shelter. No longer simply protection from the weather, we wanted the additional security. Working as a team, we collected poles, vines, and more palm fronds. Rigo helped Joanne and me add more fronds to the roof, reinforcing the quick thatching erected the day before. He also showed us how to lash the fronds down with vines so a strong wind couldn't blow our roof off.

Tom and Robbie dug holes for the heavier upright corner posts and piled large rocks around the base to give them more stability. They lashed cross-poles to the uprights and then tied the resulting wall to the roof with fibrous vines. It was hard going, but with everyone working together, we transformed our lean-to into a sturdy, three-walled, thatched roof hut.

I stood back to admire our handiwork. "It looks good, everybody! I just have one question: what happens if we have another bad storm? Won't the wind blow rain into the shelter?" They filed out to stand next to me as though that viewpoint would provide an answer.

"You're right," Tom said. "We will sometimes need a fourth wall. Let's build one that can be temporarily lashed onto the shelter. That way, we can use it as needed."

"Great idea, Tom!" We set about collecting more poles for the removable wall. In the process, we voted to leave a doorway opening and build a smaller section of poles that could be lashed to the wall from the inside, effectively "closing the door."

By the time the shelter was finished, the removable wall and door built and stowed between two nearby trees, and new fronds added to the beds, we were exhausted. It was mid-afternoon and all we'd had to eat was fruit and coconut for breakfast. Tom, Robbie, and Rigo offered to go fishing. Joanne and I weren't about to be left out of the adventure, so after a brief rest and more fruit, the entire group set off for the lagoon.

Following our rules, each person carried a spear and wore his dive knife buckled to his leg; the convenient sheath left hands free.

The kidney-shaped lagoon was picturesque with powdery white sand, afternoon sun reflecting off deep aquamarine water that darkened to sapphire beyond the reef, and palm trees waving lightly in the breeze. Waves lapped gently at our feet as we gazed seaward. A postcard. It would be absolutely perfect without dorsal fins breaking the surface every few minutes. Sharks seemed to patrol the area regularly, very close to shore.

Joanne and I searched for crabs at the water's edge, but, after catching a few, realized we had no way to contain them. Rigo removed his wetskin and suggested we use it as a carry-all. It was perfect and we soon had enough for dinner. The next problem would be how to cook them – I was not into sushi, in any way, shape, or form and saw a lot of fruit in my future.

The men had ventured into slightly deeper water in search of dinner-sized fish but returned shortly with bad news. "We'd never see a shark coming until it was too late. We need a different plan."

31

As we stood on the beach, thinking, I said, "Look at those big rocks over there." I pointed off to our left and Tom, Robbie, and Rigo agreed it looked like a promising fishing area. We walked around the curved end of the quiet lagoon and were shocked to find a boulder-strewn shoreline buffeted by stronger waves. No one was going into the water here.

We explored around the boulders and found pools where fish had become trapped – easy targets for the spears. We soon had plenty for dinner and as we returned to camp, I pondered our next problem. Fire.

Once back at the clearing, I collected the remains of the coconuts and began pulling the strings off the shell. A mere spark would easily be fanned into flame once the strings caught. The smaller kindling I'd collected the day before was piled next to the pit. And Tom and Robbie were deep in discussion over how to create that first spark.

Once I had an impressive pile of coconut strings, Tom futilely tried to ignite them by striking two rocks together. Meanwhile, out in the open without any trees to block the sun, Robbie arranged two rocks about eight inches apart. He piled coconut strings in between and laid his dive mask, lenses upward, on the rocks. He covered all but the lenses with palm fronds. He saw me watching and explained. "I'm so nearsighted that my dive lenses are made of glass, not plastic. The glass should magnify the sun's heat enough to ignite the strings. Keep your fingers crossed."

I smiled encouragingly and said, "I will. Sushi is *not* on my list of preferred things to eat."

Robbie and Joanne stayed at camp to keep an eye on the potential fire while the rest of us took coconut shells and walked to the stream. If we succeeded in building a fire, we'd need water for cooking and cleaning up afterward. Armed and watchful, we saw and heard nothing unusual and it was just too tempting not to wash off in the pool.

Relaxed and cooled by our quick dip, we found Joanne and Robbie sitting next to a small crackling fire, huge smiles plastered across their faces. Joanne hollered, "He did it! Now we can cook dinner!"

Tom cleaned the fish and crabs while Rigo prepared the stove. He had often cooked fish this way and proudly showed us how it was done. Once the fire was big enough to spread out, Rigo washed a couple of flat rocks and laid them carefully in the fire. He added more wood so flames were blazing around and on top of the rocks. When he felt it was hot enough, he used wet palm fronds to brush the ashes away and he Joanne dropped the fish and crabs onto the surface – the sizzling said the rocks were, indeed, hot enough to cook on.

Before long, the aroma of cooking food filled the air. Stomachs growled and mouths watered. We were so hungry we could hardly wait for the seafood to finish. Finally, Rigo called out, "Es listo!" We had each found a rock to use as a plate and Rigo served the meal with the flat side of a dive knife. Without forks, we used our knives as eating utensils, too. Damn, those things were coming in handy.

Seafood was low on my list of favorites, but that meal was one of the best I'd ever eaten. I'd better get used to seafood and fruit – unless there was a restaurant on the far side of the island, I'd be eating a lot of it.

Sated, we relaxed around the pit as the sun set and darkness fell. I felt much more comfortable sitting in front of a crackling fire than I had been the night before with only moonlight to pierce the darkness. We talked and laughed and shared diving stories as though we were at a neighborhood barbecue instead of stranded on an island in the middle of the ocean. Eventually, everyone admitted to being too tired to continue. Although reluctant to let the fire go out, we knew that as long as the sun was shining brightly, we could always start another one.

I almost asked Tom to add the fourth wall but then decided it would be a sissy thing to do. After all, the moon was bright, it was warm with only a slight breeze, and we could hear the faint sound of waves lapping at the beach. In only moments, everyone else was fast asleep.

I was the only one feeling uneasy. Snores and deep breathing sounded around me. My body tense, I lay flat on my back, ears straining for any out-of-the-ordinary noise. I could hear leaves and palm fronds rustling in the soft breeze. In the distance, gentle waves kissed the sandy shore. Nothing seemed out of place. The moon provided enough light that I could see the outlines of my sleeping friends, the fire pit with its dull and dying glow, and palm trees that thinned out with only blackness behind them. All was well. Gradually, my eyelids grew heavy, my muscles relaxed, and the silence and soft ocean sounds lulled me to sleep.

Sometime later, pulled gently from the depths of sleep, I felt a tickle on my left cheek. I twitched and relaxed again. Then I felt a tickle on my nose. I turned my head and brushed my hand over my face. At the third irritation, I opened my eyes.

A hairy little face only inches from my own bared its teeth in a silent snarl. Wickedly sharp fangs reflected moonlight. I inhaled the beast's fetid breath and screamed.

The creature scampered quickly along the wall, around the corner of the shelter, and out of sight as Rigo, Joanne, Tom, and Robbie leapt to their feet. "What? What's wrong?" "¿Leesa, qué pasó?"

I could hardly speak. Tears coursed down my face and my body shook. "It… it… had teeth… the hairy beast snarled…" I hiccupped and buried my face in Rigo's chest. He tightened his arms around me and let me cry. *How would I ever sleep again?*

Once the torrent subsided, Tom asked more questions. "Lissy, can you tell us what happened? What woke you?"

I took a deep breath, wiped away the tears, and tried to recall details. "I felt something tickle my cheek, then my nose. At the third tickle, I opened my eyes and there it was, only inches from my face." I shivered at the memory of those fangs so close to my face. "It made no noise at all – just silent snarling. It had big fangs, bigger than those of a dog."

Tom continued his inquiry. "What kind of animal was it?"

"I think it was a monkey; a dark brown monkey. It had hands and its eyes looked almost human. Big, dark eyes with eyelashes. It was so close..." I choked up and once again tears threatened. "It smelled awful – like rotten meat." I gagged, recalling its hot, foul breath on my face.

"Okay, Lissy, only a couple more questions. Where was it when you opened your eyes? You said it was right in your face." Tom was relentless but his questions actually helped me calm down – to focus on the facts rather than the terror of the incident.

"It was right between my head and Joanne's." I saw her shiver at the thought of the snarling beast so close while she slept.

"When it ran away, do you recall how it moved? On all fours? Upright on its hind legs? Or did it scamper like a monkey?"

I tried to remember. "I think it moved like a monkey. But I was so scared, I'm not sure! Oh, it had a long tail. I remember seeing it as it ran away."

Finally, the questions stopped and Tom patted my shoulder. "You did great, Lissy. We now know the island has monkeys. That might have been a monkey you saw at the pool, too."

Thinking back, I said, "You could be right. It was a small face, but in the shadows I couldn't tell whether it was hairy or not. And when it followed me back to camp, it was fast."

Robbie's comment put us on edge again. "I'm no expert on primates, but I think most monkeys eat fruit and leaves. From Lissy's description of this animal's stench and foul breath, it sounds like a carnivore or omnivore, eating pretty much whatever's available. We'll have to stay alert and should probably put the fourth wall on at night."

I sighed with relief, knowing I'd be much more comfortable in a secure space. And again I wished I had more to wear than a bathing suit and Lycra wetskin. They'd be scant protection from pointed teeth intent on rending flesh. I shivered. Rigo's warmth and strong arms were doing little to dispel my goose bumps and trembling as I recalled the furry carnivore mere inches from my throat.

We didn't get much sleep the rest of the night.

Chapter 5

Day 2

Lissy

Although the remaining hours passed without incident, we were up early. Consumed with our thoughts, we ate coconuts and mangos in relative silence. Rigo gave us purpose by suggesting we explore the island. "We must look for people. To see eef we are here alone." At that, Tom once again took charge, reminding us all to bring our knives.

We set out in our bathing suits, wetskins, and booties, carrying spears, with knives securely strapped to our legs. The tropical sun was already warm, the jungle steamy. No ocean breezes penetrated this far inland and I yearned for a hat to protect my head and the fair skin of my face. Enough dappling sunlight made its way through the trees that I could feel my skin heating up. I promised myself I would weave a hat – surely there was something suitable to work with on this lush island.

We had walked for nearly an hour when I heard rustling in the trees overhead. I looked up and saw a dark shadow swinging from branch to branch, high above. "Look! Up there!" I pointed and everyone gazed up into the canopy. Nothing moved.

"You're jumpy, Lissy. There's nothing there." Joanne squeezed my arm and gave me a sympathetic look.

"I saw something swinging through the trees! It was one of those damned monkeys." Why was I the only one who ever saw them? My friends were going to think I was losing my mind.

A short while later we encountered a well-worn trail intersecting our path. We stopped and debated about whether to continue uphill or take the new path that looked as though it might lead to the other side of the island. Since the intersecting trail was so well-used, we hoped it might lead to another encampment. The next decision: right or left?

Tom's instinctive sense of direction led him to the right. "This looks like it leads around the base of the mountain to the coast on the far side. If no one objects, I vote we go this way." No one had a strong opinion to the contrary so we turned right and continued our trek. A few mangos provided lunch, although my stomach clamored for more.

Another two hours of hiking through the steamy jungle took its toll. We were tired, soaked with sweat, thirsty, hungry, and irritable. I was thankful, though, that I hadn't seen any more monkeys. Come to think of it, I hadn't seen any wildlife at all. "Other than that monkey earlier, I haven't seen or heard any animals. Has anybody else seen anything?"

Robbie said, "I spotted a small snake slithering across the path into the underbrush a while back, but that's it."

I tenaciously continued. "Don't you find that strange? Lots of animals live in a jungle, don't they?"

No one replied and I assumed they didn't feel like talking. I had an uneasy feeling that the lack of wildlife might be connected to the carnivorous monkey. If there were more monkeys – and I couldn't imagine the island having only one – and they had eaten all of the available food, we might be in more danger than we'd originally thought. As we tromped onward, I kept my dark musings to myself.

I spotted several burrows at the base of large trees and wondered what type of animal had dug them. Rabbits, perhaps, although I hadn't seen any. Maybe they were the monkeys' favorite food and had been exterminated. Marching onward, I contemplated what other kinds of animals dug burrows and was startled when Tom rounded a sharp bend in the path and let out a shout. "Look at that! Wow!" We rushed forward to see what had caused his excitement. The trail came to an abrupt end at the tree line and rock-studded white sand stretched to the shore. A brisk ocean breeze caressed our faces, cooling our sweaty bodies – it felt delicious. Invigorated, we trotted toward the sea.

However, our exhilaration died as we noticed the sizeable waves pummeling the rocky shore. Joanne groused, "Damn. More than anything, I wanted a quick dip to wash off the sweat and grime. I guess I'll have to settle for a splash in one of those pools." She pointed to water trapped amongst the rocks and headed for one nearby.

"Hey, guys! Come quick!" Standing at the edge of a large pool, Joanne waved us over. We dashed to her side and discovered a good-sized stingray had become trapped, swimming frantically to and fro, searching for a way back to the sea.

Excited, Rigo said, "Rays good to eat. We cook heem, no?" We looked at Robbie, our firemaster, and he nodded, smiling broadly.

He then surprised us by barking orders. "I brought my mask, just in case. Somebody collect some coconuts and start pulling strings. We'll need kindling and firewood, too. Tom, come help me build a fire pit."

We scattered, hunger adding impetus to our actions. Soon, the fire pit adorned the edge of the tree line – kindling to the left, firewood to the right – and three of us eagerly pulled strings from coconut shells. Robbie set up his rocks and dive mask and we waited for the sun to ignite the dry, stringy kindling underneath. As hot as it was, we didn't wait long.

As soon as the strings began to send up small whispers of smoke, Rigo and Tom grabbed their spears. Weapons in hand, they slowly advanced on the stingray, driving it to one end of the pool. They kept a respectful distance from the tail, neither of them wanting to tangle with the venomous barb that could deliver a nasty and potentially fatal wound. After several misses, Rigo speared one wing and Tom delivered the killing blow. Cheers went up as we envisioned dinner.

Before long, the aroma of cooking fish wafted across the beach. We lined up, buffet style, and Rigo served us each a generous "ray steak." Coconut water washed it down but we were careful not to drink too much. With the freshwater stream so near our camp, we had to find a way to carry some with us; hiking through the jungle worked up a powerful thirst. I'd kept a sharp eye out for a stream but hadn't seen even a trickle.

Once we'd eaten our fill, we relaxed for a while in the shade of the trees, enjoying the ocean breeze and the beautiful, tropical view. It was idyllic, if you didn't consider our dire situation.

Sated and cooler, we were eager to explore. We followed the tree line to take advantage of the shade as well as the refreshing ocean breeze, now in much better spirits. Talking and joking amongst ourselves, we nearly ran into Tom when he suddenly stopped, focused on the scene off to his right. Words died in our throats as we followed his gaze.

The skeleton of a huge ship loomed eerily out of the water about a hundred yards off shore. Tattered remnants of fabric gave no clue as to what flag it once flew. Severely weathered wood indicated the vessel had foundered many years ago and waves still battered it relentlessly.

Excitement in his voice, Tom said, "Rigo, you and I can swim out to the ship to look for things we could use: pots, pans, any type of utensils, buckets. Robbie, Joanne, and Lissy, you watch for sharks. We'll take our knives with us, but the spears will have to stay behind. There's no way we can carry them and swim effectively in the surf."

"Sí. I sweem strong!" The two men trotted toward the water.

"Wait!" Concerned about their safety, I wanted them to have all hands free to swim as fast they could to and from shore. "Why don't you take some vines with you to tie things together? Otherwise, how will you carry them and swim in the rough surf at the same time?" Rigo grinned and hugged me. "Beautiful chica, another buen idea!"

We ran into the trees and collected long lengths of sturdy, fibrous vines. Tom and Rigo tied them securely around their waists before heading back toward the water.

Remembering the numerous dorsal fins and the shark fight we'd seen on the other side of the island, I held my breath as the guys splashed into the surf. It was rough going but both men were strong swimmers, and frankly, I had no idea what we could do if we did see a shark. I heaved a sigh of relief when they reached the wreck and clambered out of the water, waving to let us know all was well. They disappeared from sight and Robbie, Joanne, and I settled down to wait.

Chapter 6

Day 2, Continued

Tom

I swam hard against the waves, hoping Rigo had the stamina necessary to make it to the ship. When I grabbed a rail just above the water line, Rigo swam up next to me and grinned. "We do thees, no?"

I chuckled, my worries evaporating. "Yes, we do this. Let's go!" We climbed aboard, watching carefully for exposed nails and jagged wood. It wouldn't do to put blood into these shark-infested waters, not to mention fighting infection without a first aid kit. We waved to our friends on shore and explored. Nothing useful remained here on the main deck as it was continually beaten and battered by storms and waves. Heading below, we found water filled the rooms at the bow. Ducking my head under the surface, I saw metal cages of various shapes and sizes that had been demolished in the wreck. The doors stood wide open, bent and battered by the impact. In one cage at the far rear, I glimpsed stark, white bones. At least one hapless animal hadn't escaped the wreckage.

Wiping the water from my eyes, I stood with Rigo, musing aloud over the twisted metal mess. "I wonder what she was transporting. She must've struck the reef and sunk, front end first. At this crazy angle, we might have better luck searching the rooms at the stern."

We returned to the deck and Rigo and I slowly made our way upward to the stern, carefully pulling ourselves hand-over-hand along what rail remained. We soon discovered another set of stairs leading below deck. Luckily, the galley was located at the aft end and we found numerous useful items: a bucket with an intact handle; two pots and pans; metal cups with handles; knives, forks, and spoons; and the biggest prize of all – a canteen in pretty good condition.

We divided the bounty into two piles, wrapping vines securely around the flatware. Rigo lashed his items together with the vines and I tied the bundle to his back. He did the same for me. That way, we could swim freely. Just as we were about to climb the stairs to the upper deck, I spotted something strange in the next room. "Hold on a minute, Rigo. I want to check in here before we go."

I clambered over chairs, upended tables, and piles of unrecognizable junk to get to the next doorway. Inside, I spied a metal cage just like the wrecked ones in the bow, about the size suitable for a medium-sized dog. *That's odd. Why would they have a caged dog on board?* Curious, I continued my search and found a slender, plastic-wrapped log book tucked in the back of an old desk drawer. Miraculously, it had survived the wreck and remained dry and intact, protected by the waterproof covering.

Again, my thoughts ran wild. *Someone believed the information in this book was important. I can't wait to read it.* I rolled it tightly and stuffed it into the canteen. Hopefully, it wouldn't get ruined during the swim back to shore – I was eager to find out what the ship had been carrying. And why.

Rigo had returned to the main deck and I found him there, eyeing the horizon. "I no like that, Señor Tom. More storm comes. We hurry back, no?" The puffy white cottonball clouds I'd admired earlier were now a threatening shade of grey. "Yes, let's hurry. We have to start back to camp, pronto!"

We slipped and slid down the upper deck to where we'd climbed aboard. I was afraid to leap into the water with all the metal items lashed to my back – I didn't want anything whomping me on the back of the head – so I climbed carefully down the vessel's side until I could slide easily into the sea. Rigo copied my moves and we were soon on our way back to shore. The waves carried us along swiftly with minimal effort.

Just as I thought the return trip would be uneventful, Joanne screamed, "Shark! Shark! Swim faster!" Robbie ran into the waves from the beach. In chest-deep water, he grabbed my hand to help me stand, the waves nearly knocking me off my feet and the metal accoutrements further hindering my efforts. Lissy ran to Rigo and helped him. Clambering quickly out of the water, we turned and saw a large shark cruise by not twenty feet away.

"I hope you got everything you wanted this trip because you're *not* going back out there!" Lissy raved, hugging Rigo. Joanne and Robbie held onto me, terror in their eyes.

I said, "I agree – once was enough." I looked at the sky and motioned toward the ugly clouds building on the horizon. "We'd better hustle. Let's split up the goods and get moving." We piled the scavenged items into five smaller bundles and lashed them to our backs. With everything secure, we hit the trail. I wanted to return to camp and close the shelter before it began to rain. From the looks of those clouds, it was going to be a wet night.

Setting a grueling pace, I hoped everyone could maintain a good speed – we were about three hours from camp. Once the path turned from the beach into the trees, we no longer enjoyed the cooling ocean breeze. The temperature rose and we could almost see steam rising from the jungle floor. Sweat dripped constantly from our red faces and I anticipated a dip in the pool. I hoped we got back in time to relax a bit before closing ourselves into the shelter for the night. It would feel like a sauna if we couldn't cool off first.

Joanne was the first to stumble. "Can we please rest for a minute? I can't keep up this pace any longer." Lissy and Robbie both collapsed to the ground next to her, breathing hard.

"Okay, we'll rest here for a few minutes. Rigo, let's see if we can find some mangoes. The sugar will give us all more energy."

We disappeared into the trees and almost immediately Rigo hollered, "Here, Señor Tom! I bring some." He returned only moments later with his arms full of the juicy fruit. Everyone greedily munched in silence.

Knowing we were short on time, I urged the group to its feet again. Amidst growls and complaints, I coaxed everyone into another quick pace. "Come on, we have to keep moving. We're only halfway there and the storm's getting closer." I'd no sooner finished the sentence than an ominous rumble of not-too-distant thunder filled the air. I didn't have to prod anyone to move faster after that.

An hour and a half later, we stumbled into camp, exhausted, hungry, and thirsty. In the future, we'd be able to carry fresh water with us in the canteen, but right now, we needed a drink and a cooling dip in the pool. The storm would soon be upon us and we needed to prepare. I hated to goad the group into moving again so soon, but we had things to do. "I know you're whipped, but we need to get a drink and cool off. Then we have to lash the fourth wall on before the storm hits. Come on, I promise you'll feel better after a quick dip!" I helped Joanne and Robbie to their feet; Rigo grabbed Lissy's hand and pulled her up. I unscrewed the lid from the canteen and worked the plastic-covered log book out, tossing it into the shelter. I wanted to wash the canteen out and fill it with water for the night and hoped to read some of the log before darkness fell.

I'm sure everyone was thankful camp wasn't far from the creek as we filed to the pool. We didn't even bother to remove wetskins or booties, preferring instead to wash the day's sweat and grime off while simultaneously refreshing ourselves. A loud crack of thunder indicated the storm was closing fast. After only a few minutes, we crawled quickly out of the pool and dashed a short distance upstream to fill our coconut shells with water. I repeatedly filled the canteen and shook it vigorously. Convinced it was as clean as possible, I then filled it to the brim.

Our thirst quenched and refreshed by our quick swim, we hurried to camp and pitched in with the nighttime preparations. Since we couldn't cook dinner due to the weather, I said, "Robbie, why don't you and Joanne take the bucket and go find some fruit and coconuts? That's going to be dinner since we can't light a fire. Lissy, you collect the dive gear and bring the weapons into the shelter. Rigo and I will add the wall. Then we can settle in for the night and hope the storm doesn't blow our roof off."

Everyone scattered, thunder and flashes of lightning fueling our actions. Robbie and Joanne soon returned, the bucket overflowing with fruit. Rigo and I worked on lashing the front wall tightly to the sides with numerous vines, making sure the wind couldn't blow it loose. We "hinged" the door on the left, leaving it open for the time being. We could lash it shut from the inside when we were ready to relax – or when the rain started, whichever came first.

Lissy had collected the spears and clubs and stacked them in the corner of the shelter, heading back out to get the dive gear. Suddenly, I heard her voice, frantic and filled with fear. "Tom, didn't we leave all the gear over here? Some of it's missing and the rest is scattered everywhere!"

Rigo motioned for me to go help Lissy while he finished with the lashings. I walked up beside her as she reached for a dive mask hanging on a bush. "Yes, I'm positive we left it all together. What's missing?"

Tears in her eyes, she pointed out only four pairs of fins and three BCs; the masks were accounted for but one snorkel was gone. Her voice strained, she said, "I found the fins scattered around this edge of camp, the masks tossed into the bushes. The BCs are way over there." She pointed into the trees. "And look at this." She walked to the edge of the trees and gazed at the ground. There, a clear footprint was pressed into the dirt. It looked like a small, bare foot – almost, but not quite human.

"Now do you believe me? Those damned monkeys were in our camp today. Every time I close my eyes, I see those snarling fangs only inches from my face. What are we going to do, Tom? I'm scared!" She turned her tear-streaked face up to me and her lower lip quivered. Fear plain in her eyes, she leaned into me and I put my arms around her as she cried. I held her close, feeling her body tremble. My mind raced. I glanced over her head toward the shelter and met Rigo's hostile stare, glaring daggers in my direction. He tossed down the vine and stalked stiffly into the trees.

I shook my head, lamenting the fact that Rigo had obviously misunderstood what he'd seen. I had no designs on Lissy – she simply needed some reassurance. "Right now, we can't do anything but prepare for this storm. Come on, pull yourself together and let's collect the gear. We'll soon be locked inside the shelter and the monkeys won't be able to reach us. Get a good night's sleep. We'll talk about this tomorrow, okay?"

Lissy raised her head to look at me, tears wet on her cheeks, her eyes red from crying. "Okay, Tom. Thanks. Sorry I fell apart." She shuddered. A deafening crack of thunder made us both jump. "Come on. Let's get this stuff inside!"

We grabbed the dive gear and dashed for cover. Robbie and Joanne were already there; Rigo was nowhere in sight. Lissy and I ducked through the doorway just as the sky let loose and water poured down in sheets.

Joanne asked, "Where's Rigo? He was here a minute ago."

I didn't want to go into detail and said, "I saw him run off into the trees. Maybe he was headed for the loo."

Robbie said, "Let's close the door and leave it unlocked until he gets back." Everyone agreed we didn't want to lock him out. I just hoped he'd return before we settled for the night. We couldn't leave the door unsecured while we slept.

I found the log book where I'd tossed it earlier and stretched out on my bed, hoping to read, but with the overcast sky, the rain, and the roof blocking what little daylight there was, I couldn't discern the somewhat faded handwriting. Finally, I tucked it under some palm fronds and determined to tackle it tomorrow.

We talked for a while but it was clear that the day's exertions had worn everyone out. One by one, they fell asleep and, eventually, I was the only one not snoring – and I was fighting to stay awake. Rigo had still not returned and, with the unrelenting tropical downpour showing no sign of abating, I decided to lock the door. He'd have to wake us to let him in.

I lashed the door securely shut and lay back down. It seemed I'd barely closed my eyes when I heard an awful racket outside. Screaming, screeching, and Rigo's voice, "Let me een! Let me een! Por favor! Ayúdame!" Everyone leapt up and since I was closest to the opening, I ran to untie the vines holding the wood panel shut. A heavy body hit the door with a loud thud, rattling the entire wall. Rigo's voice sent chills up my spine as I clawed at the vines. "Ayúdame! Ayúdame! They keel me!" I heard an ominous thud and then he went quiet.

The last of the vines came loose and I swung the door inward. Rigo fell heavily into the shelter, landing hard and not moving. Through the heavy rain, I saw numerous dark, hairy creatures running madly around the campsite, their high-pitched screeches sounding like fingernails on a chalkboard. Using my foot, I tried pushing Rigo away from the opening and hollered for Robbie to help – I couldn't close the door.

Robbie grabbed Rigo's arms and dragged him inside. A hairy beast ran for the doorway as I slammed it shut. I leaned against it as a weight crashed into the wood and I knew I couldn't hold it if the creatures joined forces. "Robbie, tie the door shut, quick! I won't be able to hold it much longer." Robbie and Lissy tied the vines securely and after a few minutes, we heaved a collective sigh of relief when all fell silent outside. It seemed the animals had given up – for now.

Lissy knelt beside Rigo. I fetched the water canteen. Robbie rolled Rigo onto his back and we viewed the extent of his injuries. Long, bloody scratches marred his face and arms; one ugly bite dripped blood at the left side of his throat; one eye was swollen shut and badly bruised; and his wetskin was ripped in a dozen or more places, blood seeping through from the inside. I didn't see any serious damage and couldn't figure out why he was unconscious.

Joanne asked us to remove his wetskin so she could get to the wounds. "Once you have the wetskin off, rip out a sleeve so I have something to clean him up with." I did as she asked while she cleaned her hands with water from the canteen. Then she looked at the wounds and addressed the more serious neck bite first. When the bleeding stopped, her hands moved swiftly from gash to gash. Finally, she said, "I wish we could light a fire to boil some water. I have no way to really *clean* these wounds – I'm just wiping the blood away." She raised her eyes to mine. "How do we keep these wounds from getting infected? These injuries won't kill him but infection will."

"Do the best you can tonight, Jo," I said. "Hopefully, it won't rain for long and tomorrow we'll light a fire and boil some water. Until then, there's nothing more we can do."

Rigo groaned and opened his one good eye. Still kneeling at his side, Lissy took his hand in hers and whispered, "I'm sorry those beasts attacked you! And I'm glad you're finally awake. I was so worried."

His reply stunned everyone but me. "I see you weeth Tom. You cry on hees shoulder and he hold you. I not want to see heem kees you so I go into el bosque." He looked at me then, and I could still see the anger in his gaze, the jealous challenge, one man to another.

Lissy shook her head. "No, Rigo, it's not like that. Tom and I are just friends. I was upset and scared and he held me while I cried. That's all." She looked at me and said, "Tell him, Tom. Tell him there's nothing between us, that we're just friends."

"It's true, Rigo. Lissy and I are just good friends. But, somehow, I don't think you believe that."

"You are right, Señor Tom, I no believe eet."

Lissy changed the subject. "Where did you go, Rigo? Where did the monkeys attack you?"

His reply sent chills down my back. "When I run out of camp, I hear them een the trees. They follow but stay up high. Eet rain and I steel no want to come back. Then the monkeys come down and make a circle, me een el centro. I know eet ees trouble. I theenk I die." He looked up at Lissy. "I remember our kees een the water. You say eet ees a good time. I know I must fight."

Lissy squeezed Rigo's hand and he smiled, then grimaced in pain. "I run at a leetle monkey and wave arms and scream. He has surprise and move away. I break through the circle and run here, but the monkeys run, too. They run fast. Here, they attack. When I fall, they jump on me and bite and scratch. I know I must get up. I punch one een hees face and he has surprise, too. I run to the door and call for help. One monkey heet me with wood. I know nothing more until I am here."

I summarized, more for my own clarification than anyone else's. "They followed you *from* camp, stayed up high in the trees until you were farther away, surrounded you, and then followed you back here when you broke through the circle. They only attacked when you reached possible help. And you say they hit you with a piece of wood?"

Rigo nodded. "Sí. Like a club."

A slight quiver in his voice, Robbie said, "They're *thinking*. Deciding when and where would be the best place to attack. And using a club as a weapon. I don't like this at all!"

I could tell by the looks on their faces that everyone else's thoughts went to the same dark, scary place mine did. "Okay, from now on, there is *no* reason good enough for anyone to leave camp alone. We need each other. We *have* to have each other's back – our lives depend on it. This assault on Rigo proves the monkeys are intelligent, getting bolder by the day, and will attack when they feel safe enough. We have to stay alert and on guard at all times." Looking from face to face, I could see their fear, but I also saw determination. This was a good group – a group the monkeys wouldn't find it easy to defeat.

"Robbie, let's help Rigo to his bed. We need to get some sleep." We helped Rigo up, trying not to reopen the neck wound. He shuffled slowly to his bed and lay down with a groan.

I re-checked the lashings on the door. Tomorrow I wanted to find a couple of sturdy poles and add some loops of vines on either side of the opening. We could slide the poles horizontally across the door through the loops for additional security. It might not help a whole lot but it would make me feel better.

The rain was still coming down in sheets and every now and then a strong gust of wind shook our walls. As I lay on my pile of palm fronds, I fervently wished for sunshine tomorrow. We *had* to clean Rigo's wounds before they got infected. He was a valuable member of our small group and we needed him. He *had* to survive. *We* had to survive.

Chapter 7

Day 3

<u>Lissy</u>

I lay awake for a long time, listening to the pouring rain and trying to discern any other sounds in the night. The monkeys might have given up for now, but I knew they were there somewhere, waiting. The vicious attack on Rigo proved they weren't afraid to try and take us down, one at a time. They were intelligent. And they had used a weapon. There were only five of us and we had no idea how many of them there were.

At last, I slept. When I woke, early, the rain had stopped and it was already heating up. Carefully, I inched out of bed, trying not to wake Rigo. He needed rest. Tom was already up, untying the vines lashing the door shut. Quietly, we stepped out of the shelter and came to an abrupt halt. Our campsite had been vandalized – obviously, the monkeys were angry at being thwarted the night before. The rocks from around the fire pit had been tossed into the trees; the logs we used as seating had been hauled to the edge of the clearing and carelessly dumped; and feces had been tossed at the shelter and left in stinking piles around the site. Dark, disgusting streaks showed plainly against the wall's lighter wood. Human-like footprints were everywhere, the mud preserving them like unwanted talismans.

I could feel tears welling in my eyes but I determined not to cry. Instead, I found a couple of flat rocks and began scooping the repulsive piles of poop, tossing them as far as I could into the trees. Tom began rebuilding the fire pit and, once Robbie joined the efforts, they dragged the seating logs back into place. As I watched them struggle with the heavy logs, I wondered how the monkeys had moved them; there weren't any drag marks. I mentally added "strong" to the growing list of adjectives I used to describe the beasts.

Joanne came out just as we finished reorganizing the campsite and asked Robbie if he could make a fire as soon as possible. "I need to boil some water and thoroughly clean Rigo's wounds. We can't waste any more time. If they get infected, he could die." Our eyes met and I could see her sincere concern. My gut clenched at the thought of his suffering. And I didn't want to lose him.

The coconuts that had been inside during the night's deluge were still dry so I began pulling strings. Robbie set up his rocks and arranged his mask. We waited. Even though it was early, the sun was hot and we soon had a small fire blazing. Robbie and Tom removed the fourth wall and announced they were going fishing. "We need more to eat than fruit and coconuts. And since we started a fire, we might as well have fish for lunch."

Tom walked over to Joanne and said softly, so Rigo couldn't hear, "Good luck cleaning those wounds, Jo. That one on his neck looks pretty ugly." He patted her on the shoulder as she nodded.

Tom and Robbie headed toward the beach, spears in hand, as Joanne and I boiled water and disinfected the cooking pots brought back from the shipwreck. Once Joanne was satisfied that the utensils were germ-free, she boiled the sleeve Tom had ripped off Rigo's wetskin the night before and asked me to remove the other one. While those were cooling, we went to see Rigo.

He greeted us with a smile but I could tell it was forced. "How do you feel?" Joanne asked, her voice soft and full of concern. She held the back of her hand to his forehead.

"I hurt all over. Here, ees beeg pain." He pointed to the wound on his neck.

Joanne examined the bite and shook her head. "I don't like the way this looks at all. We have to get it cleaned out immediately." She looked into Rigo's eyes and said, "It'll hurt like hell, Rigo. I have nothing to give you for the pain, but if I don't clean it out, you could die from infection."

He reached out and took Joanne's hand. "Por favor, Cho, do eet. Eet weel hurt, but I am strong now. I no want to die. Hurt me and make eet better, no?"

"Okay, Rigo. I'll be as gentle as I can."

"Cho, I see a plant een el bosque last night that ees good for to heal. Es aloe vera – do you know eet?"

I perked up at the name. I kept some in a pot at my condo and used it on burns and small cuts. "I know aloe vera, Rigo. Where did you see it?"

"I run that way een the trees and I see eet near some beeg rocks. Es beeg plant. You see eet easy." He pointed into the trees, away from the creek.

I jumped up and grabbed my knife, quickly buckling it to my leg. Picking up the bucket and a spear, I said, "I'll be back as soon as I can." I jogged into the trees, following a faint trail heading in the direction Rigo had indicated. Although we'd decided no one was to go into the jungle alone, I had no choice. There wasn't anyone else and Joanne had to stay with Rigo.

Joanne's hollered "Be careful, Lissy!" was almost drowned out by a sudden rustling in the leaves overhead. I didn't look up. My heart pounded. Sweat trickled into my eyes. I gripped the spear so tightly my hand went numb. But I was determined to find the aloe.

My jogging finally slowed to a walk – I just couldn't keep up that quick pace. The overhead rustling had stopped and I didn't know whether that was a good thing or not. Had the monkeys followed me from camp? Were they now on the ground, intent on attack? My nerves were so taut I almost speared a harmless lizard that hopped down from a low tree branch, my frightened screech loud in the morning stillness.

There! Up ahead was a stand of aloe vera growing amongst some large rocks, just as Rigo had described. I leaned the spear against a tree and broke off enough aloe to half fill the bucket, knowing Joanne would want more than one application. And, frankly, I didn't want to come back again any time soon.

I glanced to the left and noticed another of those burrows at the base of a nearby tree. Whatever dug the hole must've been about the size of a large cat. *Hmm...I'd like to take a closer look but right now I have to get this aloe back to Jo. Another time.*

Grabbing the spear, I picked up the bucket and turned. Shocked, I stopped so suddenly I nearly fell forward, the sweat on my body turning cold as ice. Directly in front of me, blocking the trail and standing still as a statue, was a large ape. A chill ran up my spine. We stood there, eyeing each other for what seemed like an hour. I used the time to commit to memory every detail. It was a male. He was about four and half feet tall, very muscular and powerfully built, with arms longer than his body and no tail, like the orangutans I'd seen on TV. Unlike the smaller dark-colored monkeys, though, he was almost blonde; light-colored hair that turned reddish-orange near the tips covered his entire body. Sunlight dappling through the trees colored him a shiny, striking strawberry blonde. His non-threatening body language was also at odds with the hostile, snarling image burned into my memory.

After a while, he slowly sank to his haunches and lowered his head, breaking eye contact for the first time. My racing heart slowed. Confused at this display of submissive behavior, I was afraid to make a move for fear he'd take it as a threat.

I had heard that if you play dead or act subservient, some animals will halt an attack; I wondered if that also meant it could prevent one. Following the ape's lead, I sank to the ground, imitating his sitting position. I lowered my head. We sat like that for several minutes. When he made a soothing humming sound, I raised my eyes to find him looking at me, head quizzically cocked to one side. The look in his eyes had softened and, astonishingly, he curled his lips in what could only be called a smile. At that moment, he appeared so harmless that I smiled back.

His smile widened, showing large, discolored, square teeth in the front with wicked-looking canines at the sides, top and bottom, but I could tell his main food must be fruit, leaves, and maybe insects. Shocked and relieved, I realized this was not the same type of animal that had snarled at me and attacked Rigo. This was a vegetarian. Although large and powerful enough to inflict major damage, he was not carnivorous. Thankful that he wouldn't be appraising me as his next meal, I let out a deep sigh of relief. The orangutan sighed, too. *Imitating me?*

Now, neither of us felt threatened. The animal slowly stood and took a small step closer, whimpering slightly as though in pain. I realized he was listing to the right to avoid putting much weight on his left leg. From my position on the ground, I noticed the extreme swelling and inflammation in his left foot.

No longer in fear for my life, I pitied the suffering beast. *I wonder if he'd let me help.* Slowly, keeping my eyes cast downward, I reached toward his foot, hoping he would allow soft physical contact. When my hand touched his ankle, he sighed again and sank to a sitting position, lifting his foot off the ground. Amazed that he would permit me to touch him, I gently smoothed back the short hairs on his foot to get a better look. A large thorn protruded slightly from the side of the arch. The abscess looked extremely painful and walking had to be excruciating. I knew it would hurt to remove the thorn and wondered if he would misunderstand the pain, thinking I was somehow attacking him. I lifted my eyes to his and saw only warmth and calmness in his gaze. It gave me the courage to proceed.

Keeping my voice low and gentle, knowing he couldn't understand the words but hoping he'd sense my kind intentions, I murmured, "Okay, big boy, I'm going to pull this spine out. It's gonna hurt, but I'll be as gentle as I can and I promise it'll feel better afterwards." I took a deep breath and, using my fingernails, gripped the barely protruding thorn and pulled. A nasty-looking, one-inch spine slid out of the wound and bloody pus oozed over the ape's foot. He whimpered once.

I knew by relieving the pressure in the abscess, some of the pain would subside, however, to heal the wound completely, the infection needed to be treated. Aloe vera would help heal the wound but first, the toxins had to be drawn out of the animal's body. Without a first aid kit, I was at a loss. And my first priority was to get the aloe vera back to camp.

Gazing into the animal's eyes, I was struck by the look of gratitude he gave me. One big, hairy paw reached slowly toward me and I gritted my teeth, determined not to flinch. Using his pointer finger, he gently caressed the hand I had used to remove the thorn from his foot. He nodded his big head as if in approval and I was amazed at the clarity of his non-verbal "Thank you."

With my other hand, I stroked his paw and said, "You're welcome. But now I have to get back to my friends." I slowly stood, making no sudden movements, and said gently, "Okay, big fella, you're on your own." Picking up the spear and the bucket, I stepped carefully around him and strode purposefully down the trail. For several minutes, I walked, concentrating on any sounds from behind. Hearing nothing, I decided the orangutan had not followed me and, relieved, I broke into a lope. I was anxious to return to camp and get the aloe vera into Joanne's hands.

My mind filled with the wonder of the encounter, I paid scant attention to the sounds in the overhead canopy. Suddenly, two small, dark-colored monkeys with long tails dropped from the trees onto the path in front of me, snarling, screeching, and hopping excitedly from one foot to another. These were the animals I remembered – vicious, threatening, and foul-smelling.

I dropped the bucket and raised the spear, terrified but determined to give them a fight. One rushed me, fangs bared, and I stabbed, nicking its arm. It fell back, chattering angrily. The two beasts advanced in tandem, forcing me off the path. It was hard to keep my footing in the viny undergrowth, but I had to keep my eyes on them. They were quick and I couldn't lower my guard.

The second monkey hopped about four feet straight up into the air, screeching loudly and drawing my attention. Focused on him, I raised the spear and the first monkey darted in. Too late, I realized my mistake. The animal threw itself at my chest and I stumbled back, tripping over the vines underfoot. Both monkeys were on me and I screamed, punching and pushing at the snarling beasts. Useless in the close contact, the spear fell to the side.

An enormous roar sounded directly behind me and both monkeys scampered back, stopping about ten feet away to spit and snarl. Afraid to see what had scared them off, I slowly craned my head around. Astonished, I saw the big strawberry blonde ape standing just behind my head. Chest thrust out, hair on end, stretched to his full height, the beast waved his long arms and growled at the monkeys in front of me. He snarled, exposing his fangs in a vicious display. Although the smaller, carnivorous animals were equipped with wicked teeth and razor-sharp claws, they would be no match for the orangutan's power and reach.

The larger beast stepped around me, advancing menacingly on the two attackers. They snarled once more and ran into the trees. I heard the rustling of the leaves overhead as they retreated, knowing better than to begin a fight with such a formidable foe.

Prone on the ground, I debated my next move. With adrenaline flowing, would the big beast threaten me, as well? When he snarled viciously into the trees one last time and then turned toward me, I broke into a sweat and lay perfectly still, my raspy breathing loud in the sudden silence. He lowered his huge head toward my face and I closed my eyes.

I felt him sniffing and snuffling, his moist nostrils moving slowly across my eyes, my nose, my mouth, and down to my throat. *Would I meet my end at the hands of this animal?*

He smelled of fruit – sweet and citrusy – a sharp contrast to the putrid stench of the smaller beasts. And when he no longer snuffled, I held my breath, waiting for whatever would come next. After several long moments, I had to breathe, and dared to look. The big ape sat motionless beside me, staring at my face, concern apparent in his large, expressive eyes. When I took a long, gasping breath and gazed at his face, he again curled his lips in a smile. One large paw reached out and gently patted my leg. I couldn't help myself. I grinned and then laughed out loud, relief flooding my system. The harder I laughed, the more excited he became. He clapped his hands and then jumped to his feet, rocking from side to side, his lips curled in that absurd monkey-smile. Obviously, we were both delighted the attackers were gone and we were safe.

I stopped the insane giggling and said aloud to my new friend, "Well, BigBoy, I do appreciate your perfect timing. Thanks for saving my life. And now I have to find out what the hell I'm lying on – it's definitely bigger than a pea." I rolled to one side to find a three-inch, sort-of-round object on the ground. I picked it up, wiped off the dirt, and scratched it with my fingernail. *A potato?* I sliced it open with my knife to determine if that's, indeed, what it was. The inside was white and the right texture; tentatively, I tasted it. Yes, definitely a type of tuber.

I realized I held the solution to Rigo's and BigBoy's wounds. A potato will draw infection out of the body – I had used it myself back home a lifetime ago. Excited, I found the bucket where I had dropped it and replaced the aloe vera. I then loaded it with as many potatoes as I could find, wondering if we'd have enough to adequately treat all the injuries. BigBoy watched as I filled the bucket, confusion again written plainly on his face. As I stood and looked around, I said, "Well, I hope that's enough."

The lightbulb came on in BigBoy's brain and he began digging at the ground. Potatoes appeared in the dirt and I grinned. In minutes, we had filled the bucket nearly to overflowing and still, he dug for more. I had to stop him or he would've dug up an entire acre. "Okay, okay, that's enough! I don't think I can carry the bucket as it is." I hefted the pail and between the potatoes and the aloe vera, it was pretty heavy. I was afraid the handle would break so I raised the bucket and cradled it in my arms.

I began walking down the path toward camp and BigBoy fell into step behind me. I could just imagine how Joanne was going to react when we ambled into camp. I stifled a giggle, afraid of getting him all excited again.

When my arms began to ache, I stopped and set the bucket down. As I flexed my arms, I saw BigBoy watching and then eyeing the pail. He came to a decision and picked it up in his strong arms, cradling it as I had done. I smiled. He smiled. And we continued on to camp.

When I walked into the clearing with the orangutan right behind me, Joanne was sitting beside Rigo's bed. She looked up, froze, and screamed, "Behind you, Lissy! Look out!"

I tried to calm her but her terrified shrieking continued. Eyes wide with fear, she flattened her body against the back wall, doing her best to completely disappear. Rigo never moved, the noise not penetrating his infection-induced sleep, but the screams had a profound effect on BigBoy. He stood immobile, the bucket still clutched in his arms. He seemed to shrink in upon himself, becoming smaller and less imposing and looked from me to Joanne and Rigo. His eyes expressed confusion and fear.

Making myself heard over the commotion, I said, "It's okay, Joanne. This is BigBoy – he saved my life back there in the jungle and it seems he's adopted me. He's harmless. Jo, please stop screaming!" With a final, drawn-out whimper, Joanne fell silent. I turned to BigBoy and murmured, "It's okay, big fella. She's just surprised to see you. Nobody's going to hurt you. Here, give me the bucket." I took the pail from BigBoy who then sank down onto his haunches, keeping a watchful eye on Joanne.

I walked into the shelter to show her what I'd brought back. "I found the aloe vera right where Rigo said it would be. And I found some potatoes."

"Potatoes?" Joanne sounded surprised. Keeping one eye on the orangutan and sniffling, she looked into the bucket.

I grinned. "It's a long story. I'll tell you later. But I know potatoes will draw out infection. I've used it myself. So now we can treat Rigo's wounds with the potatoes before putting the aloe vera on." I pointed to the orangutan sitting near the fire pit and added, "I removed a thorn from BigBoy's foot. He needs to be treated for infection, too."

Astonishment plain on her face, Joanne looked at him and then back at me. "You removed a thorn…? How did you…? Never mind. We need to work on Rigo. He's been delirious and is unconscious now. His neck wound has opened up again and is oozing pus. Some of the other wounds are infected, too. Heaven only knows what kinds of bacteria live in those awful monkey's mouths. I cleaned him up the best I could with the boiled water but it's not enough. How do we use the potatoes?"

Seeing Rigo lying so still and unresponsive drove me to action. "We need to clean them and then slice them directly onto his wounds. We can wrap them with the sleeves we cut off his wetskin so they stay in place. We might have to do it several times, but the sooner we get started, the better."

I dumped the bucket's contents onto a palm frond and then put a dozen or so of the vegetables back into the container. "I'll take BigBoy and go wash these off. I'll be right back. Why don't you boil a knife and be ready to slice them as soon as we return?"

Joanne nodded and reached for her knife, watching warily as the orangutan and I headed out of the clearing. I knew I'd be safe with him at my side.

By the time we got back, Joanne had sterilized the knife and a large, flat rock to use as a cutting board. She sliced the potatoes and put them into a clean pot. I helped her scrub Rigo's wounds once more and was glad he was unconscious – the pain would have been unbearable. The neck wound was red, swollen, and oozing, with jagged, inflamed edges. I hoped the potatoes worked quickly. She placed the slices gently onto the damaged tissue and we wrapped it with one of the sleeves.

We scrubbed his other wounds and applied more slices. We didn't have anything long enough to wrap around his body to hold the potato pieces in place, but as long as he was lying flat on his back they should stay where we put them.

BigBoy sat near the fire pit, gravely watching the proceedings. When we finished with Rigo, I told Joanne I wanted to treat the orangutan's foot. She shook her head and raised both hands in front of her. "You're on your own, Lissy. I'm not going anywhere near him. Sorry."

I understood her fear and didn't press. I ripped a sleeve out of my wetskin and boiled it for several minutes. While it cooled, I walked over to BigBoy and said, "Now it's your turn, big fella. I'm going to wash your foot and then apply a slice of potato, just like you saw us do to my friend. It'll pull the infection out of your system and make you feel better. I doubt you understand a thing I'm saying but hope you know I'm only trying to help." I sat down in front of him. "Come on, let me have your foot." As I reached out, he raised his swollen foot and gently placed it in my hand.

Shocked, I gazed into his eyes. "You're amazing. I wonder if you *do* understand me." He sat quietly while I washed the still-oozing abscess and then placed a potato slice onto the wound. When I glanced away to pick up the strip of fabric, he snatched the potato and popped it into his mouth. I watched him chew and wondered if he would leave the dressing alone. It probably wouldn't help remove the infection if he just *ate* the potato.

I placed a second slice on his foot and waited. He looked at me and then at the potato. When he glanced back at me again, he raised his right hand and slowly reached toward his foot. I slapped his hand and snapped, "No!" hoping he wouldn't take offense.

He pondered what to do next – I could almost see his mind working. Once more he reached toward his foot and again I slapped his hand. "No, BigBoy, leave it alone!" At first, I saw his face harden, his eyes boring into mine, and I thought I might be in trouble. When I maintained eye contact, though, he dropped his eyes and lowered his head in submission.

Heaving a sigh of relief, I patted his hand and said, "That's better. You leave *this* potato alone and you can have this one to eat." I handed him a large spud and he grinned at me before taking a big bite. He happily munched as I dressed his wound.

Joanne came out to the far side of the pit and watched as I finished. She said, "I'm sure you have quite the story to tell once we're all gathered together for lunch. I hope the guys get back soon. I'm starved."

"Me, too. I think I'll go clean some more of these potatoes and we can toss them in the fire. We'll surprise Tom and Robbie!" I patted BigBoy's foot and placed it back on the ground. Joanne helped me put ten medium-sized tubers in the bucket and I called to the orangutan as I headed into the trees. "Come on, BigBoy! Joanne will be more comfortable if you help me at the creek."

She muttered, "Oh, yeah," as we disappeared into the jungle.

I heard rustling in the overhead canopy but it no longer bothered me – I had my own private bodyguard. When we arrived at the creek, BigBoy lowered his face to the water for a drink while I washed off the potatoes. Then we headed back to camp.

As we neared the clearing, I heard Joanne say, "Lissy has a surprise for you guys. She's at the creek but should be back any minute." Just then I strolled into sight with BigBoy at my heels.

Tom jumped up and yelled, "Lissy!"

Joanne laughed. "That's the surprise I mentioned."

"What the…? "What in hell is THAT?" Tom and Robbie couldn't contain their shock and confusion. They jumped to their feet and backed away, spears at the ready.

I wanted to defuse the situation before someone did something regrettable. "Hey, guys, put your spears down. This is BigBoy and he saved my life today – literally. You have to treat him nicely. He's someone we want on our side."

The orangutan stood just behind me, looking from face to face, assessing the situation. I knew he would protect me if he felt it was warranted – and I didn't want him protecting me from the rest of our group. I turned to BigBoy and, keeping my voice calm, said, "It's okay. Come meet my friends. You'll have to protect all of us, not just me." I reached out and the ape stepped to my side.

"Tom, put your spear down and slowly walk over here. I want to introduce each of you as a friend." As requested, Tom leaned his spear against the wall and tentatively came toward us. BigBoy's earlier reaction to a smile made me believe it would be helpful now. "Smile, Tom. And make it look real, not forced."

Tom smiled and I put my arms around him. We hugged and I made a soothing, humming sound similar to BigBoy's hum of this morning. I stepped back and said, "Okay, now reach out slowly and stroke his arm." Tom swallowed hard and gradually raised his hand to touch the orangutan, sliding his hand downward in a gentle stroke. BigBoy watched Tom's hand slide down his arm then reached out and imitated the movement on Tom's other arm. They stood there stroking each other, until I giggled. "I think he gets the point, Tom. Smile at him again and walk away."

This time, when Tom smiled, BigBoy returned the favor, offering his funny monkey-smile and everyone laughed.

I repeated the scenario with Robbie. And then it was Joanne's turn. She didn't want to get that close to the animal. I coaxed. "Come on, Jo, he won't hurt you. And you want him as a friend, believe me. We're all much safer with him in our corner."

She argued, "But what if he decides he doesn't want to be our friend? How will we know he changed his mind until he turns on us?" She had backed away until she was nearly inside the shelter. Her voice trembled and she was on the verge of tears.

During this exchange, BigBoy had watched everyone's movements and listened closely to the intonations. Suddenly, he huffed, exhaling forcefully to get our attention. All heads swiveled sharply in his direction. Staring intently at Joanne, he slowly lowered himself to a sitting position. Gazing up at her, he purposefully dropped his eyes and raised his arm, his right hand outstretched, palm up – a supplicating gesture containing no threat whatsoever. No one moved.

BigBoy sat like that, a statue, until Joanne finally stepped toward him. She extended her hand and gently touched his fingertips. He sighed contentedly then raised his face to her, baring his teeth in a humongous smile. Unable to help herself, Joanne chortled softly. BigBoy patted her hand, continued smiling, and let out a giggle-screech that had us all in stitches.

And of course, the more we laughed, the more excited he got. He leapt to his feet and repeatedly shifted his weight from left to right, clapping his hands and screeching loudly.

After an especially loud squawk, the ape ran off into the jungle. We exchanged puzzled glances and I wondered if he'd come back. But moments later, he reappeared with his arms full of mangoes and handed one to each of us. Evidently, introductions needed food to seal the deal.

When the enthusiasm finally died down, we'd become fast friends. Even Joanne appeared to have lost her fear of the big blond ape – they had a different type of bond than the rest of us. He was gentler, quieter, and more subservient. I had no doubt he would lay down his life for her just to prove he'd never hurt her.

After our strange little meet-and-greet, Tom cleaned the fish, Robbie fed the fire, and Joanne and I cooked the late-lunch meal. We enjoyed potatoes cooked in the hot coals and fish done to perfection in one of the skillets from the shipwreck. While we feasted, BigBoy wandered into the trees and found more fruit to go with his potatoes. Life would have been good except for Rigo lying unconscious from his festered wounds. But I had high hopes the potatoes would extract the poison from his system and he would soon be on the mend.

Later, we cleaned up after the meal and considered what to do for the remainder of the afternoon. We couldn't wander far from camp, leaving Rigo unprotected, so I decided to weave a hat. I'd been wanting one and this seemed the perfect time. BigBoy and I ranged through the trees around the campsite, collecting various vines and grasses. I wanted a variety of materials to work with until I figured out what would be the easiest to weave and the most comfortable to wear. I thought I'd make one for Jo, too.

Tom and Robbie collected more kindling and firewood and then found two sturdy poles and some strong vines to create additional locks for the shelter door. They rigged the loops and leaned the poles against an inside wall. Everything was in place for the night. Afterwards, Tom stretched out on his bed and opened a tattered book of some sort. Soon, he was engrossed, totally ignoring the rest of us.

Joanne found a comfortable seat against a tree and pulled coconut strings; we'd be well supplied for future fires.

It was a quiet, sunny afternoon, the breeze cool and comfortable. BigBoy took a nap in a tree overlooking the clearing and everyone was more relaxed than we'd been in a while.

I tried weaving each of the vines and grasses and found some heavy and bulky and some thin-edged and sharp. Finally, I tried a softer grass that was pliable yet strong and lightweight. It was the perfect material. Once I got the hang of it, my fingers flew and I soon had a comfortable hat with a wide brim that would keep the sun off my head and face. I even wove a chin strap. Joanne asked for one just like it so I made a second.

When we modeled the hats for Tom and Robbie, they both wanted one with a somewhat narrower brim – a more manly style. I told them it would have to wait for another day – it was time to think about dinner. As we moved around camp, BigBoy swung down from the trees and sat at the edge of the clearing. Since we'd had fish for lunch, Tom suggested hunting for crabs.

Robbie set up the rocks, mask, and coconut strings for another fire and Tom offered to stay in camp. He could keep an eye on Rigo and build the fire so it would be ready to cook dinner when we returned. I figured he just didn't want to put his book down. Meanwhile, the rest of us headed to the beach with the bucket, BigBoy trailing behind.

It was a picture-perfect beach scene and we enjoyed the view for a few moments before settling into the hunt. Being a vegetarian, BigBoy had never hunted for shellfish and didn't understand what we were doing. He watched us and finally got into the spirit of things, pawing at the sand. Soon, he realized he could find crabs, too, and before we knew it, we had a bucketful. BigBoy was having a blast and kept on digging. He looked absolutely crestfallen when we started back to camp. I had to call him twice before he'd leave the beach. "BigBoy, come on! We have enough crabs for today. Let's go!"

He hung his head and shuffled his feet like a chastised child, but fell in behind us, soon forgetting the beach when he noticed a stand of mango trees. He ate two mangos and dropped six more into the bucket on top of the crabs. Joanne and I locked eyes and she said, "He learns fast." I nodded and handed him the pail. He happily cradled it in his arms and marched on toward camp.

Tom had a blazing fire ready when we returned and he and Robbie cleaned the catch. BigBoy took his fruit into the trees. Jo and I checked on Rigo. He was still out, his forehead hot to the touch. Joanne said, "While the guys cook dinner, let's wash Rigo down and see if we can lower his temperature. He's awfully hot."

I offered to go to the creek and get a clean bucket of water. BigBoy followed – I knew he would – and as a reward, I let him carry the heavy bucket. It was a bit tricky getting him to hold the handle instead of cradling it in his arms and I wondered if we'd have any water left by the time we got to camp. However, he finally mastered the handle and we trudged toward home.

Joanne had removed the potato slices and I thought the wounds looked slightly less inflamed. Using the sleeves from his wetskin, we gently washed him down, letting the water and the faint breeze cool his body. Afterwards, he seemed to rest more comfortably and Joanne added fresh potatoes to the wounds.

The timing was perfect – dinner was ready. Tom and Robbie had thrown more potatoes into the fire so we had a side dish with the mountain of crabs. All we needed was butter and a little salt and pepper but, hey, I wasn't going to complain. It sure beat sushi! At this rate, I might even learn to *like* seafood.

After gorging ourselves on crabs and potatoes, Tom asked, "So, Lissy, how did you strike up a friendship with an orangutan, of all things? We're dying to hear the whole story!" I glanced up into the trees where I knew BigBoy was keeping watch and launched into the incredible tale. Joanne went pale when I described the attack by the two vicious monkeys but smiled widely as I recounted BigBoy coming to the rescue.

"You see how protective and eager to please he is. I feel so much safer knowing he's up there," I pointed into the tree branches, "keeping watch."

Everyone nodded and Joanne added, "At first, I was terrified of him. He's so big and powerful and after those other monkeys attacked Rigo, I just couldn't bring myself to go near him. But you can see the intelligence in his eyes. He *wants* to help us; he *wants* to be our friend. And you said it yourself, Lissy, we're much safer with him on our side. I'll sleep better tonight!"

"Yeah!" Robbie said. "Those vicious little monkeys won't get past him!"

Then Tom surprised us with a revelation of his own. "When Rigo and I swam out to the shipwreck, we saw a roomful of broken, twisted metal cages – the kind you kennel a dog in."

We nodded and waited for him to continue. "I couldn't figure out what the ship had been transporting until I found a log book in a desk drawer. It had been wrapped in plastic so it was still legible. That's what I was reading today and it explains a lot."

"Explains a lot about what?" Joanne asked.

"Our situation here," Tom replied.

We leaned forward, anxious to hear what the book said.

"It began a long time ago on a small island quite a way from here. I couldn't make out the name – it might've been Spanish. There was a facility there where they performed experiments on animals, mostly monkeys and orangutans, but a few smaller mammals, as well. Originally, the smaller monkeys were given injections of an experimental serum that was supposed to alter their brains and make them more vicious. The end goal was to create an army of flesh-eating, vicious, and intelligent monkeys that could see very well at night, could travel across any type of terrain including treetops, and would eat just about anything – fruit, insects, leaves – but preferred meat. It would be an impressive and almost-unstoppable army. They would never hesitate to kill the enemy and would never run out of food."

"Oh, my God, Tom, that's awful! What happened?" Joanne paled again.

"The scientists thought they had perfected the serum and began breeding the most vicious animals to see if the altered attributes would be passed on to the next generation. As it turned out, the offspring were more intelligent and savage than the original pairs. They started training them to follow basic commands and fed them only meat so they'd develop an insatiable appetite for it. There was one entry that clearly described how a worker got too close to a cage and was mauled. The monkeys tore off his arm and he bled to death. Later, another worker found the arm bones, gnawed clean, in the cage."

"Can you skip to the end, Tom? I don't need to hear about the blood and gore." By then, I felt as pale as Joanne looked.

"Okay, I'll skip the worst parts. Long story short, there were several documented incidents where workers were killed by the monkeys. They even had to add extra locks to the cages because the animals learned how to open the latches. One time, a monkey escaped and let the others out. The workers shot several of them before subduing the mutiny."

"So what ultimately happened? Did the monkeys kill all the workers or did the workers exterminate the monkeys?" I wanted to jump to the end.

"Come on, Lissy, let him talk. Go on, Tom!" Robbie urged. I sighed and leaned back against a rock. Guess I was going to hear it whether I wanted to or not.

"Well, the scientists decided the facility wasn't secure enough to continue the work there. They contacted the government officials and they located another group of scientists on a different island. They agreed the work was too important to risk losing the animals, the workers, or the experiment's detailed data and wanted to work together. So the facility was shut down and the animals were caged and put on a ship…"

"Oh, my God, Tom, that's not the ship that sank here at *this* island, is it?" Suddenly, I was interested again and could hardly contain my questions. "Is that where the carnivorous monkeys came from? From those experiments? When did this happen? Are these the same monkeys from the ship or their descendants? What about BigBoy? What did they do to the orangutans?" I babbled so fast, Tom didn't have time to answer.

"Lissy! I thought you didn't want to hear this." Tom smirked.

"How can I *not* be interested now that we have information on the monkeys *here*? Tom, talk!"

He grinned and said, "Okay! Okay! I think the monkeys we're dealing with here are the descendants of the original test monkeys. So I'm not sure how accurate the information is – although, we do know they're still vicious and very aggressive.

"As for the orangutans… They were part of a different experiment meant to increase intelligence, loyalty, and protective instincts. The idea was to train them to be helpers – nothing like having a butler, a gardener, or a bodyguard you don't have to pay. After all, fruit's pretty cheap."

Although still pale, Joanne smiled and said, "No wonder BigBoy's so intelligent and willing to please. At least we know he wasn't intended to be vicious."

I nodded and said, "I wonder if there are more orangutans on the island. Does the log book say how many animals were on the ship? Were there males and females? Maybe there's a whole colony of orangutans somewhere. After all, we didn't know BigBoy was here until he approached me."

Shrugging his shoulders, Tom said, "Yes, it does give a count but we have no way of knowing how many survived the wreck. And we don't know if there were young ones produced since then or if the other monkeys ate them. Also, since we haven't seen any other wildlife so far, we should probably assume the meat-eating monkeys have decimated those populations." Scowling, he added, "Of course, that means we're most likely at the top of the menu." Everyone shivered at the horrific thought and Joanne whimpered.

Then Jo surprised us. "Maybe we should hunt for more orangutans. If we have several of them living near us and feeling protective, we'd be a lot safer. If the savage ones ganged up on BigBoy, he might not fare so well – then we'd *really* be in danger."

Robbie jumped up and exclaimed, "You're right, Jo! We should find BigBoy some friends. It would make *all* of us safer – us *and* the apes! We could go fishing with one while the other stayed in camp. It's perfect."

Tom, ever the pragmatist, said, "How do we hunt for orangutans? If Robbie and I go hunting, BigBoy would have to stay here with you gals and Rigo. But our best chance of finding more orangutans would be for BigBoy to come with us. And right now we can't all go; Rigo needs someone here. Any ideas?"

Struck by another thought, I said, "If we *do* find more orangutans, how do we befriend them? BigBoy approached me because he needed help getting the thorn out of his foot. And we can't just assume they're *all* going to be as friendly and helpful as BigBoy. What if they aren't? They're bigger and stronger than the nasty little ones. If they felt threatened…"

Nodding, Tom said, "You're right, Lissy. We can't make a dangerous assumption. And even if Robbie and I went out alone, we'd be pretty vulnerable without BigBoy along for protection. I don't see a safe way to find more orangutans – at least, not until Rigo's well. And that could be a while."

Turning to Joanne, Robbie asked, "Have you noticed any changes in Rigo's condition since you applied the potatoes? I know it hasn't been long, but I'm hoping."

Joanne reached over and patted Robbie's hand. "I know how you feel. Lissy and I washed him down right before dinner because his fever was pretty high. I think we brought it down some – he seemed to be resting more comfortably. I hope it's not just wishful thinking, but it looked like the wounds were slightly less inflamed. We should know more by morning."

Rustling in the trees overhead brought us to our feet. Grabbing spears and with adrenaline pumping, we readied ourselves for an attack. The shelter's fourth wall wasn't yet up so retreating wasn't an option. Joanne shrieked when BigBoy swung down from above, landing lightly on his feet. He gave us a smile and ambled over to me, pointing to his injured foot.

"Robbie, let's put the wall on the shelter while Lissy tends to BigBoy," Tom said. "Jo, why don't you go check on Rigo and make sure he's okay for the night. It's dark — we talked longer than we should have. We ought to go inside and lock the door."

I sat down on a log in front of BigBoy and removed his bandage; the wound looked less inflamed and painful. I washed it and applied a new potato slice, giving BigBoy the rest of the tuber to eat. He munched happily while I re-dressed his foot. Sitting there watching Robbie and Tom prepare to add the fourth wall I absently stroked BigBoy's leg. My mind wandered.

We'd been in Cozumel for three days before being lost at sea and we'd been on the island for another three. Friends and family probably wouldn't start worrying about us until sometime late next week. I hadn't left contact information with anyone in the States, merely saying I was going to Cozumel on a dive trip. I sighed, wishing I hadn't been so lax. I preferred to keep my personal life personal, but, dammit, I should've told *someone*.

I didn't know if anyone else in the group had been more diligent or not. I'd have to ask. Maybe Joanne had told her parents — I knew they were close. I felt a brief glimmer of hope.

But even if concerned, would anyone have enough information to locate our dive boat? Would Captain Carlos admit to leaving fourteen divers in the water during a brutal storm? Had he come back looking for us after the storm ended? What had happened to the other eight divers? Did any of them survive?

My dark musings ended abruptly when BigBoy snuggled up to me and laid his big head in my lap. I smiled down at him and he curled his lips in a monkey-grin. I stroked his head and he reached up and played with my hair.

"Hey, you two lovebirds! How 'bout a little help?"

"Very funny, Tom! What do you need?"

76

"See if you can get BigBoy to carry the wall over," he shouted. "If he can do it, Robbie and I can start lashing it on from the top and work our way down."

"Okay. Come on, BigBoy, I've got some work for you." We ambled over to the wall and I motioned for him to pick it up. I went to the far side and hefted my end. He understood and lifted the entire wall all by himself, carrying it easily and following me to the front of the shelter. We maneuvered it into place and Tom and Robbie lashed the top to the sides and then worked their way to the ground. BigBoy carried the door over, too.

Joanne had checked Rigo's wounds and added fresh potatoes, commenting encouragingly. "Rigo's bites definitely look less angry and his fever has come down. He's resting comfortably and I'm hoping by morning he'll wake up. Keep your fingers crossed!" We cheered and I hoped dawn would bring a positive change.

It was time to lock the door but BigBoy didn't want me to go. Finally, I coaxed him to let go with a potato. "Here, this is your nighttime treat. Now, go on up into the trees and keep watch – you're our bodyguard. Go." I walked to the shelter and turned to see him standing in the clearing looking completely forlorn.

"Go on, BigBoy, up into the trees. You stand guard and we'll see you in the morning." I closed the door and Tom lashed it shut, adding the new cross poles. It looked much more secure.

As we moved to our pallets, I heard BigBoy snuffling at the door. We ignored him and he moved away. In a low voice, I asked, "Did any of you give contact information to friends or family prior to this trip? Something they could use to try and locate us when we don't come home as scheduled?" For a long moment, no one answered.

"I just said I was going diving in Cozumel – not much for anyone to go on." Joanne moaned, "If only I'd given *somebody* more information."

"I'm always going somewhere so nobody will think it's strange if I'm not home." Retired, Tom was free to come and go as he liked. His wife had passed away a few years back and he did a lot of solo traveling. "I'm always either on a dive trip or hiking in the mountains. Nobody'll miss me for quite a while, I'm afraid."

I turned to Robbie, "How about you?"

He shook his head and said, "Nope. I told one friend I was heading to Cozumel but didn't leave him any specifics." In a melancholy voice he added, "I don't talk to the kids very often. They have their lives, I have mine. If I never came home they wouldn't even notice for a while."

My heart ached for this man who'd worked long hours all his life to provide a comfortable home for his wife and children. About eight years ago, after a long day at the office, he'd found an empty house and a note saying they were leaving – she'd met someone else and was taking the teenage kids to Nebraska. We'd had a rather lengthy chat one day over drinks following a dive at a local quarry and he'd shared more of himself than he usually did. After that, I'd developed a soft spot for Robbie. He was a good man dealt a bad hand. Now retired, he enjoyed diving, puttering around in the garage, and reading science journals.

Tom's question startled me out of my musings. "What about you, Lissy? Did you leave info with people at work?"

I grimaced. "No. I just told them I was going out of town for a week. I mentioned Cozumel to a couple of friends, but I've been on quite a few dive trips and have gotten lax about leaving specifics in case of an emergency." We fell silent, the reality and seriousness of our situation finally sinking in. "If Rigo's awake in the morning, I'll ask him. Who knows, maybe Captain Carlos has reported us missing and there's a huge effort underway to find us, as we speak!"

Robbie rained on that parade. "I did a little research on Cozumel before we left. The dive operations rarely report negative experiences, fearing it will impact the number of tourists to the area, and, ultimately, their income. So I wouldn't hold my breath that Captain Carlos has reported fourteen missing divers. Who would dive with him again after *that* got out?"

Lost in gloomy thought, I lay there wishing I had told *someone* where I was going when I heard rustling overhead. I tensed and then relaxed when I realized it was most likely BigBoy settling in for the night. Soon, silence fell over the jungle. A slight breeze occasionally stirred the leaves; if I listened hard, I could hear the waves dancing lightly on the sandy beach a short distance away. Slowly, I unwound, the knots in my neck and shoulders loosening as the silence lulled me to sleep.

Screeching and screaming woke us several hours later. Leaping to our feet and grabbing spears, we heard numerous quick footfalls in the clearing outside and an occasional thud as something heavy was thrown at the shelter walls. A loud roar silenced the shrieking vandals; we could tell BigBoy had positioned himself just outside the door. A few more screeches and snarls later, silence once again enveloped the jungle.

For the second time that night, we settled into our pallets, our heartbeats slowing to a normal rhythm. I smiled to myself, envisioning our orangutan keeping watch over his family as I fell into a dreamless and restful sleep.

Chapter 8

Day 4

Lissy

"He's awake! He's awake, everyone!" Joanne's excited voice brought us to our feet early the next morning. I dashed to Rigo's bed and fell to my knees beside him. "Hi, Rigo! I was so worried about you. I'm thrilled you're feeling better."

Rigo held my hand and whispered, "I happy to see you, too, pretty chica." Then he hoarsely growled, "Agua, por favor." Joanne brought him a cup and he greedily gulped it down.

"Whoa, take it easy. Not too much all at once. You can have more later." Joanne took the cup and pressed her hand to his forehead. "You're cool! No more fever. The potatoes are working." She smiled as Rigo frowned, puzzled.

"Potatoes? ¿Qué papas?"

She eagerly explained. "Lissy found some potatoes and we sliced them onto your wounds to draw out the infection. You've been delirious and unconscious for almost two days. But now your fever's gone and you're on the mend."

"I never hear about papas use like that." Rigo looked at the slices on his chest and shrugged, amazed.

I stood and leaned down to kiss Rigo's cheek. "I'll be back soon." To everyone else, I said, "I'll take BigBoy and bring back some fruit and coconuts for breakfast." Leaving the shelter, I called, "Come on, BigBoy!" The orangutan swung out of the trees; I grabbed the bucket and a spear. We headed down the trail as Joanne jabbered to Rigo about all that had happened while he was ill. I figured we'd need another meet-and-greet when we got back.

We soon returned with a pail of fruit. I knew Joanne, Tom, and Robbie had explained about BigBoy because Rigo wasn't shocked when we sauntered into camp. The orangutan put the bucket down and smiled at everyone, but when Rigo said, "He ees beeg!" BigBoy's head swiveled in his direction. A new voice, one he hadn't heard before, changed the big ape's entire demeanor. He went from cute and funny to on edge and protective.

I darted to Rigo's side and took his hand. "Don't look him in the eye; he'll consider that a challenge." When Rigo's eyes were downcast and BigBoy stood stiffly in front of us, nostrils quivering, I said, "Now, slowly put your arms around me. I'm going to hum as we hug – that seems to indicate approval and affection." I leaned down to hug Rigo and in a few moments, I saw the ape relax. I suggested Rigo gently reach out to the animal.

"Come here, BigBoy. I want you to meet another member of my family." I held out my hand and he stepped closer.

Rigo tensed and I nudged him with my elbow. "Smile at him." He looked at me in disbelief. "Smile. I'm serious." He turned his eyes back to the big ape and smiled. BigBoy bared his teeth in his now-familiar monkey-grin and reached out to pat Rigo's arm. After some arm-stroking, the animal leaned down and sniffed at the dressing on Rigo's neck. He pointed at the bandage and then at his injured foot, looking at me with a question in his eyes.

"Yes, BigBoy, he has an infection, too. You're both wearing potatoes." At that, everyone laughed and the ape got excited. Rocking left and right, he clapped his hands and giggle-screeched. After that, he treated Rigo as another family member.

Tom, Robbie, and BigBoy removed the fourth wall and we shared a breakfast of fruit and coconuts. Joanne wanted Rigo to have protein for lunch so the guys prepared to go fishing. Before leaving, Robbie assembled his fire-making set-up and I promised to have a fire blazing by the time they returned.

I offered to send BigBoy to the beach with them, but Tom declined. "No, I'd feel better if he was here with you. Robbie and I have knives and spears and, so far, except for your encounter with the two monkeys the day you met BigBoy, we haven't had any daytime attacks – and you were deeper in the jungle at the time. We've never seen monkeys near the beach. And we'll try not to be gone too long." They waved as they headed toward the sea.

Joanne and I checked Rigo's wounds and she commented on how much they had improved. "Who'd have thought potatoes would be such a life-saver? It sure is good to know, though, since we have no first aid kit. How do you feel this morning, Rigo?"

"I am mucho better, Cho! No so much pain. You are very good doctora. Gracias."

"I'm not a doctor, Rigo, but you're very welcome. Lissy found the potatoes when she went after the aloe vera. That was the day she met BigBoy." She chattered happily, as she added fresh potatoes to his injuries. "Tonight, I'll wash off the wounds and start using the aloe. It looks like the infection is gone."

"That's good news!" I was thrilled the potatoes had done such an efficient job of eradicating the infection. "We'll have to be sure and always keep a supply on hand."

Jo surprised me again. "Do you think BigBoy would let me look at his foot? It's probably ready for some aloe vera, too."

"Sure, I think he'd be fine with that." I glanced at the big ape sitting at the edge of the clearing, gnawing on a potato. "Come here, BigBoy. Joanne needs to look at your foot." He ambled over and sat in front of Jo; she pointed at his foot and he raised it, placing it gently in her hand.

Amazed, she said, "He seems to understand what we say!"

"I think he does. He's so attuned to our emotions and body language that he knows what we want. We're lucky he introduced himself." I smiled at BigBoy and he smiled back.

After a quick look at his wound, she said, "One or two days with the aloe vera should be all he needs. Without your help, Lissy, he probably would've died from the infection or gotten so weak the ugly monkeys could've easily killed him. I don't know who's luckier – us or him."

She smeared a generous amount of aloe vera onto the wound and re-wrapped it with the wetskin sleeve. "Okay, BigBoy, you're all done." The ape didn't move.

Realizing Joanne had never handed him anything before, I said, "Oh, he expects a treat. Here." I handed Joanne a potato and she hesitated, unsure about extending her hand to him. They sat there looking at each other until BigBoy slowly reached his hand toward hers. Holding the potato with one finger and her thumb, curling all other fingers safely under, Joanne offered it. He imitated her and very gently took the potato with only one finger and his thumb. Then he smiled at her, and slowly nodded his big head. Deliberately removing his foot from her lap, he patted her leg before walking away, munching contentedly.

I smiled. He was so very gentle around Joanne. He knew how frightened she had been and always tried to reassure her. I didn't know if she even noticed how different he was with her.

A pleased look on her face, Joanne said, "How about if I tend to the fire? You go spend some time with Rigo."

"Okay! Thanks. Let me know if you need help with anything." I strode into the shelter and sat cross-legged next to Rigo's bed. He smiled at me and I was happy to see it didn't look forced. Putting my hand on his arm, I said, "I'm *so* relieved you're getting better, Rigo. We were really worried."

"I worry, too, Leesa. I no want to die." He took my hand. We chatted about things that had happened while he was ill and I broached the subject the rest of us had discussed earlier.

"Does anyone in Cozumel know where you went or that you were diving with Captain Carlos?"

"No, I no tell no one. Many times I dive on the boats, always different ones. No one knows."

My heart sank. "We don't know if anyone will be looking for us. What if no one ever finds us? We'll have to live here on this island with those God-awful monkeys forever!"

Tears overflowed. Rigo gently wiped one from my cheek. "You no cry, pretty Leesa. Someone comes – I am sure."

Sniffing, I stifled more tears. "I hope you're right." We chatted a while longer and I could tell he was fighting to stay awake. "You rest, Rigo. The guys should be back from the beach soon. I'll wake you for lunch." I kissed him on the cheek as his eyelids drooped. He was asleep before I left the shelter.

Joanne was sitting next to a blazing fire, deep in thought. She shrieked when I plopped down on the log next to her. "Oh, my God! I didn't hear you, Lissy! I thought it was one of those damned monkeys!" A long sigh escaped her and she teared up. "What'll we do if no one comes to rescue us? We can't live here with those awful beasts forever!"

"I know. I just had the same conversation with Rigo. No one knows he was diving with Captain Carlos so they won't be searching for him, either." We sat in dejected silence until we heard voices coming up the beach trail. "I think lunch is coming."

Tom and Robbie strolled into camp, laughing and joking. Joanne and I glared at them. *How could they be having so much fun when we had no idea when — or if — we'd ever get off this horrible island?* Tom took one look at our faces and stopped dead in his tracks. "What happened? Is Rigo okay? Why do you two look so miserable?"

"Because we *are* miserable!" we wailed in unison. Joanne burst into tears.

Upset, I stomped off with the bucket. Over my shoulder I said, "I'm going after some water. Come on, BigBoy." I headed into the trees, leaving the guys to deal with Joanne's tears. Maybe they'd be a little more sympathetic by the time I got back. *They were acting like they were on a damned camping trip. We need a plan — something! — to help figure out how to get back home.*

Clomping along the trail, swinging the bucket vigorously to and fro, I didn't notice I'd left camp without a knife or spear. Suddenly, the trees around me came alive with raucous noise: screeching, screaming, snarling, and growling. Smelly, dark brown monkeys dropped out of the branches and surrounded BigBoy and me. I stepped closer to him and realized just how vulnerable I was. Heart pounding, I broke into a cold sweat. Looking around, it seemed there were teeth everywhere. I screamed as loud as I could. "Tom! Help! Help!"

BigBoy roared and snarled and puffed out his chest, swinging his arms in an effort to intimidate the smaller beasts. They knew we were outnumbered and refused to retreat. It was only a matter of time before they rushed us and my faithful companion wouldn't be able to protect me.

One or two at a time, they darted forward, taunting BigBoy and causing him to swing at them, futilely. Suddenly, one rushed him while simultaneously, one darted at me. I screamed and instinctively swung the bucket, connecting with the beast's head. A solid thunk left the monkey dazed and staggering. BigBoy had forced his assailant to retreat and turned to strike at the stunned animal. With one swipe, he tossed it hard against a tree. I heard a distinct crack as something broke. The animal never moved.

The screeching increased in volume as the monkeys realized they'd lost one of their own. One younger animal played the hero and rushed BigBoy. He took one step too close and the big ape grabbed him in a crushing hold. A powerful bite to the animal's throat left another one dead. BigBoy's teeth were made for grinding vegetation and fruit, but they were big, strong, and lethal in close quarters, the large canines doing their job very efficiently.

The odds had improved, but the monkeys were smart and learned from their mistakes. Single animals never rushed BigBoy again, keeping a respectful distance from his long arms. I was the weak one, but I had proven to be deadly, too. They didn't know it was complete good fortune that the bucket had connected so solidly. That accident may have saved my life since none of the monkeys dared rush me again. It seemed to be a stand-off until I heard Tom and Robbie screaming my name. "Lissy! Lissy!"

"Over here! Be careful! We're surrounded!" I didn't want them to rush headlong into a bad situation.

The monkeys realized help had arrived and divided their attention between us and the newcomers. BigBoy took immediate advantage of their lack of focus, grabbing the monkey that seemed to be calling the shots. With one swift movement, he broke the animal's neck and threw its lifeless body at the other attackers.

At the same moment, Tom and Robbie rushed the remaining monkeys. Tom speared one in the chest and Robbie clubbed another soundly alongside the head. Both animals dropped dead where they stood and the rest of the group leapt into the trees. Rustling leaves and angry snarls and growls showed the direction of their hasty retreat.

I fell to my knees, weak with relief, and burst into tears. BigBoy turned to me with a whimper and sank down beside me. I reached out to reassure him and realized his arms were bloody and a nasty gash on his chest dripped red down his belly. *He received those wounds protecting me.* I dried my eyes. Tom helped me to my feet and, with determination coloring my words, I said, "I'm sorry. It was stupid to run off into the trees without any weapons and now BigBoy's hurt again. We need to get back to camp before the monkeys regroup. Joanne needs to look at his wounds. This is the second time he's saved my life."

After making sure none of the blood on my body was mine, we set off for camp.

Joanne anxiously met us at the edge of the clearing. Eyeing the blood, she said, "Are you okay, Lissy? We heard you scream!"

"I'm fine, Jo, but you need to take care of BigBoy. He saved my life before Tom and Robbie could get there. He's bleeding."

From the shelter, Rigo yelled, "Leesa, you are okay?"

"Yes, Rigo, I'm fine. It's BigBoy that needs Joanne's attention. I'll tell you about it later."

Jo grabbed a pot to boil water. Dinner was nearly done so she pushed the fish aside and set the container over the fire.

"Come here, BigBoy. Let me look at you." Joanne had overcome her fear and he obediently sat down in front of her. She wiped the blood away from his arms and announced that those wounds were superficial; the one on his chest, however, was more serious. It was a deep scratch rather than a bite, with one center furrow deeper than the ones on either side. She wiped the blood away and applied pressure to the wound, murmuring tenderly to the big animal that looked at her with soft eyes.

No one cared that the fish were over-cooking, wanting only to be certain BigBoy was properly tended to. When the bleeding stopped, Joanne applied a thick slather of aloe vera and said to no one in particular, "Hmm... We don't have anything to bandage the wound with, so I guess the aloe will have to suffice. We can watch it and if it gets infected, we'll have to figure out a way to put potatoes on it." She smiled at BigBoy and stroked his arm. "You keep that wound clean, now, you hear?"

Snuggling his big hairy head against Joanne's chest, he made a contented sound low in his throat, like a cat's purr. She scratched the side of his face and said, "Okay, you big beast, here's your potato. Now move, so we can eat lunch. Go on!" She slapped him affectionately on the shoulder as he ambled away.

We fixed our plates and moved into the shelter to sit with Rigo. Although everything was overdone, no one complained. While we ate, BigBoy foraged in the nearby trees for mangoes and papayas. After lunch we again discussed the feasibility of hunting for more orangutans.

Tom suggested, "Why don't we keep a low profile until Rigo's better? Then we can lock all our stuff in the shelter – not that there's much of it, but it's precious, nonetheless – and go, as a group, into the jungle and see if we can find more apes."

Robbie said, "Say we do find more of them. How do we know BigBoy will allow other orangutans anywhere near us? He seems to think we're his and he might feel he has to protect us from them. What then?"

Feeling strongly on the subject, I said, "I don't see that we have much choice. BigBoy can't protect us much longer all by himself. The monkeys are smart and learn from every encounter. Next time, I bet there will be more of them and they'll have a *plan*. They're angry – and they're hungry!" I saw Joanne shudder at the thought of being attacked and eaten by the nasty beasts and I softened my voice, although determination underlay my words.

"I agree with Tom. We wait until Rigo's better, lock up our stuff, and arm ourselves to the teeth. We go into the jungle and look for more orangutans. If we find some, we'll figure it out as we go, depending on how BigBoy and the other apes behave. We know pretty much how to introduce a new *person* to BigBoy; we'll have to hope other apes have the same kind inclination toward humans. Then we'll just have to be sure the apes get along."

Softly, Joanne said, "It could end up being a bloodbath."

"It could be a bloodbath if we *don't* do this, Jo." I put my arm around her shoulder and tried to lend her strength. She wasn't cut out to be a warrior. She was a gentle, nurturing soul and violence of any kind made her cringe.

"You are all een danger because I am stupeed. I run een the jungle alone and have surprise by bad monkeys. I sorry. I owe you much." Rigo hung his head, shame apparent in his demeanor.

"No, Rigo, we don't blame you for anything." I took his hand and said, "Look at me."

90

He raised his eyes to mine and I smiled and shook my head. "It's not your fault. When you're well, we'll go orangutan hunting to find BigBoy a friend."

"Okay. I help. Ees my fault we dive een the strong current first. You have plans with Captain Carlos and I make eet deeferent. I sorry, but I help you now."

Robbie stood and patted Rigo's shoulder. "We accept your offer, Rigo. When you're strong again, we'll go ape-hunting. You rest and regain your strength." They smiled at each other and the tension dissipated.

We left him alone and went our separate ways. Tom sat with his back to a tree with the log book while Joanne and I cleaned up the lunchtime mess. Robbie suggested we collect more potatoes while the monkeys' defeat was still fresh in their minds. I offered to go with him, with BigBoy in attendance, of course.

Once armed, we let everyone know where we were going. I grabbed the bucket and called, "BigBoy! Do you want to go get more potatoes?" The ape swung down from the trees and moseyed over, a half-eaten mango in one big paw. In spite of the skirmishes that always seemed to draw blood – usually his – the orangutan obviously enjoyed our forays into the jungle. We set off at a quick pace, anxious to get there and back without incident. According to my mental calculations, we shouldn't be in the jungle for more than an hour, but past experience had proven that could be fifty-five minutes too long.

I was more familiar with this path than Robbie, so I took the lead, however, once I spotted the aloe vera patch, I realized we'd come too far. Since we were there, I broke off a few fresh aloe branches and put them in the bucket. Retracing our steps, we located the spot where I'd been attacked by the two monkeys and found the potato field off to one side. "Okay, BigBoy, scratch up some potatoes." This time, he knew what I wanted and began pawing at the ground. Robbie shook his head in amazement, watching as the animal cleared away the dirt.

"You'd think he spoke English, he understands you so well."

I grinned. "Yep, you only need to show him something once and he's got it."

In no time at all, we had a bucketful, even though the orangutan ate a fair amount in the process. Then he threw in a few mangoes and a coconut he collected nearby. He'd learned quickly how to take full advantage of the situation.

"Okay, let's go home." I smiled as BigBoy picked up the bucket and cradled it in his arms. Halfway back to camp, leaves rustled overhead but we maintained a quick pace and made it home without incident. I didn't realize I'd been holding my breath until we entered the clearing and I let out a huge sigh of relief.

We found Rigo sitting on a log next to the fire pit, enjoying the sunshine. "Hi, Rigo! It's nice to see you up and about. You must be feeling better." I went over and sat next to him.

"Sí, I feel much better, Leesa. I have hunger, too." He eyed the bucket BigBoy clutched in his arms.

"Okay. Bring that bucket over here, BigBoy." The ape ambled over and set the bucket at my feet. "How about a mango? I don't think BigBoy would mind sharing. After all, there's no shortage of fruit on this island." I handed Rigo a nice, fresh mango and watched as he devoured it. "Want another one?"

"Sí. Es very good!"

I turned to address everyone and asked, "What do you think we should have for dinner? Fish?" I grimaced at the thought, but then decided it was better than going hungry. And protein would be good for Rigo – he needed to regain his strength.

Tom looked up from his book and said, "Robbie, that sounded like a hint. Wanna go fishing?"

"Sure. Lissy and Joanne can get the fire going while we're out. Maybe we'll get lucky and find another ray trapped in a pool. Those ray steaks were really good!"

They grabbed spears, knives, and the bucket and headed for the beach.

Joanne hollered, "Be careful, you two!"

Rigo, Joanne, and I sat by the pit, talking and tending the small fire. Tom and Robbie were gone quite a while and I was just beginning to worry when I heard voices.

"Dinner has arrived!" Tom announced as they strolled into the clearing. "We lucked out and caught another ray trapped in a pool. I guess it's a common occurrence."

Joanne said, "The fire's ready whenever you are, Chief Cook!" She laughed and poked Tom in the ribs.

"Okay, I'll clean this baby and get steaks on the fire. How 'bout some potatoes to go with?" Tom was definitely a meat-and-potatoes kind of guy.

I grinned. "We have you figured out, Tom. We cleaned some earlier so we'll toss them into the fire now. They ought to be done by the time the steaks are. What I wouldn't give for some butter, salt, and pepper, though." My mouth watered.

"Cut it out, Lissy! When we get home, you can have whatever you want. For now, be happy we have what we have." Robbie then added, under his breath, "But I'd kill for a big slab of chocolate cake."

In unison, we yelled, "I heard that!" and laughed when Robbie's face turned bright pink. He ignored us and concentrated on helping Tom get the ray onto the cutting board stone, saying nothing more about his gastronomic yearnings.

Soon, dinner smells wafted through the clearing. As soon as Tom said, "Soup's on!" we scrambled to the buffet line. Everyone except Rigo, that is; I fixed his plate so he wouldn't have to move around too much.

Although not a fish-lover, I had to admit the ray steaks were delicious. And the potatoes were good, too, even without the butter, salt, and pepper. At least, we weren't going hungry.

Everyone was in a good mood and I enjoyed the laughter and stories told around the fire that night. I think it was because Rigo was on the mend and we had a plan in place to find more orangutans. Dare I say that it seemed things were looking up?

We had learned our lesson about waiting until dark to put the fourth wall on, so shortly after dinner, we began our nighttime preparations. Tom and Robbie lugged the wall over instead of asking BigBoy to do it. He was injured and we wanted his wounds to heal without complications. He didn't put in an appearance by the time we were ready to lock up so I raised my eyes to the trees and said, "Goodnight, big fella. Rest easy."

Rigo made it to his bed without help and said, "Tomorrow I want to go to the pool. You go, too, Leesa?"

"Yes, Rigo, I'd love to go to the pool with you. In fact, I think we could all use a relaxing swim. There's safety in numbers, after all!" I smiled to myself as the entire group agreed.

Before long, snores and deep breathing surrounded me, soft nighttime jungle sounds floating in from outside. More relaxed than I'd been in a while, my last thought as I drifted off to sleep was of BigBoy. I pictured him draped over a sturdy tree branch, leaves tucked under his big, hairy head. *Do orangutans snore...?*

Chapter 9

Day 5

<u>Lissy</u>

Slowly, I opened my eyes. Lying on his side, Rigo faced me with a sexy smile on his lips. Quietly he said, "Hola, Leesa. You are beauteeful een the morning. I like to watch you sleep – you sometimes make leetle noises, like a cat."

"Oh, stop it! I am *not* beautiful in the morning and quit watching me sleep!" I grumbled. I stretched and sat up, finding that everyone else was already awake and out of the shelter. Alone with this sexy Lothario who was, obviously, feeling much better, I wasn't quite sure how to react. After not shaving for five days, Rigo's dark stubble was very pronounced, giving him a dangerous, bad-boy look. Tousled, black hair flopped forward over his forehead, not quite hiding the gleam in his dark eyes.

My pulse quickened and I found myself staring at his full lips, wondering how they'd taste in the morning. I chided myself. *Stop it, Lissy. Your friends are just outside – don't start something you can't finish!* I raised my gaze to his eyes and his lips curled in a slow, sensual grin. *Dammit, he knows what I was thinking.*

"Come on, Rigo. You'd better move around so you don't get stiff." I leapt to my feet, realizing how my comment sounded; his deep-throated chuckle told me where his thoughts had gone.

"See you at breakfast!" I dashed out of the shelter and nearly knocked Joanne off her feet.

"Whoa, Lissy! What's the rush?" She grinned knowingly and I stammered something incomprehensible. She added, "Rigo's feeling better this morning?" and laughed. I flushed scarlet.

Tom looked up from slicing a mango and said, "Yep, that's a sure sign the fellow's on the mend!"

"Stop it, you guys!" I picked up a chunk of fruit and said, "I wish we had coffee. I miss that more than anything else, especially in the morning."

Jo's murmured, "Mhmmm" sent everyone laughing again.

I ignored them and ate another mango. About then, Rigo sauntered out of the shelter, still looking dangerously gorgeous and sexy. I averted my eyes. Wanting to point the conversation in a safer direction, I asked, "Has anyone seen BigBoy yet this morning? He's usually down by now."

The orangutan had been conspicuously absent thus far and I gazed up into the trees, hoping to catch a glimpse of him. I called out. "BigBoy! Come down and have a mango." Nothing stirred and I felt a frisson of apprehension. Maybe his wounds were more serious than we thought and he was lying somewhere, helpless. Or maybe the ugly monkeys had attacked him and he was too weak to defend himself. I shivered.

Moving toward Rigo, Joanne said, "Good morning, Rigo! Have a seat over here and let me look at those wounds. You look good today. Are you feeling better?"

"Sí, Cho, I feel mucho mejor. You are very good doctora." He smiled at Joanne and she blushed, surely remembering the topic of our earlier banter. "Maybe I go to the pool today. Ees okay for the bad bite to get wet?"

Smiling, Joanne replied, "Yes, it's healing nicely now that the infection's gone, but we'll have to clean it really well afterwards and apply more aloe. I think we could all use a swim today."

"Let's finish this fruit," I suggested, "and then head to the pool before it gets too hot." They murmured assent and I handed out more mangoes, still wondering about BigBoy. He wasn't one to miss a meal.

We downed the fruit then collected our weapons. Once more I called out to the orangutan. "Come on, BigBoy, we're going to the pool. Don't you want to come with us?" Nothing stirred in the branches above. This was the first time he hadn't responded to my voice and knowing he loved to venture into the jungle with us, I was more than slightly concerned. I was downright scared. *What would we do without him?*

I kept a watchful eye on the canopy during the short walk, but nothing moved. Before entering the water, we laid the weapons around the pool within arm's reach. Feeling exposed without our bodyguard, I said, "It might be a good idea to take turns standing watch. Without BigBoy, we're much more vulnerable. I'll go first."

"You're scaring me, Lissy," Joanne said. "Do you think they'd attack us here?"

I didn't want to worry her further, but figured it was better to be on edge than complacent. "It was here that I heard the monkeys for the first time. Remember, I heard that twig crack and thought it was you guys? Then I saw that face behind those vines over there. So, yeah, this place isn't off limits at all!"

Taking a position on the highest rock, I had a good view all around. Nothing could sneak up on us. I had a spear in one hand and my knife lying on the rock, easily accessible. The group splashed and played, relaxing in the water and sunshine.

Finally, Tom clambered up on the rock next to me and said, "Okay, Lissy, it's your turn to relax. Go get wet."

I turned to Tom with tears in my eyes and said softly, so the others couldn't hear, "What if something's happened to BigBoy? He could be hurt... or dead. What would we do without him?"

Tom patted my shoulder. "I'm sure he's okay, Lissy. He's a wild animal. It's perfectly natural for him to go off by himself. Who knows, he may have a girlfriend somewhere. He'll come back when he's ready. Go enjoy the water." He smiled and motioned toward the pool.

Not completely comforted, I knew there was nothing we could do about BigBoy's absence. I nodded and said, "You're right. Thanks, Tom." I crawled down and stepped into the pool. I hadn't realized how hot it was on the rock, exposed to direct sunlight, and the water felt refreshingly cool. Rigo floated over and took my hand.

"You are alright, Leesa? You worry about BeegBoy, no?" His concern made me smile.

"Yes, I'm worried. He's never left like this and I feel something might be wrong. He could be in danger. Those ugly monkeys know he protects us so if they could get rid of him, we'd be sitting ducks."

"We are ducks? Why are we ducks, Leesa?" Confused, Rigo had obviously not heard the saying before.

I tried to explain. "It's an American expression. It means we'd be easy targets."

"Oh, sí. Ees not good to be ducks." He shook his head in all seriousness and I stifled a giggle, not wanting to hurt his feelings.

To dispel the gloomy mood, I splashed Rigo and said playfully, "Come on, let's float in the middle of the pool." I swam to the center and stretched out on my back, placing my woven hat over my face to avoid a sunburn. Rigo floated up beside me and took my hand. Water in my ears muffled the sounds from my friends and I concentrated on the physical sensations: heat from above; coolness below; tiny waves lapping all around me; Rigo's warm hand holding mine. I made a conscious effort to relax, beginning with my toes and working upwards – ankles, calves, knees, thighs, buttocks, belly – feeling the tension gradually drain away. By the time I got to my shoulders and neck, I felt looser than I had in a while. I needed this and was grateful my friends had agreed to a morning swim. Maybe it would be a good day, after all.

Suddenly, I heard Tom's muffled voice, low but full of urgency. "Lissy. Lissy! Slowly turn toward my voice." Something in his tone made me shiver. I expected to see a ring of ugly monkeys surrounding the pool. I slid the hat from my face to my head, gripped Rigo's hand tightly, and we slowly lowered our feet until we were vertical in the water. Making no sudden movements, we turned as one toward the big rocks.

At first, all I saw was Tom sitting atop the rock, spear held tightly in his right hand. The look on his face showed concern and surprise, but no fear. *What was going on?* When our eyes met, he tilted his head slightly toward the trees. I glanced in that direction and did a double-take. There were *three* orangutans standing at the tree line, watching us. One was BigBoy and he smiled at me from his position between the other two.

Both new orangutans were males. One was slightly smaller and the other a tad larger than BigBoy. And whereas BigBoy was strawberry blonde, the larger ape was a dark, rusty-red color and the other a muddy chocolate brown with only hints of red in his hair. Both were very muscular and seemed to be in good health. Neither exhibited threatening behavior, but then, neither did they seem overly friendly. I wondered how we should react. I looked at Tom and raised an eyebrow; he shrugged. The five of us faced the three animals, silent and doubtful about our next move.

I thought, *Well, we wanted more orangutans, now we have some.* Making up my mind, I let go of Rigo's hand, breast-stroked to the edge of the pool, and slowly crawled up onto the rocks. The animals watched intently and BigBoy made low, soothing noises.

Lowering my eyes, I took three deliberate steps toward the trio and stopped, lowering myself to a sitting position. I sat there for a minute with downcast eyes, giving the animals time to accept my closer proximity. Then I raised my arm toward them, palm up, supplicating, as BigBoy had done when I introduced Joanne. Nobody moved for several minutes and I didn't know how much longer I could maintain the position; my muscles quivered with the strain. Just as I decided this wasn't going to work, BigBoy and both of the new apes moved toward me. I forgot the pain as I watched them through lowered eyes.

They stopped directly in front of me and I held my breath. BigBoy reached out and stroked my arm, humming quietly. After a moment, the red ape extended his arm and touched his fingertips to mine. I could feel his apprehension and, wanting to put him at ease, began humming like BigBoy had done. It seemed to have the desired effect and the ape gently stroked my arm. He stepped back and the smaller orangutan hesitantly reached out to my fingers. But instead of stroking my arm, he lowered his big head and sniffed, snuffling all the way to my elbow. His face was only about six inches from mine and I couldn't help myself – I raised my eyes and looked into his. I could swear I saw intelligence and soul in that animal.

100

When he dropped his eyes and shuffled back, I lowered my aching arm. BigBoy then took my hand and pulled me to my feet, wrapping his long arms around me in a tender hug. He held me, humming, and patted my shoulder. He moved away and motioned toward the red ape. Rusty, as I thought of him, took me in his arms and crooned, holding me gently. No pat from him.

The chocolate-red ape liked to do things his way. He moved toward me, but when he was about three feet away he reached out and took my hand in his, pulling me close. He then snuffled my face from eyelids to chin and lipped me, moving his lips over my cheek in a monkey-kiss. My eyes flew open in surprise and he giggled softly, put his arms around me and hugged me tighter than the others had. He was quite the flirt. I named him Frank after Sinatra's hit, *My Way*. It suited him.

When Frank moved away, BigBoy stepped into the trees and brought out some mangos. Since introduction ceremonies included eating, the four of us shared a mango, passing it from one to the other. Although part of me cringed at the idea of taking a bite of fruit that had just left an ape's lips, I quelled the feeling and did my part. At that point, all was well and we were family.

I knew Rusty and Frank also had to be introduced to the rest of the group and motioned for Tom to come down from the rocks. This time, I took the initiative and hugged Tom first, breaking the ice for the new guys. As our ambassador, BigBoy hugged, hummed, and patted and things went smoothly – the apes readily accepted all three men. However, one look at Joanne's face told me she wouldn't be able to approach the beasts. They'd easily sense her fear. Heck, *I* could sense her fear!

Once more, BigBoy came to the rescue. Leaving Rusty and Frank standing with us, he moseyed over to the edge of the pool and offered Joanne his hand. She took his hairy paw and he easily pulled her up out of the water. Looking into her eyes, he hummed softly then wrapped his long arms around her in a gentle hug. When he released her, he nodded his big head.

Joanne's relationship with BigBoy had changed dramatically since that first traumatic introduction. He treated her with obvious respect and deference. He clearly loved her. She trusted him to protect her and loved the big guy in return. That confidence enabled them to get through the next few minutes.

Holding Joanne's hand, BigBoy led her over to Rusty and Frank, stopping about three feet in front of them. He screeched at the newcomers and pointed to the ground. Puzzled, I didn't know what was going to happen next since this had never been a part of an introduction. When the two apes didn't move, he screeched a second time and puffed out his chest, once again pointing to the ground. Acknowledging his superior rank, I guess, both apes lowered themselves to sitting positions, eyes downcast.

BigBoy then led Joanne up to the larger orangutan and placed her hand atop Rusty's head, stroking his hair softly. He released her hand and although her face expressed abject terror, she continued the stroking motions. After several minutes, Rusty's body relaxed and slouched and he began to hum. Approval had been given. I let out the breath I didn't realize I'd been holding.

Frank had watched the proceedings and, true to form, again did his own thing. He reached out and took Joanne's hand from Rusty's head, placing it on his own. And instead of humming he giggle-screeched when she stroked his chocolaty-red hair. The rest of us smiled at the ape's reaction to her touch.

Then suddenly, Frank jumped to his feet, eliciting a shriek of pure terror from Joanne and startling us all. She backed away, unable to tear her eyes from the unpredictable ape. Tears welled as she faced him, continuing to back up until she encountered the rocks. Trapped, she whimpered.

Frank slowly moved toward her and I glanced at BigBoy to see if he sensed a threat. Surprised, I saw he looked relaxed and not at all threatened by this new behavior.

Joanne pressed against the rocks, trembling. Frank swaggered over until he stood directly in front of her. By then, tears coursed freely down her face but she remained silent. She turned her head away and screwed her eyes tightly shut as the ape slowly reached toward her face. Gently, he wiped a tear from her cheek with one long, hairy finger. He looked at the droplet, sniffed it, and then raised his face to snuffle at Joanne's cheek. I thought she was going to pass out as he snuffled her left cheek, then her right. Pulling back and cocking his head in confusion, he gazed at Joanne's face and once more looked at the tear on his fingertip.

Slowly, he dropped to a sitting position, lowered his eyes, and hung his head – the very picture of shame and remorse. It seemed that Frank had come to the conclusion he was scaring Joanne and not knowing how to reassure her, wanted her to know he felt bad for frightening her. He sat at her feet, motionless, for several minutes. Finally, when she sensed no further movement, Joanne opened her eyes. Seeing the orangutan hunched at her feet, head hung, she looked over at me for some indication of what to do. I mimed petting motions and she shook her head in a vehement "no." I nodded with conviction and she hesitantly placed her trembling hand on the animal's head. As she gently stroked, he sighed deeply and began to hum.

BigBoy clapped and screeched his approval, smiled widely, and rocked back and forth. Rusty joined in and we laughed at their antics. Frank never even twitched, perhaps afraid of scaring Joanne again. When she finally stopped petting him, he raised his face and gazed into her eyes. She gave him a tentative smile and he grinned back. Some of the tension had left her body during the petting session and when Frank smiled, she relaxed further. The ape slowly stood and wrapped his long arms around her in a tender hug. I held my breath, wondering if Joanne was ready for the close contact, but when she awkwardly patted his back, I knew the crisis was over. Of course, further introductions signaled more mangoes, so we shared fruit to cement the new relationships.

Tom came and stood next to me as I watched the interactions between the apes and my friends. Frank and Rusty kept handing Robbie, Rigo, and Joanne more mangoes. They'd even found some papayas and coconuts to add to the feast. Tom's comment echoed my own thoughts. "The timing makes you wonder if BigBoy understood what we said about needing another ape."

I smiled. "Yep. And then he took it a step further and figured if one was good, two would be better. It's scary, he's so smart. I wish we knew how much he actually understands."

With a thoughtful look, Tom said, "Maybe we could try training him. That should indicate how quickly he catches on to things and might prove whether or not he actually understands what we say or just knows a few of the words."

Excited at the prospect, I grabbed Tom's arm and exclaimed, "That's a great idea! Just think... We might actually be able to communicate with him. With *all* of them!" I turned away, my thoughts in turmoil. Whirling back to face him again, I said, "Let's give Rusty and Frank a day to settle in and then we can start regular classes. I'll work out a lesson plan as a starting point. If it's too simple or too advanced, I can adjust it as we go along."

"Whoa, Lissy! Slow down. Take it step by step and see what happens." Tom grinned. "Jumping in with both feet works with some things; for others, you need to be more systematic."

Knowing he was right, I tried to reign in my enthusiasm and channel it constructively. "Does that log book say whether they did any training after injecting them with the serum to see how much faster they learned?"

Tom thought for a minute. "Not in what I've read so far. The handwriting is faded and kind of hard to read." His brow furrowed and he thoughtfully added, "Maybe the last half of the book will shed some light on what you're asking. I'll let you know if I come across anything you can use." We stood there grinning at each other, possibilities racing through my mind. I wondered if Tom was thinking along the same lines. It would change everything if we could *converse* with the orangutans!

"Hey, you two! Get us out of here. I'm stuffed!" Robbie hollered for help as Frank handed him more fruit.

Tom and I laughed. "We'd better go rescue them!" We collected the weapons and joined the group. "Are you guys ready to head back to camp?" I asked, already knowing the answer.

"Yes! Let's go!" Joanne rolled her eyes as BigBoy offered her another papaya. "No more, BigBoy. No more, please!"

We started up the trail to camp and the three orangutans fell into line behind us. I figured we'd eventually have to teach one to walk in the lead in case of a frontal attack; the other two could bring up the rear. We had some work to do but I was thrilled at the prospect of finding a way to communicate with the apes. At one point, I had considered going into teaching. Although this wasn't what I'd had in mind, I was up for the challenge.

Upon returning to camp, Rigo said, "I must sleep more," and went off to take a nap. Joanne cleaned his neck wound and added more aloe vera. He fell asleep before she finished.

As she exited the shelter, I asked, "How does the bite look?"

She said, "It's fine. He's healing quickly now that the infection's gone. He just needs to regain his strength and stamina. In a few days, he'll be ready to go fishing."

"We need to explore more of the island once he's up to it, too. With three orangutans, we shouldn't have much trouble with the ugly monkeys and we need to find out if there are any other inhabitants. Who knows? There could be an entire village on the other side of that mountain!" I laughed. "Wouldn't that be ironic? We've been living here like deserted island castaways and there could be a hundred people a day's walk away!"

BigBoy showed Rusty and Frank around camp and then they disappeared into the trees. I liked knowing they were close by.

Robbie came and sat next to us on the log by the fire pit. "I know none of us is hungry right now after all that fruit, but Tom and I were thinking of going fishing. If we can talk two of the apes into staying here at camp, we can take the third one with us. That way, everyone's protected and we can take our time at the beach. What do you think? Can we separate the trio?"

"We can try," I said. Looking up at the leafy canopy, I hollered, "BigBoy! Come here, BigBoy!" The leaves rustled and three big, hairy bodies dropped from above. BigBoy came over and I explained, not knowing how much he understood. "Tom and Robbie are going fishing and they want one of you guys to go with them. The other two stay here in camp. Okay?"

The ape grinned, nodded, and screeched. *Yes? Who knows!* I figured we'd find out when the guys headed toward the sea.

"Collect your fishing stuff," I said. "And if you want, we can have a fire going when you get back. We'll fix potatoes, too."

"Okay. Do you think he understood about two of them staying here?" Robbie looked at the trio with skepticism.

"We'll find out soon enough." I hoped BigBoy could help instruct Rusty and Frank. I knew I could make him understand; I wasn't sure about the other two. Would they want to split up?

"Okay, we're ready to go," Tom said, eyeing the apes.

"Start down the trail. If all three follow you, I'll see if I can explain it so they understand." I grinned at Joanne. "This ought to be interesting."

As the guys took the path toward the beach, BigBoy followed. And right behind him sauntered Frank and Rusty. I was about to call out to BigBoy when he stopped and turned to face the other two. Pointing to his own chest with one hand, he motioned down the path toward the sea with the other. He then pointed to Frank and Rusty and shook his head no. He waved them back toward camp, uttering a conversational "Woo, woo, woo." When he continued down the trail, Frank and Rusty turned and came back to the clearing.

Joanne and I gaped at each other in astonishment. Recovering her voice, Joanne said, "Did you see that? He told them to stay here!"

"So BigBoy clearly understood what I said earlier. Oh, my God, this is incredible!" Weak in the knees, I dropped down next to the fire pit, my mind in a whirl. Joanne plopped down beside me. Frank and Rusty climbed up into the trees and we heard them settle for a nap – or whatever orangutans do up there in the trees.

After several minutes of individual contemplation, I shared what Tom and I had discussed at the pool. "I'm going to create a lesson plan and start holding regular classes for BigBoy, Rusty, and Frank. We need to know how much they actually understand, which words they recognize. Wouldn't it be amazing if we could just *talk* to them?"

Joanne giggled. "I feel like I've been transported to *Planet of the Apes.*"

I nodded and joked, "Yeah, as long as BigBoy and Company don't start talking back!"

We checked on Rigo and found him fast asleep. Joanne said, "That looks like a great idea." and headed for her pallet.

Camp was exceptionally quiet at the moment, so I decided to make a couple of hats for the guys, keeping my hands busy and freeing my mind to wrestle with structuring classes for the apes. I dug out the supply of vines and grasses and, using my own hat as a guide, began weaving. To get a more manly design, I created an Indian Jones-style that I thought they'd like.

With fingers flying and mind a-whirling, I soon completed one hat and began another. When Frank dropped out of the trees a few feet away, I yelped in surprise and he froze. I giggled at his reaction and he slowly moved toward me, staring at my face for a long minute. I think he was checking to see if I was crying as Joanne had earlier. Reassured there were no tears, he picked up the completed hat and examined it inside and out. When he plopped it on his head at a rakish angle and swaggered back across the clearing, I hollered, "Hey, Frank! That's not for you, you big lug! Bring that back here!" Ignoring my directive, he climbed up into the canopy. I sighed, hoping I had enough grass on hand to make hats for everyone, figuring once BigBoy and Rusty saw how debonair Frank looked they'd want one, too.

Sure enough, I was halfway through the second one when Rusty climbed down a nearby tree and ambled over to watch me work. He looked around for a hat to filch, but the only completed one was on my head. He ogled mine and sidled closer.

Humming a monkey-tune, he slowly reached toward my hat, avoiding my eyes. When his hand was only a few inches from the brim, I slapped his fingers and said, "No!" Surprised, he backed off a foot or so and continued to watch me work, but I knew he hadn't given up hope of making off with his coveted prize.

We covertly watched each other and he finally sauntered into the trees, wearing a sneaky look. I wondered what he was up to. I removed my hat and tucked it under my knees so he couldn't grab it from behind in a snatch-and-run blitz.

I heard rustling in the bushes behind and to my left and knew Rusty was up to something. Totally ignoring him, I plucked another long strand of grass to weave into the hat. A hairy red-brown arm reached around my body, fingers grasping for the brim of the hat I had tucked away. Once more, I slapped his hand, harder this time, and said, "No, Rusty!"

The arm disappeared. I didn't hear him climb back into the trees so I knew he was still skulking nearby. He certainly was persistent. *What would he try next?*

When a long stick slid out of the brush behind me, I grabbed it, jumped up and turned toward the ape. I yelled, "Stop it, Rusty! You cannot have my hat!" Stepping out of the trees, he rose up to his full height, chest thrust out, and stopped a few feet away. My heart pounded and I thought maybe he was going to take the hat by force. *How far would he go to get what he wanted?* After all, this wasn't BigBoy.

I met his gaze and tried to stare him down. If I wasn't in charge, he was — and that would not be a comfortable situation. He glared steadily back at me and slowly raised his lip in a silent snarl. I got a glimpse of his long, right fang and broke out in a cold sweat, wishing BigBoy would miraculously appear and save me once again. For one prolonged moment, neither of us moved.

Rusty slowly took a step forward, but I held my ground and he stopped, unsure. A loud screech split the air and Frank dropped gracefully from above. He quickly ran to my side and stood tall, slightly to the left and in front of me, his eyes glued on Rusty. He growled low in his throat and shook his big head no. Although the smaller of the two apes, Frank seemed older and wasn't going to take any nonsense from this arrogant kid. Rusty once again curled his lip in a challenge, flashing both fangs in an effort to intimidate Frank. That was his undoing.

In a blur of motion, Frank leapt on Rusty and knocked him to the dirt. Screeches, snarls, growls and nearly-human screams filled the air as the two rolled, ran, and jumped around the clearing. I hid behind a thick bush as Frank thoroughly trounced Rusty before chasing him into the trees. Distant screams continued for several more moments before the jungle fell silent.

Rigo and Joanne blasted out of the shelter and came running toward me, concern written all over their faces. "I'm fine, you guys. I'm fine."

"Leesa, you are okay, no? Those monkeys no hurt you?" Rigo put his arms around me in a consoling hug.

Joanne, almost in tears again, said, "What happened, Lissy? I heard a loud screech and then Rusty and Frank fighting!"

It would've been funny if I wasn't so frightened. I told them the whole story.

"Oh, Lissy, you're so brave! I would've dissolved into screams and tears," Joanne said.

"When Rusty snarled at Frank, that's when the real ruckus began. You saw Frank chasing Rusty all over camp. I'll bet he gives him a good thrashing."

"I hope he does! Rusty has to know he's supposed to protect us, not threaten us. How will we feel safe with him around?" Joanne had a point.

"You are brave chica, Leesa! I no like that monkey growling for you." I smiled at Rigo and patted his hand.

"I'm fine, really. Hopefully, Frank will teach him a lesson and we won't have any more problems with him." I gazed at the disheveled campsite. "We'd better straighten things up before the guys get back. And it's probably time to start the fire. Hope they're catching some fish – I'm getting hungry again."

I cleaned up my grass, vines, and half-finished hat, restacked the rocks Robbie had set up for the fire – they'd been scattered in the earlier free-for-all – and added the dive mask. The scorching hot sun wouldn't take long to ignite the coconut strings.

By the time Tom, Robbie, and BigBoy strolled into camp, all was normal once again. A nice fire blazed in the pit and I'd tossed in some potatoes when I heard voices coming up the trail.

"I hope you guys are hungry! We brought back a feast! BigBoy helped us find some clams, we caught several fish in the pools, and found a small ray. It'll be a buffet tonight!" Tom was jovial after a relaxing day spent fishing with the boys even though he and Robbie were both sunburned and glowing a bright pink.

Joanne came to their aid. "Before you do anything else, I'm putting aloe on your faces. You guys are fried!" Tom and Robbie grumbled but submitted to her ministrations, later admitting their faces felt much better with a cooling layer of gel.

And once her nursing duties were done, she ordered Tom to start KP. "We're starved! So get those fish cleaned. And Lissy has another story to tell over dinner tonight."

"Now what?" Tom whipped his head around and said, "We can't leave you alone for one hour without you having an adventure. What happened?"

I grinned and put him off. "You'll just have to wait until we're all together for dinner. The fire's ready so any time those fish are cleaned, we can cook 'em." He groused some more but I'm sure his stomach was rumbling, too. In no time at all, fillets, small ray steaks, and a skillet of clams were tender and steaming hot. We raked the potatoes out of the fire and filled our plates.

No one spoke for a while; everyone concentrating on the bounty before us. Then, one by one, we set our plates aside. Finally, Tom looked at me and said, "Okay, Lissy, out with it."

I began with our astonishing discovery earlier in the day. "When you and Robbie started down the trail to go fishing, BigBoy, Rusty, and Frank were right behind you. I was about to holler for BigBoy when he stopped and told Rusty and Frank to stay in camp."

Joanne said, "It was as plain as if he'd spoken English. Right, Lissy?"

"Yep. So BigBoy understood what I said after we got back from the pool. And I only said it once – it's not like I pantomimed or showed him what I wanted. He understood the words, Tom. And he explained it to Rusty and Frank."

Still skeptical, Tom asked, "So what did the apes do when they came back to camp?"

"They climbed up into the trees and stayed there… for a while." I was slowly leading up to the later brouhaha but wanted Tom and Robbie to understand the importance of what had transpired earlier before getting into it. "I think BigBoy understands a lot more than we give him credit for. After this morning… I don't know, it's like we can just *talk* to him and he *gets* it. I'm not sure about the other two, but BigBoy is amazing!"

"So that's the story?" Tom almost sounded disappointed.

"Noooo. I said the apes stayed up in the trees for a while."

"Okay, so what happened when they came down?" Tom was getting exasperated, so I caved and told them about Rusty's rebellion. "When he rose up to his full height and snarled at me, I thought I might have a problem."

With concern in his voice, Tom said, "He snarled at you?" I nodded and he added, "Then what?"

"We just stood there, scowling at each other."

Shaking his head, Tom said, "Lissy, sometimes you're too fearless for your own good. What would you have done if he'd grabbed you?"

"I don't know. But he didn't. Frank leapt down out of the branches and proceeded to kick the snot out of him."

Joanne added, "Yeah, Frank chased him into the jungle and we haven't seen either of them since."

After a few moments I said, "Today was a real learning experience. We found out BigBoy understands more than we thought; we know Frank will protect us, even against other orangutans; and we know Rusty's a wild card. It'll be interesting to see what kind of shape he's in when – and if – he comes back. We don't know how badly Frank might punish him."

About then, BigBoy dropped down from above and wandered aimlessly around the clearing. When he stopped and stared into the jungle in the direction Frank had chased Rusty, I said, "He's probably wondering the same thing."

Worn out from the exciting day, we put the fourth wall on and retired early. Joanne examined the scratches on BigBoy's chest and announced they were healing nicely. And since he seemed to be looking for something to do, we asked him to carry the wall and door over. After having a couple buddies around for a while, he was probably feeling lonely.

Calling to him, I scratched his head and shoulders until he relaxed. I handed him a potato and said, "Okay, big fella, it's time for bed. Maybe your friends will come back tomorrow."

He stood in the clearing until we closed and locked the door, then we heard the leaves rustling in the trees as he made himself a nest. I felt comforted, knowing he was there.

Joanne applied another layer of aloe vera to Tom and Robbie's faces and we settled for the night. I floated to sleep to the soft sounds of snoring and deep breathing.

Chapter 10

Day 6

<u>Tom</u>

I awoke early to barely breaking dawn. In the murky light, the sleeping shapes of my friends looked like huge anthills scattered throughout the shelter. Rigo had snuggled closer to Lissy during the night and had draped one arm across her body. I grinned to myself, thinking, *I wonder how she'll react to that?*

Stretching, I realized the aloe had taken the sting out of my face. I'd always tanned easily, but I knew Robbie and I had both spent way too much time in the sun yesterday. If my face looked anything like his, Jo was right – we were *fried.*

Needing to visit the latrine, I carefully tip-toed through the maze of bodies. Then it took a few minutes to get the vines undone so I could open the door. After the surprise attack in camp that night, I never exited without first checking the clearing.

My eyes widened and I stopped short in the doorway. Rusty lay face-down next to the fire pit, immobile. Knowing he'd been somewhat aggressive the day before, I hesitated to approach him; he might also be in pain from Frank's whooping. Was he asleep or unconscious? It wasn't like the apes to sleep on the ground but I could see his back moving with each breath. He wasn't dead.

My bladder reminded me why I was up so early and I took a few cautious steps, pulling the door closed behind me. I continued tip-toeing across the campsite, made it to the tree line, and figured this was far enough. Two steps into the trees and I relieved myself. *Ahhh, that's better.*

As I turned to reenter the clearing, Rusty stirred. The ape was between me and the doorway and I hadn't brought a weapon. I watched from behind a tree as he rolled over and sat up. Even from here, I could see missing patches of hair and long bloody welts. Frank had really worked him over. Would it change his behavior for the better or make him resentful? The last thing we needed was an unpredictable and angry orangutan in camp.

Then I noticed the pool of blood on the ground. Evidently, Rusty had at least one serious wound. I didn't know if Joanne would be able to force herself to get close enough to help him or not. And would Rusty *allow* anyone close enough to help?

I pondered my predicament and watched the animal slowly get to his feet. Just then, the door opened and Joanne, Lissy, Rigo, and Robbie piled out of the shelter, laughing at some private joke. In the lead, Jo spotted Rusty standing in the clearing and came to an abrupt halt. The others bumped into her from behind. She pointed and all eyes turned to the ape.

An intimidating animal to begin with, Rusty now looked slightly deranged. The hair on his head poked out wildly at odd angles and he sported a long, raw scratch running from the left

116

side of his forehead, over his eye, and down across his nose. It ended in the middle of his right cheek. His upper lip was swollen and, now that he was standing, the missing patches of body hair were more evident. The blood pool on the ground must have come from the gash on the back of his head – it looked like Frank might have clubbed him.

Although large and imposing, Rusty was none too steady on his feet. He took one drunken step toward Joanne and fell flat on his face, not moving. She squealed.

I sprinted from the trees. "Get your weapons," I said softly. "If he comes to, we don't know what he'll do." Everyone scattered and regrouped at the doorway. For a long moment, we stood there. Finally, I decided I had to do something – I couldn't stand there and watch him die. "I'm going to check on him. Robbie, come with me. Everyone else, stay alert."

Robbie and I slowly approached the prone figure and took a good look at the gash on his head. It definitely needed attention, probably even stitches, but I had no idea how we'd accomplish that. And a concussion would explain the wooziness.

"Lissy, can you get BigBoy down here?" I asked softly.

She called, "BigBoy? BigBoy, come here, fella." Her voice sounded strained. I hoped the orangutan would respond quickly.

Amidst a rustle of leaves overhead, two orangutans dropped to the ground. Frank was in much better condition than Rusty. Obviously, the fight was mostly one-sided.

Keeping my eyes on the injured ape, I said, "Jo, can you come over here and assess his injuries?"

When she didn't move, I glanced up and saw Jo shaking her head. She then babbled, "No, no, no... I can't."

Keeping my voice low, I said, "Jo, he needs help. We can't just let him lie here in the dirt in the middle of camp. BigBoy and Frank are here to protect you. Come over and look at the head wound and tell me what we should do. Come on." Without taking my eyes off the ape, I held out my hand. Lissy put her arm around Jo's shoulder and walked her over.

I guess her nurturing instincts kicked in despite her fear and she said, "We'll need clean water, clean rags if you can find any, and more aloe vera. It should have a couple of stitches but I don't have anything to sew him up with – and I don't waaa-aaant to…" She sobbed or hiccupped or something just as Rusty stirred again. Joanne shrieked and backed up several steps. The ape rolled over and looked up at the group encircling him.

Frank pushed past Joanne and Lissy, stopping beside the still-prone form. Rusty momentarily locked eyes with Frank but quickly lowered his gaze, submitting to the older animal. He lay still until Frank took a backwards step, evidently giving permission to sit.

Just as the woozy animal attained a sitting position, Robbie returned with the water, rags, and aloe vera. "Here, Jo. Here are the things you wanted." He tried to hand them to her, but she held up both hands to stop him.

"I don't want them. I'm not going to doctor him. Someone else can do it." She darted past Robbie and fled into the shelter.

"Give them here, Robbie," I said. Putting the rags in the water, I spoke softly, hoping to keep the ape calm. "Alright, Rusty, I'm going to clean this gash on your head and try to stop the bleeding. No wonder you're dizzy." I wiped at the blood oozing down the back of his head and he flinched. "It's okay. I'm not going to hurt you." Rusty slapped at my hands, whimpered, and tried to stand up. Frank stepped forward and put his hand on Rusty's shoulder. He pushed him down, woo-wooing softly.

Rusty stopped struggling and sat still as I cleaned his head. While I was at it, I continued on to the other wounds, too, not knowing if I'd have a chance to address them later. Although there were a lot of them, none were as serious as the head laceration. Pressing his wild hair back into place, I soon had him looking slightly less maniacal.

"He probably needs water and fruit." I wanted to replenish his fluids and thought a mango would help balance his sugar and electrolytes. Robbie darted off and returned shortly. I unscrewed the cap on the canteen and poured a few drops of water onto the ground so Rusty would know what it was. When I held the canteen up to his face, he eagerly opened his mouth and I poured water onto his tongue. We repeated this several times and then he reached for the mango. He munched on the fruit while I smeared aloe on the head wound. He flinched once, but all in all, was quite well-behaved as I coated the other scratches. I'd prefer that nothing got infected so I wouldn't have to treat him again.

There was nothing more I could do so I stood and backed away. Rusty struggled to his feet and although he swayed a bit, remained upright this time. Frank said, "Woo-woo," and Rusty calmly followed him into the jungle. I heard leaves rustling in the canopy as the apes climbed into the branches. He needed rest and would be safer up there than on the ground. BigBoy hung around the clearing a minute or two longer and then followed the others into the trees.

I spied Joanne peeking out the door. "Is he gone? Is it okay to come out?" We laughed and I said, "Yes, he's gone. Come on out."

On the way back from a group trip to the loo, we picked mangos, papayas, and coconuts for breakfast. I secretly craved something more substantial and my mouth watered as I thought of my favorite foods. *When we get home, I'm going to have a stack of French toast with both ham and bacon for breakfast and a huge filet mignon for dinner. I might not eat fruit or fish again for a month!* With those

119

images playing in my head, I bit into a mango and my taste buds shriveled at the fruity flavor. I made a sour face.

We finished breakfast and lounged around camp. I didn't think Rigo was strong enough, yet, for a lengthy jungle foray, and Rusty certainly wasn't, so it looked like we'd have another quiet day at home. At least, I hoped it was quiet.

I propped myself against a tree trunk and opened the log book. Maybe I could find some answers to Lissy's questions about training the orangutans. She was so enthusiastic about learning how to communicate with them that I wanted to help.

She sat at the fire pit, no doubt creating her lesson plans for the apes. Too bad we didn't have anything to write on – or with, for that matter. Joanne had gone back to bed. Robbie was cleaning up the mess after the morning's doctoring session and had offered to boil the rags I'd used to clean Rusty's wounds. Good idea. It seems we never knew when we'd need to bandage someone. Rigo was resting. And the apes were nowhere to be seen, probably napping in the trees overhead.

I dove into the hard-to-read handwriting and everything else faded into the background. Two hours and many pages later, I came across the information Lissy had inquired about. The scientists *had* done some training with the orangutans after they'd been injected with the serum. And, as they'd found with the ugly monkeys, the offspring also showed the effects of the drug. In fact, the level of intelligence and traits of helpfulness, empathy, and kindness actually *increased* in several generations.

Looking up into the trees, I mused. *Hmm… That might explain BigBoy. I wonder how many generations removed he is from the original subjects.* Reading on, I found some of the intelligence tests they had administered with results corresponding to Subject 1, Subject 2, and so forth. Of course, that didn't help because we had no way of knowing which subjects were which – or which orangutans were descended from them. But the results were astounding. The injected apes had the intelligence level of a six-year-old human child and their offspring were even *more* intelligent.

As I turned the page, a blood-curdling scream rent the air. I leapt to my feet, scanning the clearing for dark monkeys or a rampaging orangutan. Another scream pierced my ears and I ran toward the source of the sound – *inside* the shelter. We'd removed the fourth wall earlier so the front was open and I knew Joanne was napping. However, when I dashed inside, I was shocked to find Joanne cowering against the back wall and Robbie wrapped in the coils of a humongous, yellow snake. It was at least eighteen feet long and as big around as my thigh. Wrapped tightly around Robbie's legs, the loops also engulfed his abdomen. I could see its muscles ripple as it squeezed, then loosened, only to squeeze again. One of Robbie's arms was trapped against his side and he beat futilely at the reptile with his other as the coils moved inexorably up his body. Robbie's face was red and he gasped for air. We didn't have much time before the snake crushed ribs.

Rigo darted to my side and thrust a spear into my hand. "Aim for eyes. Bite no ees dangerous, squeeze ees dangerous." We advanced on the snake. It followed us with its dead black eyes, tongue darting in and out. Rigo stabbed at the snake's left eye, but the beast shifted and the point lodged behind its head. It pulled to the right, jerking the weapon out of Rigo's hands.

Lissy ran up with more spears and handed Rigo another. He smiled widely at her, the hot-blooded Latin knight slaying the dragon for his fair maiden, and darted toward the monster again. This time, he succeeded in burying the spear in the snake's left eye and it loosened its grip on Robbie, writhing in pain. I stabbed again, drawing blood.

Sprinting to Robbie, Lissy helped him out of the snake's loosened coils. They crawled out of the shelter while Rigo and I pressed our advantage over the injured reptile. But without Robbie in its grip, the deadly tail whipped around like a live electrical wire. We not only had to stab a moving target with some degree of accuracy, we had to do so while avoiding the lashing tail. Our strikes went wild, more often than not, until I told Rigo, "I'm going to let it catch me in its coils. When you don't have to worry about that tail, you can move in for the kill. Make it quick!"

Focused and deadly, "Ciudado, Tom!" was Rigo's only response.

The next time the tail whipped in my direction, I didn't move away and once it felt the warmth of prey, it probed closer and coiled tightly around my legs. I couldn't believe the strength of this beast and hoped Rigo could put it down quickly. The power of the snake and the number of coils wrapped around my limbs kept me mostly upright even though I no longer felt the ground under my feet. I thrashed as best I could, trying to distract the reptile from its concentration on Rigo.

Suddenly, BigBoy and Frank charged into the fray. Working in tandem, they diverted the snake's focus. Frank threw rocks at the reptile's head while BigBoy poked bloody divots in its side with a spear. Blind in its left eye, the beast had to turn its head fully in their direction to see its attackers.

Rigo darted closer and stabbed a spear deeply into its exposed right eye. Once again, the coils loosened and I wriggled free. The apes both jumped on the snake's body just behind the head, straddling the incredible girth. Rigo stabbed again and again, going for the already-bleeding eyes.

I snatched another spear from the ground and rushed in to help Rigo. "Go for the left eye! I'll try for the right!" Now blind in both eyes, the snake flicked its tongue more rapidly, trying to sense our location, forcing it to remain immobile for longer periods of time. It darted toward Rigo, paused, and we pressed our attack. Both spears found the eye sockets and drove deeply into the beast's brain. Its movements became sluggish and twitchy, the tongue no longer darting from its cavernous mouth. Copious blood stained the bright yellow scales a sickly orange.

Finally, with the added weight of the two apes riding its neck, the beast dropped heavily to the ground. Soon, it stopped moving altogether. Side by side, Rigo and I bent over, hands on knees, gasping for breath. I heard Joanne crying hysterically in the far rear corner of the shelter. Lissy retched into the brush at the edge of the clearing and then came to Rigo and slipped her arms around his waist. He turned and pulled her close. I glanced up and saw Robbie sprawled on the ground, leaning against the back wall. He looked shocked, pale.

On shaky legs, I staggered slowly to the far corner. Pausing and putting a hand on Joanne's shoulder, I asked, "Are you okay, Jo?" She nodded and continued crying, although the hysteria had subsided. I lurched over to Robbie and dropped to my knees beside him, turning unsteadily to sit with my back against the wall. We sat silently for several long moments and he finally angled his head slightly in my direction.

Hoarsely, he whispered, "I thought I was dead. I've never felt so helpless. He was more than Goliath; I was less than David." His voice broke and a lone tear made a wet track down his cheek. "How much more can we survive, Tom? How much more?"

I sighed. "I don't know. We keep fighting until we can't." I put my hand on his arm and said, "We won this battle, though."

His eyes darted to the motionless beast lying in the dirt. "Yeah. Yeah, we did." A small smile twitched the corner of his mouth and I knew he'd be alright. I patted his arm and forced myself to my feet. My legs were a tad less shaky and my heart had resumed a normal beat. Walking rather than lurching, I moved toward Rigo and Lissy. "Are you guys okay?"

Lissy nodded and said, "Yeah. You guys were amazing. You're both so brave — we never would've survived this long without you. Thanks." She stepped close and gave me a grateful hug, returning to Rigo's arms quickly thereafter.

"You're no slouch yourself, Lissy. You were right there in the thick of things, too, dispensing spears and helping Robbie out of the snake's coils. You did good." I smiled and turned to Rigo.

"And you. Thank you." I didn't know what else to say — emotional stuff didn't come easy to me. "I want to shake the hand of one of the bravest men I've ever met." I thrust out my hand and looked him in the eye.

Rigo unwrapped his arm from Lissy's shoulder and grasped my hand in a firm grip. "You, too, Señor Tom. You are one brave hombre! Thees snake ees no match for us!" We laughed, easing the tension of the adrenaline-packed event.

Lissy, Rigo, and I sat down around the fire pit and soon, Robbie and Joanne joined us. Robbie was still pale and Joanne had post-hysteria hiccups, but after a drink of water — too bad we didn't have something stronger! — we shared our stories.

Robbie said, "One minute I was sitting on my bed thinking about taking a nap and the next minute, something nudged my foot. I couldn't figure out what this yellow thing was until it coiled around my legs and I saw the rest of the beast. Then I screamed."

Joanne took over and said, "I was asleep until then. I couldn't believe my eyes — that thing was *huge!*" She shook her head and reached out to pat Robbie's hand. "I didn't know what to do, how to help. I'm sorry I'm such a coward."

"You're not a coward, Jo. You're just made more for nurturing and healing than battling. We all have our weaknesses and our strengths." Lissy grinned at her friend. "You may not be the one I want standing next to me in a fight, but you *are* the one I want patching me up afterwards!" They giggled.

I turned to my battle partner and asked, "Rigo, where'd you learn to fight a giant snake? I wouldn't have known to go for the eyes – I'm really thankful you were there to lead the fight."

"Mi padre teach me and my brothers. We find one een the jungle een Mexico and he show us how to keel eet. We eat eet. We eat thees one, too, no?" He looked around at our shocked faces and added, "Es good! I weel cook."

It might not be filet mignon, but I was game to try it, curious about the taste. "Does it taste like chicken?" Robbie and I laughed, the joke sailing over Rigo's head. Joanne grimaced in distaste and Lissy looked skeptical. Luckily, Robbie only had a few bruises to show for his encounter and was all for turning the tables and eating the snake instead of the other way around.

Later, after we'd regained our strength and sense of humor, I said, "Well, I guess the snake isn't going to skin itself. Rigo, you want to take the lead again?"

The apes helped us drag the thing outside and Rigo showed me how to skin it and remove the meat from between the many vertebrae. By the time we finished, we had enough to easily feed ten people. All that activity had worked up a powerful hunger so as Robbie set up his fire-making kit, Rigo and I went to the pool to wash up. Snake-butchering was messy business.

When we returned, the fire was blazing and Rigo took charge of cooking the snake – pretty much like any other meat. It smelled good and I could see Joanne taking more of an interest now that it wasn't slithering around on the ground. When it was done, we filled our plates and I could see the girls hesitating. I tried a bite and found it tasty.

"Come on, Lissy, Joanne. You have to try it. It's good." I coaxed until Lissy took a bite.

A trouper, she exclaimed, "Wow! I never would've expected it to be this tasty." Turning to Joanne, she said, "Try it, Jo. One bite and we won't be able to hold you back. It's actually more tender than I expected."

At last, Joanne took a nibble. Then another. "Okay, you're right. It is good. But I would never want you guys to have to fight another snake just so we could eat something other than fish."

We ate well, with potatoes on the side, and I figured snake wasn't bad. I definitely liked it a lot better on my plate than wrapped around my legs. So much for a nice quiet day at home.

After our late lunch, I told Lissy what the log book said about testing the apes. She leapt up with enthusiasm. "Can I see the book? Maybe I could replicate the intelligence test for BigBoy and Frank – and Rusty, too, once he heals."

"Sure, why don't you read it now? I'm going to go clean up the shelter – I'm sure it's a mess." I held out the log book and grinned as she greedily snatched it from my hands.

"Thanks, Tom. Take your time. I'm not going anywhere near the shelter until it's been freshened up." She settled down with her back to my favorite tree and I strode across the clearing.

Robbie, Joanne, and Rigo stared at the mess. Shredded fronds littered the space and numerous dark stains marred the earthen floor. I felt Joanne tremble beside me and I said, "Why don't you go collect some fresh fronds, Jo? We'll do this."

I saw her eyes glitter with a new wave of tears as she turned away, mumbling, "Thanks, Tom."

Robbie took a deep breath and strode inside, fiercely collecting armfuls of stained palm fronds. I said, "Robbie, Rigo and I can do this if you want to go help Joanne."

"No. I can do this, Tom. I *need* to do this." I admired his fortitude. For a man who'd spent his entire working life in academia, sitting behind a desk or instructing a classroom, his willingness to engage in physical activity and face adversity at his age gave me hope. In a few years, I'd be well into my golden years and I wanted to spend them doing what I loved – outdoors, hiking, diving, camping. Robbie inspired me whether he knew it or not.

Turning my attention to Rigo, I said, "Let's use the old fronds to rake the floor." We each grabbed a handful and used the stiff ends to rake the earth. The dirt had absorbed the blood and raking helped move it out of the shelter. When Joanne returned with an armload of fronds, we helped reassemble the beds. Soon, the shelter looked clean and fresh. You'd never know it had been the scene of a life-and-death battle just a few hours earlier.

Once the shelter was clean and the reptile carcass disposed of, I thought about our weapons. The battle with the snake had convinced me we needed more than one spear per person – and we needed to replace those broken in the skirmish. So Robbie and I collected more sticks and spent the rest of the afternoon sharpening points on ten additional spears. I also honed all the knives on a large rock, feeling much more prepared with sharp blades and additional weapons. I just hoped we wouldn't need to use them for a while – it seemed that nearly every day was a battle for survival. What I wouldn't give for a *normal*, stress-filled day.

Later, we reheated leftovers and potatoes for a quick and easy meal. And, hallelujah, a day without fish! We lingered around the fire pit, rehashing the day's battle, and at dusk I looked up into the trees and hollered, "BigBoy! Can you come help, please?" He and Frank came running and easily set the wall and door in place. It was great not having to do the heavy work.

I tossed them each a potato and told BigBoy to take one back to Rusty, but I'm pretty sure I saw him eat it before he climbed back into the canopy. I chuckled. It was kind of like having a big, hairy kid in camp.

We settled for the night and I hoped tomorrow would be quieter, easier, dare I ask for boring?

Chapter 11

Day 7

<u>Lissy</u>

In the morning, all I could think about was the log book. The tests the scientists had administered to the original subjects could be easily replicated, but I believed our apes were well beyond those.

Slipping out from under Rigo's arm, I thought, How dare he snuggle up to me during the night! I'm going to have to talk to that man.

Quietly, I undid the ties at the door and poked my head out, seeing nothing out of the ordinary. Great! Ordinary was a welcome change.

I munched on a mango and plopped down onto a log in front of the cold fire pit, my mind a-whirl. Before long, the rest of the gang was up and about.

"You're up early, Lissy," Tom commented.

"That log book has me anxious to get started testing the boys," I said. "Once Rusty's feeling better, we'll need to go exploring again, so I figured I'd see what I can get done now. I'm dying to find out how much the apes understand."

"I see that – you're all fired up." Tom grinned.

Frank joined BigBoy in the clearing and they wandered off to find breakfast. We knew they didn't roam far – we could hear them in the brush – and I looked up into the trees to see if I could spot Rusty. We hadn't seen him since Tom's doctoring. I'd like to take a look at his wounds to be sure nothing was infected.

"Rusty? Rusty?" I called out to the orangutan but nothing moved above. About then, BigBoy and Frank bounded back into camp and I decided to see if I could make BigBoy understand what I wanted. "BigBoy, go get Rusty. Go on, go get Rusty." Looking intently at my face, he seemed to be processing my request.

He made up his mind and climbed the nearest tree. Frank waited at the edge of the clearing. Leaves rustled overhead and I heard a soft, "Woo-woo," followed by a grumble – not quite a growl. We waited to see what would happen next and I held my breath.

Then, both apes dropped lightly to the ground in front of me. BigBoy smiled and rocked from left to right. I smiled back at him and said, "Thank you, BigBoy. That's exactly what I wanted." I turned my attention to Rusty and found he had obviously not been grooming himself. His hair was matted in places and blood still caked the back of his head. He seemed very subdued. I talked softly to him as I moved closer.

"Be careful, Lissy," Joanne muttered.

I reached out to stroke Rusty's arm and he shied away from my touch. Trying to reassure him, I murmured, "It's okay, big fella. I'm not going to hurt you. I just want to look at your scratches and that head wound." As I patted his arm, he relaxed and I coaxed him into sitting down.

"Somebody get me a mango or a potato – let's give him something to munch on." Robbie came over with one of each. I held the mango out and Rusty gently took it from my hand. As he nibbled, I examined his wounds. The scratches had healed nicely. When I walked around behind him, though, he pivoted to face me. I walked to the rear once more and he turned again.

"Okay, Tom, would you look at his head wound, please? I'm going to stay in front of him and try to hold his attention. He must associate the pain in his head with someone being behind him. Robbie, can I have some more fruit?" I fed Rusty another potato and a mango while Tom took a closer look at the wound.

"I think it's healing okay. It doesn't seem infected. But it has oozed a bit more blood. I wonder if he'd let me clean it up. His hair's all matted."

Robbie brought a clean rag and the canteen to Tom and he dribbled water onto the fabric. As he touched the rag to the back of Rusty's head, the ape screeched loudly and leapt to his feet, whirling to face Tom with panic in his eyes. BigBoy and Frank ran over to flank the frightened animal, one on each side. Frank woo-wooed and pressed on Rusty's shoulder, forcing him back into a sitting position. BigBoy patted Rusty's back. Either their presence had a calming effect or Rusty acquiesced to Frank's superior rank, but he soon relaxed, sitting between the other two.

Once the panicky ape had calmed down, BigBoy reached for the rag in Tom's hand. Surprised, Tom gave it to him and we all watched in astonishment as he cleaned the blood from the back of Rusty's head.

"Well." Tom watched with wide eyes, speechless.

"Yeah, I think those simple intelligence tests are light-years behind what we need for him." I grinned at Tom and shook my head in wonder. "Every day he does something that amazes me."

At a loss as to what type of intelligence test to use on BigBoy, I decided to talk normally to him and try to figure out how much he understood. I announced to everyone that we were going to the beach. "I want to get him away from distractions – and the other apes – so we can concentrate. We'll probably be gone about an hour. You guys keep Frank. I want to test them separately at first. Maybe later, if I'm doing some training, I can work them together." I started down the Beach Trail and called for BigBoy to follow me. "Come on, BigBoy, let's go to the beach."

Frank ambled along behind BigBoy, his hat perched at a rakish angle. "No, Frank, you stay here." I stopped and put my hand on Frank's chest, pointing back to camp with the other. "You stay here." When BigBoy and I headed down the path again, Frank stayed and watched us go.

We arrived at the beach and BigBoy immediately started digging for clams. "No, we're not here for clams this time." The ape stopped and cocked his head. I knew he understood the words we used all the time: no, yes, come here, go, help, mango, potato, eat, water, stay. But I didn't know how he understood words strung into sentences. For example, how did he know that I had asked Tom to clean the blood from Rusty's head? It wasn't something we'd said before; the sentence contained words not used every day; and I hadn't simplified the sentence.

"How do I figure you out, big fella?" I gazed into his warm brown eyes and saw intelligence and love in their depths. "If only you could talk." BigBoy sat down next to me, putting his big, hairy paw into my lap. I took his hand and held it, looking out over the aquamarine sea, wondering how to navigate the communication maze. This amazing, wonderful animal had saved my life numerous times and had proven he would put his life on the line to do so again. I owed him so much, yet I couldn't even talk to him. Tears trickled from my eyes as my heart swelled with love for this incredible ape. He wasn't a pet – he was a loyal, loving friend.

He hummed softly and I smiled through my tears, turning to look at him. As he saw the wetness on my cheeks, he stopped crooning and leaned closer. As Frank had done with Joanne, BigBoy wiped one tear from my face with a long, hairy finger. He examined it, sniffed it, and looked quizzically into my brimming eyes. Raising his face to mine, he snuffled the tear tracks and then licked a tear from my skin. His tongue was slightly rough and warm. The gentle slurp startled me – it was the first time any of the apes had licked me.

The salty taste appeared to surprise him and he gazed again at my damp cheeks. He clucked softly, a new noise that seemed to express concern and caring, and stroked my arm. It appeared he was trying to comfort me. I patted his arm and said, "It's okay, BigBoy, I'm just feeling emotional. You are such an amazing animal and I love you so much. My heart's so full of love it's running out of my eyes." I giggled at the thought and figured, "What the hey, he doesn't understand this, I'm sure."

In college, I had written a paper on whether or not animals shed emotional tears. Obviously, they could express sadness or grief over losing a companion or being separated from their mother, but the most commonly-held belief is that animals do not cry, as we know it. So it came as no surprise to me that my tears confused BigBoy.

"Okay, enough of this blubbering. Let's get to work." I dried my eyes and turned my mind to the situation at hand. I thought I'd ask him to do a variety of tasks and see how easily he

1) understood the words or 2) caught on when I showed him what I wanted. I knew from past experience that once I had shown him something, he'd never forget it.

"BigBoy, bring me a clam. Go bring me a clam." He went over to the spot where he'd originally started digging and carried one over.

"Thank you. Now bring me two clams." I didn't recall ever asking him for a specific number of things, so had no idea if he'd get this or not. Without hesitation, he ran back over to the disturbed sand and brought me two clams.

Astonished, I kept going. Obviously, the boy knew his numbers since three was as easy for him as one and two. I continued the sequence and he made it to twenty-nine before getting confused. I knew it would be a simple matter to teach him higher numbers, but what would be the point? I might as well teach him things that could be useful. I doubted we'd ever send him to the beach to collect fifty clams.

I gave him one of the mangoes I had brought along as a reward. "Good boy! You are one smart cookie. Ready to do something else?" He looked eager and I thought it must be fun for him to do something challenging.

"BigBoy, dig a hole. Can you dig a hole?" One step ahead of me, he ran to the hole he'd been digging for the clams. "Yes, that's a hole. Good boy. Now, put five clams into the hole."

Eager to please, he ran over to the pile we'd accumulated and counted out five clams, one at a time. Then he ran over and dropped them into the hole, looking up at me with a satisfied grin. I laughed and clapped my hands. "Yes! That's good!"

"Alright. Now, take this and put it in the water." I handed him the core of the mango he'd dropped onto the sand. He trotted to the shoreline, waited for the next wave, and dropped it into the water. He screeched as the water poured over his feet and ran back to where I was sitting. He sat down beside me and raised one foot, pointing to the drops of water clinging to the hair on his ankles. "Yes, that's water, too. You got wet." He grinned and giggle-screeched happily as I tickled him.

Next, I tried something a little more difficult. Holding a clam in the palm of my hand, I asked, "How many clams, BigBoy?" He looked from my hand to my face and back to my hand again, confusion showing in his eyes. This had him stumped. I held up one finger and said, "One. This is one clam." I pointed at the clam and held up a finger again. "One clam."

He pointed at the clam and held up one finger. "Yes! Yes! That's one clam." Then I put two in my palm. I pointed at them and held up two fingers. "Two. This is two clams." BigBoy pointed at the clams and held up two hairy fingers. I was ecstatic. We continued in sequence to ten and then I tried random numbers. Five. Two. Eight. Four. He never once made a mistake.

I wanted to try it with something other than clams to be sure he understood the concept of numbers, not just numbers of clams. So I picked up a handful of sticks off the beach and tried it again. He never missed.

We'd been at it for a little over an hour, so I decided we should head back to camp. I couldn't wait to tell everyone how well BigBoy had done. I gave him the last mango and he munched contentedly on the walk back to the clearing. I was trying to think of a dramatic way to show everybody what BigBoy could do – something with impact.

"Well, how'd he do?" Joanne was the first to ask.

"He ees smart, no?" Rigo added.

I nodded and said, "I want to show you something. Joanne, you and Robbie stand next to the fire pit."

135

"Why?" Robbie grumbled at having to get up from his comfortable position. "Can't you just tell us? My old bones are happy where they are."

"Humor me, Robbie. You'll see why in a minute." When they were standing by the pit, I asked the ape, "How many people, BigBoy?" I pointed at Joanne and Robbie. "How many?" The ape held up two fingers. Robbie's mouth dropped open.

Tom said, "Try it again," and eagerly joined the other two.

"How many, BigBoy?" Three hairy fingers came up. I laughed and BigBoy screeched and grinned. We all lined up at the pit and I asked again. Five fingers.

"That is amazing! How did you teach him to count?" Joanne wanted details.

"He already knew numbers up to twenty-nine. All I had to do was teach him to show me how many fingers it was. So now he can tell us in addition to us telling him, how many." I excitedly explained the various exercises we'd done at the beach and asked if they would please try and think of things that would be useful for him to learn. He was a quick study and I was sure he could master just about anything we threw at him.

Frank dropped down from above to see what the ruckus was about. Tom and Robbie wanted to go fishing so I suggested they take him this time. "We ought to vary it so the apes don't get stuck on only doing it one way."

After collecting their gear, Robbie said, "Come on, Frank, you're coming with us this time."

When BigBoy tried to follow them, I called, "No, BigBoy, you stay here with us." And it was as easy as that. One went, one stayed. Rusty was still up in the trees. I hoped he recovered quickly – we needed to explore more of the island – but I was also excited about working with BigBoy. And maybe tomorrow I'd see what Frank could do.

With Frank at the beach with Tom and Robbie and Rusty recuperating from his bash over the head, camp was again quiet. Rigo rested inside the shelter. I wanted to finish hats for the guys and set up under my favorite tree.

Joanne hunkered down next to me in the shade. "Lissy, would you show me how to make a hat? With both of us working at it, we might be able to make enough for the guys and the orangutans before dinner arrives."

"Sure, Jo. Here." I handed her some grass and demonstrated how to start the weave. "Your first hat might be better suited for one of the apes. It takes some practice to get the brim even all the way around and the apes won't care what it looks like. The guys might be a little pickier."

We worked in silence and after a while, I heard Rigo stirring. He strolled out of the shelter and sat next to the fire pit.

At his inquisitive look in our direction, Joanne said, "We're making hats. Want one?"

He grinned. "Sí. My hair ees long and I don't like eet een my eyes. A hat weel help, no?"

"Yes, it will. Here you go." I tossed him the one I had just finished – the one that had been interrupted by Frank and Rusty's altercation a couple days earlier. He snatched it and placed it carefully on his head, low over his eyes and tilted off to one side.

"How do you see eet? Good?" He smiled that slow, sensual grin and I felt myself blush. He looked incredibly sexy and raw with his dark stubble, the hat at a jaunty angle, and his teeth white against the olive skin.

"Yes, it looks good, Rigo. I'm really happy you're feeling so much better. Soon, you can go fishing with Tom and Robbie." I had to keep talking so he wouldn't look at me like that. My fingers stumbled and I growled as I tore out an inch of awkward weaving. There had to be something he could do other than sit and stare at me. "Rigo, could you go collect another armful of this grass, please?" I pointed across the clearing. "I found it around the trees over there."

"Sí, Leesa, I get more." He strolled off in the direction I'd indicated and Joanne gave a knowing glance.

"You just wanted him to do something other than sit and stare, didn't you?" Her voice was low and teasing.

"Yes. It makes me uncomfortable when he sits and looks at me. He's so doggone sexy my fingers kept tripping over themselves. I figured he ought to make himself useful." She giggled and I elbowed her in the ribs. "I woke up this morning and he had his arm thrown over me like we're an old married couple. I don't know what to do with him."

"I know what I'd do with him if I were you." Her wicked chuckle told me exactly what she was thinking. I blushed.

"Stop it, Jo! If we were at home living normal lives, I'd know how to behave. But we're not – we're stranded here on this island and God only knows when we'll be rescued. I really like him, but I can't just have a fling. What if it doesn't work out and we end up disliking each other? I can't avoid him."

"That's true. It would be pretty awkward."

"Besides, neither of us has any protection. We were going diving, for Pete's sake – I'm sure he didn't tuck something into his dive boot just in case I wanted to get frisky at sixty feet!" I heard Rigo heading back through the brush and dropped the subject.

"Ees enough, Leesa?" He leaned down and dumped an armful of grass on the ground beside me. I looked up and smiled.

"Yes, Rigo, that's plenty. Thanks." As he stood there smiling at me, I saw something move. A spider every bit as big as a man's hand, crawled slowly into view up and over his left shoulder. Spiders were my worst nightmare. I froze, paralyzed with fear, and broke into an icy sweat. I stammered, "A...a... sp...sp..." I gulped and tried again. "There's a... a... spi...spi..." At the look of terror on my face, Rigo spun around to look behind him, surely expecting to see monkeys filling the clearing.

As he turned, the gigantic spider lost its grip on Rigo's Lycra-clad shoulder and slid off, landing right beside me on the ground. The paralysis left me. I screamed and scrambled backwards, nearly bowling Joanne over. Rigo still had no idea what had frightened me and Jo tried to regain her balance as I continued screaming. When I struggled to my feet, I backed up against a tree and tried not to hyperventilate, my eyes glued to the enormous arachnid.

The spider crawled slowly across the depression my butt had left in the dirt, apparently unfazed by the hysteria it had caused. Rigo finally spotted it. He picked up a flat rock and reached down to pick it up. "No-no-no-no!" My insane screams stopped him.

"Leesa, ees no dangerous. I can move eet away." Confused, Rigo didn't comprehend my terror.

"No-no-no!" I shook my head frantically, willing him to understand that I didn't want him to touch it. I wanted it to go away. I wanted it dead. I wanted it to stop moving!

Joanne had recovered from my bull-dozing escape and stepped to my side. Putting her arm around my shoulder, she gently said, "It's okay, Lissy. Rigo can take it away. You want it out of camp, right?"

I nodded, eyes wide with fear.

To Rigo, she said, "Okay, without touching it, can you carry it out of camp?"

"Sí. I take eet een the jungle."

"Okay, Rigo, take it away." Joanne wrapped her arms around me, trying to ease my uncontrollable trembling, as I burst into tears.

"Don'ttouchit-don'ttouchit," I chanted in between hiccups.

At my initial shriek, BigBoy had dropped from the canopy and scanned the clearing for danger. Seeing nothing, he ran to my side. To him, a spider was no cause for alarm and he was obviously confused by my panic. The tears worried him. He woo-woo-wooed and alternately patted me on the back and stroked my arm.

When Rigo and the spider were out of sight, my hysteria slowly subsided and Joanne walked me over to the fire pit. We sat down and BigBoy huddled against my legs, wrapping one long arm around my knees. Frightened by the unknown, he was almost as upset as I was.

Finally, the trembling stopped and my breathing returned to normal. I apologized. "Jo, I am so sorry I nearly ran you over. I have a phobic reaction to spiders and that one was so big. It was an instinctual fight-or-flight response and obviously I opted for flight." I grinned sheepishly and hung my head.

"It's okay, Lissy. I've just never seen you react like that. You can stare down a snarling orangutan or chase sharks around the bottom of the ocean with nothing but a camera, but you get hysterical over a spider. I guess there's no logic to our innermost fears, huh?" She hugged me again and said, "It's okay."

I reached down and stroked BigBoy's shoulder and he finally relaxed enough to croon. And that's how Rigo found us when he returned – the three of us sitting in a pile on the log, humming a tuneless monkey-song.

Seeing him stop at the edge of the clearing, I figured I should apologize to him, too. He had to be as confused over the whole thing as BigBoy. I smiled at him and he slowly walked toward us, his body language saying he still didn't know what to expect.

"You got rid of it? And you didn't touch it?" I couldn't help but ask.

"No, Leesa, I no touch eet. Ees far away and he no come back. Why you afraid?" His sincere concern touched my heart and I thought once again that he was worth having in my life. I patted the log next to me and he sat down.

"I don't know, Rigo. It's something I can't control. I've always been afraid of spiders and that one was huge. I'm sorry. Thank you for taking it away." I smiled at him and kissed him on the cheek. He brought his right hand up and cupped my chin, raising my face to his. Looking into my eyes, he lowered his lips to my mouth and gently kissed me.

"You are brave chica, Leesa. I weel save you from spiders. No worry more." He kissed me once again, a quick peck on the lips, and stood. We all untangled and Joanne went to find some coconuts to collect strings for the fire. I cautiously approached the hat-making, spider-chasing area and, seeing no further intruders, gathered up the grass that would have to wait for another day.

Before long, a fire crackled in the pit. Voices and laughter preceded the guys up the trail and Joanne and I tossed some potatoes into the flames. We had it down pat, now, and knew exactly how long it would take for the potatoes to cook. I hated half-baked potatoes.

It looked like another buffet: a small ray, clams, and a few medium-sized fish. Tom got busy cleaning the day's catch and the rest of us collected our plates and dinnerware. BigBoy and Frank wandered into the trees. We tossed them a few potatoes to take to Rusty. We still hadn't seen much of the injured ape and I hoped he would soon be well enough to come down from the canopy. I was anxious to see how Frank's thrashing would affect his behavior. We needed to trust him if he was going to be allowed to stay. And I had concerns about how we'd get rid of him if he proved untrustworthy.

Once we'd filled our plates and dug into the seafood feast, Joanne said, "Lissy had another adventure today."

Tom looked up and said, "You're kidding! Not more monkeys, I hope."

Joanne snickered and said, "Nope. This had eight legs."

I shot her a sour look and said, "Well, you guys battled a huge snake. I battled a huge spider."

Joanne retorted, "Battled?"

I shrugged and said, "Well, not exactly battled. I guess you could more accurately say I got hysterical over a huge spider." I blushed. "What can I say? I've always been terrified of the damn things and this one was huge."

"How huge? Bigger than a fifty-cent piece?" Tom scoffed.

"Oh, yeah, way bigger! It was every bit as big as your hand." Joanne now came to my defense. "Lissy's one of the bravest women I've ever known. She just has issues with spiders."

"So what happened to the spider?" Robbie asked.

"I take eet een the jungle. He no come back." Rigo gave me an encouraging smile. "Leesa ees brave chica, but no like spiders."

Under his breath, Tom muttered, "I'll have to remember that," as though he might plot to scare me with one. I knew he sometimes had a twisted sense of humor.

I jumped off the log, nearly spilling my dinner, and shouted, "Tom, if you ever try to scare me with a spider, I promise you, you'll be looking at the business end of my dive knife!" Still emotional over the earlier incident, I burst into tears and darted into the shelter. Feeling foolish, yet unable to help myself, I curled up on my pallet and cried.

Silence engulfed the diners and I heard Joanne say, "Go on, Tom. You owe her an apology."

Soft footsteps approached and Tom's voice, filled with remorse, said, "I'm sorry, Lissy. I had no idea you were so afraid of spiders. I promise, I will never joke around with one. Ever. And if I'm anywhere nearby, you won't have to deal with one on your own. Okay? Forgive me?"

Sniffling, I said, "Okay, Tom. I know you'd never go back on a promise." I sat up and he brushed a tear off my cheek.

"Alright, now come finish your dinner. Robbie and I risked life and limb for that seafood – I won't see you let it go to waste." He helped me to my feet and gave me a hug. "I am sorry, Lissy."

"Okay, let's drop it. I'm sick to death of thinking about spiders." I dried my eyes and we headed back to the fire pit.

"Friends again?" Joanne joked.

"Yes. He promised to never, ever scare me with a spider. You're all my witnesses. And if he does, I get to kill him." And with that, I sat back down to my dinner. Everyone laughed and to my great relief, dropped the subject.

The rest of the evening passed without incident and we retired early. I lay down on my pallet but couldn't relax enough to sleep, visions of that huge spider crawling repeatedly through my mind. I dozed off once but jerked awake moments later, feeling something soft and warm tickling my bare arm. I froze, adrenaline pulsing through my veins, my heart pounding wildly. I forced shallow gasps in and out of my lungs and a small whimper escaped my lips.

I was facing Rigo's back and he quietly murmured, "Qué es, Leesa? You are okay?" When he rolled to face me, a lock of his silky black hair slid softly across my skin.

"It's okay, Rigo. I thought something was crawling on my arm, but it was only your hair." I'm sure he could hear the residual fear in my voice.

Facing me, he scooched closer and placed his hand on my waist. "I weel hold you, eef you want. You weel be safe, Leesa. For to sleep."

Normally, I would've said no, but lying there in the dark of night with the spider's memory looming so large in my mind, I agreed. "Okay. Just for tonight." I rolled over and slid my back to his front, his arm strong and warm around me.

"Just for tonight." His lips brushed my hair as we snuggled together. I felt warm, safe at last, and fell almost immediately into a deep and nightmare-free sleep.

Chapter 12

Day 8

<u>Lissy</u>

Giggle-screeches and woo-woos sounded in the clearing. As I stirred, so did everyone else. Joanne muttered, "Sounds like the kids are up." Tom laughed and I rolled away from under Rigo's arm. He'd held me throughout the night, keeping the nightmares at bay. I felt a strong surge of affection and knew I would soon have to face the physical attraction that had drawn me to him initially. I glanced at him and he smiled that slow, sexy grin that never failed to set my pulse to racing. Time to get up!

Tom untied the vines at the door and we peeked out to see what the apes were up to. Frank's hat sat rakishly askew his head while he sashayed around the fire pit to an unheard tune. Maybe it was some kind of early-morning monkey dance? I was relieved to see Rusty joining in the fun for the first time since Frank worked him over, his clapping and grinning interspersed with high-pitched giggles. BigBoy watched Frank's antics and chomped on a mango, every now and then waving at the main act like a slightly inebriated and eccentric fan.

"They're having fun! If Frank breaks into an ape's rendition of *My Way*, I'll know we've all lost our minds." I couldn't help but compare him to some arrogant performer cutting up on stage.

When we opened the door, the shenanigans came to a halt as all three orangutans turned and smiled at us. I greeted them warmly, "Good morning, guys. You seem to be having fun. Is everyone invited to this performance or is it for apes only?" BigBoy sauntered over for a hug while Frank stroked our arms and patted us on the back. Rusty remained seated but grinned and giggled as we said hello.

I walked over and rubbed his back so he wouldn't feel left out. "Is your head feeling better, Rusty? Let's have a look." He still didn't want me behind him but when I held out a mango, he turned his head enough that I could see the wound. It was healing nicely even without stitches. He'd probably be shy of anyone walking behind him for a while but it was good to see him up and about and having fun. Now, we needed to assess how the incident would shape his interactions with us.

"How about a group trip to the latrine?" I hollered.

"You read my mind. We can collect fruit on the way back." Tom grabbed the bucket. Joanne snatched a spear and led the way down the Loo Trail. BigBoy brought up the rear.

More comfortable and in less of a hurry on the return trip, we fanned out and collected a bucketful of mangos, papayas, and coconuts, gathering enough to share with our furry friends. They seemed to eat constantly, but their protection was worth every piece of fruit I could find.

As we dined, I broached a subject we hadn't discussed in a while. "Now that Rigo and Rusty are feeling better we should probably plan another exploratory trip around the island. What do you say we go tomorrow, weather permitting?"

Tom added, "Good idea. We need to see if there are other people on this island; look for additional fresh water sources along the way since we only have the one canteen; and maybe we can find some new fruits and/or vegetables to eat. I'm getting tired of the same ol' stuff every day. What do you think?"

"I agree! I like mangos, but enough is enough. Shouldn't there be bananas on a tropical island? And it would be great if we could find some onions or carrots or squash... something other than just potatoes." Joanne nailed it. We wanted variety.

"Sí, bananas should be here. And maybe piñas. Mm-mmm!" Rigo smiled at the thought of bananas and pineapples.

Robbie said, "I know it's too much to ask, but I'm dying for some chocolate." We laughed.

"I can just imagine an Oreo cookie tree," I said with a giggle.

Tom murmured, "M&Ms – what I wouldn't give for a big bag of M&Ms."

"I'm back to the chocolate cake you all scolded me for a few days ago. That's *my* chocolate craving." Robbie closed his eyes and inhaled deeply. "I can almost smell it."

Rigo surprised us. "Chocolate cheep cookies! Mi amigo visit U.S. two years ago and hees abuela send some chocolate cheep cookies back weeth heem. He share weeth me. Hees abuela make good cookies. No can find cookies like that een Mexico."

I moaned with frustration. "Alright already. Stop it! My mouth's watering for chocolate and all I have is a papaya."

"Yeah, this is getting us nowhere," Robbie said. "The cake will have to wait."

"Let's clean up the fruit mess and then I'm going to take Frank to the beach to see if he can measure up to BigBoy. You keep the other two guys here."

As everyone pitched in to clean up coconut shells and fruit leavings, I wondered how it would go with Frank. He was older than BigBoy and not quite as affectionate, but I knew he had accepted all of us as his family and would defend us to the death. He was quite a character and loved to make us laugh. I was anxious to see how well I could communicate with him.

I tucked a few mangos and potatoes in a wetskin sleeve and tied one end in a knot. I then tied the other end to a nylon weight belt around my waist making an effective carry-pouch that left my hands free. Strapping on my dive knife, I snatched a spear and hollered for Frank. Of course, BigBoy and Rusty came running, too. I pointed at Frank and said, "You come with me, Frank." Then I pointed at BigBoy and Rusty and instructed them to "Stay here. You two stay in camp."

When I started down the trail, Rusty and BigBoy watched us go. I smiled. I had wondered if we'd have trouble separating the three apes when we wanted one or two to do one thing and the remaining one or two to do something else, but so far, there hadn't been any objections. They seemed to understand that we'd all come back together later.

Since we'd never taken Frank clam-digging, he didn't think that's why we'd come to the beach. I sat on a log and stared out over the blue water, watching puffy white clouds scudding across the azure sky. Frank hung out nearby. I had always loved the beach: views of white sand and swaying palm trees; views *from* the beach of blue water, white clouds, and rolling waves; silhouettes of sailboats with an orange, setting-sun backdrop.

With my mind wandering, it took a minute for the unusual sound to penetrate. I looked up and saw an airplane up high and several miles off shore.

A plane! I jumped up and ran to the shoreline, stopping at the water's edge, visions of hungry sharks stopping me from going farther. Screaming and waving, I jumped up and down in the sand like a maniac until my throat was raw and my legs trembled from the exertion. The plane never deviated from its course and as I collapsed on the sand, I realized how silly I'd been – the plane was too far away. Tears left salty tracks on my cheeks. I hung my head and sobbed, the desperate hope that had leapt into my heart withering in the tropical heat.

I pulled myself together and looked around for Frank. I'd forgotten he was there in the excitement and despair of the last fifteen minutes or so. I spotted him standing out in the open a short distance from the shoreline, gazing upwards, much as I had been earlier. I stood and walked a few steps towards him. Then my jaw dropped and goosebumps roughened the skin over my entire body – I couldn't believe my eyes!

While I'd been performing my useless leaping and screaming and waving at the plane, Frank had written the word "HELP" in the sand. The letters were about ten feet tall, all capitals, and contained dark rocks and driftwood carefully placed to help define the letters on the light-colored beach.

How...? Who...? What...? Questions raced through my mind as I gazed at that very human word spelled out in the sand. Obviously, someone had taught Frank what to do if an airplane flew over. But who? And when? And where was he now?

Suddenly, Tom, Robbie, Rigo, Joanne, BigBoy, and Rusty blasted out of the trees at a dead run.

"Lissy!" "Leesa!" "Are you okay?" "You scream!" Everyone was talking at once, but when I turned to face them, my stricken countenance and demeanor stopped them in their tracks.

In a low voice, Tom said, "Lissy? Are you alright? What happened?" He walked slowly toward me and I pointed at Frank. "What? What's wrong? You're as pale as a ghost. Talk to me."

Again, I pointed. "What did he do?" Tom's voice grew hard as he added, "Did he hurt you?"

"No. Tom. Look." I pointed to the word written so clearly in the sand and he finally saw it.

"Why did you write 'help' in the sand, Lissy?" He saw it but didn't understand.

I whispered, "I didn't write it." I paused and added, "Frank did."

Silence engulfed us. The only sound was the gentle waves lapping at the shore. No one could grasp the enormity of that single word carved so carefully into the sand by an ape.

My knees gave out and I sank down onto the beach. One by one, the others knelt, too, and there we sat: five people, three apes, and one huge word. HELP.

Finally, Joanne said, "You mean *Frank* wrote 'help' in the sand? By himself?" I nodded. "Why?" she said. "Why did he write 'help'?"

"A plane flew over, several miles out there." I waved a hand toward the open ocean. "I suddenly thought we could be rescued and acted like an idiot, jumping, screaming, waving. As though they could see or hear me. But not Frank. Oh, no, not Frank. *He* wrote the word 'HELP' in the sand. Something useful. Something that might actually work."

"But how did he know how to do that?" Robbie asked, as mystified as the rest of us.

"Obviously, we aren't the first people Frank has befriended on this island," Tom answered. "Someone taught him what to do if a plane flew over. I wonder what he'd do if a ship sailed by."

"And I wonder what happened to the people who taught him what to do," I said, voicing my earlier thought. "I'm done with lessons today. I'm so shocked I couldn't teach him anything if my life depended on it. Let's go back to camp." Everyone agreed. "I'm more certain than ever that we need to explore the rest of the island – as soon as possible." The determination in my voice left little space for argument and we lined up, single file.

We were almost at the clearing before I noticed BigBoy had taken the lead with Frank and Rusty bringing up the rear. I felt a frisson of apprehension run up my spine. *Who was really in charge here? Us? Or the apes?*

Filing into camp I almost missed the multitude of bare, human-like footprints in the dirt of the clearing. "Stop!" I commanded. Everyone halted and looked around, confused. "Check out the footprints." I pointed downward and we all stared at the ground, frightened at the implications. Nearly every square inch of dirt contained imprints of bare toes and heels, heading in all directions, as though a huge group of monkeys had stampeded wildly through our camp. Obviously, they'd been watching from the trees and saw everyone dash out of the clearing, taking the opportunity to invade our space.

Examining the campsite more closely, we noticed things had been moved: the logs by the fire pit were at odd angles; the bucket of fruit had been knocked over and many papayas, mangos, and potatoes were gone; and our bed fronds were scattered around the shelter. But most chilling of all was the realization that our spears were missing. Only Tom and Robbie had thought to grab one as they bolted toward the beach. With the extras made following the battle with the snake, we'd had a total of thirteen, so ten spears were now in the hands of the ugly monkeys.

"Oh, my God! This just goes from bad to worse – now we've armed the enemy!" Joanne burst into tears.

"Well, the good news is their aim will be way off." I tried to make a joke so Joanne would stop crying. It didn't help.

"Their aim will only be off until they practice on *us*!" She hiccupped and fled into the shelter. "I'm throwing these fronds out. Somebody will have to come with me to collect more. I'm not sleeping on a bed those beasts have touched!" Fronds flew out of the shelter as Joanne vented her frustration on housecleaning.

"Why don't you go with her, Tom? Take BigBoy. Rusty and Frank can stay here with Robbie, Rigo, and me. We'll straighten up while you're gone." I handed him the bucket and added, "And while you're out, you might as well pick up more fruit." I smiled wanly and shook my head. "Will they ever give up?" Tom took it as a rhetorical question and left to deal with Joanne.

"Come on, Jo, let's go find some more fronds." He took her by the hand and hollered for BigBoy. All three apes dropped down from the trees and I told Frank and Rusty to stay in camp. Robbie, Rigo, and I began cleaning the campsite, using the old fronds to rake the dirt free of monkey-prints. If nothing else, it would make us feel better to not see reminders of their visit.

By the time Tom and Joanne came back, their arms full of palm fronds with BigBoy hauling a bucketful of fruit, camp was clean and neat once again. Everything was back to normal – except for the empty corner that used to house our weapons.

Protection being our number one priority, Tom suggested he and Robbie address the issue immediately. "Robbie, let's collect more spear-wood. When we get back, you and Rigo and I can sharpen them. We can't spend the entire day with only three spears – and if we're going to explore the island tomorrow, we *have* to be well-armed. Especially now."

"BigBoy! You come with us." Tom looked at me and motioned toward the other two apes.

I said, "Stay here, Frank, Rusty." Tom, Robbie, and BigBoy entered the trees and the rest of us stayed behind, hoping they wouldn't be gone long. We had one spear, our dive knives, and two apes, but at least we could go into the shelter where the monkeys couldn't surround us. Tom, Robbie, and BigBoy were more vulnerable, but better-armed.

On pins and needles, Jo, Rigo, and I sat around the fire pit chatting, knives conveniently at hand and the one spear nearby. Frank and Rusty ascended into the canopy but we could hear them above and knew they'd rush to our defense, if needed.

"What do you think we should do about lunch? Or should we just wait and fix a big dinner tonight?" Joanne, the nurturer, was concerned about feeding everyone.

"We'll have to wait until the guys get back and sharpen some spears. Maybe they'll go fishing. Hopefully, they won't be gone long." My stomach growled. "Does anyone want a mango or papaya? I'm hungry now." I headed to the fruit-laden bucket.

"I'll take a mango," Joanne said.

"Me, too," Rigo added, then said, "I go fishing with Señor Tom and Robbie. I feel good now."

I said, "That's great, Rigo! I'm really happy you feel well enough to go fishing."

We ate and relaxed in companionable silence until Rigo chuckled to himself. "What?" I asked.

"Eef we are een Cozumel and I am weeth two beauteeful chicas, we would have fun. Not seet and talk. We eat tacos and drink tequila!" Rigo laughed and reached for my hand.

"Well, Rigo, if you want to whip up some tacos and pour us a shot, we'll join you!" I squeezed his hand and smiled. "If we have time when we get back to Cozumel, we'll have some fun, okay?"

"Okay, Leesa. You weel not go back to U.S. right in the moment? You weel stay some time?" The tender look on Rigo's face made me want to snuggle into his arms and forget we were stranded on an island. I didn't want to think about heading back to the States without finding out where our relationship could go.

"I can't think that far ahead right now, Rigo. We have to deal with things here, first. Alright?" I gazed into his dark eyes and felt my heart skip a beat. *Damn, he's hot!*

We reached for our weapons as the brush at the edge of the clearing rustled. When Tom, Robbie, and BigBoy strolled into view, we relaxed, and I said, "Welcome back. No trouble?"

"Nope. Didn't see a single monkey. Found lots of wood for spears, though." BigBoy dropped his load on the ground by the pit and wandered over to the bucket to filch a mango. He swung up into the trees to join his buddies, leaving us to people-things.

The guys pulled out their knives and began sharpening the sticks. Before long, we had ten new spears and lots of tiny kindling chips for the evening's fire.

After glancing around the clearing, Tom said, "I think we should keep the spears in a different place now. The monkeys know where we used to keep them, so let's think about another location – maybe even two different places so they aren't all in the same spot." We nodded.

"And," Tom continued, "I want to find some good strong vines to lock up the shelter tomorrow. When we head off to explore, I don't want to leave the shelter open and exposed."

"I go fishing with you and Robbie. We look for vines then."
Rigo offered his help and the guys nodded.

"Perfect plan, Rigo. Thanks. So you feel up to fishing, huh?"
Robbie seemed pleased that Rigo was getting back to normal.

"Sí, I feel good now." He smiled and showed the guys his
healing wound. "Mucho better."

"It'll be nice to have you fishing with us again. And who
knows when we might encounter another snake. I'd certainly
want you along if that happened!" Robbie grinned at Rigo, surely
recalling the terror of that day.

Soon, the guys gathered their fishing gear and I suggested
they take Frank this time. So off they went, leaving BigBoy,
Rusty, and ten brand new spears behind. Oddly enough, I felt
much safer even though it was only Joanne and me.

We collected the remaining potatoes – the monkeys had
taken or eaten most of them during the morning raid – and set
up Robbie's fire-making kit so we'd be ready to cook when the
fishermen returned. We hadn't had much "girl time" so it was a
rare treat for us to be alone in camp. Somehow, a testosterone-
free environment seemed very relaxing.

"What are you going to do about Rigo, Lissy? He *really* likes
you," Joanne asked.

"I really like him, too, but I don't know what to do. Like I
said before, I don't want to have a fling with him here on the
island. And when we get back to Cozumel, we'll have to head
home asap – we've already been gone longer than we expected to
be. I'll need to get back to work if I want to keep my job so I
won't be able to stay and date him." I shrugged sadly. "It's kind
of an impossible situation. If we had time, I'd love to see where
things might lead. He's a *really* nice guy. And sooooo hot!"

"Yes, he *is* that! When he looks at you with that smoldering heat in his eyes, even *I* get too warm." She giggled and then sighed. "I don't think a guy has ever looked at *me* like that."

We finally ran out of girl-things to talk about and went to take a nap. It was a hot, tropical afternoon and, without the guys, really quiet. I knew BigBoy and Rusty would keep an eye on things so it was easy to relax. Before long, I felt myself floating away…and awoke later to voices in the clearing.

"Where is everybody? Lissy? Joanne?" Tom called.

"Leesa? You are okay?" Rigo's voice rang with concern.

"Here. Taking a nap," I answered, groggy with sleep.

"Me, too," Joanne said. "Oh, crap, we forgot to start the fire! Sorry, guys." She jumped up and ran out to the pit where Robbie was setting his mask on the rocks. "Guess you can't leave us in charge of the fire, huh?"

"That's okay. It's been a rough day." Tom held up a good-sized ray. "Ray steaks, coming up!"

The sun was so hot we soon had a nice fire blazing, easily fueled by the little wood chips left over from sharpening the spears. We tossed the few remaining potatoes into the flames and Tom put steaks into the skillets. A few sizzling minutes later, the smell of cooking fish filled the air. Our stomachs growled.

As soon as the food was done, we crowded around the pit and wolfed down another delectable meal. Afterwards, we relaxed and hashed over the day's happenings. Still blown away by Frank's writing in the sand, we speculated about what could've happened to the person or people that had taught him.

"Maybe they were rescued!" Joanne was optimistic.

"Maybe they die." A rare expression of pessimism from Rigo.

"If they were still here, wouldn't Frank be with them instead of us?" Robbie mused.

"We may never know. I'm just thankful we have him now."
I couldn't imagine not having Frank in our little family.

As daylight faded, Tom suggested we close up for the night.
Tomorrow was going to be a long – probably grueling – day, and
we needed a good night's sleep.

"BigBoy! Come help with the wall, big fella!" I called to the
ape and, of course, got all three. They made short work of adding
the wall and the door to the shelter. I tossed them each a mango
as a thank you and said goodnight. They went up, we went in,
and everyone settled for the night.

In spite of the hectic day, it didn't take long for deep
breathing and snores to punctuate the night air. I fell asleep
quickly, my last thoughts of the up-coming day and what
adventures it might bring.

Chapter 13

Day 9

Lissy

We awoke as the sun rose and started the hike in the cool of the early morning. Filling the canteen at the creek, we munched fruit on the trail. BigBoy led, followed by Robbie, me, Rigo, Joanne, and Tom. Frank and Rusty brought up the rear. Everyone had a dive knife strapped to his leg, a spear in hand.

Thinking ahead, Tom had also made short spears – about a foot and a half long – for each of us to tuck into our belts. There could be occasions where a long spear simply wasn't feasible.

A curious-looking bunch, we all sported hats, including the apes. Rigo's wetskin was missing both sleeves and mine was missing one – all of them used in treating injuries. But the non-attached sleeves were being used as carry-pouches, tied to our belts and containing fruit for snacks. Whenever we encountered a mango or papaya tree, extra fruit was added to the pouches for later. The apes, of course, ate constantly.

We followed the creek as far as we could to have sufficient drinking water or a quick dip to cool off. It seemed logical that if there *were* other people on the island, they would probably be living near the water, too. A small trail ran parallel to the creek and we were able to maintain a fast but not grueling pace.

Occasionally, I heard rustling overhead however I never saw any monkeys. But I knew they were there, watching, and it gave me the creeps. Again, I thought it odd that we saw no signs of wildlife, only an infrequent bird or small snake. I mused to myself. *What are they eating, those damned monkeys?* Then I shivered. Were they looking down at us thinking, "Aha, a living, breathing, always-fresh buffet!"?

We spoke little, saving our energy for the hike, the nearly-complete silence eerie in the jungle. Sunlight filtered through the canopy and shadows jumped and swayed as we moved along the trail. I smelled the rich soil, still slightly damp and springy underfoot, and every now and then, the perfume of some exotic flower. No breezes reached this far from the beach and the air hung still and heavy amidst the trees.

In one area, I noticed a lot of those base-of-the-tree burrows, some quite large, some smaller. I almost hollered back to ask Tom if we could stop and inspect one when we met a thick, ropy vine drooping like a low valance across the trail – it forced us to duck beneath it. As I stooped to go under, I spied a repulsive, eight-inch-long black centipede with a bright red stripe down its back, its numerous legs carrying it slowly across the trail. In my opinion, centipedes ranked right up there with spiders and I let out a shriek, stumbling into reverse and nearly up-ending Rigo in line behind me. Everyone whirled, hands on knives or spears. Frank and Rusty pushed past Rigo to face my attacker. When they saw the centipede, they actually smiled and I wanted to slap their hairy ape faces. Rusty reached down and scooped the thing up. With all its myriad legs wiggling in the air, he folded it in half and popped it into his mouth, closing his eyes and chomping in delight.

Horrified, I turned off the trail and puked up my breakfast. It was going to be a long day.

Once my stomach settled and I could look at Rusty without retching, we continued along the path. I saw another centipede sometime later but refused to acknowledge its existence, not wanting to prompt another snack-fest.

Suddenly, BigBoy came to a halt and turned to look at Robbie who turned to look at Tom. We'd come to a fork in the trail: one branch continued on along the creek, the other angled sharply to the left, uphill. "What do you think, Tom? Straight along or up the hill?" Robbie called back.

"It might be a good idea to gain some altitude. We could see farther and maybe pinpoint where we want to go. I'm for uphill. What do you guys think?"

He made sense. Maybe we could see a village from up there. "I'm with Tom. Let's go up," I said.

It was unanimous, so Robbie pointed BigBoy to the left-hand path. For a while, it meandered slightly uphill and wasn't too difficult, then became steeper and rockier. We had to pick our footing carefully so as not to lose our balance. The trail zigzagged up the side of the mountain and we made slow, but safe, progress.

When we reached a somewhat level stretch, we stopped for a break, fruit, and a drink. Above many of the trees, we enjoyed a slight breeze, but wished for some cool water to splash on our faces. The canteen was half empty already and we hoarded it, hoping we'd soon find a creek or spring in the rocky hillside.

Feeling somewhat refreshed, we continued the upward trek. In places, the trail was plenty wide enough to feel comfortable, even with the steep drop-off immediately to our left. In others, it narrowed so much we could hardly put both feet side by side. In those areas, we hugged the side of the mountain and shuffled carefully, not looking down, relieved when the path widened again. The apes didn't seem to care how wide or narrow the path was – they swaggered along, enjoying the outing.

As the afternoon wore on, we became more and more exhausted and thirsty. "Where should we spend the night?" I asked. "I'm not keen on sleeping on this path. I'd probably roll over and wake up dead at the bottom of the mountain. And what if the ugly monkeys found us? There's no way to fight them here."

Tom answered. "I've been watching for a cave or wide spot in the trail where we could sleep close together, but haven't seen anything. Let's keep going – a cave would be ideal."

"Okay. I like the cave idea much better than a wide spot in the trail," I concurred.

"Sí. I no like open place – too easy to be ducks." Rigo liked the duck reference and used it at every opportunity.

Joanne was vehement. "I do *not* want to sleep out in the open! I'll walk until midnight if I have to. Let's keep moving."

Robbie said, "I agree. It's too easy for the monkeys to sneak up and attack from both sides." He urged BigBoy forward and we moved ahead, eyes alert for the smallest opening.

An hour or so later, BigBoy woofed and Robbie let out a hoot. "Water! There's a spring up ahead!" We raced forward, anxious to cool our sweaty faces and take a long sweet drink. Again, Tom rinsed and refilled the canteen, wishing for the umpteenth time that we had one for each of us.

After Robbie slaked his thirst, he and BigBoy wandered up the trail. His excited shout reached our ears just as we sat down for a rest. A cave? Jumping up, we nearly tripped over each other in our eagerness to see what he'd found.

A short distance beyond the spring, a small opening tucked between some large boulders beckoned invitingly, but with no flashlights to illuminate the darkness within, we were loath to enter. We grouped around the mouth, peering futilely into the darkness. I called to BigBoy. "Hey, big fella, go inside and check it out, okay? Go on."

Not sure if he understood, we watched the big ape crawl in through the opening. We listened, holding our breath and hoping we hadn't sent our friend into enemy territory. Soon, pebbles rolled as the dusty orangutan crawled back out. He woo-woo-wooed and waved at the cave mouth. Assuming that meant it was safe, Tom knelt and wriggled inside. After a moment we heard, "It's okay, come on in. I think it's big enough for all of us. Not the Taj Mahal, but, hey, all we asked for was a cave."

One by one, we clambered inside and found it roomy enough for everyone to sit and lean against the walls – and each other – legs out-stretched. It would be a cozy night. But at least we'd be in a secure space with our orangutan protectors guarding the door. I felt a bit claustrophobic and suggested we lounge on the trail outside until dark. We'd be stiff and sore after sitting on the hard ground and leaning against a rock wall all night, anyway, so now that we knew we'd fit, we crawled back out.

Relaxing near the spring, we sprawled in all directions and stretched our overly-tired muscles. Dividing up the last of the fruit, we enjoyed dinner and speculated about what tomorrow might bring. Joanne rested her head on her knees and moaned. "I sure hope we don't meet any of those ugly monkeys." she mumbled. "Maybe we've left them behind."

"I never thought I'd miss my earth bed and palm fronds, but that sounds like heaven compared to sitting up, crowded together, in a rock cave." I pasted a grin on my face. "But it's 100% better than sleeping out in the open! I'm not complaining."

Finally, as darkness fell, we each visited the loo around the bend, took a last drink of water, and crawled back into our night's sanctuary. Sandwiched between Joanne and Rigo, I squirmed and wriggled, trying to get comfortable. Digging a few pebbles out from under my butt I thought about *The Princess and the Pea* and giggled.

"What?" Jo said.

"Nothing," I replied, nesting into my pebble-free zone.

With the dim twilight backlighting BigBoy, Frank, and Rusty, I could see them sprawled in the doorway and felt comforted. Our guards were on duty, we were together, safe in our little cave, and water was just a stroll away. What more could we want?

Exhausted by the day's exertions, I soon dropped off to sleep. And in spite of the rocky surroundings, I slept like a baby, awaking only when I felt someone stir. The apes were up and I could see Tom wriggling toward the cave mouth, trying not to wake anyone else. But one by one, heads came up, eyes opened, and soon everyone was stretching and moaning.

"Oh, my God, I am so stiff," Joanne groaned.

"Me, too. Ow!" Robbie bumped his head on the low ceiling on his way out. "I'm too old for this."

"I don't think age has much to do with it, Robbie. Anyone who trekked up the side of a mountain and slept sitting in a rock cave, crammed together with four other people would be stiff and sore. I know I am."

"Come on out, everyone. We have a long day ahead of us." Tom urged us along and we slowly moved toward the light. He helped everyone stand as we exited.

I said, "Thanks, Tom," as he pulled me to my feet, and then took a closer look at his face. I frowned and asked, "What do you have on your cheek?"

"Where?" He reached up and wiped across his cheek. The black spot moved and spread out.

"Oh, my God! It's spiders! No! No!" I looked down at my arms and saw hundreds of little black spots about the size of the flat head of a straight pin running across my skin. The thought of sleeping in that spider-infested cave literally made my skin crawl and I retched. "Get'emoffme, get'emoffme!" I screamed, beating at my arms and frantically trying to remove my wetskin. I could feel them crawling in my hair and under my clothes. I ran for the spring, pulling at the Lycra, screaming hysterically. I managed to get the zipper undone and the wetskin down to my ankles but the booties were in the way. Not thinking clearly, I tugged and pulled and sobbed until Joanne stooped down next to me and said, "Lissy. Lissy, let me help, okay? I'll help you. Here."

She undid the Velcro on the booties and I kicked them away, using my feet to push the wetskin off, too. I pulled the bathing suit straps down and wriggled out of the suit, needing to be free of anything infested with spiders. Then I stuck my head into the small waterfall created by the spring and scrubbed at my scalp. "Jo, get'emoffme, please get'emoffme," I whimpered. Coherent thought ceased as I imagined thousands of spiders crawling on my body – my absolute worst nightmare come true.

Once I'd scrubbed my scalp raw, I tried to physically climb into the spring and ended up sitting in the mud. I scratched and clawed at my skin. "Get'emoffmyback, Jo! I can't reach it. Get'emoffmyback!" Much gentler than I was being, Joanne rubbed water on my back to remove the spiders.

From around the bend, Tom yelled, "Can I help, Jo? Is she okay?"

"She'll be alright, Tom. Just keep everyone back until I get her dressed again." Joanne, more than anyone else, was aware of my phobia and knew I wouldn't be able to dress again until both bathing suit and wetskin were thoroughly washed and inspected.

I rubbed mud and tiny stones into my skin to remove the bugs until Joanne said, "They're gone, Lissy. They're all gone. You can stop scrubbing now. You're bleeding, Hon, please stop." She took both of my hands in hers and held them tightly. "Look at me, Lissy. Honey, look at me."

Slowly raising my eyes to hers, I said, "Are they gone? Are they gone?"

She nodded and fresh tears flooded my eyes. "Are you sure, Jo? Every last one? Are you sure?"

"Yes, Honey, they're gone. Here, stand up and let me rinse your hair one more time. Then we'll clean off the mud."

Joanne gently rinsed my hair again and sluiced water down my body to remove the mud. Bloody scratches crisscrossed my arms, legs, torso, and even my face where I had clawed at the spiders. Once I was mud-free, Joanne picked up my bathing suit and I backed away. "I can't put it on, Jo. I can't." Sobbing and hiccupping, I whispered again, "I can't."

Patiently, she said, "We'll wash all the spiders out, Lissy. You don't have to put it back on until it's clean, okay?"

I nodded and watched closely, my arms wrapped around my body protectively, as she rinsed and inspected every inch of the suit, inside and out. When she was done, she said gently, "Okay? Can you put it on now?"

Knowing I was being unreasonable but unable to stop myself, I said softly, "Can you clean it again, Jo? Please? There might still be one in there. Maybe…maybe you missed one."

Joanne smiled patiently and said sympathetically, "Okay, Lissy, I'll clean it again, very carefully. I won't miss any. Then you'll have to put it back on." I nodded.

She went over every inch of the suit again and then reached out to hand it to me. Our eyes met and I hesitated, frozen with fear. "It's okay, Lissy, it's clean. I promise," Joanne coaxed.

Slowly, I took the suit and looked at it like it might grow fangs. "Put it on, Lissy. You have to put the suit back on before we can hike up the mountain. Everyone's waiting for you."

"They're waiting for me?" Rational thought was slowly returning, the fear reluctant to loosen its grip.

"Yes, of course they're waiting for you. Put that on and I'll wash out the wetskin."

Inspecting the suit, I found no creepy-crawlies, and donned it while Joanne thoroughly cleaned the wetskin. She handed it to me to examine and I found it spider-free, too. I smiled at Joanne, appreciating her patience and understanding of my incomprehensible fear. I put it on while she cleaned the booties.

When we returned to the group, I shrugged sheepishly. "I'm sorry, everyone. Having spiders crawling all over me was more than I could handle. Does anyone else need to use the spring? It's a muddy mess, but the water's still flowing."

Robbie, Tom, and Rigo went to get a drink and wash up. I found out later, they'd simply squished the small arachnids with their hands and needed to clean off the remains. They didn't want to mention it and send me off the deep end again.

BigBoy, Frank, and Rusty greeted me enthusiastically, evidently relieved I was no longer running around screaming like a banshee. I'm sure the whole incident confused and upset them.

Once we were clean and the canteen filled with fresh water, we set off up the trail. I knew I would never be able to sleep in a cave again and trudged ahead, trying not to think about nightfall and what it might bring.

We plodded along while it was still morning-cool, in pretty good spirits considering the way the day had begun. I longed for some fruit or a coconut, my stomach voicing its opinion on being ignored and slightly upset at the earlier flood of adrenalin. Still, I felt my confidence returning, the embarrassing spider episode becoming a thing of the past.

After several hours of uphill exertion, the path wound around a sharp up-thrust of solid rock, leading between a pile of boulders to the right and a solid wall on the left. As we followed BigBoy's lead, I glanced to the right and saw an opening between two large boulders. "Wait a minute, guys. There's an opening here."

I turned to the right and stepped into the mouth of a cave. My mind flashed on tiny spiders crawling on my skin and I shivered. I took a step back and away from the opening.

"Lissy." Tom came up beside me and said quietly, so the others couldn't hear, "You don't want to go in there. After this morning's episode, do you think you can handle it? We don't know what might be inside."

Although my stomach clenched and my heart raced, I knew I needed to face my fear. I hated coming unglued every time I met a spider. "I need to get over it, Tom. I'll be okay as long as I know we aren't going to sleep in there. And if we find spiders, we'll turn around. I promise you won't have any trouble getting me to leave." I grinned, resolute in my decision to face my fear.

He studied my face and said, "Alright. We'll take BigBoy."

I hollered for the ape and said to the others, "We're going to check inside. You guys wait here, spears ready."

"Leesa, you no need to go een there. I weel go weeth Señor Tom." Clearly, Rigo was afraid for me and I loved him for it, but

167

I was going. After all, I was the one who'd spotted the opening –
and I wanted to face my terror. I didn't want to add caves to the
currently short list of unreasonable fears.

"It's okay, Rigo. I'll be alright." I smiled at him, but he
wasn't happy. "Thank you for offering to go, but I need to do
this."

BigBoy led the way and as Tom and I walked into the cave,
it took a moment for our eyes to adjust. We paused and I
scanned the ground for any sign of small creatures crawling
around in the dim light. I could hear the big ape up ahead and
moved forward, knife in hand. If something should appear in
front of us, there wasn't enough space to use the spear – it would
be hand-to-hand combat. Rounding a bend, I realized the light
was still dim but not as dim as it should've been this far from the
entrance – there must be another opening up ahead or a chasm
in the ceiling.

The ground, littered with large and small rocks, made
precarious footing. We moved slowly and while watching the
floor, I almost hit my head on a low spot in the ceiling. In places,
the opening narrowed and I felt claustrophobic, but then it
widened again and my heart slowed its wild race. Around another
bend, the light dimmed even more and I could hardly hear
BigBoy up ahead. I called out, "BigBoy? Where are you?"

Suddenly he materialized right in front of me and I gave a
yelp of surprise. For a large animal, he could move on silent feet.
From behind, I heard Tom stumble and curse. "You okay,
Tom?"

"Yeah, I turned my ankle, but it's nothing serious. Why'd
you yell?" he asked.

"BigBoy just suddenly appeared right in front of me. He can
be so quiet – I feel like a bull in a china shop compared to him.
Are you okay to keep going?"

"Yeah, but go slow. My feet are bigger than yours and I'm having a hard time on all these loose rocks." He grumbled something under his breath I figured I was better off not hearing.

"Okay, BigBoy, let's go." I urged the orangutan on and he moved silently away while I slowly tripped along behind him, rolling rocks and pebbles every which way.

When the floor suddenly dropped out from underneath me, I pitched forward. Landing hard, face down, with the wind knocked out of me, I lay there, desperate for a deep breath. A large black beetle crawled past my face and I shrank back in disgust. I forgot about the insect when Tom landed on top of me, squishing any remaining air out of my lungs. He'd landed heavily, but his fall was broken by my poor battered body and the breath hadn't been knocked out of him. He apologized profusely saying, "Oh, God, Lissy, I am so sorry! Are you alright? Lissy? Lissy!"

I gasped, "I'm okay. Gimme a minute."

Tom sat up and helped me into a sitting position beside him. The air was stale with more than a trace of something distasteful, but I was eternally grateful when a deep breath finally filled my lungs. We sat there for a minute, breathing heavily, and I realized we had only fallen a couple of feet. This larger cavern was eerily lit by a crevasse in the ceiling, the sun's rays visible shafts shining into the huge space. As I looked around, I saw hundreds of white-ish rocks, all more or less the same size, littering the floor. *That's odd – why are all the rocks the same size and color?*

Looking closer, my stomach clenched and my body stiffened in horror. I put my hand on Tom's arm and stuttered, "T-Tom."

"What?"

"Those rocks." I was having a hard time forging a sentence.

"What about them?"

"They're not rocks."

"What do you mean they're not rocks?" He sounded confused.

"Look at that one, right there. That's not a rock." I pointed, paused, and gave him time to consider. "It's a skull. We're surrounded by hundreds of skulls!" We gazed around the huge cavern, the floor literally buried in skulls, several feet deep in places. Eye sockets stared vacantly in all directions and it dawned on me what that "something distasteful" in the air was – decomposition. I had a feeling I'd discovered what had happened to Frank's last friend.

"Tom, we have to get out of here. NOW! This must be where the monkeys bring their prey. Let's go! We don't want to be trapped in here." I scrambled to my feet. "BigBoy! BigBoy!" I frantically whispered his name, afraid of conjuring something other than our friendly orangutan.

When he silently appeared at my side, I stifled another screech and said, "Let's go, BigBoy. That way." I pointed back the way we'd come and he effortlessly hopped up the two-foot ledge, turning to offer me his hand. I grasped his big paw with both of mine. He curled his fingers around my left wrist and easily lifted me to his side. I moved out of the way and he helped Tom up, too. I was constantly amazed at the ape's strength.

Although in more of a hurry now than on the way in, we maintained a snail's pace to avoid turning ankles or falling and incurring a more serious injury. I couldn't help but look over my shoulder every now and then, afraid I'd see eyes in the dim light. We were nearly at the opening when I heard distant screeches.

"Hurry, Tom! I hear them." I urged Tom forward and we exited the mouth, breathless, dusty, and horrified at what we'd seen. "The monkeys are coming!" I told the rest of the group. The chattering and snarling grew louder as they headed our way.

I called to the other apes. "Frank! Rusty! Come up here with BigBoy!" We positioned the orangutans just at the mouth of the entrance, BigBoy and Frank in front with Rusty centered behind them. We fanned out along the trail on either side of them, spears at the ready. The orangutans were tense and agitated, occasionally snarling into the dim light, rocking from left to right.

Suddenly, an awkwardly thrown spear flew out, missing BigBoy by more than a foot. It clattered harmlessly to the dirt and Tom darted forward to pick it up – one less weapon for the monkeys, an additional one for us. Another spear sailed past Frank and skittered over the edge of the trail. I heard it slide down the steep embankment. The monkeys had obviously not practiced with the stolen weapons.

By losing two of the spears, the monkeys learned not to throw them away – no more spears flew out of the opening and the moments ticked by as we awaited their next move. There wasn't enough space for the beasts to rush the orangutans in a group but two came darting out and simultaneously launched themselves at BigBoy. He knocked one to the ground and it immediately jumped back up, unhurt, looking for an opening to pounce again. With its eyes glued to BigBoy, it never saw Frank swing one powerful arm in an arc. His fist slammed into the side of the monkey's head, sending the small animal sailing over the edge of the trail. It thunked into a wide tree trunk and lay still.

The other landed on BigBoy's shoulder. He reached up with both hands and easily broke the animal's neck, tossing it over the embankment where it landed not far from the body of the first.

Two more animals rushed Frank. He caught one in mid-jump, broke its back and tossed it over the ledge in one continuous movement. BigBoy reached out and deflected the other monkey's trajectory, sending it flying over the edge without ever making contact with its intended victim. Impaled on a stiff branch, it struggled weakly and died.

Again, a pause as the monkeys regrouped. Then, four snarling beasts charged out of the dimness, one attacking BigBoy, one launching itself at Frank, and two darting past the orangutans to try and reach us. Tom accurately stabbed a spear into the chest of the one that ran to the right. He kicked it over the edge. The one that dashed to the left dodged Rigo's spear and only received a grazed arm. It kept coming. As it leapt for Rigo's jugular, I stabbed it in the throat with my short spear, showering us with hot monkey blood. I kicked it away in disgust and turned back for the next onslaught.

Suddenly, Rusty roared and charged past BigBoy and Frank, disappearing into the darkness. Screeches, snarls, roars, whimpers, and screams met our ears as the simians collided, just out of sight.

"No, Rusty! Come back!" We yelled over the cacophony. We listened to the awful sounds, imagining the battle in our minds. The powerful roars grew less frequent and less forceful, the screeches becoming louder and more animated. Finally... silence. I hung my head and cried as Rigo put his arms around me in a consoling hug. No one moved, hoping against hope the rusty-red ape would appear in the opening. He was a pain, but he didn't deserve this.

Then I heard pebbles rolling and held up a hand, pointing toward the interior. I'd seen vague movement in the dim light. We faced the mouth of the entrance and saw a dark, smelly, nasty monkey walk into the sunlight. He stopped and snarled, showing his imposing red-stained fangs. He stood there for a moment, challenging us with his eyes, then quickly raised his chin in an insolent move and gave a sharp bark. As he turned to go, he carelessly tossed something that rolled our way, coming to a stop at Tom's feet. Rusty's head, blood still oozing from the gaping wound of his neck, stared skyward with wide, unseeing eyes.

Joanne turned away with a sob, retching. I closed my eyes and made a vow to *end* those nasty, wicked beasts. Tom reached down and gently grasped the rusty hair.

"I'm not going to let them have Rusty's head to add to their macabre collection. Let's bury it and be on our way. I think they're done for now." I admired Tom's strength. I couldn't have touched the head if my life had depended on it – even though the ape *was* our friend.

Despondent, we continued up the incline. The monkeys evidently believed they'd lost enough members and inflicted sufficient damage on us for one day since we heard nothing more. Besides, they surely feasted on the body they'd claimed.

Before long, Robbie spotted a deep depression at the side of the trail and we loosened more of the pebbly soil with our spears. Tom dug the free dirt out of the hole, gently placed Rusty's head inside, and we said a silent prayer for the willful young ape. He'd caused us some grief but had lost his life protecting us. Once the hole was filled with earth and covered with a mound of rocks, we moved on, our hearts heavy.

We rounded a sharp bend and came face to face with a nearly-vertical rock climb. We either dug in and clambered up the steep and dangerous trail or turned and headed back down. None of us wanted to lose the ground we'd gained – or feel that Rusty's death was in vain – so Robbie motioned for BigBoy to proceed. He made it look easy. He would scamper up a ways and then turn to lend a hand to everyone else in line. In this way, with numerous climb-and-wait shifts, we finally made it to the top of the steepest part of the trail.

Without room for more than one person – or ape – on the path at a time, BigBoy maintained his place in the lead with Frank bringing up the rear.

Turning to look out over the treetops, we saw little but unbroken canopy, punctuated here and there by rocky up-thrusts. Giving a collective sigh of disappointment, we continued upward. Maybe we'd see something more inspiring once we reached the summit and could look out over the other side.

One advantage of the higher altitude was the cooler temperature. A fresh breeze blew in from the ocean and we could smell salt in the air. We continued to climb and, rounding a curve, encountered a spring bubbling out of the side of the mountain, forming a miniature waterfall. First in line, BigBoy gave a triumphant "Woof!" before ducking his head into the cool wetness. One by one, we drank our fill and then doused our heads and sweaty faces, letting the water run down our necks to dampen the Lycra wetskins. They'd dry out in no time, but for now it felt good.

I hadn't noticed before, but wet ape smelled a lot like wet dog with a bit of fruity muskiness. I wouldn't want to be in an enclosed room with soggy orangutans, but out here in the open I was glad they could cool down, too.

Once the apes had finished bathing, Tom rinsed the canteen and filled it with fresh water. Resting by the spring, we enjoyed the soothing creek-trickling-over-rock sounds. It was amazing how much better we felt after rinsing the sticky sweat and monkey blood off our bodies. Soon, we were ready to move.

"I wonder how much farther it is to the top," I said. "I'm dying to see if we can spot a village or campsite. Wouldn't it be great if we could find more people?" I was excited at the prospect of new friends with new ideas of how to get off the island. "Maybe they'll know how we can contact someone to rescue us!"

"Not to rain on your parade, Lissy, but don't you think if they knew how to contact someone to get rescued, they'd have left the island?" Robbie made a good point. "It would be nice to be in a larger group, but I'm not holding my breath."

Crestfallen, I grumbled, "You're right, Robbie. I just wish you weren't."

We fell into line and silently headed upward once again. After trudging for another hour, our leg muscles complaining with the constant uphill exertion, we encountered another steep rock climb. There didn't seem to be a way around the rock and it overhung the trail too far to climb without a safety line. With no other choice, we literally put our lives in BigBoy's hands, asking Frank to remain at the rear of the line in case someone needed help. Past experience had shown that Frank sometimes rushed to the fore and we didn't want him inadvertently pushing someone off the ledge.

BigBoy scrambled over the seemingly-smooth, solid rock out-cropping and found a niche where he crouched and dug his finger-like toes into a small crevice. Reaching down with one long, powerful arm, he waited for Robbie – first in line – to secure his hold. Gripping the ape's wrist with both hands, he closed his eyes. BigBoy grasped Robbie's left arm in his huge paw, his fingers completely encircling the wrist, and swung him out over the precipice and around the out-thrust rock. We all gasped as our friend momentarily dangled in mid-air. Then, in one smooth motion, the ape brought Robbie back to solid ground and deposited him gently on his feet. He waited until Robbie steadied himself before letting go. One by one we trusted our friend to bring us safely past the out-cropping.

When it was Joanne's turn, she cowered just out of BigBoy's reach. Unable to brave the mid-air dangle, she whimpered and trembled with fear. Just as we thought she'd refuse to go on, BigBoy leapt down onto the trail in front of her where he squatted and looked up into her face, making a low cooing sound deep in his throat. Reaching up, he gently brushed a tear from her cheek. He knew she was afraid and did his best to reassure her. The tears and trembling stopped, an occasional hiccup punctuating the silence as we waited to see what would transpire. Suddenly, he giggle-screeched and gave Joanne a huge, toothy grin. She laughed and extended her arm to pat him on the cheek. Smoothly, BigBoy stepped toward Joanne, wrapped his arm around her and hefted her up over his shoulder in the monkey version of a fireman's carry. Holding her in a firm, one-armed grip, he turned and scrambled up over the out-cropping before she realized his intent. She shrieked as he softly deposited her on the trail.

Furious, and with adrenaline flooding her system, Joanne whirled to face BigBoy and slapped him hard across the face, screaming, "How *dare* you do that, you big ape? You could've killed us both!" She beat at his chest with her fists and screamed again, "How *dare* you?" The orangutan hung his head and endured her abuse without flinching.

Robbie reached out and caught her fist, saying gently, "Jo. Jo, he didn't mean to scare you. He was trying to help."

She turned her tear-streaked face to Robbie and whimpered, "I saw the ground. When he held me upside down and climbed up over the rock, I saw the ground far below. I thought I was going to die." She sobbed and leaned into Robbie. He wrapped his arms around her and held her as she sobbed.

BigBoy stood rooted to the ground, head low, eyes downcast.

When Joanne stopped crying, she said, "I'm sorry I'm such a coward." She dried her eyes and looked at Robbie apologetically. He tilted his head toward BigBoy.

She looked at the dejected ape and under her breath, breathed, "Oh." I could feel the heartbreak in that one syllable. She stepped over to the despondent orangutan and stood close in front of him. Still, he didn't raise his eyes to hers. Putting her hand on his arm, she softly said, "I'm sorry, BigBoy. I didn't mean to hurt your feelings. I was scared. *Really* scared."

BigBoy darted a glance at her face and then lowered his eyes again. He clucked softly.

Joanne stroked his arm and murmured, "I'm sorry I hit you. Please forgive me."

BigBoy began to hum. Joanne hummed with him and he rocked slowly from left to right. She put her arms around him and rocked in sync, holding him gently and stroking his back as she crooned in his ear. Finally, BigBoy grinned and patted her on the back. His giggle-screech plainly demonstrated his forgiveness and he looked at Jo with such adoration that we laughed.

I said, "Looks like he's forgiven you, Jo. You are once again his BFF." We laughed. BigBoy laughed. And all was again right with the world.

BigBoy positioned himself once more and helped Tom over the outcropping. Frank quickly followed them up and over.

Settling into formation, we plodded along the trail, hoping we'd soon reach the summit. BigBoy appeared to be taking the day's events in stride and, now that Joanne had apologized, was again a happy ape. He raced along the trail and then waited for us to catch up; he scrambled nimbly over rocks and large boulders; once he hid from us and giggle-screeched when we spotted him peeking around a rock. Obviously, he sensed no further threats.

Frank took his duties seriously and behaved as the more mature of the two apes. He brought up the rear and maintained a reasonable distance between himself and Tom, never once disappearing from sight. Losing Rusty seemed to have aged the orangutan, his quirky sense of humor temporarily suspended.

BigBoy rounded a bend in front of Robbie, out of sight, and barked a series of sharp "woof-woof-woofs" – not the woo-woos we were familiar with but not a danger call, either. We stopped, wondering whether the ape wanted us to follow or wait for him to reappear. After a moment, Robbie said, "I'm going to go see what he's up to. Be right back." He disappeared around the bend and we waited. And waited.

Next in line, I called, "Robbie? Robbie! Are you okay?" Spear in hand, I prepared to venture around the bend and see what had happened to my friends. Suddenly, Robbie and BigBoy both appeared with smiles on their faces.

"Come here! Come on!" Robbie urged us to follow. Eager to see, we surged forward. The vista ahead held us speechless – we'd reached the summit. The rocky trail in front now led downward, eventually disappearing into the trees. Looking out from the mountainside we watched hawks soar and play on up-drafts, their regal calls sending shivers up my spine, white puffy clouds a backdrop to their graceful choreography. At the horizon, the aquamarine blue of the ocean met the azure of the sky, tropical sun glinting off the unbroken expanse of water. Directly below us, the green canopy was a velvet cloak, bunched and folded, hiding…what?

No villages or campsites beckoned. No city with telephones and Starbuck's and restaurants. No people to commiserate with. And no place to buy a damned T-shirt. Initially enthralled by the beauty of the vista before me, I sank to the ground and sobbed. I'd been certain the other side of the mountain held the solution to our problems: people, food, coffee, methods of communication, *rescue*. And now that I faced the stark reality of our situation, I collapsed, heartsick with disappointment. Unable to contain myself, I cried and ranted and sobbed and howled.

"We're going to die here on this god-forsaken island! We're monkey bait. It's only a matter of time before our heads end up in that bone pile in the cave. I don't want to die heeeeere." Rigo lowered himself to the earth beside me and I buried my face in his chest. His arms were warm and strong but still I felt alone and scared and hopeless.

"Leesa, eet weel be okay. We not die here. All together, we are strong and not for monkey food. We are no ducks, Leesa." He stroked my hair and wiped the tears from my face. At his duck reference, I smiled and sniffed.

Ashamed of my outburst, I dried my eyes and said, "You're right, Rigo, we're *not* ducks. Thank you for reminding me." Forcing myself to my feet, I thought, *I am not a coward. I will not give up. And I will not be food for those damned monkeys!*

As Rigo and I rejoined the group, Tom asked, "Do you want to rest a while or start down the mountain? I know you're tired, but we probably won't find anything more to eat until we hit the tree line." He pointed. "And it'll probably be fruit for lunch and dinner, too." He smiled when we all groaned. "But who knows? We might find more of a variety on this side of the mountain!"

"I'm ready to head downhill. How about you guys?" I'd had enough uphill; I was ready to strain the downhill muscles.

"Let's go! I wanna see what's down there."

Once again, it was unanimous. You'd think trekking downhill would be much easier than going up, but after thirty minutes or so, I actually wished for an uphill stretch. I figured I'd suck it up and keep moving, however, I was relieved fifteen minutes later when Joanne said, "Can we take a short break? I thought this would be easier, but it's not. My muscles are screaming already."

Everyone else found places to sit on the rocks. I turned and walked a short distance back up the trail just to stretch those muscles again. Frank followed me while BigBoy remained with the group. Staring out over the beautiful vista and absorbing the sight, I sighed. *It really is a gorgeous view from up here.* Just as I turned to head back, a flash of light caught my eye. *What the heck?* I stared once more at the spot where I thought the flash had originated, but saw nothing. Convinced it hadn't been my imagination, I took a couple steps farther up the trail and looked intently down the mountain. Nothing.

Shaking my head and wondering what it could've been, I turned to descend toward my friends. Again! *There!* I stopped and stared hard toward the flash of light. I yelled, "I see something, Tom. Come up here, quick!" I heard pebbles rolling as Tom scrambled to his feet and rushed up the path.

"What is it, Lissy? Monkeys?"

"No, not monkeys. Look. There!" I pointed as a flash of light flickered in the far distance. "What is it?" It flashed again and again; stopped; flashed, flashed, flashed; stopped. A pattern?

"Wait. It's an SOS. It's someone signaling for help." Retired Navy, Tom was quite familiar with the international distress signal. "Robbie, did you bring your dive mask?"

"Yeah, here it is." Robbie handed Tom his mask and we all watched in amazement as he tilted the mask at an angle to reflect the afternoon sun, communicating with the flasher below. After several minutes, the flashing stopped and Tom said, "Evidently, he only knows how to signal for help since he can't answer my questions. But obviously he's alive – we need to get down there asap. Is everyone ready to move?"

"Of course!" It was unanimous.

We headed down the mountain with new purpose in our stride. Wondering about the man's story, I couldn't wait to hear how he'd ended up on the island. And maybe there were others!

When we encountered a vertical rock slab, BigBoy did his thing and helped each of us down, one by one, but thankfully, we didn't find any more out-thrusts that would force the ape to dangle us in mid-air. I didn't think Joanne would allow the orangutan near enough to institute another fireman's carry.

Our self-imposed lively pace was grueling enough, but when we hit the tree line and lost the cool ocean breeze, we melted. Sweat dripped from our chins, wet our hair, and soaked our wetskins; our faces colored an unhealthy red; and we desperately needed more drinking water – water that simply wasn't available.

One advantage, though, to leaving the exposed trail was shade provided by the canopy. Our overheated, sunburned faces resembled lanterns bobbing along in the shadowy jungle and, in spite of the heat, I was happy to be out of the sun. I hoped we'd soon find a stream or spring to splash around in – we needed to lower our body temperatures before someone passed out. Joanne looked especially wan and Robbie's white hair contrasted sharply with the red of his face.

BigBoy and Frank both seemed alert and jumpy in this new environment. I hoped it wasn't because they sensed nearby predators. I shivered. Looking up into the canopy, I half expected to see eyes gazing back at me. But nothing moved – no birds, no lizards, no small mammals. I would even have welcomed one of those creepy centipedes. This side of the island seemed even more lifeless than the other, if that was possible.

My stomach growled, reminding me how long ago we'd consumed the last of the fruit. I stared into the jungle, trying to spot a mango or papaya tree. Suddenly, BigBoy and Frank both darted off the trail. *What the…?* I kept my eyes glued to the apes, desperately hoping they weren't deserting us. Not here. Not now.

When they stopped moving away and began collecting something from the ground, my spirits soared. *Food?* I ran toward the orangutans, the rest of the group hot on my heels. Bananas! Finally something other than mangos and papayas. My mouth watered, my stomach growled, and I tore a slightly over-ripe banana from a bunch lying on the ground. Peeling the skin back, I sank my teeth into the luscious sweet fruit.

"Mmmm… This is so good. I didn't realize how much I love bananas." Joanne mumbled, her mouth full.

"Yeah! This is almost as good as that chocolate cake I've been fantasizing about," Robbie exclaimed.

Tom said nothing, too busy eating. Rigo sighed happily, gobbling his second one. The apes ate banana after banana, tossing the skins onto the jungle floor. They would rot and add further richness to the already fertile soil.

After we'd eaten our fill, we tucked as many bananas as we could into the carry-pouches on our belts and relaxed for a few more minutes. Sitting in the shade of a tall tree, I stared off into space, fantasizing about being rescued. Suddenly, I realized what I was staring at – a large aloe vera plant. "Jo! Look. An aloe vera."

We ran over and broke off a few branches. I saw a large burrow at the base of a nearby tree and said, "Hey, Jo, what do you think made that hole?" I pointed. Small bones littered the entrance. "Whatever it was, it's eating well. Look at those bones." I walked over and scattered the remains with my toe.

"I don't know, Lissy. Leave those bones alone – they give me the creeps." Turning her back, she said, "Come on."

We rejoined the group and Joanne said, "Okay, everyone. You all get aloe on your sunburned faces. Line up." No one complained as Jo applied a thick layer of the cooling gel to our hot skin. "Does anyone have anything else that needs attention?"

I had a few scrapes received from the fall in the cave and the self-imposed scratches created when I'd desperately scraped the spiders off; Tom had a deeper scratch on the side of his neck; everyone had bug bites. The apes should benefit from this bonus, too, so I called them over. Joanne applied a thick coating to a minor scratch on BigBoy's neck; Frank appeared unscathed.

Jo tucked a small aloe branch in a carry-pouch, just in case.

Although tired, we were united in our desire to find The Flasher and discover how he had come to be on the island. We returned to the trail.

The path was much less steep now that we were in the heavily-forested part of the mountain and was softer underfoot, the rocks and precarious footing left behind on the uppermost portion. Silence engulfed us, the only sounds an occasional birdcall or the crack of a twig.

BigBoy and Frank had relaxed and since the apes seemed calm, we also loosened up, welcoming the tranquil, jungle setting. Every now and then, I spotted a glorious orchid growing from the trunk or branch of a tree, the beautiful flower a bright touch of color amidst the varied browns and greens of the forest.

We trudged, silent and determined, until I heard rustling overhead. I tried to ignore it, hoping it would go away, but the sound followed us. Finally, I looked up, dreading the sight of ugly monkeys gazing back at me. Shocked, I saw instead a large family of orangutans moving about in the canopy above.

"Tom, take a look up in the trees." I didn't quite know how to react, however, since BigBoy and Frank seemed at ease with the animals' presence. Tom stopped and stared upward. The rest of the group did likewise.

Frank came to stand beside BigBoy and the two apes gazed into the branches. "Woo. Woo." BigBoy greeted the newcomers.

Adding his voice, Frank woofed, too. Whatever they said must've been an invitation because eight female orangutans, four with youngsters clutched to their breasts, dropped to the ground a short distance away. I hoped we wouldn't need the traditional meet-and-greet ceremony – I couldn't begin to eat enough fruit if our past introductions were the norm.

BigBoy and Frank moved closer to the females who quietly huffed and lowered their eyes. The males sniffed and pawed the females and they all performed brief grooming rituals in acceptance of each other. Then BigBoy came over and took my hand, leading me to meet what seemed to be the head female. He hugged me, hummed, and patted my back, then placed my hand on the female's arm. I stroked her gently and she relaxed, finally humming in approval. She then led me to the next female while BigBoy led Tom up for his introduction.

In this way, each of us was introduced to the females. Even Joanne seemed more at ease, perhaps because of the presence of the babies. They were inquisitive, reaching out with tiny, human-like hands to touch us and grasp our hair, their big eyes wide with curiosity. The sounds they made reminded me of human infants and I smiled at their antics.

There were no males in the group and I recalled a documentary I'd once seen. The females and young of both sexes traveled and lived together in a large group. Adult males normally lived solitary lives, seeking out females only for mating. Babies depended on their mothers for the first two years of their lives and were weaned around the age of four. Youngsters stayed with their mothers and often helped raise the next generation, although females only gave birth once every eight years.

I wondered what we would do if all eight females joined our family. I glanced at Tom and raised my eyebrows; he shrugged. Anxious to be on our way, I said, "Come on, BigBoy, Frank. We have to get moving. Say goodbye to your new friends." We lined up and prepared to go. I watched the apes' behavior and noticed that one orange female was being particularly friendly with Frank. She flirted; he flirted back.

When BigBoy led the queue down the trail, Frank's girlfriend followed behind. The rest of the females climbed up into the trees and I could hear them in the canopy, trailing us. I didn't mind if the female accompanied us as long as Frank didn't forget his duties. I'd rather she joined *us* than have Frank leave us for her.

I named the coquette Gigi and thought the two of them made a cute couple. Having her along turned into an asset when she led us to a nearby stream we would've missed. She woo-wooed once and then again when we didn't stop. When Frank woofed we all turned to see Gigi leave the trail and motion for him to follow. Torn between his desire to please her and his duty to us, he stood on the trail, confusion apparent on his hairy face.

"What do you think, Tom? Should we see what she wants?"

"Yeah, it would probably be easier than trying to get her to change her mind. And we don't want to lose Frank." Tom motioned for him to go ahead and the ape bounded off, happy to have our blessing to follow Gigi.

A short distance away, we found the pair frolicking in a stream. Thrilled with an unending supply of water, we joined the apes in the creek, cooling our overheated bodies and splashing the welcome wetness on our red faces. Robbie stretched out full length in the ripples and sighed with pleasure. He looked so contented, the rest of us couldn't resist. Before long, five people lay in the creek while three apes romped happily upstream.

Once we'd cooled off and refilled the canteen, Tom asked, "Is everyone ready to move on?" We nodded and looked at Frank. He sat with Gigi under a tree as she groomed him gently. "I hope they're ready to go," Tom added under his breath. "Come on, Frank! Bring your girlfriend."

Reminiscent of his namesake's era, Frank stood and took Gigi's hand, gallantly helping her to her feet. I giggled. BigBoy giggled. And before long, we all had a good old-fashioned belly-laugh. It felt good – we hadn't laughed like that in quite a while.

With the giggles out of the way, we traipsed along the trail, cooler, wetter, no longer thirsty, and full of bananas. It wasn't perfect, but it was better than before. An hour passed uneventfully and I began to wonder how we'd find The Flasher. "Hey, Tom," I hollered back, "How will we find the guy?"

"He knows we're on the trail leading down from the mountaintop. If he's familiar with it, he'll know where it leads. I'm hoping he'll be waiting along the path somewhere." Tom sounded optimistic so I tried not to have too many doubts. After all, what could possibly go wrong? I snorted. *Yeah, right.*

Here in the trees, it would get dark earlier with the sun setting behind the mountain. *Where would we sleep? We couldn't start a fire and we had no shelter.* The doubts set in and I again voiced my concerns. "Tom, where are we going to sleep tonight? Shouldn't we put a camp together before it gets any later? I'm not comfortable sleeping out here in the open and do *not* want another cave."

Joanne agreed, "Me, either!"

"I'd like to build a shelter, even if it's just a lean-to," Robbie added.

"Sí, we no should be ducks." I smiled at Rigo's duck reference, but he now had the correct meaning.

Tom stopped and said, "Alright. As badly as I'd like to find our friend, we do need to put safety first. Let's look for a good campsite."

"I wish we could locate another creek. But I guess for one night, it won't be too bad without water," Robbie commented. "How about right here?"

We looked around the small clearing where we'd stopped to talk and Tom said, "It's okay with me. Anybody have any objections?" Nobody voiced any problems with the location so Tom, Robbie, and Rigo set out to drag poles back for the shelter. Joanne and I began collecting vines and fronds for the roof and bedding. The guys located some heftier poles for the corners and recruited BigBoy and Frank. Gigi found some mangos, papayas, and more bananas. We hadn't brought the bucket but it's amazing how much fruit an orangutan can carry when she wants to. She brought fruit back by the armful and then returned for more. We wouldn't go hungry.

With the apes' help, the shelter went up faster than the original one and soon the guys were lashing the roof fronds on. "Since it's not yet getting dark," I said, "do you think we could make a fourth wall, too? We're not familiar with this area and I'm sure we'd all sleep better knowing we're secure."

"Sure. Let's do it. We'll need more poles and vines." Tom's comment had Robbie and Rigo ranging in search of poles while Jo and I collected more vines. I felt much safer once we had the front wall in place. We didn't bother with a door since this was a one-night stay.

By the time the depressions were dug and palm fronds laid for our beds, the light was fading. We brought some of the fruit inside and said goodnight to our hairy friends. As I lay my weary head down on the fresh palm fronds, I hoped Frank and Gigi weren't planning to elope.

Chapter 14

Day 10

Lissy

I had worried I might have nightmares about the spiders but exhaustion took me to a much more pleasant place. Sleep rejuvenated me and I awoke to sunshine and soft woo-woos just outside the shelter. Everyone else stirred about the same time and we untied the vines holding the front wall shut. When we shoved it to the right enough to slip out of the shelter, we saw Gigi and Frank sitting together on a felled tree, grooming each other, Frank's hat perched on her head and a vine hanging around her neck like an organic necklace. A gift from Frank? What a charmer!

Quietly, we giggled and the apes looked up and grinned. BigBoy appeared with bananas in his arms. He ambled over and handed one to each of us. When he got to me, he held up three fingers and pointed to the three bananas left in his hands. I said, "Yes, BigBoy, you have three bananas." I took one and asked,

"Now, how many bananas are there?" He held up two fingers as he scampered over to deliver them to Gigi and Frank. Then he darted back into the jungle for more. I guess you could say room service delivered breakfast.

After enjoying our meal, we were eager to hit the trail, knowing we should find The Flasher later today and hear his story. We formed our now-familiar queue, with Gigi accompanying Frank at the rear. Concerned that he might be distracted, I pulled Tom aside and said, "You may want to keep an eye on Frank today and be sure he's not too preoccupied with Gigi. If he's in love, he might not notice the presence of the ugly monkeys until it's too late."

"I was thinking the same thing. After the disaster with Rusty, Frank seemed very focused and protective. It's amazing what a pretty face can do to turn a guy's head, huh?" Tom was quite amused by Frank's flirtatious behavior, but a bit concerned also, that he might not have our backs. "I'll keep an eye on him."

We set a quick pace and even though it was morning-cool, we soon worked up a sweat in the still air amidst the trees. A couple of hours had passed when Gigi woofed and scampered off the trail at a right angle. Frank bounded after her and we soon heard his woof, too. I hoped Gigi had discovered another creek. We followed their voices and soon found them cavorting in a shallow pool fed by a cold-water mountain stream. Joining them in their splash-fest, we laughed at their watery antics.

Soon, however, we were cool and ready to head downhill with a newly-filled canteen and wet hair to keep us comfortable for a while. The apes obediently fell into line and off we went.

The hours passed uneventfully and around noon, with our stomachs growling again, we stopped for lunch. Gigi and Frank brought more bananas and mangos. Thankful for something to put in my stomach but less than overjoyed at the same fruit, I said, "What I wouldn't give for a ray steak. Doesn't that sound good?"

Teasingly, Joanne said, "Thought you didn't like seafood, Lissy."

"Well, it would be a welcome change from fruit. I've eaten more fruit in the last week and a half than I have the entire rest of my life. I'd turn around and climb that mountain again if there was a cheeseburger waiting on the other side." I closed my eyes and imagined a hot, thick, juicy burger, a generous serving of fries on the side, and a chocolate shake to wash it all down. My mouth watered at the vision and I could almost smell the delectable aroma. I licked my lips and sighed. "Guess I'll have another banana, instead. The burger will have to wait." Tom tossed me some fruit and everyone laughed as I peeled it, the image of the cheeseburger still fresh in my mind.

After lunch, we trekked along the path in silence and I wondered how much farther it would be before we'd find The Flasher. I was so intent on my thoughts that I nearly plowed into Robbie when he suddenly stopped. "What?" I switched to high alert, raising my spear and searching the trees for monkeys.

Robbie whispered, "There. In the trees off to the right. Is that our flasher?"

A man sat on the ground leaning against a tree, sound asleep, his chin resting on his chest, legs outstretched in front like a couple of long toothpicks. We took the opportunity to study him: tall, he was thin to the point of emaciation with a bushy white beard and a long, unruly mop of silver-white hair. His clothes, what was left of them, were ragged and filthy, and there was barely enough material left in his shoes to hold the soles to his feet. A sturdy, four-foot wooden staff lay on the ground next to him.

I whispered, "He looks like Moses. I know this is the Caribbean and not the Red Sea, but maybe he could part it and we could walk home."

Robbie snorted. "I wish."

Tom moseyed toward the sleeping figure, not wanting to startle him – he looked so fragile. But when Tom stepped on a twig, the man leapt to his feet and raised the staff, eyes wide, prepared for battle. The speed with which he'd moved amazed me – his appearance belied his agility and apparent strength.

BigBoy and Frank raced toward the man, intent on protecting Tom. He yelled, "No, BigBoy! Frank!" The apes stopped, looking confused, and Tom motioned for them to fall back. They retreated to Tom's side and he spoke to the man. "Whoa, take it easy, everybody. We signaled you from up the mountain yesterday. At least, I assume it was you." Tom smiled and took a couple more tentative steps forward.

"Moses" was loath to lower the staff with the orangutans so close. "Will they attack?"

Reassuringly, Tom said, "No, they're okay. We'll introduce you in a minute so they know you're a friend. You'll be alright as long as they don't sense a threat."

"Okay." In a deep and sonorous voice, he said, "I must've nodded off while I was waiting. I'm Morley." He gave a small wave to Tom, continuing to eye the apes suspiciously.

"Nice to meet you, Morley," Tom said, giving a casual salute in return. "I'm Tom and my friends here are Robbie, Lissy, Rigo, and Joanne. These big fellas are BigBoy and Frank. That's Gigi over there."

Morley gazed in wonder at our friends and said, "Did you tame them?"

I giggled and Morley looked at me with a question in his eyes. I replied, "We didn't tame them. They came to us – they're more friends than pets and more intelligent than we ever could've imagined. Here, let me show you." Keeping a respectful distance from Morley since he hadn't yet been properly introduced, I said, "BigBoy, come over here a minute, please." While the orangutan ambled over, I picked up six twigs from the ground. Holding them out in front of me, I said, "How many sticks are there?" BigBoy held up six fingers. "Good boy. Take two sticks." He reached out and plucked two twigs from my hand. "Good. How many people are there?" I pointed around the clearing. He looked and held up nine fingers." *Nine?* Astonished, I looked at Tom and I could see from his expression that he had the same thoughts racing through his mind. BigBoy had included himself, Frank, and Gigi in the people count.

"Nine people?" I asked BigBoy. He nodded. "Not six people and three orangutans?" He shook his head no and once again held up nine fingers. I wondered to myself when BigBoy had begun to think of himself and the other orangutans as people.

His voice filled with amazement, Morley said softly, "Well, I'll be damned. They still have the enhanced attributes."

I said, "We're dying to hear your story, Morley, but first, I think we'd better formally introduce you to the apes so they consider you part of our group."

We performed the meet-and-greet ceremony, complete with fruit, and found comfortable seats on some nearby logs. Morley settled himself, spread his knees and stood the walking stick upright between them. Both hands clasped the stick and he leaned slightly forward as though eager to share his tale.

"So, Morley, how did you come to be on the island?" I couldn't wait to hear.

He cleared his throat and said, "Well. Let's see. I guess I'll start with my parents. They were scientists. The facility they worked for had been hired by the Spanish government to develop an army of small, vicious monkeys. You've met some of the descendants?" He glanced at us with raised brows.

We nodded and, as a group, murmured, "Oh, yeah."

"Figured as much." With a commiserating nod, he continued. "They were also working on creating an intelligent, helpful, and protective group of orangutans – these guys must be their offspring." He inclined his head toward BigBoy and Frank who were being surprisingly quiet and attentive – for the moment, at least. He stared at the apes for a long minute and I could almost see his mind wandering. The pause lengthened and Joanne and Robbie glanced at each other. Robbie shrugged.

Morley shook his head and turned to meet my eyes. He said, "Sorry. I'm out of practice talking to people other than myself. Where was I? Oh, yes. After the monkeys killed some of the workers, that facility was closed. All of the experimental animals were caged and loaded onto a ship to go to another island.

"My mother told me they were hit by a terrible storm – a typhoon, really – that blew their ship off course. It was late at night when they hit the rocks and began to sink. Some of the monkey cages came open and those animals must have unlatched the other ones. She said the sounds were horrible: wind and waves beating against the ship; groans and cracks of the vessel breaking apart; metal bending and twisting; people screaming; animals growling and screeching."

His eyes once again took on that far-away look and, along with him I imagined the horrific scene in my mind. I shuddered and then jumped as Frank shoved a mango into my hand. "Thank you, Frank. You and BigBoy go explore. Go on." At his name, BigBoy dashed over to me for a hug and I sent the two of them off. I didn't want them intruding.

I said, "Sorry for the interruption. The apes don't usually sit still very long. Go on. How did your parents get off the ship?"

He watched the orangutans scamper into the trees and then turned his attention back to the tale. "They were lucky. Their cabin wasn't near the doorway to the hold. When the monkeys escaped, they attacked everything in their path. My mother said by the time she and my father made it to the upper deck, there was blood everywhere. They were afraid to jump into the water but couldn't stay on the ship – it was sinking fast. So they jumped. She couldn't swim but my father never let go of her – she said he saved her life several times that night." He smiled to himself and drifted away from us again.

Although impatient to know what happened next, I sat silently, the picture he'd painted vivid in my mind. I looked at the rest of the group and everyone seemed as impatient as I. However, we waited for him to begin again and when he rejoined us he smiled and continued as though there'd been no break.

"My parents were among the lucky forty or so that made it to shore. Between the monkeys on the ship and the sharks in the water, many didn't. The monkeys and apes that survived the waves fled into the jungle. When the storm ended, the people found a favorable spot along the creek and made camp, hoping they'd soon be rescued.

"Time passed. No ships came. No planes. And they realized they might never be found. So they concentrated on making themselves comfortable – and that was when my mother found she was pregnant. With me. They were terrified – who wouldn't be? – but they loved each other and couldn't end the pregnancy." He lowered his eyes and growled, "Sometimes I wish they had."

My heart ached for this lonely old man. A tear trickled down his weathered cheek, disappearing into his bushy beard. He

BEVERLEY SCHERBERGER

brusquely wiped the dampness away and said, "Please forgive an old man for tearing up over his memories. They're all I have."

Walking to him, I knelt at his side and placed my hand on his. I gazed into his pale blue eyes and said, "It's okay, Morley. Take your time and tell your story the way you want. We're not going anywhere." I smiled at him and his eyes overflowed again.

"Child, you have no idea what your kindness means to me. It's been many years since…" His voice broke and his breath caught in his throat. I slowly reached up and put my arms around his thin shoulders. At first he resisted. Then he surrendered to the emotion and pushed the walking stick away to free his hands. He wrapped his arms around me in a tight embrace, buried his face in my hair, and sobbed.

We sat like that for many minutes. No one spoke. No one moved. When the torrent subsided, Morley leaned back and whispered, "This is the first human touch I've felt in forty years. Thank you. Thank you." His eyes met mine and I saw a myriad of emotions in his face: joy, loneliness, fear, and gratitude.

Hugging Morley was the single most emotional moment of my life. Eyes brimming with tears, I whispered back, "You hold on as long as you need to, Morley. As long as you need to."

He patted my shoulder and said, "Why don't you sit here beside me? If it's okay with you, I'll hold your hand for a bit. I'd nearly forgotten how wonderful it felt to touch someone."

I scooted up onto the log and placed my hand in his big, gnarly one. He smiled a smile that lit up the world and said, "Now. Where was I?"

Thoughtfully, he sighed and said, "Ah, yes, my mother. She never completely recovered from my birth and suffered poor health until her death several years later. My father was inconsolable and I was raised mostly by the village as a whole. Thankfully, they were an educated group and took it upon

196

themselves to see that I learned to speak properly and how to write my name. My father passed on at a relatively young age – I think he died of a broken heart. I was eight."

We murmured condolences and he said, "It was a long time ago, but thank you."

Shifting his position and rearranging his spindly legs, Morley resumed. "Several other women bore children about the same time I arrived and growing up, we became a close-knit group. Although we played on the beach, we were forbidden to enter the water because of the sharks.

"Back then, there was a lot of wildlife in the jungle and the monkeys didn't bother us. For many years, we enjoyed a peaceful, very basic existence, living mostly on fruits and vegetables.

"When the other children and I became older teenagers, we weren't content to stay in our small community – we wanted to explore. So we'd take off for days at a time, camping in the forest, climbing the mountain, visiting the beach. I guess we were lucky the monkeys had plenty of food and didn't attack us."

He hadn't mentioned the orangutans and I was curious. "Did you ever see orangutans while you were exploring?"

Staring intently at the ground, he pondered. "No, I don't recall ever seeing any."

Shifting on his log, Tom said, "I wonder why they stayed so well hidden then, yet approached and befriended us."

Morley cleared his throat and said, "I don't know, Tom. If they had, perhaps things could've been different."

After a short pause, Morley buried his fingers in his bushy beard, scratched his chin, and resumed. "Eventually, we discovered another small village on the far side of the island. They, too, had been ship-wrecked and survived much as we had.

"I met a young woman there and she and I took a liking to each other. I began spending a lot of time there and, with both of my parents gone, I eventually moved to that side of the island to be near her. Her folks didn't like us being together too much so I usually camped in the jungle outside their village. She'd come find me in the morning and we'd spend the day wandering the forest and playing in the creek.

"We fell in love and wanted to be together but her father forbid it and told me to stay away from Caterina – I called her Kit. We didn't, of course, and after a time she ran away from her parent's home to live with me in the jungle. We built our own hut and scratched out a meager existence, living on love until she got pregnant. Young and scared, she talked about going home to have the baby. We fought. She left. Living in our jungle house alone, I was miserable and eventually went to see her. Her father told me to stay away, he'd kill me if I came back. I could hear Kit crying in the house and I knew she wanted to see me – I couldn't just walk away from my only love and my child."

Feeling his pain and wanting to distract him, I squeezed Morley's hand and said, "What did Kit look like, Morley? I bet she was beautiful."

He smiled and his eyes glowed as he answered. "She was beautiful. She had long blond hair that curled around her face and hung over her shoulders – it gleamed like gold in the sun. And it was soft, so soft. Her skin was pale and she always wore a hat to protect her face, but the sun brought out the freckles sprinkled across her nose. We used to chase each other through the jungle and she could run like a deer – she had long legs and could climb a tree better than me! Her laugh sounded like joy itself. We laughed a lot until she got pregnant." His countenance changed and the remembered happiness turned to sadness as he continued.

"Kit lived with her parents until the baby was born – I wanted her to have her mother's help during the birth. It was a boy and she named him Alex. I'd peek in the window opening to talk to Kit when her parents were busy and one day she let me hold him. He was beautiful! I wanted the two of them to come live with me, but she was afraid and refused to come away. Again, we fought and she told me not to come back. She said she'd tell her father if I returned.

"After that, I'd sneak up to the window at night and watch the two of them sleep. Kit and I never spoke and I never again held my son. I'd see her walking around the village, carrying him strapped to her back or feeding him at her breast."

Again he fell silent, lost in his memories. We honored his need to revisit them and remained quiet. Moments passed and we watched a myriad of emotions parade across his wrinkled face. He sighed deeply. "Oh." He looked around at us, seemingly surprised to find he had an audience. "Sorry. Where was I? Oh, yes. I became a hermit, avoiding people from both villages, watching Kit and Alex from a distance. I knew I'd never be a part of Alex's life, but that didn't mean he couldn't be a part of mine. I thought of myself as his private guardian and one day he was sleeping in the sunshine on a pile of soft blankets on the ground next to Kit's house. Thinking him safe, everyone had drifted off. I saw movement in the shadows – a constrictor was slithering toward him. It would only take a minute for the beast to crush the life out of my son, so I grabbed a big stick and beat the snake to death. Kit and her parents came running. I left the dead creature lying on the ground near my baby and darted into the jungle. Kit scooped Alex up and crooned to him, tears on her face. When her parents dragged the snake away, she looked into the trees, and said, 'Thank you, Mor.' I knew she knew and I was grateful."

A coughing fit interrupted the story and Tom brought the canteen over. Morley took a few long swallows and said, "Thank you, Tom. This is more talking than I've done in my whole entire life. It's taking a toll, I'm afraid."

Concerned, I said, "Do you want to stop? We could finish the story later."

"No, no, young lady. I see you hanging on every word – you're dying to know what happens next."

I giggled. "You're right, Morley, I am. But if you need to stop…"

He squeezed my hand and said, "Nope. Let's finish the tale, okay?"

"Okay." I grinned at him and added in a whisper, "Thanks."

He winked at me and took up where he'd left off. "For years, I watched over them. I saw my son take his first steps; I saw him run and play in the clearing; I heard him talk to his mother. I think Kit purposely took Alex into the clearing beside the house so I could see him. She was afraid to try and raise him in the jungle with me, but she wasn't heartless. If her parents had been willing, I'm sure she would've welcomed me into our son's life.

"Then I noticed the wildlife in the jungle had decreased dramatically. There were fewer birds, snakes, and small mammals, and I rarely saw larger animals any more. It was quieter, emptier, and I saw more and more monkeys.

"I became concerned about the friends and neighbors I'd left behind in the village where I was born, so I decided to go back to the other side of the island and check on them. During the two-and-a-half-day trek, I had several close calls when the monkeys surrounded me. I'd always used a walking stick and switched to a heavier one – one I could use as a club. It came in handy!

"When I arrived, I found the homes totally destroyed. Everyone was gone, the shelters torn apart and overgrown. It was obviously not new destruction – the jungle had already reclaimed much of the clearing. I never saw any of them again and figured the monkeys had slaughtered them. They'd decimated the other animal populations and had their eyes on the humans.

"The people in Kit's village didn't know the monkeys were carnivorous so I started the long journey back, pushing myself as hard as I could. I had to warn Kit and her family and protect Alex! But when I arrived, exhausted, it was too late. I found no bodies and no survivors. Kit's house was a pile of sticks with monkey-prints everywhere. I was devastated and vowed to kill the animals that had taken them. I spent a week prowling the jungle, searching for the murderous beasts, but they were nowhere to be seen."

Tom interjected, "I think I know where they take their victims. We found a cave on the far side of the mountain that has bones and skulls several feet deep. That's probably where they feed, leaving the bones. We lost one of our orangutans there."

"Poor Rusty," Joanne murmured.

Morley's eyes narrowed and he growled, "I might have to pay that place a visit. I've killed more than my share of monkeys but it doesn't make up for them taking my son." His voice held determination and deep hatred.

He paused and I watched him rein in his emotions, forcing himself to calm down. When he continued his tale, his voice was even with no trace of the previous anger. "There I was, alone at the age of twenty-five. My son was dead, the love of my life, gone. All I had left was a burning desire for revenge. So I spent the next ten years or so hunting monkeys, half out of my mind with grief. I didn't care what happened to me. My attacks took the animals by surprise and I got really good at killing the things.

"Then suddenly, the overwhelming grief dissipated. Revenge no longer governed my every waking thought. I was alone and lonely, with no hope of ever having another friend, another love. I actually thought about walking into the sea and letting the sharks have at it, but couldn't abide the thought of those teeth dragging me under, drowning in excruciating pain, blood, and salt water." He shivered.

"And I refused to allow the monkeys the satisfaction of taking my life. They stole Kit, Alex, and everyone I knew growing up – they couldn't have me, too.

"Even though Alex never knew his father, I needed to be the kind of man he could be proud of, not a quitter, not the type of man who would give in to despair and allow Death to take him easily. So I faced each long and lonely day, wondering how many years I'd have to endure, and prayed that God Himself would end my suffering and loneliness."

He hung his head and sighed. My heart ached along with his and I closed my eyes, picturing this brave soul trying to live up to a dead child's expectations. Lost in my reverie, I jumped when he continued.

"I explored the island in all directions and found no other human inhabitants. I ate when I had to. I slept in small caves and rolled a big stone in front of the opening so nothing could get in without waking me up. I battled the monkeys when they attacked – and I waited. Now I know I was waiting for you. God sent you with your smile, your touch, your kind and helpful ways, and did, indeed, put an end to my suffering and loneliness. Not in the way I expected, but the Lord moves in mysterious ways, does He not?"

He gave a small, sad smile and looked into my eyes. I saw a little less grief, a little more satisfaction, and was glad we'd pushed ourselves to get here as soon as possible. And surprisingly, I found myself thinking I needed him as much as he needed us.

"The other day when I glanced up the mountain and clearly saw *people*, I thought I was hallucinating. I found my father's spectacles and flashed an SOS, hoping you'd see it and understand. He taught me how to do that when I was six, just in case, and I've never forgotten." He choked up and tears filled his eyes. "I waited sixty years to use it." Tears trickled down his weathered cheeks, following wrinkles and creases like floodwaters in gullies. He lowered his chin to his chest and sobbed.

My eyes overflowed as I tried to imagine living completely alone on this miserable island for over forty years. My heart went out to this man who'd had so little control over his destiny and once again I wrapped my arms around him as he wept.

When Morley's tears turned to the occasional sniffle, I said, "I'm so sorry about Kit and Alex. You all deserved better."

"Thank you, child. It was a long time ago but the pain is as fresh as if it was yesterday." He forced a smile and I noticed how tired he looked.

"Why don't you take a nap, Morley? All that talking must've worn you out." I stood and helped him up, watching as he slowly collected his gangly legs.

"That's a splendid idea, Lissy." He pointed and said, "I'll be over there under that tree, if you should need me." He shuffled across the clearing to settle against the trunk. No sooner had he closed his eyes than a gentle snore filled the air.

Morley's story had deeply touched our hearts. Wanting to celebrate, Tom asked, "If we're not too far from the coast, would you guys want to walk there and go fishing? I'd love something special for dinner to welcome Morley into our family."

We unanimously agreed and I said, "Let's give him an hour to nap, then we can ask him how far it is." We relaxed and pondered the old man's story until Frank and BigBoy scampered up with a bunch of mangoes. Trying to keep them quiet, we each took one and moved farther away from the slumbering figure. When we'd found comfortable seats, the apes climbed up into the trees, evidently realizing we weren't going anywhere.

Eyeing Morley, I said, "How sad that he lost Kit and Alex to those murderous beasts."

"Yeah," Tom said, "And he's not bitter. I would be."

Robbie said, "He was for a while. I wonder how many monkeys there'd be if he hadn't wiped a lot of them out."

"He's really taken a shine to you, Lissy," Joanne said. "Just think, forty years without touching another human being."

Meeting her eyes, I whispered, "I didn't think he was ever going to let go." My heart ached and my eyes burned with fresh tears. "I feel pretty selfish wanting all the things that I didn't think I could do without – when all he wanted was to hear a human voice, to feel the touch of a caring hand.

"I don't think I ever told you guys this, but I never knew my father. He died shortly after I was born – but I'd like to think he was as nice a person as Morley. I'd be proud to call him Dad." The tears spilled over and I stood, turning away from my friends. I left them chatting amongst themselves and quietly walked toward Morley. I wanted to be near him.

Finding a comfortable spot nearby, I sat with my back against a tree and watched the old man sleep. My eyelids grew heavy as I contemplated his long and lonely life.

A hand shook my shoulder and I jerked awake. Joanne squatted next to me and said, "You've been asleep for a while, Lissy. Should we wake Morley, too?"

"Yes, we'd better find out if he feels like heading for the coast. If we don't start soon, we won't have enough time to get there and go fishing. I'm dying for something other than fruit."

I knelt beside Morley and gently put my hand on his arm, not wanting to startle him. "Morley. Hey, Morley."

His eyes opened and he smiled. "Have I died and gone to Heaven? You're the most beautiful waking sight these eyes have beheld for many years, Lissy."

Grinning back, I said, "No, this is surely not Heaven, Morley." He held out his hand and I helped him to his feet, saying, "How far to the coast? Can we get there in a few hours?"

"Sure. Even these old bones could make it in a few hours. What do you have in mind?"

Maintaining my hold on his hand I said, "We want to go fishing and fix a special meal for dinner tonight. If you can lead us there, we'll take care of the rest. Is it a deal?"

"It certainly is a deal! How soon can you be ready?" He smiled another of those light-up-the-world smiles and my heart swelled with affection.

I turned to look at Joanne and said, "Looks like we're going to the coast!" I hollered for the rest of the group and added, "BigBoy! Frank! Gigi! Let's go!"

We collected our spears and formed another queue, this time with Morley in the lead behind BigBoy.

From the rear, Tom shouted, "Just point the way, Morley, and BigBoy will get us there."

For the next couple of hours we trudged through the thick jungle on a well-worn path. The still and steamy air felt thick. Few bird calls broke the silence. Mostly, the only sounds were our footsteps and heavy breathing. I imagined a beach scene similar to our little lagoon with palm trees and gentle waves.

Suddenly, the trees ended and a fresh, salt breeze dried the sweat on our faces. Unlike the peaceful, scenic lagoon I had anticipated, unceasing sea winds buffeted the coast. Strong waves drenched the rocky shoreline; driftwood and the occasional piece of rubbish that had drifted here from far away littered the beach. If you could even call it a beach – it was comprised mostly of rocks with a smattering of sand. Scenic in its own way, it should contain many pools where fish and rays could become trapped.

I saw Robbie, Tom, and Rigo exchange a hopeful look. "Let's go get dinner."

Robbie tossed me his dive mask and I said, "I'll set up – you guys bring back something substantial."

We watched them trot toward the shoreline and with concern in his voice, Morley said, "They're not going into the water?"

"No, they're searching for pools in the rocks where fish have become trapped. Don't worry, Morley, they know what they're doing. And we'll have fish for dinner tonight."

"Fish. I don't remember the last time I ate fish." He shook his head and added, "You guys are a God-send." With tears in his eyes and a huge smile on his wrinkled face, he said again, "Fish!"

Joanne and I grinned at each other and I said, "Hey, Jo, why don't we take BigBoy and dig up clams to go with the fish? We can have a seafood buffet to celebrate meeting Morley."

"Okay! You want to join us, Morley?" Joanne asked.

"No, you kids go ahead. I'll watch from here. Might even take another nap."

"Alright. Come on, BigBoy. Let's go to the beach." The three of us headed for the shoreline and left Morley sitting on the ground, leaning against a tree. Even though the nasty monkeys never seemed to venture this close to the water, I told Frank and Gigi to keep an eye on him.

BigBoy soon dug up more clams than we could carry in one trip. "Okay, BigBoy, no more. No more!" When I finally convinced him to stop digging, I loaded his big hands with clams and we picked our way across the rocky beach toward Morley. We found him sound asleep with a contented smile on his lips.

Leaving him to his dreams, we set up the fire pit a short distance away and made a second trip to bring back the rest of the clams, then set off to collect dry wood. BigBoy, Frank, and Gigi located fruit and coconuts so Joanne and I pulled strings for kindling. Before long, we had a small fire blazing, ready for whatever bounty the guys brought back for dinner. Lacking the skillets from camp, we washed flat rocks for cooking and collected additional ones for plates.

Soon, we heard laughter approaching and looked up to see Tom, Robbie, and Rigo hauling two rays and a stringer of fish – they'd taken a length of vine and strung it through the fish's gills.

Morley awoke and called, "It's been many a year that voices woke me. What a lovely sound!" He collected his lanky legs and strolled over to join us. "There's a stream not far from here, if you need fresh water for dinner. I'd be happy to go get some if you'll pass me that canteen, Tom."

"Sure, that would be wonderful, Morley. BigBoy, you go with him." Tom sent the ape along, just in case, and the old man looked pleased to have the company.

We watched the two of them disappear into the jungle and I turned to Tom, my eyes welling with tears. "I can't imagine living alone in this God-forsaken place for forty years. It's a wonder he hasn't gone insane from loneliness. And it's so sad that those damned monkeys killed his son. Wouldn't it be incredible if we could get rescued and take Morley home?"

"Home? Lissy, this *is* his home. He wouldn't know what to do or how to fit in anywhere else." Sadly, Tom added, "I think he'd be even more miserable there than here."

Shocked, I said, "I never thought about it like that. The poor man – to have to call *this place* home." I shook my head and said, "What are we going to do, Tom?"

Shrugging his shoulders as he cleaned the fish, Tom said, "There's nothing we *can* do, Lissy. And it's irrelevant, anyway, unless we can get rescued ourselves."

I nodded and turned to wipe away the tears that had dampened my cheeks.

By the time Morley returned with the canteen of fresh water, the smell of cooking fish filled the air. "Now *that* smells *good!*" He turned a beaming smile on Joanne at the fire pit and added, "It's been so long since I've eaten anything other than fruit, I hope my system can take it. Do you think the fish will settle okay?"

She nodded and said, "You're right, Morley. Take this advice from the resident nurse: eat slowly, chew well, and don't eat too much all in one sitting. I'd hate for you to get sick on your first real meal in years. You may not be able to assimilate the protein very well. Take it easy and we'll have fish again tomorrow. Okay?"

"It'll be hard not to feast, after so many years without, but I respect your advice." He smiled at Joanne. "Thank you."

When the meal was ready, we lined up with our stone plates and Joanne served generous portions to everyone except Morley. With a gentle smile, she said, "Here you go. Try a few clams and this small piece of ray steak. Tomorrow you can have more, if this settles alright."

"Yes, ma'am, nurse-lady. You're the boss." He grinned and accepted his meager portion without complaint. At his first bite, he closed his eyes and chewed slowly, savoring the flavor. He took Joanne's suggestion to heart and made it last. Finally, he swallowed and said softly, "Now I know what Heaven tastes like."

Tom made a toast, raising the canteen. "Morley, this is to you. We are blessed to have met you and call you our friend. Cheers!" He drank and passed the canteen around the circle.

I handed it to Morley and he added onto the toast. "And this is to *you*, my friends. You've made a long, lonely life worthwhile. I couldn't be happier than I am at this very moment. Cheers!"

Dinner was a joyful affair, filled with laughter, camaraderie, and contentment. My heart filled to overflowing and I felt blessed to have met this amazing man who had survived so much hardship and loneliness in his lifetime, yet was still kind and loving. A lesser man might be bitter and filled with hatred, cursing God for his lot in life. In spite of our situation, that night I enjoyed good friends, good food, laughter, and an inner joy I hadn't experienced in a long, long time.

When we'd finished eating and cleaned up the mess, addressing no one in particular, I said, "Where are we going to sleep tonight? Any suggestions?"

Morley spoke up first. "The monkeys don't like to come near the water. It may be because of the trauma of the shipwreck – the fear of the ocean has been passed down through the generations. I've never seen them near the shore."

"We never saw them near the lagoon, either," Tom said. "Let's build a temporary shelter here at the tree line."

"I think that's a good idea, Tom," I said, and then added, "Morley, do you want to stay on this side of the mountain or would you like to come with us to our camp on the other side? There's plenty of room for one more and we have a really sturdy shelter that I'm sure you'd like. What do you think?" I was hoping he'd want to come back with us – I missed our pretty little lagoon – and hated to think about leaving him here alone.

"That's a very generous offer, Lissy, thank you. But, you know, I've gotten so used to living in the moment that I find it difficult to think about the future. Can we discuss it later?"

"Sure, Morley. First thing tomorrow. We can talk about it over more fruit. Ugh." I made a face and then grinned at the old man. His smile warmed my heart.

Tom started barking orders. "BigBoy, Frank, Gigi, we need poles. Joanne, Lissy, vines and fronds. Robbie, Rigo, we can lay out the shelter and dig the corner post holes and then make sure the apes are collecting what we need. We only have about two hours before it starts to get dark so we don't have time to waste." Everyone scattered.

Morley approached Tom and said, "I want to help, too. You've done so much for me – what can I do?" Tom sent Morley to help collect vines and fronds with us, leaving the heavier work to the apes and younger men.

"Come on, Morley. You can show us how you make *your* bed. It might be more comfortable than what we do." Joanne and I showed him which fronds we used and he suggested another, softer type. Soft sounded great so we collected armfuls of those. Then he pointed out another larger, more durable frond for the roof. We learned a lot and respected his experience and wisdom.

With everyone working at top speed, we soon had a pile of poles, a mountain of palm fronds, and what seemed like miles of vines, all waiting to be assembled. The apes helped place the corner posts and then held the horizontal poles while Tom and

Rigo tied it all together. Once three walls were up, they laid the foundation for the roof fronds. Rigo helped Joanne and I add the roofing. Done before dark, we even made a fourth security wall, sans a door, so we could sleep comfortably and not worry about uninvited nocturnal visitors.

Joanne and I showed Morley how we dug a depression in the earth for bed fronds and he approved, saying, "That's how I did it, too. Makes things softer and at my age, a soft bed is a necessity – too many aches and pains, otherwise."

Finally, we filled the canteen, said goodnight to the apes, and tied the front wall on. Prior to settling into our respective beds, we sat and chatted, safe and secure in our new shelter. Morley's reaction to my earlier touch had had a profound effect on me and weighed heavily on my mind. No one should go forty years without being held by another human being. So I got up and walked to his pallet. "Morley, if you wouldn't mind, I'd like to give you a goodnight hug. Would that be alright?"

The old man looked like I'd offered him the moon and said softly, "There's nothing in the world I'd like more, young lady." He opened his arms to me and I snuggled up next to him. Moments later, a single tear dripped onto my arm and I knew I'd done the right thing by sharing another touch with this kind old man. Knowing I was where I needed to be, I relaxed and soon fell into a deep and dreamless sleep.

Chapter 15

Day 11

<u>Lissy</u>

Initially disconcerted to find myself lying next to someone, I then recalled hugging Morley and sitting with him before falling asleep, offering him the human touch he had lacked for most of his life. I smiled to myself, recalling the tear of joy he'd shed. I carefully inched away from the slumbering form and found the others awake, as well.

We collected fruit for breakfast and I anticipated peppering Morley with more questions about his survival over the years. Maybe he knew more about the monkeys that would help us avoid or defeat them in future attacks. There was much I wanted to know.

When we returned to the shelter, I checked on the old man. He hadn't moved. Something in his utter stillness caused me to go to him. I sat down and took his hand, now cool to the touch. Tears coursed down my face as I thought how unfair it was that

Morley'd had such little time with us, certainly not enough to make up for all those years of deprivation.

Tom peeked in and I glanced up. Seeing my tears, he came to me and asked, "He's gone?"

I nodded. "It's not fair, Tom. He missed out on so much in his life. He could've lived with us and joined our family."

Older, wiser, Tom said, "Lissy, life isn't fair. But you made him happier than he'd ever been just by offering him your time, your generosity, and your touch. Holding him was the greatest gift he'd ever received. He died happy."

Tom was right. Morley had passed away in my arms, knowing I cared. I sobbed and held onto the old man's hand, loath to let go – it had meant so much to him. Finally, Tom murmured, "Come on, Lissy. He's gone. We might as well bury him and head back to the other side of the mountain – there's no reason to linger here."

Reluctantly, I released Morley's hand and placed it on his chest. I wiped away my tears and went with Tom to tell the others. One look at my face and they knew. I said, "Morley died in his sleep" and Joanne wrapped her arms around me and cried along with me. We'd known him only a short time but he'd made a huge impact on us. We'd miss him. I thought back to last night's dinner and recalled the utter contentment on Morley's face, the joy in his laughter – he'd had so little to laugh about in his life – and the happiness in his eyes when I'd asked if I could hug him. He wouldn't want me to mourn him. He'd prefer that I celebrate the fact that he was no longer alone and lonely, no longer missing his son, and no longer fighting, waiting, regretting his life.

I dried my eyes and said, "Let's find a peaceful place to lay Morley to rest. He said the monkeys don't like the ocean – how about right here?"

"That's a good idea, Lissy. He seemed very content last night. And when you asked if you could hug him, I thought he was going to cry. You made him happy." Using our knives, we dug a depression at the edge of the tree line. A flat rock aided in removing more of the dirt and when BigBoy realized we needed a hole, he helped, too – dirt flew everywhere.

When the hole was deep enough, we lined it with rocks and sand topped with the soft fronds Morley liked for his bed. Tom and Rigo gently lowered the body into the ground and I handed them his walking stick. We covered him with more fronds and rocks before refilling the hole with dirt. A mound of small boulders the guys wrestled into place on the surface served as a headstone.

Although Robbie and Rigo hadn't said much since we'd discovered Morley had passed in the night, Robbie wanted to say a few words. Holding hands, we encircled the fresh grave and bowed our heads. "Lord, Morley had a hard life and only You know why. He lost his parents at an early age; lost the love of his life and his only son Alex in a horrific way; lived alone and lonely for forty years, hungering for the sound of a human voice, the feel of a caring touch, and the joy of laughter. And in spite of the hardship and deprivation, he was a good man and never turned his back on You. Welcome him to Heaven, Lord, and give him the love and joy he never knew here on earth, reunite him with his son, and let him hold him again. He'll live on in our memories but his soul belongs to You. Amen."

"Amen."

"Amen."

"Amen."

"Vaya con Dios."

"That was lovely, Robbie. Thank you. I do think he's in Heaven, now, watching over us and smiling. He'd like this spot as his final resting place." I hugged Robbie, feeling a deep fondness for this kind and gracious man.

He hugged me back and murmured into my hair, "I liked him, too, Lissy. He was very special."

I turned once more to the grave. "Goodbye, Morley. I would've liked to know you better, but in our short time together, you felt like the father I never knew." I blew him a kiss and joined the others.

With heavy hearts, we headed up the trail. Visiting this side of the island had been quite a bittersweet experience. We'd found the monkeys' main feeding cavern; lost Rusty; Frank fell in love with Gigi; we met and lost Morley; discovered there were no other people anywhere on the island; and found that bananas grew over here but not on our side of the mountain. And we weren't even home yet. I couldn't help but wonder what adventures we'd have on the return trip.

The day had already heated up by the time we hit the trail and it wasn't long before our faces grew red and sweat dripped from our chins. The air was moist and heavy in the jungle and by noon we could hear thunder rumbling in the distance.

BigBoy, Frank, and Gigi served us bananas, papayas, and mangos for lunch. Afterwards, they took us to a nearby stream for a cool drink and a refreshing dip – from the sound of the approaching thunderclaps, we'd soon be drenched, anyway.

Rested and refreshed, we resumed the hike. The canopy overhead blocked a lot of the sunlight even on a clear day and before long, it dimmed to near-twilight in the trees. We heard the first pitter-patter of raindrops falling on the leaves but it took several minutes for the water to work its way to the jungle floor. At first, walking along the trail with a misty drip from the leaves seemed pleasant – cooler and not so steamy. However, before long, the rain became a deluge and the misty drip became a constant and heavy trickle pouring off every leaf overhead. Thunder crashed and lightning flickered, creating weird shadows that jumped and loomed in the dim light. Underfoot, the path turned slick in places and thick with sucking mud in others. We often had to stop while someone pulled a dive bootie out of the muck.

"Can we stop for a while out of the rain? This is absolutely miserable," Joanne moaned. "I'm muddy to my knees."

"I've been looking for a cave, but haven't seen any – just trees and mud. If we're going to be out in the rain, anyway, we might as well keep walking." Tom sounded just as discouraged.

BigBoy, Frank, and Gigi had all picked large palm fronds to hold over their heads like jungle umbrellas. None of them looked as wet as we did. Again I wondered who was smarter.

We continued to slog through the mud. The storm showed no sign of abating and, if anything, increased in intensity. I shivered. It reminded me of the storm that had gotten us into this fix in the first place. At least we were above-ground and not under water where a rogue current could carry us away.

Then, over the noise of the storm, I heard a train-like roar that seemed out of place here in the jungle. We stopped and listened. "What's that?" I asked.

BigBoy, Frank, and Gigi suddenly turned and fled toward a nearby hill. Tom screamed, "Run! It's a flash flood!" We dashed toward the apes, not knowing where the water would come from, but hoping to get out of its path. All of a sudden, the ground was squishy underfoot, our feet splashing in water instead of smacking in mud. "Hurry! Run, faster! We're almost there!" Tom continued to yell encouragement as the water around our ankles rose higher and we dodged left and right through the trees.

By the time we reached the foot of the hill, the water had risen nearly to our knees and it was difficult to stay upright. I was astonished at the force of the current as it swirled around my legs. Tom positioned himself with his back to a broad tree and, with the current helping hold him in place, grabbed our hands as we came within reaching distance. He hauled on my arm and then shoved me upwards, reaching back for Joanne.

I heard a scream from behind and turned to see Jo being swept away in the frothy water. She thumped and bumped into the trees as the water churned and grew deeper, swifter. I screamed, "Jo!"

BigBoy nearly knocked me over as he ran down the hill and plunged into the water, his strawberry blond head immediately disappearing in the turbulent floodwaters. "No! BigBoy!" I shouted. We stood on the hillside and stared into the distance, watching the water grow deeper and more treacherous, our friends quickly disappearing from sight.

Rigo came and put his arm around my shoulder. "BeegBoy weel save her, Leesa. He ees strong and brave. You weel see."

"I hope so, Rigo. We can't lose them both. Not like this," I cried into his chest.

We clambered higher up the hill and joined Frank and Gigi at the summit. Looking around, I thought *This isn't a very big hill. I hope the water stops rising soon.* Drenched, despondent, and terrified for our friends, we sat and watched the rushing torrent. Boulders, trees, logs and debris of all kind swept past as our patch of ground at the top grew smaller and smaller. We even saw several dead monkeys float by and I couldn't help but rejoice at their demise.

As the water rose, we inched closer together, finally standing in a tight knot at the very top of the hill. When the water lapped around our ankles and we had nowhere else to go, I took Tom's,

Robbie's, and Rigo's hands in mine and said, "I love you all, you know that. This has been an amazing, wonderful, horrible experience and I wouldn't have wanted to be with anyone else. It's because of who you are that we got this far, but there's nothing you can do to save us now. It's up to God whether we live or die. I just wanted you to know how I feel." I hugged the three of them, closed my eyes, and let out a deep sigh.

I realized it really was up to God and, in that moment, I gave all my concerns and worries over to Him. A calm peacefulness settled into my heart. I knew things would happen as they should. I didn't have to fight, I didn't have to cry; all I had to do was *be*.

"Lissy. Lissy, look!" Robbie squeezed my hand and I opened my eyes. The water had receded a bit, exposing the very top of the hill; we no longer stood ankle-deep. The rain had lessened to a drizzle and the thunder echoed from off in the distance. I could actually see the floodwater receding and my spirit rejoiced.

I raised my eyes to the heavens and said, "Thank you."

Now, we needed to find Joanne and BigBoy. "Let's go!"

I released their hands and started down the hill. Tom grabbed me. "Wait, Lissy. We can't go into the water. It's still running fast and is far too dangerous."

"Tom, we have to find Joanne and BigBoy. The water's receding. We can't wait." I hollered for Frank and Gigi. "Come on, Frank! Go find BigBoy and Joanne!" The apes took off, loping right at the upper edge of the receding water line, and I hurried along as fast as I could. With little choice, Tom, Robbie, and Rigo followed. I heard Tom mutter, "Damn stubborn woman," and I smiled, thinking, *If that's what it takes...*

We trudged along the side of the hill until the water receded enough for us to reclaim the lower trail. Actually, the trail was a mud slick – we slogged through the wet leaves, rocks, and debris at the side of the trail, skirting boulders and logs that had become wedged amongst the trees. It was rough going, but I was determined not to stop until we found Joanne and BigBoy.

Two hours later, I heard another roar. Not the train-like roar from before, but the bellow of an orangutan. It was Frank. We followed the sound and came upon an unlikely scene. My heart leapt into my throat and tears filled my eyes. Frank and Gigi sat at BigBoy's side. Joanne lay across the ape's lap, his arms supporting her carefully. She was bruised and battered, her face bloody; one eye was swollen shut and she seemed lifeless. Then I saw the slight rise and fall of her chest. She was alive!

BigBoy, too, was battered and bloody, but nothing seemed to be broken and he woo-wooed and gave me a huge monkey-grin. "Good, boy, BigBoy! You're such a wonderful guy. Thank you for saving my friend." I hugged him and scratched his head and he monkey-kissed my cheek.

Leaning down beside Joanne, I asked, "Jo. Jo, honey, are you okay?" I touched her face and one eyelid fluttered open. A lop-sided grin split her lip and blood oozed down her chin.

"I think I'll live, thanks to this big galoot. You should've named him SuperApe." She groaned as she shifted on BigBoy's lap. "I thought I was a goner until he showed up. Ow. Can you ask him to put me down? He's not as soft as he looks." Joanne wriggled again and he gently stood and set her on the ground. She stretched out flat on the soft, muddy earth and said, "Ah, that's better." She looked at the ape and said, "Thank you, BigBoy." She reached out her hand and the orangutan took it in his paw. Raising it to his mouth, he lipped her hand and made low clucking sounds. Then he lowered his eyes and sat at Jo's feet. From the look of him, it would take another flood move him away.

I asked the question foremost in my mind. "Is anything broken? Do you think you might have internal injuries? You're the nurse, Jo, what do we do?"

"I've done an inventory of all movable parts and everything's sore but intact. Aside from the bloody lip, the swollen eye, some bumps and scrapes, and I'm sure, some pretty nasty-looking bruises, I think I'm okay. It's a miracle, Lissy. I really thought I was going to die. I kept going under water and banging into rocks and trees. I figured I'd be impaled by a tree branch and that would be it – once the water receded you'd find my lifeless body hanging in a tree somewhere.

"Then this ape appears beside me, grabs me around the waist, and latches onto a tree branch. It's a wonder his arm wasn't yanked out of its socket. He pulled me up out of the current, climbed a bit higher, and held me in his arms until the water started to recede. Then he climbed down and wouldn't let me go until you got here. Frank found us and roared – I assume that's how you knew where we were.

"If BigBoy were a man, I'd marry him in a heartbeat. No man would do what he's done for me." Joanne blushed and said, "Seriously, Lissy, find me a man like him." We laughed and I knew she was going to be okay.

Tom, Robbie, and Rigo crowded around and congratulated Joanne on her miraculous swim.

"I'm glad you're okay, Jo. You scared us all really bad," Robbie kissed her cheek and squeezed her small hand in his.

"Pretty Cho, you are okay. I know BeegBoy weel save you." Rigo had his tenses mixed up but the sentiment was sincere.

"Okay, okay, thanks, everybody! I'm alright and I think we should try and find a place to spend the night. It's getting late." Joanne brought us back to our present predicament. "No matter where we go, it's going to be soggy and I can't hike any farther. I'm open to suggestions."

BigBoy suddenly raised his eyes to mine and huffed. I said, "What, BigBoy?" He loped to a big tree and pointed upwards.

I said, "I don't know what... Oh! He wants us to spend the night in the trees." I looked at Tom and said, "Can we do that?"

Thoughtfully, he said, "Maybe. With the apes' help in building a nest, we might be able to sleep okay. It's worth a try. I don't know how we'd find a safe place down here, out in the open. At least up there, the apes would be with us."

Joanne said, "Let's do it." Then, looking at BigBoy, she said, "Go ahead, show us what to do."

BigBoy recruited Frank and Gigi and the three of them found a stand of trees grouped closely together. They scampered up and proceeded to weave vines and palm fronds into the boughs, pulling small branches together, creating sleeping nests. Our biggest problem was going to be how to get up there. I didn't see any way we could climb the trees – especially Joanne.

But once again, BigBoy solved the problem. When the apes finished building the nests, they dropped back to the ground. BigBoy looked at me with a question in his eyes. "I think he wants to know if we're ready to go to bed." I laughed.

I said to the apes, "Why don't you guys go collect mangoes while we're getting ready for bed?" The orangutans scampered off while we took care of business and by the time they returned, we were ready.

BigBoy hauled me into a fireman's carry and clambered up the tree. Upside down, I clung to the ape's back and viewed the ground from a different perspective. He gently deposited me on an ape-bed and dropped to earth for another passenger.

One by one, we arrived in our treehouse beds, munched on mangoes, and settled for the night. The apes relaxed one tree over, keeping watch. I felt as safe as I had in our shelter at the lagoon and after the day's excitement, it didn't take long for soft jungle night sounds to lull me to sleep.

Chapter 16

Day 12

Lissy

My eyelids fluttered. Blue sky peeked through the canopy above and I felt the heat of the early morning sun dappling my face. I'd slept amazingly well here in the trees and decided the apes made very nice beds.

I heard the others stirring and a soft monkey-chuckle from the next tree over. Frank and Gigi snuggled together, soft giggles and clucks sounding like lovers' pillow talk. I looked away, feeling like a voyeur, and my eyes met Rigo's. His slow, sexy smile told me he'd noticed the affectionate scene, as well. My face colored slightly. "Good morning."

Rigo's throaty "Buenos días, pretty chica," sounded very much like a proposition. "You are beauteeful een the morning."

"Thanks, Rigo. We'd better get a move on. Seems we all slept well after yesterday's exertions." I wanted to deflect any early morning banter sprinkled with sensual innuendos. I looked over at Joanne. Her eyes were open – at least, the one eye that wasn't swollen shut was open. "How are you feeling, Jo?"

She slowly turned her head in my direction and said, "Like I played pinball with every rock and tree in the jungle. Ow. Even breathing hurts. But nothing's broken – I'm just really sore. And probably black and blue all over – sounds like a sick joke." She rolled onto her side and groaned.

BigBoy appeared below us, his arms filled with fruit. His eager woo-woo-woo was an unmistakable call to breakfast. I laughed. "Okay, BigBoy. But you do realize you're going to have to come get us, don't you?"

He chuckled and easily scaled the tree, landing beside me for a morning scratch and a hug. Then he scooped me up into the now-familiar fireman's carry and hauled me to the ground. When it was Joanne's turn, I saw him pause beside her as she scratched the side of his face and spoke softly to him. He lowered his big head and clucked quietly. Taking her time, she gradually got to her knees with many moans, groans, and the occasional curse. BigBoy gently picked her up and, with as little jolting as possible, carried her to the jungle floor. Placing her softly on her feet, he ran to distribute the fruit. He seemed to enjoy playing waiter.

Frank and Gigi took their time descending from the trees and I wondered how much longer she'd be with us. I knew orangutans usually only came together to mate and then went their separate ways. I'd gotten used to the shy female and enjoyed Frank's adolescent antics. I figured we'd all miss her.

Finally, after a fruit buffet, we were ready to hit the trail. Still soggy from the flood, the treacherously muddy path made for slow going. We picked our steps carefully and BigBoy trudged leisurely along, even in the drier, flatter stretches. Knowing we could spend the night in the trees took the pressure off trying to cover as much ground as possible.

We strolled, enjoying the scenery. I spotted numerous exotic orchids and small yellow flowers that had bloomed like a carpet between the trees, seemingly overnight. Purple posies poked their faces up from amongst the roots and rotting logs.

Snakes and spiders washed out of their holes by the floodwaters roamed the forest floor in search of new homes. We saw more of the critters than I would've liked and kept a sharp eye out for eight-legged creatures crossing our path. A mouse darted across the trail directly in front of me and I gave an involuntary cry, coming to an abrupt stop. Heads whipped in my direction and hands grabbed for spears. "Just a mouse. Not to worry." I gave a short bark of laughter and raised my right foot to continue.

Six inches from my bootie-clad left foot, a black, hairy spider the size of a Chihuahua dashed across the trail in pursuit of the mouse, disappearing into the foliage. Blood froze in my veins and icy sweat popped out on my forehead. My heart stopped and then resumed a furious pounding beat, driving adrenaline into every cell in my body. A scream pierced my ears and it took a minute before I realized the raw, carnal shriek had come from my own throat. Trembling, I stood rooted to the path as tears and sweat mingled to drip down my cheeks.

Rigo leapt to my side. When he touched my arm, I yelped and jerked away, my eyes wide with terror. "Qué es, Leesa? Qué pasó? You are alright?"

Slowly, I turned to face him. Pale, trembling, I opened my mouth but my knees buckled and I started to fall. Rigo caught me and between him and Tom, they helped me to a nearby rock. Before sitting, I frantically scanned the area around the boulder for any sign of a huge arachnid, holding tight to Rigo's arm.

"Lissy? Lissy. Look at me." Tom's voice penetrated the layer of panicky, adrenaline-induced fog clouding my brain. "What

225

happened?" He took my hand in a firm grip and his eyes held mine. "Tell me. What did you see?"

I swallowed and blinked before answering. "A gi... gigantic spider. It chased the mouse."

"The spider chased the mouse?"

I nodded. "Just as I raised my f-foot to take a step, the spider ran ac-across the path after the m-mouse. It was as big as a small d-dog!"

"That's pretty big for a spider, Lissy. Are you sure you're not exaggerating because of your fear?" Tom had obviously not seen the monster.

"I am *not* exaggerating, Tom! It was only about six inches from my foot – I got a real good look at it!" I shivered again at the vivid memory of the huge arachnid so close to my foot.

Rigo came to my defense. "Eef Leesa say eet was beeg, eet was beeg!" He glared at Tom.

I took several deep breaths and forced myself up. "Alright! I'm done with spiders! We've had small ones, large ones, and huge ones and I'm sick to death of dealing with them. Let's go."

"You are alright, Leesa? You weel not fall?" His reference to my earlier near-fainting episode brought a flush to my cheeks. *Somehow I had to get this fear of spiders under control.*

"I'm fine, Rigo, really. I just want to forget about the beast and move on." I reached up to run my fingers through my hair and realized I'd lost my hat, but the very last thing I wanted to do was reach into the foliage searching for it.

Just then, Joanne hobbled up and said, "Here's your hat, Lissy. You don't want to leave it behind."

I smiled ruefully at my friend and took the hat. "Thanks, Jo. At least I didn't run you over this time." We grinned at each other, remembering the day in camp when I'd nearly knocked her flat getting away from a spider much smaller than this one.

Wanting to talk about something else, I said, "How are you holding up?"

"I hurt. But it'll fade – moving helps, actually. I'd be really stiff if I was just sitting around."

"Are you okay, Lissy? Ready to move on?" Tom patted my back as I nodded. "Okay, let's go."

We queued up and resumed the hike. I kept a sharp eye out for more spiders but soon relaxed when no more furry bodies dashed across the trail.

Joanne was a trouper and, in spite of her pain, kept up with the group for several more hours before requesting a break. We perched on rocks and logs, watching Frank and Gigi cavort amongst the trees like flirtatious teens. Yes, he would miss her. I just hoped he would remain with us and not try to follow her. I felt much safer with more than one orangutan in our group and didn't want to rely solely on BigBoy again to keep us safe. It was a huge responsibility and was far too dangerous for him.

As we resumed our trek, I wondered about the ugly monkeys. They seemed to spend more time on our side of the mountain, perhaps because numerous orangutan groups lived on this side. Or perhaps because we lived there – with their animal food sources nearly depleted, we'd soon be their sole focus. *Would we have a confrontation attempting to pass the feeding cave?* I certainly didn't want to lose another ape on the trip home – or have one of us end up being dinner. What a horrific thought.

The trail began an upward slant and I knew the hike would soon become more difficult. We also wanted to spend the night in the thick, jungle trees before hitting the tree line – farther up the mountain they became smaller and sparser. If we could sleep in the trees on this side and make it to the tree line on the other side before dark tomorrow, we wouldn't have to risk spending the night in a cave. I didn't think I could handle that, especially after my latest encounter. It would also eliminate sleeping anywhere near the feeding cave. That would be a tremendous relief to us all.

By late afternoon, we were well above the flood line and the trail had dried out considerably – no more mucky mud or slippery slopes, just hard-packed earth that had dried out in the heat of the day. Thankfully, the wetskins had dried quickly so we didn't have to slog about in wet clothing, but I'd give a year's pay for something clean to wear. We'd become a tattered and unkempt group.

"What do you say we start looking for a place to spend the night? Now that we know we can sleep in the trees, we don't have to hunt for a cave – I'm done with that for as long as I live!" I hollered back to Tom.

He yelled back, "That's the plan. BigBoy, let's find some trees to sleep in, okay?" Tom grinned as the ape woo-wooed and started scouting the area, Frank and Gigi following close behind.

Before long, we heard his familiar call and located him a short distance away in a thick stand of trees. It looked good to me.

The apes collected fruit for dinner. Surprisingly, I found myself looking forward to getting back to the lagoon and having seafood again. We relaxed and hungrily devoured the fruit while Gigi searched for a nearby stream. Her triumphant woof meant we'd have plentiful fresh water. Her presence in our small group had become quite an asset.

I was anxious to get home, but worried about the feeding cave. It seemed we were all on edge, keeping our thoughts and feelings to ourselves, spending the evening in quiet reflection.

Losing Rusty and Morley both on this expedition was a huge blow and I still reeled from the losses. I realized the pain showed when Rigo said, "You are sad, Leesa. You mees Morley, no?"

In a sudden rush of anger and despair, I replied, "Yes, I miss Morley. And Rusty. And Sarah. And who knows what happened to the rest of our group? Instead of a fun, carefree vacation, this has become a dreadful nightmare. When will we wake up? I'm ready for it to be over so I can go back home to a normal life and put it all behind me."

Rigo's face fell and I suddenly understood how it must've sounded to him. My voice soft and full of remorse, I said, "I'm sorry, Rigo. I'm glad I met *you* – that's the one good thing that's happened. I just wish we could've enjoyed getting to know each other and spent time diving, eating tacos and chimichangas, and drinking margaritas. It would've been fun, huh?" I smiled sadly at this gorgeous hunk of a man who clearly cared for me. But there was so much sorrow and stress associated with our relationship that I didn't think I could let it go any further. I cared for him, yes, but that caring was so intertwined with danger, death, mourning, and regret that I couldn't look at him and feel the normal exciting emotions associated with falling in love. Our budding relationship was doomed that day the current swept us away.

I put my hand on his and, with tears overflowing, said, "You're a good man, Rigo. One day you'll find your perfect chica, but I can't be that girl for you. My heart's too full of sadness – there's no room for love and happiness right now. I'm sorry." I saw pain fill his eyes and added that to my long list of regrets.

His face hardened, his eyes became dark, burning coals, and he growled, "You want Señor Tom, no? You want heem to hold you when you cry on hees shoulder. I can love you better, but you no see eet." He pushed to his feet and stalked off into the trees.

The tears came in torrents, violent sobs wracking my body. I wept for hurting Rigo; for the death of my friends; for Morley; for brave, foolish Rusty; and for being stranded on this God-forsaken island in the middle of nowhere. Joanne came and wrapped her arms around me. In spite of her physical pain, she knew I was suffering. My spirit was bruised and bloody, my heart breaking, and caregiver Jo was there for me, as always.

Holding onto her I sobbed, "I want to go home, Jo. I don't want anyone else to die." I cried on her shoulder and choked out my pain and frustration. "Poor Sarah and the rest of our group – they could all be dead. Those ugly monkeys killed Rusty because he was protecting us. And poor Morley... Morley shouldn't have lived his whole life alone and died when he could've been part of our family. I never knew my father, Jo, and Morley felt like the dad I should've had. It's not fair that he was taken away so soon! And Rigo wants me to fall in love with him – but I can't. I'm too sad and scared and full of regret. I just want to go home."

Joanne sat with me until I was all cried out. We sat together under a big tree, the bark digging into our backs, until BigBoy came and sat in front of us with bananas in his hands. He clucked and whined, obviously distressed at my emotional outburst. I scratched his cheek and said, "It's okay, big fella. I'm alright."

He woo-wooed and we smiled. For BigBoy, all was once again right with the world. I wished it was really that easy.

I appreciated the others giving Joanne and me some space to handle our emotions and when I'd dried my eyes and felt ready to face the world again, we rejoined the group. Rigo was conspicuously absent and once more, I felt guilty for hurting him. I just hoped he wouldn't run into the ugly monkeys. He was alone and vulnerable without a bodyguard.

Tom came over and asked, "Is everything okay with Rigo? He gave me an angry glare when he stalked out of here while ago. Any idea what his problem is or where he went?"

I sighed deeply and said, "Nope. He doesn't understand that it's hard to fall in love when all those happy feelings are mixed up with sadness, regret, fear, and death. So, as a result, he still thinks you and I have a 'thing' and he's jealous." Shrugging, I added, "I just hope he doesn't run into the ugly monkeys – he didn't take an orangutan with him."

"Well, if he doesn't come back soon, maybe we should send BigBoy or Frank out to look for him. You'd think he'd have learned his lesson about going off alone after his last episode." As he walked away, he muttered, "Hot-headed Latino."

We dined on fruit and relaxed in the shade amidst the trees, conserving our energy for tomorrow's climb up and over the summit. The apes ascended into the trees and built our night-time nests. When they dropped back to the ground I told BigBoy, "Go find Rigo, BigBoy. Bring him back so we can go to bed. Go on!"

The ape scampered off and I hoped he'd find Rigo safe and sound. He could brood all he wanted, but I needed to know he was safe. We sat for a while until twilight chased the sun away. BigBoy and Rigo had yet to return and Joanne and I felt uneasy on the ground, wishing we could climb up into our nests.

Still seemingly irritated by Rigo's disappearance, Tom said, "Robbie and I are going to take a walk around this area and see if we can find Rigo. Maybe he didn't go very far and just doesn't want to sit here with us." He pointed and said, "I'll go this direction and Robbie can circle around that way."

I didn't want *them* wandering around without an ape, either. "You guys take Frank – we'll be okay here for a few minutes –

you're just going to circle this big stand of trees and will be able to see if anything approaches. And you'd easily hear us scream."

"Are you sure? I hate to leave you girls without protection."

"We'll be fine, Tom. We're not helpless, either." I grinned at him and raised my spear.

He smiled back and said, "No, you're not helpless, Lissy. In fact, you're one of the most capable women I've ever met. And we won't be gone long. Come on, Robbie, Frank."

I watched the three of them separate – Frank went with Robbie in one direction while Tom headed the opposite way. Joanne and I sat on our rock and talked for a few more minutes until Joanne said, "I'm going to the loo – be back in a few."

"Do you want me to come with you?" I hated the thought of everyone going off alone.

"Not necessary. Unless you have to pee."

"No. I'll wait here." I sighed and said, "We need more apes." I leaned back against a sun-warmed rock and closed my eyes, enjoying the solitude. Under normal circumstances, I loved having time to myself – I couldn't remember the last occasion I'd spent five minutes alone since washing up on the beach.

Drowsing in the silence, I barely heard Joanne's fearful call. "Lissy. Lissy, help me! Bring spears."

Something in the purposely controlled tone of her voice told me she was terrified. *Monkeys?* Surely she would've screamed. *But what, then?* I leapt to my feet, grabbed two spears and my dive knife and darted into the foliage. The hair on the back of my neck rose like hackles on a dog.

"Jo? Jo, talk to me." I needed to home in on her voice to head the right direction.

"Here. Please hurry."

I could sense her terror and barely-suppressed tears and had no idea what I was walking into.

The trees thinned and I walked into a small clearing, but saw nothing out of the ordinary. Thick foliage flanked the trees to my right, flowers bloomed profusely under the saplings to my left. I spotted a burrow at the base of a tree but no sign of Joanne.

Keeping my voice low, as she had, I called, "Jo?"

"Here, Lissy. Behind the big tree." Her strained voice came from the foliage cloaking the rear of the huge tree to my right, the one with the burrow in front of it.

Slowly, I approached. Reaching out with my left hand to part the vegetation, I raised the spear in my right. Blood froze in my veins when I saw Joanne trapped in a thick spider web. She had stepped into the foliage for privacy and crouched to pull her wetskin down. When she brushed against the web, her body was caught in the sticky strands and her hands became entangled when she tried to tear the web loose. Now hopelessly ensnared, she could only move one foot.

Rooted to the spot, my heart raced and icy sweat oozed down my temples. A wave of nausea swept over me and I swallowed hard as I noticed the mice and small birds that had become trapped in the web. Their carcasses were a visual reminder of Joanne's grisly fate if I couldn't free her.

"Lissy!" At the sharp urgency in her voice, I raised my eyes to hers and she darted a wide-eyed glance behind me. I spun to the right and saw a hairy, Chihuahua-sized spider exiting the brush. It stopped about four feet away and leaned slightly onto its back legs; its front ones pawed the air in a definite challenge over the prey caught in the web. Its mandibles gnashed and dripped a clear liquid onto the dirt. *Poison?*

Every cell in my body screamed, "Run!" My mind fought the physical urge to flee – I couldn't leave Joanne. Trapped between fight and flight, I stood frozen in place until Joanne tearfully whispered, "Lissy, do something. Please."

I had to face my greatest fear to save my friend. Turning completely toward the spider, I filled my lungs to capacity, then exhaled forcefully, loosening the terror that had taken tight hold. I shook my shoulders, stretched my back, and focused on the beast before me. Bracing myself and swallowing hard, I raised the spear and stepped forward.

The spider didn't retreat. Instead, it lowered its front legs back to the ground and crab-walked sideways about a foot. Then it tensed for the attack. Moving much faster than I expected, it darted toward me. Surprised, I retreated and the beast halted.

"Don't back up any more, Lissy, or you'll get caught in the web, too." I heard Joanne's voice directly behind me and realized what the spider was trying to do – it was herding me into its web. If we were both ensnared, our only hope would be to scream for Tom and Robbie and hope they found us in time. Determined, I vowed to vanquish this nightmare, once and for all.

Slowly, I moved forward; the spider held its ground. Evidently, it wasn't used to prey fighting back. Using that to my advantage, I crept ahead again, raising the spear into a striking position. The creepy thing once more reared up to challenge me, exposing its vulnerable belly. I threw the spear at its underside, praying for accuracy at such a short distance. The spear impaled the beast, the tip protruding from the beast's back. An unearthly, high-pitched scream rent the air as the animal flailed, bled, and died a mere three feet away.

I let out a deep sigh and leaned over to rest my hands on shaky knees, relief sapping my strength. But as I rose up and turned toward Joanne, she shrieked. I whirled and found myself face to face with two new adversaries. Adrenaline again flooded my system and I confronted the spiders with less terror and more confidence and determination. *I killed the first one. I can do it again.*

They exhibited the same type of behavior as the other, rising up and pawing the air, gnashing their fangs, and dripping poison from their formidable fangs. Trying to force me to back into the web, they advanced in tandem, but I refused to give ground. When they paused, I pressed ahead and they slowly retreated.

Wanting one to dart forward alone, I stopped and quickly backed up a few steps. As I'd hoped, the larger of the two dashed ahead, evidently thinking it had me on the run. I stopped and it reared up. I threw the spear and once again found my mark.

Now armed only with my knife, I needed to close the distance between me and my attacker. Determined, I strode toward the last remaining spider, hoping no reinforcements would appear before I could kill it and free Joanne. This last foe didn't have its brethren's self-confidence. After watching its companion die, it fled. I kept an eye out to be sure it wouldn't circle back and saw it dart into the burrow. *Now I know what lives in those holes.*

Feeling like I'd slain the dragon, I yanked both spears from the arachnid carcasses – no need to leave them behind. Using my knife, I carefully hacked at the web and pulled it away from Joanne's body. Tearfully, she threw her arms around me and nearly squeezed the air from my lungs. "Thank you, Lissy! I know how hard that must've been for you. You're the bravest person I've ever known."

Hugging her back, I said, "The little spiders won't bother me anymore, Jo, but I wouldn't recommend this as 'arachno-therapy'!" We grinned at each other and I said, "Come on. Let's go."

Holding back, Joanne said, "I never did pee, Lissy. Can we stop here for a minute? I promise I won't go into the bushes."

Figuring I might as well take care of business, too, but staying alert, we paused behind a tree and then dashed back. We arrived just as Tom, Robbie, and Frank did. Tom asked, "Where'd you two go? You were supposed to stay here at the tree stand."

Sheepishly, Joanne said, "I had to pee. I didn't go very far."

When Tom scowled at Joanne, I said, "We found out what lives in those burrows – hairy, Chihuahua-sized spiders like the one that chased that mouse across the trail. I think they're poisonous." Finally feeling the effect of all that adrenaline, I sank down onto a rock, trembling.

Joanne continued the story. "Like I said, I had to pee, so I went into some brush for privacy. When I bent over to... you know... I backed into something soft and sticky. I reached behind to brush it away and next thing you know I'm stuck in this humongous spider web. All I could move was my left foot."

Tom and Robbie sat down next to me on the rock, but Joanne was still agitated and paced back and forth as she talked. "I didn't want to scream or thrash around, not knowing where the spider was, so I called for Lissy and told her to bring spears."

At that, the guys glanced at the spears I'd tossed to the ground and noticed the blood. Their expressions hardened.

"You should've seen her, Tom. She was Athena, she was Zena, she was Super Woman! And you know how afraid of spiders she is. She's the bravest person I've ever known. She killed two of the monsters and the third one ran away." Joanne stopped pacing and stood in front of us, hands on hips, a huge smile on her face. "She was amazing!"

Turning to me, Tom asked, "Why do you think they're poisonous?"

"They didn't seem to be afraid of me even though I'm a lot bigger. They reared up on their hind legs and pawed the air, gnashed their teeth, and dripped a clear liquid from their mandibles. I assumed it was poison. It would be a visual warning to anything considering an attack." I shuddered, remembering the encounter. As unpleasant as it was, though, the memory didn't elicit the terror that it would have in the past. I'd faced my fear and conquered it. It felt good!

"We'll have to keep an eye out for areas that have a lot of those burrows. And not go crawling into vegetation – for *any* reason. Right, Jo?" I got up and gave her a hug.

"I'll give up a little privacy for safety reasons. Being trapped in that web was awful. I felt so helpless. Thank you, Lissy." Another hug and we were ready for bed.

I called to Frank and said, "Can you carry us up into the trees?" I pointed to the nests in the canopy. Frank chuckled and nodded, imitating my finger-pointing. He stepped closer, hoisted me over his shoulder, and off we went. He seemed as agile and capable as BigBoy and I felt totally safe in his arms.

Joanne was next, then Robbie. Agitated and concerned, Tom wanted to linger on the ground until BigBoy and Rigo returned but I convinced him to wait from the safety of the trees. Rigo wouldn't be happy to see Tom, anyway, and I dreaded another clash before retiring for the night.

A short while later the two strode into sight with no obvious wounds. I heaved a sigh of relief as the ape hauled Rigo up into the trees to the sound of Spanish curses and muttered threats. He was still unhappy, that much was clear, but perhaps a good night's sleep would ease his mind.

With everyone safe and present, we settled into our nests and snores soon filled the night air.

Chapter 17

Day 13

<u>Lissy</u>

The sun warmed the canopy at dawn and I stretched and opened my eyes. Crawling to the nest's edge, I awaited my turn for BigBoy to carry me to the jungle floor. The apes collected fruit for breakfast and then we lined up to begin a long day's hike over the summit.

Armed with knives and spears and alert to any odd noises, we soon approached the tree line where the vegetation thinned. Uncharacteristically, Gigi hung back and woo-wooed to Frank. I saw him look at her and then at us, torn. I refused to give him permission to go with her, afraid she might be returning to her ape family and not wanting to lose Frank at this crucial moment. If we encountered ugly monkeys at the feeding cave, we'd need him.

The temptress returned to Frank's side, softly clucking and stroking his back, and once again ran into the trees. She stopped to see if Frank followed, but when he stayed in line, she woofed once and dashed away. The courtship was over and Frank would never know his offspring. I yelled back, "Keep an eye out, Tom. We can't lose him now."

We'd only been trekking for an hour when BigBoy stopped and barked, turning to look at Tom at the rear of the queue. I'd been watching a particularly pebbly area of the trail so as not to turn an ankle and hadn't noticed the large congregation of apes up ahead. Astonished, I counted almost fifty orangutans in various shades of orange, red, brown, and rust before Tom said, "Lissy, come up here with me. You understand the apes better and can communicate with BigBoy. We need to find out what's going on."

I followed Tom to BigBoy's side and realized there were even more apes lining the trail farther ahead – there must've been almost a hundred of them. I shivered. Was this a friendly meeting? I certainly hoped so.

BigBoy was deep in ape-conversation with a dark brownish-red orangutan that seemed to be the leader of the group. Tom and I waited patiently. Finally, BigBoy turned to me and pointed up the mountain, baring his teeth in a snarl. Using his hands he indicated a short height and I deduced he was talking about the ugly monkeys. But I wanted more information. "Are the monkeys going to attack us again today?"

BigBoy nodded and held up all ten fingers. "There are ten of them?" The ape shook his head no and repeatedly held up ten fingers at a time. Tom and I looked at each other, fear etched on our faces. It was perfectly clear that many, many monkeys were waiting to attack and without help, we'd never survive.

The leader of the apes, Choco I decided to call him, huffed and I turned my attention to him. He seemed to have understood the communication between BigBoy and me and was aware of my concern. Waving his arm expansively, he indicated the large group of orangutans and pointed up the mountain. He, too, bared his teeth in a vicious snarl and all of the other apes growled in unison, facing the summit.

I said, "Tom, I think they're going to come with us to fight the ugly monkeys. Let me see if I can clarify it through BigBoy." Turning back, I said, "This is really important, big fella. Are they all coming with us to fight the monkeys?"

Before answering he woofed at Choco and pointed at the group. Choco bobbed his head. BigBoy looked me in the eye and nodded, using his arm to indicate the entire ape troupe. Amazed, I whispered to Tom, "This is going to be one helluva fight."

Tom explained the plan, if you could call it that, to Robbie, Rigo, and Joanne and I could see the dread on Jo's face. She whispered, "Lissy, if the orangutans think we need that many of *them*, how many little monkeys are there?"

"I don't know, but we have a legion of apes on our side and we've seen how powerful they are. We're armed and able-bodied, too, so I think we have a really good chance of getting through this." I wanted to sound positive to keep her spirits up. In reality, I had no idea how we'd fare against an entire army of the nasty, vicious things. But I had no doubt we were going to find out.

When we resumed the hike, half of the orangutans ranged ahead and half fell in behind our little group. I felt somewhat comforted, knowing the beasts couldn't sneak up on us. However, that comfort was short-lived when I realized they could attack us on the narrow mountainside trail, coming down the slope from above. With the steep drop-off on one side and the solid wall of rock on the other, there wouldn't be anywhere to go and our whole troupe would be strung out along the path.

As the trees began to thin and the incline grew steeper, we stopped for a rest and lunch. It wouldn't do to be faint from hunger and overly tired at a crucial moment. A throng of apes stayed with us while others roamed and collected fruit. Soon, mountains of bananas, papayas, and mangos appeared alongside the trail. We joined the groups of orangutans at the buffet.

A few apes had scouted ahead and returned with news. If I understood BigBoy and Choco correctly, we would begin encountering small pods of monkeys scattered along the path in another hour or so. I suspected the feeding cave would be the location of the main battle – it was the ideal spot for a large contingent of monkeys to gather out of sight. They could then attack from the front or exit the cave at the back somewhere and fall upon us from the rear.

Refreshed but anxious, we followed the lead group of apes back onto the trail, flanked by the rest of the orangutans. Before long, I heard snarls and roars up ahead and knew the leaders had met the first of the little beasts. The queue barely even slowed. Eventually, I spotted small, dark bodies tossed over the edge – the apes had made short work of them. At this point, neither side had the element of surprise for the main battle – we were coming en masse and they knew it.

The orangutans quashed several pods of the monkeys and finally it seemed they decided the small groups were too ineffective to be worthwhile. We trudged along, unchallenged, and ultimately neared the summit. The feeding cave was a short distance over the pinnacle. We'd have to cross the out-cropping, too, but I hoped with all the extra apes, it wouldn't be an issue.

We stopped for a short break and then continued past the vista where we'd spotted Morley's SOS. My heart ached and I allowed myself a few moments to think of the old man as I glanced out at the view. Then I focused on the trail. Up and over the summit we filed, beginning the descent.

At the out-cropping, the apes barely paused. When it was BigBoy's turn, he faced Robbie and held out his arms. Taking a deep breath, Robbie stepped close to the ape and screwed his eyes shut as he was hauled into the fireman's carry. He grasped big handfuls of the animal's hair and clung for dear life, his spear jutting out at an odd angle as BigBoy clambered over the rock.

Frank pushed his way forward and tossed me over his shoulder before I realized he was there. With a shriek, I buried both hands in his hair and almost dropped my spear. I rearranged my hold on hair and weapon and held my breath, but in no time at all, he set me gently on my feet on the far side of the rock.

BigBoy climbed back up for Rigo while Frank was setting me down; once I had my footing, he turned and went back for Joanne. As expected, she shrank away and whimpered in terror, slapping at Frank's paws so he couldn't pick her up. He finally stopped and sat at her feet, head hung low, eyes downcast. He'd learned he couldn't bully Joanne, he had to coax her. When he quit reaching for her, she stopped resisting and eventually sat down in front of him. She spoke to him and he raised his eyes to hers. He clucked, she talked, he crooned, and she acquiesced. Simultaneously, they stood and Frank carefully took Joanne in his arms like they were going to waltz over the rock. She squealed when he hefted her over his shoulder but other than that, made no further sound. Her knees almost buckled when her feet hit the ground, but Frank supported her until she was steady. It was quite endearing.

The rest of the apes scrambled over the rock as the queue continued down the trail. The feeding cave wasn't far, now, and I knew the battle was imminent. I could feel the electricity in the air, could smell the nasty little beasts. Their stench was bad enough, one on one, but a large group of them together created a fetid miasma that made my eyes water.

The battle began with a distant snarl, a roar, and a single large boulder bouncing down the mountainside. A dust cloud rose into the air as large and small simians clashed. I couldn't see the fighting around the bend, but I could hear the screeches and roars, screams and snarls, the thud of bodies hitting rock. A small crevasse in the side of the mountain was just large enough for Jo and me to squeeze into; Rigo, Robbie, and Tom crowded against us with a row of apes in front of them. Frank and BigBoy had positioned several large, powerful orangutans to guard us and had moved out along the trail, side by side with the other animals. We were as protected as we could get in the crevasse and, although not very comfortable, I was grateful for the scant security it provided. And frankly, I didn't want a ringside seat to the bloody battle, anyway. Thankful for the orangutans' help, I hated to think of them suffering and dying on our behalf.

The main skirmish kept most of the lead orangutans busy, but suddenly, a wave of small monkeys washed down over our heads. They'd clambered down the rock face and attacked the apes positioned in front of Rigo, Robbie, and Tom – way too close for comfort. Far from an ideal battlefield, the trail was too narrow for a fight. A few of the apes were knocked off balance and plunged to their deaths, briefly leaving an unprotected gap in front of us. Immediately, though, the apes to the rear moved up to fill the void. Most of the monkeys were shoved over the edge without ever touching the trail and I could clearly hear their bodies thudding against the rock, a sound I feared I would hear in my nightmares – if we survived to live one more day.

Another solid wave of monkeys pounced from above, focused on the five orangutans directly in front of us. We watched in horror as they fell away over the edge, leaving us

244

completely exposed and vulnerable. The monkeys had learned that the apes to the rear would move up to fill the gap so this time they'd simultaneously attacked farther down the line, as well. As the apes fell, another wave of monkeys landed on the open trail directly in front of us, gaining a foothold for the first time. Joanne screamed as the beasts bared their fangs a scant two feet away. In such tight quarters, spears were out of the question, but I saw Tom shift his grip on his dive knife in preparation for the inevitable attack.

One monkey lunged at Tom and another charged Robbie. Joanne and I both screamed as Tom's knife slit the one animal's throat, spraying us all with a hot, red shower, and Robbie's short spear penetrated the other's chest. Somehow keeping its footing, it stared into Robbie's eyes, bared its teeth in a final defiant gesture, and grabbed the spear-shaft with both hands. Blood stained its dark fur and pooled at its feet.

Then, in a freakish chain of events, a lone monkey pounced from above and landed directly on the spear that was still firmly embedded in its brethren's chest. The new beast snarled nearly in Robbie's face and he leaned backwards, already off balance from the impact. The trio teetered on the narrow ledge, but Robbie maintained his vice-like grip on the spear shaft, obviously high on adrenaline and fear and not thinking clearly. The impaled animal's legs suddenly collapsed, changing the trio's precarious balance and sending all three of them pinwheeling over the edge. They seemed to hover in space before disappearing from sight.

Robbie's eyes met mine in that second before he fell from view and I could see the look of utter shock on his face. "Noooo!" Joanne screamed and clutched my arm, her nails leaving bloody divots in my flesh.

Rigo stepped up beside Tom, his knife in one hand and his short spear in the other, as the next two monkeys filled the void left by their dead cohorts. No sooner had they bared their glistening fangs, than the rearward orangutans advanced, led by BigBoy. Long, powerful arms grabbed, punched, and pushed the smaller beasts, driving them up the trail or over the edge. Once more a wall of orange hair closed in front of us and I was extremely thankful to see BigBoy, alive and well.

The nasty monkeys weren't the only ones that learned from experience. The orangutans protecting us now stood with their backs to the rock wall, facing outward, arms upraised. As the next wave of monkeys descended upon them, they simply used the animals' own momentum to push them over the edge. No more apes were lost and wave after wave of monkeys plunged to their deaths. Finally, they quit coming and the battle raged solely at the front of the queue. It seemed to go on forever.

All of a sudden I felt the ground shake subtly under my feet and thought the ledge was about to slide down the mountain. I grabbed Tom and Rigo and said, "What's that? An earthquake?" Jo, Rigo, Tom, and I clutched each other's hands and closed our eyes as a putrid powder billowed from the bowels of the mountain, thick, dry, and smelling of decomposition. It was the smell from the cave, intensified. I gagged and tried to cover my nose and mouth against Rigo's back. Jo, farther inside the crevasse, coughed and choked on the heavy dust.

A thunderous rumble belched from deep inside the mountain and the fighting stopped. An unearthly silence settled over the battlefield, as loud in its way as the sound of war. The apes stood motionless, paralyzed with fear. For many moments, the only noise emanated from the mountain itself, the only movement the tremors underfoot.

Then, as the rumbling ceased, so did the vibrations. The dust slowly settled and the apes came back to life, prepared to continue the battle. A few snarls, screeches, and roars floated back to us on the dusty air but gradually tapered off to utter stillness. We waited.

Finally, a barely audible whisper began at the front of the battlefield. It grew in intensity as each ape passed information on to the ape behind. I thought briefly about the childhood game we used to play and wondered if the info we received would be anything like the original message. When BigBoy received the news, he turned to Tom and curled his lips in a huge smile. Indicating the height of the small monkeys, he shook his big head in a vehement no and raised his arms in the air, shaking his narrow hips. He looked silly, performing his Super Bowl boogie there on the narrow ledge. However, the victorious performance spread and soon all of the apes up and down the trail danced and giggle-screeched. The ugly monkeys had been defeated.

The rumbling had not been an earthquake – the ceiling of the feeding cave had collapsed, burying the bulk of the monkeys' army under tons of rock and rubble. Only a few of the beasts were seen fleeing the battlefield.

Frank dashed up beside BigBoy and joined him in his victory dance, adding his own special twist. As always, he did it his way. I smiled, watching them, although my heart was heavy and tears threatened. Robbie had been a good man, a good friend, and we'd miss him terribly. I could still see the shocked realization in his eyes as he disappeared over the edge.

I heard Joanne's voice, choking, from inside the crevasse. "Is it over? Is it safe to come out?"

"Yes, Jo, come on out. Here, take my hand." I reached inside and helped her out into the less-dusty air of the trail.

After a brief coughing spell, she noticed the gyrating apes and said, "What are they doing? Are they okay?"

I laughed and said, "It's the ape version of a victory dance. BigBoy started it and it caught on. I think they like it."

"They probably like knowing they won't have to deal with the ugly monkeys anymore," Tom added and I had to agree.

"You're right, Tom! That *is* worth celebrating!" I performed a happy jig, too, and Joanne, Tom, and Rigo joined me, arms waving, hands clapping, and feet shuffling carefully on the narrow ledge. It was quite a triumphant moment.

When the hullaballoo quieted down, Choco made his way toward the crevasse to speak with BigBoy. After a few moments, both apes turned to Tom and me. BigBoy waved his arm to indicate all of the apes and then pointed toward the other side of the mountain. They were going home.

I spoke to BigBoy. "Tell Choco thank you from all of us. We would never have survived without them." BigBoy woo-wooed and clucked and Choco gave me a big ape-grin. I reached out and stroked his arm and said, "Thank you. Thank you to *all* of your orangutans!" Choco imitated my movement and stroked my arm, bobbing his head.

Then he started back toward the summit, the other apes falling into line behind him. We watched them go, knowing they had lost many of their members and feeling their pain. None of us had escaped the day unscathed.

Joanne examined everyone to be sure no one had been injured in the fray. Miraculously, none of us had sustained so much as a scratch.

We didn't want to linger on the narrow ledge, so queued up and resumed our journey down the mountain. When we reached the tree line, we stopped in the shade to rest, grieve, and cool down from the heat of the exposed upper trail. Missing Robbie, we remained silent, each mourning in his own way.

Frank sat down a short distance from the group and continued to stare up the path, no doubt hoping Gigi would return. I went and sat next to him. "It's hard to lose someone you care about, isn't it, big fella? I hate to tell you, but I don't think she's coming back. She returned to her family to have her baby, *your* baby." He gazed into my face and I could see the sadness in his eyes. "Thank you for staying with us, Frank. We needed you back there. You're an important part of *our* family. You know that, don't you?"

He nodded, curled up on the ground next to me, and laid his big hairy head in my lap. I scratched his ears and stroked his back; his fingers rubbed small circles on my knee. Although outwardly different, our hearts suffered much the same over losing our friends. My tears dripped onto Frank's chocolate-y red fur and we mourned.

After a while, Tom said, "I hate to disturb everyone, but we really should get moving." We grumbled but got to our feet. He was right. Although the monkeys had been defeated, we'd sleep much better, safe and secure, in our shelter tonight.

Tom set a swift pace and I was glad to reach one of the streams Gigi had shown us. Stopping there was bittersweet. The last time, we had watched the couple cavort flirtatiously in and around the water – now, Frank was glum and listless. To divert his attention, I sent him and BigBoy off to find fruit. We needed energy for the rest of the trek home.

Relaxed and fortified, we once again hit the trail. Arriving at our shelter just before nightfall, we were relieved to find everything as we'd left it. I'd been concerned that the ugly monkeys would trash our site and destroy the shelter, but evidently they'd had other things on their minds. A chilling thought struck me – if the food source wasn't at the campsite, the shelter might have been of no use to them. And on a brighter note, perhaps we'd have no further trouble with them now.

Tom and Rigo untied the vines holding the door shut and Joanne and I collected fresh palm fronds. Nothing like "changing the sheets" after a few days away from home. I hated the idea of insects settling into the fronds in our absence.

It was too late for a fishing expedition so we ate fruit for dinner, finishing off the last of the bananas we'd brought from the other side of the mountain. Tomorrow we'd have fish for lunch. Amazed, I found myself looking forward to it.

We retired early, exhausted from the eventful day. As my eyes closed, I hoped tomorrow would be dull and boring.

Chapter 18

Day 14

<u>Lissy</u>

When the sun warmed my face, I opened my eyes. Everyone else was still asleep and I lay there, my thoughts whirling. We'd been on this island for a full two weeks and had no idea if anyone was looking for us or if they presumed we were dead. We'd battled ugly monkeys, giant snakes, spiders large and small, and I was more than ready to go home. But how?

Morley had explored this island his entire life and assured us there were no other human inhabitants. We had no way to communicate with the rest of the world. And we were outside the regular shipping and flight patterns. I doubted anyone would stumble upon us – and if they did, they'd most likely be as stranded as we were. Tears filled my eyes.

A soft voice intruded on my thoughts. "Why you cry, Leesa?" I hadn't realized Rigo was awake.

Wiping the dampness from my face, I forced a smile and said, "I just want to go home, Rigo. We've been here for two weeks and we're no closer to being rescued than we were the day we washed up on shore. What are we going to do?" I sniffed as tears threatened once again.

"They come for us, I know thees," he slid closer and put his arms around me. Today I couldn't fight it and welcomed his consoling hug.

"How do you know they're looking for us, Rigo? None of us told anyone where we were going. We're a long distance from where Captain Carlos took us to dive and he probably didn't say anything for fear of losing business. Why are you so certain?" I admired Rigo's faith that someone would come for us, but couldn't understand how or why he was so sure.

"Een here, I know eet." He patted his chest over his heart. "They come, Leesa. You no cry." He pulled me close and held me tight. His certainty calmed my fears and I thought of the more positive aspects of our situation. No one was injured or sick; we had plenty of food and fresh water; the ugly monkeys had been decimated; our relatively comfortable shelter kept us out of the hot sun and the rain; tropical day and nighttime temperatures weren't extreme; we had BigBoy and Frank as our trustworthy bodyguards; and we had each other. This list was longer than the other so I guess you could say the good outweighed the bad.

The tears retreated and I relaxed, comfortable in Rigo's arms. If things were different, I could give in to the attraction that had drawn us together. He was a good man. But I had to concentrate on the most important aspects of our situation – namely, survival and rescue. Love and sex would just have to take a back seat.

STRANDED

Others stirred and I sat up. "You and Tom should go fishing after breakfast, Rigo. We can have a seafood buffet for lunch."

"But you no like seafood." His teasing tone made me blush.

"It's grown on me!" I playfully slapped his arm and everyone laughed. When we opened the door, BigBoy and Frank were waiting for us with a mountain of mangos, papayas, and coconuts.

Suddenly, Tom cried, "Oh, no! Robbie had his dive mask with him when he fell. We have no way to make a fire!"

"Relax, Tom. When we buried Morley, I kept his father's spectacles as a memento. They're glass so we can still make a fire." I pulled them out of my pouch and held them up.

"Good thinking, Lissy!"

"I wasn't thinking, Tom. I was feeling. I wanted something to remember him by – and he had very little." I hung my head and looked at the glasses, my heart full of sadness for the man I had felt so much for in such a short period of time.

"So today we go feesh, Señor Tom!" Rigo extended an olive branch, but I knew he still harbored a deep resentment.

After breakfast, the guys headed toward the lagoon. Frank went with them and BigBoy stayed with Joanne and me. Inevitably, we discussed Robbie's death and tears flowed freely. We cried and ranted and raved over the needlessness of it and then moved on to being stranded and helpless until I finally told Joanne about my conversation with Rigo that morning. "He's certain someone is looking for us, Jo. I mean, *absolutely certain.* And when he held me, I felt calm and sure that things would work out, too. Maybe they will. Maybe someone *is* looking for us."

"But who, Lissy?"

"I don't know, Jo. But Rigo says he knows *here*." I patted my chest like he had. "I hope he's right. I want to go home."

"Me, too, Lissy." Joanne and I changed the subject and then later pulled coconut strings for the fire. We soon had a big pile and I set up the rocks in the fire pit.

"You know, Jo, I bet everyone would love to have potatoes with the fish. Let's take BigBoy and go digging. The guys took the bucket, but if all three of us carry some, we'll have plenty for lunch and dinner. What do you think?"

"Sure. Come on, BigBoy. Let's go dig up potatoes!" She called the ape and we grabbed our spears. The monkeys might've been defeated, but we weren't taking any chances.

BigBoy enthusiastically dug up the spuds, so it wasn't long before we had more than we could carry. I'd brought my pouch, so since we were there, I suggested collecting a few aloe branches, too. "It's just a bit farther along the trail." We piled the tubers into three small mounds and left them for the return trip.

We found the aloe and Joanne broke off a couple branches. I tucked them away and we headed back to the potato field. There, we filled our arms with the earthy-smelling vegetables and trudged toward the creek. After washing them, we returned to camp and organized the fire-making set-up. With coconut strings in place, we waited for the sun to ignite the dry strands.

Soon, a nice fire blazed cheerfully – all we needed was the fish. Our timing was perfect and we heard the guys' laughter before they emerged into the clearing. Tom carried a bucket of crabs; Rigo hauled a stringer of fish and a small ray.

I tossed potatoes into the fire, Tom cleaned the fish, and Joanne and I dug out the plates and silverware. Then we waited impatiently for the food to cook. The delectable smells wafted through camp and before long, silence fell as we gorged on the tender fish, ray steaks, and crabs, washed down with clear mountain spring water.

We had enough leftovers for dinner and put them into the freshly-scrubbed bucket. Joanne stretched her wetskin over the top and secured it with a vine and we suspended it from a shady tree branch to keep critters out.

Our hunger sated, we relaxed. Tom read the log book in the shade of a tree. Joanne took a nap. Rigo and I sat and talked but I felt antsy and couldn't sit still. "Why don't we go for a walk along the beach? It's a beautiful afternoon."

"Sí, es un buen idea. Come, pretty chica." Rigo stood and held out his hand. I hesitated only a moment. For the first time, we were doing something normal. BigBoy dawdled along behind us as we meandered down the trail to the lagoon and then along the shoreline. We spotted a few dorsal fins patrolling the area but other than that, it was picture perfect.

Knowing the ugly monkeys had taken such a severe thrashing gave us a sense of security we hadn't felt for quite a while. We strolled along the beach hand-in-hand, enjoying the sunshine and companionship. We laughed and flirted and collected a few pretty seashells along the way.

Rigo picked up a stone and threw it far out into the water. We watched it splash, tiny waves washing the ripples away. Suddenly, a shark erupted straight up out of the water at that very spot, its tail clearing the surface before the animal splashed down and disappeared from sight. Shocked, we locked eyes.

Intrigued, Rigo tossed another stone into the wavelets a fair distance from the first. Another shark leapt from the water.

I threw the next stone and a third shark leapt in the lagoon. Was it one shark or three different ones? To answer that question, we each threw a stone simultaneously and waited. Two sharks exploded from the lagoon, one a huge beast, the other slightly smaller with scars marring the right side of its body.

Curious, I said, "Let's both throw several stones in quick succession. I want to see if there are numerous sharks that will do this, or just a few." We each collected a handful of stones and I said, "On the count of three. One. Two. Three." We each threw three stones one after the other into different areas of the lagoon. Six different sharks erupted from the depths of the bay, splashing back down and leaving no trace that they had temporarily disrupted the peaceful scene before us.

I shivered. Looking at Rigo, I said, "That is *not* normal shark behavior. Why would they attack a small ripple on the surface of the water? And why do such large sharks patrol this small lagoon? It's pretty deep, but not very big – certainly not large enough to support all those sharks.

"I wonder..." A thought skittered through my mind. Rigo looked at me, puzzled.

"What if the experimental drug the scientists were using on the monkeys got into the water when the ship wrecked and affected the sharks?" My mind awhirl, I continued theorizing. "Maybe it made *them* more aggressive, too. Obviously, they'll attack anything that moves. We were incredibly lucky the day we washed ashore – they must've been feeding elsewhere or we'd have been attacked long before making it to the beach."

Rigo seemed to be thinking along the same lines. "Sí, maybe eet make them smart, too. They know we are here and theenk we come eento the water. They wait for us."

Standing there on the beach, our thoughts on deviant shark behavior, we stared into the distance with unseeing eyes. Suddenly, I focused on a speck on the horizon. I grabbed Rigo's arm and pointed. "Look! On the horizon. Is that a ship?"

"Sí, maybe a sheep. Eet ees too far." Excited, he rattled off something more in Spanish that I didn't understand.

"Let's go back and tell the others. Come on, BigBoy!" We ran up the trail and burst into camp, startling Joanne and Tom. Frank leapt down from the trees, ready for an attack.

"A ship... A ship on the horizon." Out of breath, I could only make short sentences and wave for them to come. Tom and Joanne both scrambled to their feet and dashed toward the lagoon, Frank and BigBoy bringing up the rear.

The speck was still there and Tom said, "Yes, I do think it's a ship. Nothing else would be out there on that expanse of water, but it's too far away to see us."

After watching for several minutes, Tom said, "That's odd. It doesn't seem to be moving. Maybe it's a research vessel – if so, it may be anchored there for a while. Let's light a signal fire. We can use green wood during daylight hours to make a lot of smoke and once it gets dark, we can pile on the dry wood to build up a bonfire." Pragmatic as always, Tom ordered everyone to collect firewood. "We'll need a lot. After dark, we want flames shooting high into the sky and we need it to burn all night."

We scattered and once the apes realized what we needed, they, too, collected wood. Before long, we had five impressive piles. Tom said, "We can build a fire here and cook an early dinner then build it up. It's a good thing the ship didn't sail by on a rainy day – we either wouldn't have seen it at all or wouldn't have been able to signal it. Wouldn't *that* suck?"

Afraid the speck would disappear, I said, "Maybe we should build the signal fire now."

Tom smiled and said, "We have time to eat dinner first – we can pile on the wood afterwards. I assume we're *all* going to spend the night on the beach?" Tom's question brought a chorus of affirmative replies.

He grinned. "Okay, then we should probably collect a bunch of the soft palm fronds, too. We might as well be comfortable."

Joanne and I headed back into the trees to collect the fronds. I knew I shouldn't get my hopes up but I couldn't help thinking about being rescued. *To go home! To sleep in my own bed! Be safe! Take a hot shower! Drink coffee and eat chocolate and a big, fat hamburger!* Then my thoughts shifted. *What would happen to BigBoy and Frank? Could we take them home with us?* I'd broach the subject at dinner.

Our arms full of fronds, Joanne and I returned to the beach. The speck was still there. While we were gone, Tom and Rigo had dug a pit in the sand. As prepared as we could be here, we headed back to camp for the dinnerware and leftovers. I didn't want to be away from that speck any longer than absolutely necessary and I figured everyone else felt the same way.

Collecting what we needed, we locked the shelter door and headed back to the beach. We kept the blaze small while reheating dinner, ate quickly, and then built the fire into a roaring inferno. The late afternoon sun blazed brightly but when we tossed on the green wood, black smoke billowed skyward.

Unable to sit still, we wandered the beach picking up more wood and keeping an eye on the speck. Time crawled. One by one, we settled into comfortable positions arrayed around each end of the fire – everyone wanted a seaward view – and I shared what Rigo and I had seen earlier. "We witnessed some pretty unusual shark behavior while we were at the beach today," I said. "Bizarre, actually." Tom and Joanne hung on my words.

I told them about the number of sharks we'd seen. "I had a thought about the experimental drugs used on the ugly monkeys. It was designed to make them smarter and more aggressive, right? What if it leaked into the water when the ship wrecked and had the same effect on the sharks? They're definitely more aggressive than any sharks I've ever read about. And Rigo thought maybe they know we're here and patrol the lagoon waiting for us to go into the water." I paused.

"Tom, does that log book say anything about the drugs being used on other types of animals?" I held my breath.

"No, not so far – and I'm nearly done with it." He shrugged. "But it's not a far stretch to think it would have the same effect, especially on animals that are aggressive to begin with."

"Okay, so the drug might explain the unusual behavior of the sharks. Now, I had another thought, too." I figured this would be a good segue. "If the people on the ship see our fire and sail to the island, we might actually be rescued before long. Whether on this ship or on another one, we could be going home.

"What do we do about BigBoy and Frank? Can we take them with us? I'd love to have one of them live with me."

Joanne said, "That would be amazing! They'd probably be on Oprah! The whole world would see how wonderful they are."

"Whoa, whoa, you two," Tom cautioned. "If the world finds out about Frank and BigBoy, they'll live the rest of their lives in a cage at some experimental lab. The army or government scientists or somebody will swarm this island and capture all of the orangutans for testing. They're much better off here. We can't tell *anyone* about them. Not about how smart they are or about how they saved our lives or how much they understand. Nothing."

"But what if…" I started.

"No, Lissy. You don't want BigBoy in a cage, do you? He calls himself an orangutan *person*. Hell, he's more human than some people I've known. We can't be the cause of his being treated like a guinea pig. This island would be overrun with

259

people who want to *use* the orangutans, not treat them like the amazing creatures they are. We have to protect them. And the only way we can do that is to say *nothing* to *anyone*."

I sighed. "You're right. They are amazing creatures and people would perform horrendous experiments on them. I couldn't live with myself if that happened. I love BigBoy and Frank. I swear I'll *never* mention them to anyone." I had only thought how wonderful the apes were, how amazing they would seem to the world.

"I promise! I'll never mention Frank and BigBoy to anyone, ever." Joanne agreed. We all turned to Rigo.

"No me! Never weel I say their name. They are safe to me!"

Tom said, "Alright, this may sound corny, but let's make a pact that we'll never mention the apes or the ugly monkeys to anyone. Repeat this: 'I swear on the Bible to never tell anyone about the orangutans or the monkeys on this island. I'll protect them as long as I live.'"

We raised our right hands and solemnly swore an oath to protect our orangutan friends. And then I cried. They had repeatedly risked their lives for us, loved us, served us, and helped us without asking anything in return. And when we get rescued, abandoning them is the only way we can save them. It didn't seem fair. There was a lot about this experience that didn't seem fair.

Tom added, "When and if the ship comes to the island, we have to keep BigBoy and Frank out of sight. The crew members can't see them. It would raise too many questions. We can say we survived on fruit and fish and don't have to go into detail about anything else. In fact, we should probably not volunteer information – just answer the questions asked and our answers should be very similar. No contradictions."

My excitement about the ship had been replaced with sadness as I thought about the apes. Frank and Gigi were happy for a while and then she left him. Now, if the ship sees our signal fire, we'll leave him, too. BigBoy was, indeed, an orangutan person – in some respects, he was more human than animal and we had become his family. I would miss them both terribly. I wondered how they would deal with our departure.

The conversation had put a damper on the earlier enthusiasm, but as twilight fell, we continued to feed the fire. Obviously, in the dark we could no longer see the speck on the horizon – only a slight twinkle of far-off lights. On the other hand, though, they should be able to see the blaze. By dawn, we'd know if they'd seen it and were heading our way. Regardless, it would be a long night – and I'd be crushed if the ship was no closer in the morning.

Settling into our temporary beach beds, we chatted, and finally fell into a reflective silence. The waves lapping at the shore and the breeze gently rustling the leaves of the trees lulled me into a light sleep. A pop from the fire startled me awake and I realized the others had dozed off, as well. The fire had burned down to a small, cheery blaze suitable for roasting hot dogs and singing Girl Scout songs – not at all fitting for our needs. I leapt to my feet and tossed more wood into the small flames, coaxing them higher. Tom and Rigo came awake with a start – Jo seemed dead to the world – and helped me rebuild the fire. No need to conserve wood – we wanted this fire to be *seen*.

Concerned that we might again fall asleep and miss our chance to signal the ship, I shared my thoughts. "Maybe we should take turns keeping watch and feeding the fire. If we all fall asleep, the fire could die out. I'll go first."

"Good idea, Lissy. Are you sure you want to go first? I'd be happy to stand watch." Tom was also wide awake.

"No, I'll do it. I'm as alert as I'm going to get and don't think I could go back to sleep right now, anyway. I'll wake you in an hour." I looked at my watch and saw that it was shortly before midnight. "At 1:00."

"I can seet weeth you, eef you like," Rigo suggested.

"No, thanks, Rigo. You'll have to stay awake later." I smiled at his generous offer, but it wouldn't be fair. "Go back to sleep."

He grumbled, but was snoring soon after putting his head down. The silence enveloped me once again. Afraid I'd get drowsy curled up on my fronds, I strolled along the beach. It was a beautiful night with the faint moonlight reflecting off the calm water of the lagoon. I stopped and stared seaward, willing myself to see the silhouette of the ship cruising in our direction. I stood there for several minutes, the fire to my back, hoping my eyes would adjust more fully to the darkness and see what I so desperately wanted to see. No luck.

I sighed and continued my leisurely ramble, following the gentle curve of the shoreline, shuffling my feet in the warm sand. Glancing back at my sleeping friends, I decided to add more wood to the blaze. As I approached the pit, a large shadow materialized from the darkness and I nearly screamed before realizing it was BigBoy. My heart thudded loudly in the silence.

Tossing a few more branches into the flames, I heard BigBoy huff to get my attention. When I turned to face him, he motioned for me to come to him. I took a few steps in his direction and he pivoted and headed toward the trees at a slow lope.

"BigBoy, where are you going?" I whispered, loath to wake anyone before my hour was up. He didn't slow, but waved me on with one long arm. "Okay, I'm coming. This had better be good." I trudged after him across the sand and into the trees. Darkness wrapped around me like a thick blanket and I struggled to see him, the moonlight hardly filtering through the canopy. A faint rustle ahead gave me direction and I headed that way, hoping it was him.

When a hairy hand touched my arm, I shrieked and jumped back, slamming my shoulder into a tree trunk. BigBoy woofed and, rubbing my sore shoulder, I said, "Don't *do* that, BigBoy! You scared the crap out of me! What are we doing here, anyway? I need to watch the fire."

Agitated, the ape clucked and woofed, rocking left and right. For a moment, I thought it might be ugly monkeys but surely he wouldn't bring me into the trees, alone, if there was danger. "What is it? Why are you all upset?" I stroked his arm but my touch only seemed to stir him up more.

Suddenly, he hauled me into a fireman's carry and scrambled up the nearest tall tree. I held on for dear life, not expecting this, and said, "What are you doing? Why are we climbing a tree when I need to watch the fire?"

He set me down in the fork of the tree, high above the ground, and faced seaward. He was so intent, I turned to see what had him all a-twitter and there it was. The ship. I could see its lights cruising toward us across the waves. They'd seen our fire! I had to tell the others. "BigBoy, take me down to the ground." Staring out to sea, he ignored me.

"BigBoy! Take me down to the ground right this minute! Come *on*!" I grabbed his arm and he finally turned his gaze on me. His stricken appearance stopped me cold. His eyes were tormented, haunted. He bared his teeth in an anguished grimace and wrinkled his brow in a terrible frown. He snorted and grumbled, whined and whimpered – sounds I'd never heard him make before. I reached out to stroke his arm and he pulled away, refusing my touch. He turned his back to me and faced seaward again, his eyes glued to the ship.

I realized he understood what the approaching vessel meant. We would leave. His family would go away and he'd be a lonely orangutan person again. My heart broke and I didn't know how to comfort him. Really, what solace could I offer when I was the cause of his pain?

Placing my hand flat against the strawberry-blond hair on his back, I murmured softly, "BigBoy, please don't push me away. I love you, you know that. But I can't stay here – and you can't come with me. They'd lock you away and I couldn't protect you. Please, look at me."

Finally, he swung his big head to face me. Huge tears overflowed his eyes, wet tracks matting the fine hair on his cheeks. My research that said animals couldn't cry or grieve like humans obviously didn't pertain to this creature standing in front of me. There in the fork of the tree, I wrapped my arms around him; he held me in his ape-embrace, and we cried.

Eventually, I sniffed and whispered, "Come on. We have to go back to the others so I can check on the fire." I pulled out of his arms and we both sniffled and wiped our eyes. He slowly and sadly hefted me over his shoulder and descended to the ground.

I checked my watch and saw it was nearly time to wake Tom. BigBoy walked me to the beach and then turned toward the trees. I had little doubt he would go back up to watch the approaching ship. I trudged to the fire, my earlier enthusiasm about the vessel dulled by the deep sadness that had settled into my heart. Tossing branches into the flames, I thought about the pros and cons of taking BigBoy and Frank home with us and knew we were right to keep them a secret from the rest of the world. Our friends would miss us, yes, but they'd live here free of human persecution and experimentation. These incredible apes would live on in our memories forever.

Touching Tom's shoulder, I said softly, "Hey, it's your turn to stand watch." Once he was awake and we stood together staring out at the sea, I told him. "It's coming – I saw it."

"What? How did you see it?" Incredulous, he seemed to think I might have imagined it as he scanned the ocean intently.

"BigBoy came to get me and carried me up a tall tree. I saw it. And BigBoy cried. He knows we're going to leave and he cried."

"Animals can't cry, Lissy. You said so yourself."

"Yes, I did. But you didn't see him, Tom. It was the most heartbreaking thing I've ever seen. His face was full of anguish and tears streamed from his eyes. He *cried*." I choked up and tears trickled down my face. "I think the drug that was supposed to enhance the attributes of kindness and helpfulness also enhanced their emotions. You've seen how happy and excited he can get – he feels sadness just as keenly. He *is* an orangutan person."

"He'll be okay, Lissy. He'll miss us, but he'll be free. He's much better off here than he would be if we took him with us."

"I know. But it breaks my heart to see him so sad." I turned and walked to my pallet, leaving a trail of tiny wet drips in the sand. I curled up and rested my head on my arm. My last thought as I fell asleep wasn't of home. I saw BigBoy rocking left and right in excitement, a big ape-grin on his face; I recalled him roaring and baring his teeth at the ugly monkeys as he protected me on the trail; I remembered that first day when he meekly approached me, the thorn in his foot, asking for help; I saw him doing the Super Bowl boogie after the battle at the feeding cave; and I saw the tears wetting his cheeks as he thought of us leaving him. My tears that night weren't the tears of joy I had anticipated when rescue was imminent.

Chapter 19

Day 15

Lissy

When I felt the heat of the sun, I awoke with a start. *Had everyone fallen asleep? Did the fire go out? Why didn't anyone wake me?* I sat up abruptly and found my friends sitting around the small fire talking quietly.

"Why didn't you wake me for my turn?" I mumbled, groggy.

"You were sleeping like a log," Joanne said, "and we were all awake, anyway, so what was the point? We decided to let you sleep. Besides, you already know the ship's coming, right?" I could hear the excitement in her voice.

"Yes, I do. Where is it? Can we see it?" I climbed to my feet, looking beyond the lagoon. The vessel was clearly sailing toward us, much larger now than the original speck on the horizon.

"They should reach the island in a couple of hours. Maybe you should go have a talk with BigBoy and Frank so they don't put in a surprise appearance." Tom's suggestion was valid. We couldn't very well say we were alone on the island and nothing unusual happened and then have the two orangutans come bounding up to say hi – it could lead to questions we didn't want to answer.

"Okay. Do we have any fruit on hand?" I needed something to get the muzzy morning taste out of my mouth.

"Yep, here you go." Tom tossed me a mango and added, "The apes came by while ago with breakfast. I think they headed back to their nests."

Trying to decide what I was going to say to BigBoy and Frank, I nearly walked past the trees where they'd spent the night. I heard a familiar, "Woo-woo," and looked up to see two pairs of eyes looking down at me. "Hi, you two! Can I come up? Or, rather, can one of you come get me?"

BigBoy dropped to the ground and came over to hug me. "Hi, big fella. Are you feeling better than you were last night?" I looked into his eyes and saw sadness, but not the haunting torment I'd seen before. "Come on, let's go up and see Frank."

BigBoy hefted me to his shoulder and scrambled up the tree. Frank woofed enthusiastically and lowered his head for a scratch. "Hi, Frank! Did BigBoy tell you about the boat?"

The ape excitedly woo-woo-wooed and pointed toward the sea. "Yes, I guess he did. Now, we need to talk about the boat." The word elicited more woo-woos and pointing. "Okay, Frank, come here and sit down." I patted the spot next to me and he dashed over to take a seat. "You, too, BigBoy. Come here."

When both apes were seated next to me and relatively calm, I said, "The boat is bringing more people to the island and even though that might seem exciting, I need you to stay away. Do you understand? You can watch from the trees while we talk to them." I tried to think of a way to emphasize the importance of keeping their distance.

"This is very important: some people are good and some are bad. We don't know if the people on the boat are good or bad so you both have to stay away. I don't want them to hurt you. Do you understand, BigBoy?" The strawberry blonde ape nodded his head so I added, "Then you explain it to Frank so he understands, too." Another nod.

"After we meet the people on the boat, I'll come and explain what's going to happen next. I want you to stay in the jungle until I tell you it's okay to come out." Both apes nodded and I believed they understood the need to stay hidden.

"Alright, BigBoy, you can take me back down to the ground now. Let's go!" The ape hauled me up onto his shoulder and down the tree we went. He made it seem so easy. "Thank you, big fella. You stay here with Frank."

When I got back to the beach, Tom said, "Well? Do they understand they can't come to the beach?"

"I think so. I told them they could watch from the trees but could not come to the beach until I told them it's okay. And I asked BigBoy to explain it to Frank."

Tom nodded. "Good. The boat should be here within the hour. Then we'll know what we're dealing with. If they only speak Spanish, Rigo can translate."

Time passed slowly as we watched the boat gradually grow larger and larger. Tom confirmed his supposition that the ship might be a research vessel and as it cruised into the mouth of the lagoon and dropped anchor, a Mexican flag fluttered in the gentle breeze. The crew lowered a small dinghy into the water and three swarthy, uniformed men climbed aboard. They rowed in unison toward the beach.

Suddenly a tall dorsal fin broke the surface a few yards in front of the dinghy. The three men screamed as a huge shark raised its blunt snout and opened its mouth wide. Desperately trying to reverse the small craft's forward momentum, the men rowed frantically but were no match for the speed and agility of the beast. It enveloped the front of the small vessel and bit it nearly in half, the lone man in front bisected by the razor-sharp teeth. The upper half of his torso slid wetly into the lagoon.

A second dorsal fin surfaced and sped toward the foundering craft, the two screaming crewmen clinging helplessly to the stern. We watched in horror as the shark crunched the remains of the wooden craft, staining the water an even darker red and leaving only bits of timber afloat on the surface. Numerous other fins cruised the bloody water, the sharks occasionally snapping at the drifting debris.

Spanish curses floated across the lagoon as the ship's crew watched their friends die. We knew there would be no more attempts to reach the island and our hopes sank. Tom said, "Rigo, tell them we're sorry about their friends and ask them to radio for another ship. You can't let them leave without asking for help!"

In Spanish, Rigo conferred with the captain. At first, they blamed us for their friends' deaths. Rigo begged and pleaded and, finally, the captain agreed to radio for help. He said they'd remain anchored at the mouth of the lagoon until nightfall – by then he should know whether another ship would be sent to rescue us. If he didn't... I tried not to think about this ship sailing off into the darkness without giving us an answer.

Time had never passed so slowly. Tom and Rigo fished, catching enough for lunch and dinner, and we built another small fire. I went into the jungle to visit Frank and BigBoy, returning with fruit so no one would suspect I might have another reason for leaving my friends at the beach. In the heat of the afternoon, we moved into the trees at the jungle's edge to get out of the sun. And we watched the crew watching us as the minutes crawled by.

When the sun hung low in the evening sky, the captain spoke to Rigo with his loudspeaker. He had received a reply from the mainland and said they would be sending another ship to rescue us. It should arrive in two days. He had provided the coordinates of our location and explained about the sharks, so the vessel would also carry a helicopter to fly from the boat to the island. Sharks would no longer be a problem.

We yelled many thank you's to the captain in both English and Spanish, apologized again for the crew members' deaths, and watched the ship sail away into the twilight. Now, we could only hope nothing went awry with the other rescue attempt.

In case the crew still watched, we lingered on the beach until dark. Then I hollered for Frank and BigBoy and we all walked back to the shelter together. The apes were happy to see us and I made sure to thank them for not coming to the beach, telling them they were very good orangutan people. Since we hadn't spent time with them during the day, we sat around the fire pit and shared fruit with them, including them in our conversations.

At bedtime, we bid the apes goodnight and entered the shelter, tying the vines to lock the door – old habits die hard. We simply felt safer with the door locked. Frank and BigBoy nested in the trees above and life went back to normal – for two more days.

I thought I'd have difficulty falling asleep, but my eyelids quickly grew heavy. Snores filled the shelter in only minutes and images of home filled my mind as I drifted off.

Chapter 20

Day 16

Lissy

Morning dawned wet and dreary. I fervently hoped the weather wouldn't impede the rescue vessel's journey. I envisioned blue skies, calm seas, and a smooth rescue, but as much as I wanted to go home, I dreaded the thought of leaving BigBoy and Frank. It would be an emotional departure.

The apes brought us fruit for breakfast so we didn't have to go foraging, leaving the shelter only to visit the latrine. We rested, listening to rain pound, patter, and drip on the ceiling.

Shortly after noon, the clouds parted. Rays of sunshine peeked through, heating the ground and causing steam to rise from the jungle floor. High humidity left our skin feeling damp; each breath seemed like it was sucked through a wet sponge; and clouds of biting bugs appeared in the moist and heavy air.

To avoid the insects, we remained inside even though it was a few degrees cooler outside. When BigBoy brought more fruit, we noticed the thick swarm of pests hovering around his head. He swatted and snorted as the bugs flew near his nostrils. I said, "Do you think we could invite the apes inside until the humidity dies down? They must be miserable."

We took pity on the apes and Joanne said, "Sure, Lissy. But tell them to leave the bugs outside." She was not a fan.

"BigBoy, where's Frank? Go get Frank!" I sent the ape off to get his friend and waited by the door. Soon they came bounding back. "Come in here, you guys!" I called them in before they stopped running, leaving the insects no time to congregate around their bodies. Hesitant at first, the apes soon made themselves at home, enjoying the bug-free zone.

By late afternoon, the sky had cleared and a brisk breeze blew the bugs and humidity away. We chased the apes back outside and Tom and Rigo collected their fishing gear. They took BigBoy to the beach with them and Frank clambered into the trees. Joanne and I performed housekeeping duties, shaking out the palm fronds to plump up the beds. It felt good to be outside. Everything smelled fresh and new after the cleansing rain.

We decided to join the guys at the beach and called to Frank. The three of us ambled down the trail and surprised Tom and Rigo. BigBoy had dug up some clams, the guys had caught a few good-sized fish, and a large ray had been trapped in a pool during the morning storm. He wasn't going anywhere and would be fresher if they speared him just prior to heading back to camp.

Watching the dorsal fins cruising the lagoon brought to mind the horrific scene of the night before. I shuddered. Thankful the new rescue ship was bringing a helicopter, I sighed with relief knowing we wouldn't have to brave the water. No way was I putting even *one* toe into those waves!

We cooked dinner and sat and relaxed around the fire. This was one of the most leisurely days we'd had since washing up on shore. Knowing the rescue ship was on its way, the ugly monkeys were unlikely to bother us, and we had a comfortable shelter and plenty of food and water added up to a stress-free time. I looked forward to another easy day tomorrow, perhaps our last on the island. Maybe we could go to the pool. After all, we didn't have much to pack for our journey home.

As darkness condensed around us, we called it a day and said goodnight to Frank and BigBoy. I settled into my bed and glanced over at Robbie's pallet – we hadn't had the heart to throw his palm fronds out. My spirit momentarily ached at all of our losses, but soared once again at the thought of heading home.

I closed my eyes and imagined my condo and my very own bed – my last sensation one of peace and security.

Chapter 21

Day 17

<u>Lissy</u>

For a moment I didn't know where I was. With my last thoughts before sleep of my bedroom at home, I nearly panicked. Sitting up, I frantically gazed around the shelter and the entire three-week ordeal came rushing back.

I let out a sigh and lay back down. Rigo stirred. His lazy morning grin set my pulse to pounding, his sexy, "Hola, beauteeful Leesa. You are okay thees morning?" making me yearn for a bit more privacy.

He reached for my hand, his touch warm and inviting. Although I had told him I couldn't be his girl, I had terribly mixed feelings about him. Was I physically attracted to him? Oh, yeah. Did he have many of the qualities I admired in a man? Definitely. Was he brave and strong and willing to protect me? He'd proven he was. And I knew he cared for me. But could I get past the fact that the beginning of our relationship was fraught with fear, danger, and death? Now that we were soon to be heading home, could I let that go and just enjoy being with him? I had no answers other than my body's response to his touch.

"Yes, I'm fine, Rigo. You know, this might be our last full day on the island. By tomorrow, we may be sailing back to Mexico." I smiled, my hand clasped in his.

"Sí, and you weel leave." The sadness in his voice tore at my heart. His fingers rubbed small circles on the back of my hand. "You weel take my heart weeth you."

"We can stay in touch. You have a computer, don't you? We can email every day. And Skype!" I envisioned long Skype sessions with him, keeping us close, allowing our relationship to grow.

"No, Leesa, I no have a computer. What ees thees Skype?" My hopes fell and without a computer, I saw no easy way for us to stay in touch. I certainly couldn't afford to fly to and from Mexico all the time. It might be better to retreat now rather than build up Rigo's hopes and extend his pain and disappointment.

"Come on, let's get up and go to the pool! We haven't been swimming in a long time." I jumped up and dashed for the door.

Joanne said, "I heard that! Sounds like fun! Come on, Tom."

We darted out the door and grabbed our spears. I hollered to the apes, "Come on, guys! We're going to the pool!" As the orangutans dropped from the canopy, we skipped down the trail toward the stream, laughing and teasing each other.

Tom and Rigo entered the water with mighty cannonballs, sending droplets flying in all directions. Joanne and I were more sedate, stepping into the water from the rocks and adjusting to the coolness bit by bit. The sun was already hot, promising a scorching day to come, and the water felt good. The guys roughhoused while Jo and I floated on our backs on the far side of the pool. The apes foraged in the nearby jungle and brought us mangos and papayas.

We crawled from the water and lounged on the rocks as we munched the sweet fruit. "What's the first thing you're going to do when we get back to Cozumel?" I asked Joanne.

"The very first thing? I'm going to get down on my knees and kiss the ground!" She sounded serious. "And the first thing I'm going to do when I get to the hotel is take the world's longest shower. You guys won't have *any* hot water by the time I'm done!" She sighed and luxuriated, mimicking rubbing soap on her arms. "I can imagine it now... Hot water. Shampoo. Scented soap. A fluffy bath towel. And a toothbrush. I'm going to brush my teeth until they shine! Ahhhhh. Heaven!"

I laughed. "I'm with you on that shower! Isn't that going to feel *wonderful?*" I closed my eyes, better to imagine the feeling. "And the bed! I can't wait to lie on a real mattress. We'd better not have an early flight the next morning – I might not make it."

Tom said, "You girls go ahead and use up the hotel's hot water. I'm going to find a hamburger! I don't care what time of the day or night it is – I want a burger and fries with a cup of hot, black coffee." He smiled and then added sadly, "And I'm going to eat a big slab of chocolate cake, for Robbie."

"You bring chocolate cake back to the hotel and we'll help you celebrate Robbie." Joanne and I nodded, serious about eating it in Robbie's memory and salivating at the idea of chocolate. "What about you, Rigo? What's your first thing?"

"I go see mi madre and mi hermano. They worry, for sure." He hung his head and added, "Mi padre es muerte and I bring money to mi familia. Never before do I go away for so long."

"Yes, I'm sure they're worried about you. We need to call our families in the States and tell them we're okay, too, that we're coming home. I guess *that* should be before the shower." Jo and

I looked at each other and I said, "You shower, I'll phone home. When you're done, I'll shower while you phone home."

She grinned and giggled, "It's a plan, ET!" After a thoughtful moment, she said, "Can you believe it? We're finally being rescued. I certainly didn't want to end up like Morley. How did he *do* it for forty years?" With a stricken look, she touched my hand.

"He was a special man, Jo. We only knew him for a little over a day, but he touched my heart. I loved him. I wish he could've become my dad." Tears filled my eyes. "I'm glad I kept his father's glasses – they'll be a reminder to me to *never* give up. After all he endured, Morley never quit hoping, never quit waiting for someone to come along." The tears overflowed and the salty drops collected at my chin, dripping onto the damp wetskin.

"I think we'd better head back to camp before you girls get sunburned." Tom looked us over and said, "You're already getting pink. You didn't wear your hats."

"Okay, let's go." I scrambled up and dried my eyes. Enough blubbering.

Back at camp, we relaxed for a while before going fishing. We wanted a nice meal our last night on the island.

Tom leaned against his favorite tree, log book in hand. It looked like he was almost finished.

Rigo said, "Now eet ees safe, me and Frank explore the jungle." I thought it sounded like the perfect thing for him and his sexy smile to do.

Joanne went to take a nap. I think she liked the leisure time – and feeling stress-free enough to enjoy it.

I wanted to make BigBoy and Frank each another hat. The other ones were tattered and the apes really seemed to like wearing them. I'll bet that's what made Gigi fall for Frank. He looked so debonair with his hat sitting at a rakish angle – that and his "my way" attitude. I smiled as I dug out the weaving supplies.

Parking in the shade, I let my thoughts wander. Visions of Rusty filled my head as my fingers wove the grass in, out, over, and under. I smiled as I recalled the day he dropped out of the trees and tried to steal my hat. That was the day Frank whooped him. Poor brave, foolish Rusty.

The orangutans had become a *huge* part of our lives here on the island. We never would have survived without them. We had a better shelter; we ate better; we were safer; and they were an endless source of entertainment, delight, unconditional love, and astonishing discoveries. Life at home would seem pretty dull after this exciting adventure. I might have to take up sky diving just to keep the adrenaline flowing!

Several hours and two hats later, I put the weaving supplies aside and woke Joanne. Tom had fallen asleep leaning against his tree and awakened just as Rigo and Frank wandered back into camp. "You weel love thees for deener, Leesa! See what Frank found!" We gathered round the fire pit as they laid their bounty out for all of us to see: carrots and onions.

"That's fantastic, Rigo! Where were they?" My mouth watered in anticipation of the long-missed flavors.

"That way." He pointed in the opposite direction from the pool – an area we'd never explored. We could've been enjoying carrots and onions with our potatoes the entire time. Well, we'd have a feast tonight to celebrate the up-coming rescue.

"Frank like carrots but no onions." I grinned as Frank munched on one of the smaller carrots from the pile and smiled at us with orange bits between his teeth.

"We'd better hide them or we won't have any left for dinner. Once BigBoy sees them, they'll be history." Tom gathered the new veggies and took them into the shelter. Normally, we didn't tie the door shut from the outside but this time, he used a vine to lock the door after he exited and said, "Now that I have a veritable banquet in mind for dinner, let's go fishing, Rigo. It's too bad we couldn't have found something to season the food with, but we'll have spices at our fingertips soon enough. Come on!"

"Jo, do you want to go to the beach, too?" She nodded. I hollered for BigBoy and we all tromped to the lagoon.

While Tom and Rigo searched the pools for trapped fish and rays on the left side of the lagoon, Joanne and I wandered along the beach in the opposite direction. Never before thinking it safe to wander away from the guys, we felt free and adventurous, especially with Frank trailing along behind. BigBoy stayed with the men, digging up clams and chasing crabs.

We rounded the curve that created the right edge of the kidney-shaped lagoon and continued along the coastline. The sand became coarser and more littered with driftwood and debris – this area was battered by the open ocean waves. Making our way around a particularly large pile of tangled wood, kelp, and unidentifiable flotsam, we failed to notice the seaward view.

Joanne looked up and said, "Oh, my God, Lissy. Look!"

Something in her voice brought my head up with a snap and my gaze locked on the amazing view off shore. Numerous shipwrecks littered the coastline, masts of various lengths protruding from their watery graves. I counted twenty-three visible wrecks and couldn't even speculate how many more lined the ocean floor. In a storm, this must be an extremely hazardous area. My mind pictured the howling tempest; the sinking ship; the terrified and screaming passengers fighting for air in the violent ocean swells, striving to make it to shore; and the aggressive sharks attacking from below. Those that made it onto the sand surely thought they were the lucky ones. Lucky until they encountered the ugly monkeys.

The remnants of these vessels provided proof that, over the years, many people had landed on the island, but we knew none had survived to this day. That explained the hundreds of skulls in the feeding cave. I shuddered. On the surface, this idyllic little isle seemed like paradise with its pretty lagoon, palm trees, white sand beach, abundance of fruit – and vegetables, if you looked hard enough – unpolluted freshwater pools, and jungle flora and fauna. However, beneath that surface lurked aggressive and dangerous sharks, ugly carnivorous monkeys, and giant spiders and snakes. Landing on the beach of the tranquil little lagoon had initially given us a feeling of having survived the worst, of being delivered safely to paradise. We soon found we'd actually been transported into an on-going nightmare, Hell, if you will.

My over-active imagination pictured the ocean floor, liberally strewn with skeletons of old ships; cargo spilling out of the broken hulls; human bones scattered haphazardly amongst the rock and coral, now a part of the reef itself; and skulls here and there, the vacant eye sockets doorways for small fish and crustaceans calling the now-empty space home.

A chill ran up my spine. "Let's go back, Jo. This place gives me the creeps."

She trembled. "Me, too. All those poor people. Let's go sit on the pretty beach and enjoy the tranquil view from there."

We picked our way back to the cleaner sand of the lagoon and spotted the guys sitting in the shade. As we approached, I said, "So what happened to fishing? Are you okay?"

Rigo replied, "Sí, we are okay but there ees much sun. We wait for you chicas here een the shade."

Tom said, "Did you find anything around the bend? We've never been on that side."

Joanne and I took a seat under the tree. "It's a ship graveyard over there, Tom. I counted twenty-three wrecks – and those were just the ones we could see from shore. God only knows how many are sitting on the bottom of the ocean."

We sat in silence for a few moments until Tom said quietly, "Now we know where all those skulls came from."

Shaking off the gloomy mood, I stood up. "Okay, let's fish! We're about to be rescued and I refuse to spend this beautiful afternoon depressed."

Tom and Rigo headed toward the pools and Joanne and I took the bucket and collected BigBoy's impressive heap of clams, adding crabs to top it off. Once again, I thought of butter, salt, and pepper and then put it out of my mind. It wouldn't be long before I could indulge in all those flavors I'd missed.

Soon, the guys had caught a good-sized ray and a stringer of fish and I called to the apes. When they bounded up to us, I handed BigBoy the bucket and he cradled it carefully in his arms, a huge smile on his hairy face. I smiled back but my heart ached.

Arriving in camp, I dumped the bucket of clams and crabs next to the pit for Tom and Rigo to clean when they gutted the fish. Joanne and I unlocked the shelter and refilled the pail with the onions and carrots; we carried them to the creek to scrub off the dirt. We took Frank with us and left BigBoy in camp, hoping to ward off the ape-munchies since Frank had eaten a fair share of the carrots earlier. But in spite of that, we still had to slap his hand a few times so we'd have enough for dinner.

Later, sitting around the pit and savoring the taste of carrots, onions, and potatoes cooked perfectly over the fire, we commented on the exquisite flavor of the ray and today's catch of fish, clams, and crabs. "I don't even *like* seafood and this is absolutely delicious!" I smacked my lips and popped another clam into my mouth. "I guess I'm going to have to quit saying I don't like seafood, huh?" I giggled when everyone laughed.

Tom said, "The way you're downing those clams, I never would've suspected you weren't a seafood lover, Lissy!"

"Yeah, well, it grows on you. A cold beer would round it out perfectly." I grinned as Tom groaned.

"Don't start that again! Before long, we can indulge in everything we've missed. Tonight, I'm going to enjoy this feast. It doesn't *get* any fresher than this." Tom refilled his plate and started on seconds. There was plenty of food to go around – at least we hadn't gone hungry during our forced stay on the island.

When everyone moaned and complained about being too full, we laughed and I said, "People aren't going to believe we were stranded on a deserted island when we go home plump and well-fed. Usually, survivors look emaciated and scraggly. Aside from needing a shower and a toothbrush, I don't think we look bad!"

Tom's solemn comment brought us face to face with reality. "On this island, I guess you either survive well or you don't survive at all." Thoughts of Sarah, Morley, Robbie, and Rusty flashed through my mind and I wondered for the umpteenth time about the rest of our group. Would we ever know their fate?

After cleaning up the dinner mess, we sat around the fire for a while, each of us lost in our own private thoughts. Daylight grew dim as the sun crept low in the sky. I broke the silence. "Tomorrow may be the day we get rescued. Are we going to sit at the beach all day, watching for the ship? Or is there something someone wants to do?"

No one responded so I continued. "I want to spend part of the day with BigBoy and Frank. I need to explain about the helicopter and impress upon them again the importance of staying out of sight." My heart ached and I added sadly, "This is going to be the very hardest part of going home."

Joanne said, "I'd like to say goodbye to BigBoy and Frank, too. Could I go with you tomorrow?"

"Of course you can. I think they'd like that."

"Thanks, Lissy. I'm going to miss them." After a thoughtful pause she turned to Tom. "Are we going to light another fire on the beach? Or do you think the ship will come during the day?"

He said, "We should probably collect a bunch of firewood again and be ready to light a signal fire if the ship doesn't arrive during daylight hours. We certainly don't want it to end up number twenty-four!"

Joanne and I both shuddered, the image of the maritime graveyard too fresh in our minds.

With the next day's plan set, we filed into the shelter and settled for the night. As my eyes closed, I felt a myriad of emotions: excitement at going home; dread at hearing the fate of our friends; sadness at leaving BigBoy and Frank; and a sense of accomplishment at having survived the whole ordeal. Obviously, many had not. I sighed and drifted off to the snores of my companions. Would I ever be able to sleep alone again?

Chapter 22

Day 18

<u>Lissy</u>

I awoke to an urgent "Woo-woo! Woo-woo!" BigBoy and Frank were both agitated about something and I wondered if they'd spotted the ship. We leapt to our feet and ran to the door. Tom fumbled with the vines and we spilled into the clearing. BigBoy pointed excitedly toward the lagoon while Frank ran circles around us and woofed.

Knowing we could see farther from up high, I said, "BigBoy, take me up into the tree like you did the last time you saw the ship. Let's go up into the tree." I was ready to follow him into the jungle but instead, he swept me off my feet and into his arms. Cradling me like a child, he dashed into the forest. I bounced along in his hairy arms hoping my head wouldn't smack into a tree trunk somewhere along the way.

Finally, he stopped and without even putting my feet on the ground, heaved me over his shoulder and scampered up a tall tree. I should be used to this by now, but it affected me the same way every time – I shrieked and hung on for dear life. Setting me down gently in a sturdy fork, he turned and faced the water. I stood beside him and spotted the speck, still very far out to sea.

Frank clambered up beside us, woofing and stroking my arm. I stroked back and he calmed down. BigBoy, however, was not to be calmed. He ignored my attempts to get his attention and remained focused on the ship, every now and then uttering a low "woo." I could feel the tension in his body – his arm was as rigid as a two-by-four and once in a while a tremor ran through him.

"BigBoy, please sit down and listen to me. Come on." I tugged on his arm and he jerked out of my grip. Frank took my hand and clucked, patting the branches beside him. I sat down and crooned to Frank, talking softly and stroking his arm. Finally, BigBoy whimpered and squatted next to me. He took my other hand and the three of us sat in the tree together making soft soothing noises. When I felt BigBoy's body relax, I said, "Okay, fellas, we need to talk. You know another ship is coming..." At the word ship, Frank pointed out to sea and woofed.

"Yes, Frank, that's the ship. It's coming here and is going to stop out there where the other ship stopped. But this time, a big, noisy machine called a helicopter is going to fly from the ship to the beach. It'll make lots of noise and will be very windy. You don't have to be afraid of it – it won't hurt us. You do not have to protect us from it. Do you understand?"

Frank nodded and I looked at BigBoy. "Do you understand, BigBoy? You do *not* have to protect us from the noisy machine." Finally, he nodded and pointed toward the beach. "Yes, it's going to land on the beach. We're going to get into the machine and it will go back up into the air and fly to the ship."

At that, BigBoy leapt up and woo-wooed, turning first toward the sea and then toward the beach, rocking left to right. Agitated again, he obviously didn't like the idea of us getting into the helicopter and flying to the ship. He pointed at the lagoon, shook his head no, and made vicious chomping motions with his teeth. I finally understood. "It's okay, big fella, the sharks won't be able to get us. They have to stay in the water and we'll fly too high for them to reach us. We'll be safe. I promise."

I could see him processing the information and again I wished I knew how much he truly understood. When he pointed to the beach and then straight up into the air, I grasped his question. "We'll fly from the beach up into the air away from the sharks. We'll be safe." He relaxed and sat down, taking my hand.

"I need you guys to stay in the trees from the time the ship stops at the lagoon until it leaves and especially when the helicopter comes to the beach. This is *very* important, so I want you to tell me you understand. Frank? Will you stay in the trees the whole time?" He nodded his head solemnly and I turned to BigBoy. "Will you stay in the trees from the time the ship stops at the lagoon until it leaves and when the helicopter comes to the beach?" I waited and looked into his dark eyes. I saw the intelligence there and knew he was thinking about more than just my question. Finally, he nodded.

"Okay, that's good. I want you guys to know I love you very much. You're *wonderful* orangutan people. You're very smart and very helpful and you've been a big part of my family. But I can't stay here on the island; I have to go home to my people-family. And I can't take you with me. You have to stay here. This is your home." Tears filled my eyes and I stopped talking, knowing my voice would break if I continued.

BigBoy huffed and when I looked at him, he placed his hand over his heart and whimpered. "Yes, I know it hurts. My heart hurts, too." I placed my hand over my heart and whimpered the same way. Once more, tears filled his eyes and I marveled at his expression of such human emotions.

Frank whimpered and touched his chest, too, and the three of us sat together grieving over our impending separation.

At last, I said, "Alright, you guys, I need to go back down there." I pointed downward. "I'll come see you again before I get on the helicopter, okay?" I stroked their arms and told BigBoy, "Come on, we need to go." He picked me up and nimbly scrambled to the ground.

Once I was safely on my feet, BigBoy climbed into the tree to be with Frank. I headed toward camp.

As soon as I entered the clearing, Joanne asked, "What did you see? Is it the ship?"

"Yes, the ship's coming. It's still just a speck, but it's on its way. Tom, how long do you think it'll take to get here?" I had no idea how long it would take to go from speck to full-blown ship anchored at the mouth of the lagoon.

"It should be here before nightfall, but it depends on how hard they push it. The weather's clear so they don't have to outrace a storm – they might just cruise along and plan on picking us up in the morning. I think we should collect some firewood, though. We could build a smoky daytime fire and have wood on hand to signal them after dark."

"Okay." I was still feeling overwhelmed by the orangutans' emotional display and it must've shown on my face.

"What's the matter, Lissy? Are the apes okay?" Joanne picked up on my melancholy mood.

"They're okay physically, but BigBoy's taking our leaving very hard. He placed his hand over his heart and whimpered, saying his heart hurts. Then he cried, Jo. He cried actual tears. It breaks my heart to see him like that."

Confused, Joanne said, "I didn't think animals could cry."

"They can't. But BigBoy can. He's so human, it's scary. I made them both promise to stay in the trees from the time the ship arrives until it sails away, especially while the helicopter's here. And I vowed to go say my final goodbye before boarding."

"Well, I guess we're on our own for breakfast this morning," Tom said. "The apes are focused on watching the ship. Let's take a walk through the trees and collect some fruit, then we can head to the beach to gather firewood. Do you want fish for lunch?"

"I guess there's no point in starving ourselves all day. Why don't we build a cooking fire on the beach and then add damp wood later to make it smoke?" I didn't see any point in building fires in two separate locations.

"Es un buen idea, Leesa!" Rigo gave me a huge grin.

I smiled back and said, "I have my moments."

Tom led the way and we collected fruit, munching all the way from the jungle to the beach. There, we dug a pit in the same location as our previous signal fire and then scattered to find driftwood and dry twigs. As before, we created five large piles of wood; afterwards, we stood together, staring out to sea. The speck was there and I thanked the weather gods for sunshine and clear skies. It was a perfect day to be rescued.

Now that I knew the ship was imminent, I was anxious to get on with it. More than ready to go home, I was antsy and found myself pacing the beach, looking at my watch every few minutes. Finally, I couldn't stand it any longer. "I'm going to the pool. Anyone want to come with me?"

Everyone else must've been feeling the same way. I got two "yeses" and a "sí" in reply and we trudged into the jungle. I hollered for Frank and BigBoy, not knowing if they'd join us or not. We hadn't seen any ugly monkeys since The Battle, but I'd still feel more comfortable with our bodyguards present.

The apes swung down from the canopy, happy to see us, and I thought they might've gotten bored watching the speck on the ocean. They gobbled fruit on the hike and left pits and cores along the trail like Hansel and Gretel's breadcrumbs.

This time we'd worn our hats and although the sun was hot, avoided a sunburn. We swam and splashed and then sat in the shade and talked about going home. "My parents must be sick with concern, like Rigo's mom. I always call them the minute I walk in the door." Joanne was close to her parents and, under normal circumstances, talked to them nearly every day.

"I call my mom as soon as I get home, too. She must be crazy with worry. I've never been gone this long without talking to her."

We glanced at Tom and he shrugged. "Like I said before, nobody's wondering where I am. I come and go so often the neighbors wouldn't fret if I was gone for several months."

Rigo said, "I see mi madre first thing. She worry, for sure."

My thoughts wandering to the other eight divers, I said, "I wonder if the rest of the group made it to an island somewhere. Maybe they've been stranded, too. All we know for sure is what happened to Sarah and Robbie. Oh! We should probably decide what we're going to tell the authorities about Robbie. How do we say he died?"

Joanne spoke up. "We can say he fell off the edge of the cliff while we were crossing back over the mountain. That's true – we just won't add that we were in a horrific battle with carnivorous monkeys at the time."

"What if his children insist on coming back to claim the body?" Tom asked. "There could be restrictions on life insurance if there's no body. Maybe we should say he was attacked by a shark." He grimaced. "As long as we all tell the same story, no one should be suspicious."

Nodding, I said, "I think you're right, Tom. We don't want any family members insisting on coming back here."

After an hour or so, we decided to go back to the beach and fish – we needed lunch. Depending on what time the vessel anchored at the lagoon, we might possibly have dinner aboardship. *Maybe they'd have coffee!*

The speck was considerably more noticeable when we arrived at the beach but was still pretty distant. The apes disappeared into the trees. Tom and Rigo caught lunch and after dining on clams and ray steak, we built up the fire and tossed some damp wood into the flames. Watching the dark smoke billow skyward, I knew the rescue crew would see it and head straight to the lagoon. A direct approach would be safer by the looks of the maritime graveyard around the bend.

We arranged palm fronds in the shade of the trees so we'd have ringside seats to watch the ship approach. Jo and I could also easily slip away for our final visit with BigBoy and Frank. I wanted to be with them when the chopper lifted off from the ship to ease their fear and confusion over the noisy machine. It was crucial that they remain hidden and not freak out, feeling they needed to protect us from the mechanical beast. Their safety today and the future well-being of the island's entire orangutan population depended on them staying out of sight.

Suddenly, I saw a flash. "Tom, did you see that?"

"What?" Engrossed in the final pages of the log book, Tom hadn't been looking out to sea.

"A flash. Like Morley's SOS. Maybe they're trying to contact us!" Excited, I nudged Joanne. "Did you see it? There it is again!"

This time, Tom was watching. "Lissy, do you have Morley's dad's glasses with you?"

"Yeah, here." I handed the spectacles to Tom and he flashed out a reply. I watched as they exchanged several communications. When he sat back down in the shade, I said, "What did they say? When will they arrive?" I was so keyed up I could hardly sit still.

"They thanked us for the smoky fire and said they should be here in about two hours. They'll pick us up tonight." He grinned. I jumped up and performed a happy dance there on the beach, out-shimmying BigBoy's hip-shaking victory dance. Joanne and Rigo joined me and we teased Tom so badly, he boogied, too.

"In about two hours we'll no longer be stranded on a deserted island. I hope they have coffee!" I couldn't help but say it out loud. Everyone laughed.

Joanne said, "I hope they don't serve fish for dinner."

"Hamburgers. I hope they have hamburgers and cold beer!" Tom was definitely yearning for a burger. "I doubt they'll have chocolate cake on board, though. That'll probably have to wait till we get back to Cozumel."

Always wanting to be prepared, I said, "Well, we have two hours left. Why don't we go get our dive gear and pile it up on the beach? That's all the packing we have to do."

"Good thinking. Let's go!" Tom jumped up and tucked the log book under the palm fronds so it couldn't blow away. Jabbering like a bunch of excited school kids on the first day of class, we headed back to camp. Since the monkeys had vandalized our dive gear, we didn't have a huge amount to haul to the beach, but nobody wanted to leave anything behind. We'd had a traumatic experience, but I was sure none of us would give up the sport we loved so much.

Once everything was ready to go, I turned to look at the shelter that had been our home for the past eighteen days. It represented security, safety, camaraderie, and comfort – we had survived by working together and having each other's backs. And by adopting two exceptional orangutans, of course. I smiled. We had an amazing story that could never be told.

Back at the beach, the ship loomed even larger in the distance. I said, "Jo and I are going to go say goodbye to BigBoy and Frank and make sure they stay put. Don't leave without us."

We ran into the trees and when we approached the area where I'd viewed the ship earlier, I hollered for BigBoy. He immediately dropped to the ground in front of me and clucked, taking my hand in his. He grinned at Joanne and woofed hello. "Do you want to carry us up into the tree one more time, big fella?" He hauled, I screeched, and up we went. He deposited me next to Frank who uttered a friendly woo-woo and then climbed back to the ground for Joanne.

Sitting between the apes, we each took a big hairy paw. I said, "I have something for you." I pulled out the two new hats I'd made and handed one to each of them. They smiled and took the old, battered hats off, placing the new ones on their heads. Frank's, of course, was set at a rakish angle. BigBoy wore his straight on, the brim pulled as low as it would go – sometimes I wondered how he could see where he was going. I smiled and said, "You're both the most handsome orangutan people I've ever seen." I stroked their arms and they giggle-screeched happily.

Joanne smiled forlornly and said, "I'm going to miss you guys." She put her arm around Frank and gave him a hug, scratching his back gently. We were quite the foursome, sitting there in the tree.

Sadly, I said, "The ship is almost here." Frank pointed. "Yes, it's nearly at the lagoon. After they anchor, the noisy helicopter will start. Remember, I told you not to be afraid and not to try and protect us from it." Both apes nodded. "Good. When it starts, we have to go back to the beach and you guys need to stay here. Okay? You watch from up here." They nodded again.

Joanne and I stood and my throat tightened as tears filled my eyes. "I love you. I love you both. You remember that." Both apes wrapped their long arms around us and held us close in a group hug. Tears spilled over and ran down my face, dripping onto Frank's arm. He leaned back and looked at the drop. Inspecting my cheeks, he scooped up a tear and looked at the wetness on his finger. Placing the drop on his own cheek, he whimpered and placed his hand over his heart.

BigBoy sniffed and I saw tears running down his face, too. Simultaneously, he and I put our hands over our hearts and I burst out bawling. Sobbing, I heard the chopper rotors start and knew we had to go. I placed my hands on either side of Frank's face and kissed him on the cheek; he ape-kissed me back. When I turned to BigBoy, he lipped my cheek and pulled me into a bear hug. He held me tightly and I wondered if he was going to let go.

I heard the sound of the chopper growing louder as it soared over the lagoon. Joanne took my arm and said, "Come on, Lissy, we have to go." It was time. I murmured, "I love you, BigBoy," and started to pull away. Without releasing me, he leaned back and stared deep into my eyes. I could see his thoughts churning, some inner turmoil tearing him apart.

Then he let go and I said, "Goodbye, BigBoy. I'll *never* forget you! Now, take me down. Hurry! Frank, you carry Joanne." BigBoy hefted me over his shoulder and scooted to the ground with Frank right behind us. But instead of setting us on our feet, the apes dashed through the trees toward the beach. I said, "No! No, BigBoy, Frank, you have to put us down. Stop!" I struggled futilely in his gentle yet iron grip.

When we were about twenty feet away from the tree line, the orangutans stopped and placed us safely on the ground. I turned and said, "Go! Go back!" I saw the tears in BigBoy's eyes as he turned away. I watched until they made the bend in the trail and I dried my eyes as Jo and I dashed onto the beach.

Tom was slowly picking up dive gear and carrying it to the chopper, giving us time to rejoin the group. Under his breath, he said, "What took you two so long? I was about to tell them you had diarrhea or something."

"Sorry." Pasting a smile on my face, I turned to the rescue crew. "Sorry we're late. We had to make a last-minute trip to the latrine. We're just so excited to be going home!"

"No problem! I'm glad you're all okay. Bet you have one helluva story. Here, let me take that." The crewman grabbed my dive gear and stowed it in the rear of the chopper. We were ready. The last to board, I sat next to the window and would have a clear view of the beach, the lagoon, and the trees where I knew BigBoy and Frank watched. Joanne and I locked eyes, both of us still fighting tears over the poignant goodbye.

The engine revved, rotors whirled, and in only moments I felt the skids leave the sand. We rose lazily into the air and turned to face the water, swinging slowly out over the shoreline. From this height, I could see numerous sharks cruising the lagoon and was very thankful we weren't attempting a boat rescue.

Relieved yet emotional at leaving the whole ordeal behind, I sighed and leaned my head back against the seat. With an uninterrupted view of serene blue water, a white sand beach ringed with lightly swaying palm trees, and the thicker green of the jungle, I thought, *It's beautiful, but I am sooooo ready to head home.*

Just then, an enormous shark leapt straight up out of the water toward the helicopter. I shrieked as the cavernous open mouth exposed glistening, razor-sharp teeth. I grabbed Rigo's arm in terror and shouted at the pilot, "Higher! Go higher!" He pulled back on the stick and gunned the engine. It screamed and the craft shot toward the sky. I could no longer see the shark from this angle, but felt a distinct jolt as his snout slammed into the underside of the chopper.

"Oh, my God! Oh, my God!" Joanne fell to pieces as the pilot struggled to regain control of the wildly gyrating craft. We spun and twirled, quickly losing altitude. I feared another shark would leap from the lagoon and snatch us out of the sky.

The helicopter finally leveled out and the pilot once again aimed it skyward. We rose rapidly, putting substantial air between us and the aggressive beasts.

"I've never heard of a shark attacking a chopper." The pilot's voice was calmer than mine would have been, had I strength enough to answer him. We soared to the ship and settled softly onto the deck. My knees nearly buckled as the crewman helped me out of the aircraft and I staggered unsteadily to the rail, needing something sturdy to hold me up.

The four of us congregated at the rail and stared toward the island, momentarily speechless and emotionally drained. I replayed the attack over and over in my mind and it seemed that each time, the gaping jaws drew closer. I shuddered.

Turning from the rail, I watched the crew unload our gear. A crewman approached and invited us to join the captain for dinner; at that time, our questions would be answered. He then showed each of us to individual cabins with private showers that included soap, shampoo, toothbrush, and toothpaste. Jo and I immediately disappeared inside. Tom and Rigo headed to the salon for a beer, invited by another member of the rescue team.

After showering, I found a set of fresh clothes on the bed – a size too large but spotlessly clean – and I happily donned them, mentally thanking whoever had made the arrangements. I found Joanne, also clean and similarly clad, and we joined the guys in the salon. They were on their second beer, now relaxed and best friends with Julio. He'd been a member of the rescue team for five years and said, "I've never performed a rescue and found people in such good physical condition. How long were you stranded?"

Before Tom had a chance to reply, I said, "Tom, Rigo, your showers await. Please take your smelly bodies off to your rooms and come join us again after. Go!"

We shooed them away and I answered Julio's question. "We were on the island for eighteen days. Thankfully, one of our divers had glass lenses in his mask and we used the sun to start cooking fires. We found fruit and vegetables growing there, so we didn't go hungry. I guess if you're going to be stranded on a deserted island, it wasn't too bad. The lagoon was beautiful, except for the sharks. We were lucky to make it to shore to begin with."

Julio had more questions, but I was afraid we'd let something slip, so I plied him with some of my own. "What time is dinner with the captain?"

"A crewman will come to your cabin at 1900 hours to escort your group to dinner." At my puzzled expression, he added, "I'm sorry, ma'am, that's 7:00p.m."

"Okay, thanks. And I don't mean to sound ungrateful, but do you have any idea what's being served? We've had about all the fish we can handle."

"The captain thought of that and suggested hamburgers with French fries, your choice of beverage." He smiled at my reaction.

"Great! That sounds delicious." Tom will be thrilled. "Do you have any coffee?" If he said yes, my wish would be granted.

"Yes, ma'am, right this way." Jo and I eagerly followed him to a counter at the rear of the salon and watched him pour two cups of steaming black coffee. "Cream? Sugar?"

"No, thanks, Julio, black is perfect. I've missed this more than anything else." I took a sip, burnt my tongue, and didn't care. "Mmm... this is delicious. Thank you."

Julio had other chores to attend to and took his leave. "I'll see you ladies at dinner."

Tom and Rigo rejoined us, freshly showered, shaved, and clad in clean clothes. "Boy, what an improvement! Ya'll smell better, for sure!" They laughed and helped themselves to a cup of coffee.

Teasingly, I said, "Guess what's for dinner?"

Making a face, Tom said, "Fish?"

Joanne and I laughed. "Nope. Burgers and fries."

"*Alright!* My dreams have come true. If they serve chocolate cake for dessert, I'll think the island was bugged and the whole thing was a set-up." Tom grinned.

Changing the subject, I said, "Can you *believe* that shark? I swear, I looked clean down his throat and could've counted his teeth he was that close."

"I felt his nose slam into the underside of the chopper. That was *way* too close for comfort." Former Navy man Tom had seen his share of sharks, but none so up-close and personal.

Rigo said, "Eet was bad. Too close to me."

Joanne quietly said, "I nearly wet my pants when the pilot lost control of the helicopter. I thought we'd survived everything, only to be brought down on our way to the ship. That would've been too cruel."

Thinking of that nearly disastrous flight, my thoughts wandered farther back to my final goodbye with the apes. I pictured BigBoy's face, his inner turmoil and the determination in his eyes – he was definitely struggling with something. If only I could've read his mind.

Then Tom gave us some shocking news. "I finished the log book right before we left the island. The last chapter was about the newest serum they'd given to two orangutans, a male and a female. It was supposed to help them bridge the language barrier, enabling them to speak. They hadn't had any results, yet, before loading the animals onto the ship to transport them to the other facility and, of course, we know the ship sunk off the coast."

I shot to my feet, struck with an incredible thought. The words tumbled out in a rush. "Wait! What if…? We all know that BigBoy is incredibly intelligent. There were times I could tell he wanted to communicate with more than woofs and apes sounds. He often seemed to struggle with some inner dilemma." I paced back and forth, my mind a-whirl. "You know how it is when you're trying to think of a specific word that has temporarily slipped away – that's what he seemed to be struggling with. Maybe he's the offspring of those two apes. He might've been trying to speak!" I plopped back down, my thoughts racing, seeing his face, his eyes. If only I had known this was a possibility – maybe I could've helped him find his voice.

"We'll never know, Lissy. And now BigBoy doesn't have any reason to try and speak – he has no one to talk to." Tom's comment made me incredibly sad. I envisioned BigBoy trying to communicate verbally with the other apes and never receiving a reply. A deep sigh expressed my sadness and frustration.

"Dinner's not for another hour. I'm going to lie down. Someone from the crew will escort us to the Captain's quarters so I'll see you then." Dejected, I traipsed back to my room and stretched out on the bed. *Ah, a real mattress.* It felt divine and in spite of my whirling thoughts, I immediately fell asleep.

Knock-knock. *Where am I?* I nearly fell off the bed when I rolled to the left, expecting palm fronds and dirt floor. *Time for dinner.* "Just a moment, please." I ran my fingers through my hair. The bathroom mirror proved I didn't look too rumpled, certainly presentable enough for a deserted-island rescue-ee.

I went to the door and found Julio waiting with Tom, Rigo, and Joanne. My stomach growled. I was ravenous and put thoughts of the island out of my mind, determined to enjoy the meal and, hopefully, get some answers to our many questions.

Joanne asked, "Did you get some sleep, Lissy?"

"Oh, yeah. I was dead to the world in two seconds flat. That mattress is heavenly."

Julio stopped in front of a door bearing a brass plaque that read "Captain's Quarters." He rapped and a pleasant baritone invited us to enter. Julio opened the door, stepped aside, and closed it behind us.

The room was larger and better appointed than our small cabins. Dark wood gleamed throughout, a white tablecloth adorned a large dining table set for eight, and candlelight reflected off crystal water goblets situated at each place setting. A tall, distinguished-looking gentleman stepped forward and introduced himself. "Good evening. Captain Rodriguez at your service. I hope you find your quarters sufficiently comfortable?"

"Absolutely, Captain! After living on a deserted island for three weeks, the cabins are downright lavish. Thank you." Tom addressed the captain and introduced everyone. "Captain, this is Rigo, Joanne, and Lissy. I'm Tom. It's an understatement to say we're thrilled to see you and your ship."

"We're happy to be of service. Sit down, sit down. Let's eat while the food's hot." Captain Rodriguez took the chair at the head of the table and we seated ourselves to his left and right. He rang a small bell and a white-apron-clad server appeared with a large tray. Thick, juicy hamburgers spilled out of fresh buns nestled alongside mountains of steaming French fries. Lettuce, sliced tomatoes and onions, and condiments of all kinds waited to garnish the feast. My mouth watered at the heavenly aroma.

As Tom added some of everything to his burger and fries, he said, "This is the meal I've dreamed of for the past several weeks. You've made me a very happy man, Captain."

Beer, coffee, soft drinks, fruit juice, and water were available to wash down the meal. No one spoke as we enjoyed the burgers done to perfection and the lightly salted, crispy-on-the-outside-but-well-done-on-the-inside fries. Manna from Heaven couldn't have tasted better.

When we'd eaten everything in sight, the waiter returned to collect plates and serve coffee and chocolate chip cookies. At this point, Tom asked the question foremost in our minds. "Captain, has there been any news of the other eight divers from our group? Was anyone else rescued?" We held our breath.

"Yes, Tom, several other divers were rescued. They said there were others in their group but that everyone had gotten separated in a ferocious down-current and violent thunderstorm. The dive boat operator, Captain Carlos, left you all in the water and returned to the mainland to avoid losing his ship. Why don't you tell me your story and I'll fill in the blanks."

Tom proceeded to tell the captain our tale, explaining how Sarah, Joanne, Robbie, and himself had ended up the last group to enter the water; how the down-current had pushed them toward the bottom of the sea; how they'd climbed the rocky up-thrusts before hurling themselves back into the current; how they'd seen their friends rushing by, possibly to their deaths. He told how Sarah had bolted for the surface and they'd watched her lifeless body wash away on the storm-tossed waves.

Then he turned the narration over to me and I described how Rigo and I had survived the storm; how we'd ridden the current into the lagoon and up onto the sandy beach. I portrayed how the sharks had almost attacked Tom, Robbie, and Joanne as they rode that same current into the lagoon.

"And that's how we all came to be stranded together on the same island. But we had no idea where anyone else from our group went or if they'd survived the current and the storm. Can you tell us who survived?" I waited, hoping it was a lengthy list.

The captain said, "Just a moment. I knew you'd ask – I have the list here." He stood and retrieved a paper from his desk at the back of the room. He adjusted his wire-rimmed glasses and held the paper up to better read the names. "Joe and Melissa Barber, Andy Zhoersky, Johann Chimanzo, and Piper Holmes. Those are the other survivors."

I hung my head, mourning the deaths of an additional three from our group. That made a total of five out of fourteen that had perished. It could have been worse, but that was nearly a third of us and it pained me to think of their families.

"Did the others wash up on shore somewhere or were they rescued at sea? Were they together or rescued separately?" Tom asked. We were still assembling the missing pieces of the puzzle.

"Joe, Melissa, and Andy washed up on an island. Johann and Piper were picked up at sea by a Mexican fishing boat." Captain Rodriguez was more than willing to answer our questions and we were grateful. "Joe, Melissa, and Andy were found the same day of the storm; Johann and Piper spent the night at sea and were spotted early the next morning. They were lucky." He pointed at us and said, "You folks were missing the longest. Your families are very concerned."

I needed to know. "Is everyone alright? No one was attacked by a shark or suffered the bends or an air embolism?" Again, I waited tensely for the answer.

The captain smiled. "Everyone's fine. They've all gone home. We'll weigh anchor in the morning and then high-tail it back to Cozumel. You ought to be on your way to the States in three days.

"I wish I could use the chopper to transport you to the mainland but I have strict orders. 'Only in the event of a life-threatening injury can the helo be used for transport.'" He smiled ruefully. "We're happy to help, but it comes with restrictions."

Tom said, "I'm retired U.S. Navy, Captain. I know all about restrictions. Believe me, we're just happy to be going home – an extra day or so isn't going to make any difference."

"Especially since we have beds to sleep in, hot showers, and something besides fish and fruit to eat." Joanne added.

"And coffee!" I smiled and took another sip.

The captain said, "I understand you lost two members of your group. You mentioned Sarah – who was the other?"

Tom continued his narration. "Robbie Thurmann. He was a retired professor and a good man. We went fishing one afternoon about two weeks into our stay and a wave knocked him off his feet. Before I could get to him, the current dragged him away and he was attacked by a shark. He never resurfaced. He had two adult children, but wasn't close to them and I doubt they even know he hasn't returned home."

After a moment of silence, the captain said, "I'm sorry about your friends."

We remained silent, adhering to our agreed-upon "say nothing if not asked" and waited for the captain to resume his questions.

Finally he said, "Well, I'm sure you're all tired. If you don't have any more questions for me, we can retire for the evening. If you want to sit up and discuss the new information, feel free to use the salon – there are more cold beers in the refrigerator."

"Thank you, Captain. We appreciate your hospitality." We stood and Tom shook the captain's hand.

"The meal was delicious!" I grinned with real gratitude. "Thank you so much for not serving fish." Everyone laughed.

"We'll weigh anchor at daybreak. Breakfast will be served at 0800 hours – 8:00a.m. Good night. Sleep well." The captain held his door open and we filed out, heading directly to the salon.

Too wound up to sleep and needing to discuss the new information, we found comfortable seats. Tom and Rigo grabbed a beer while Joanne and I opted for soda. Everything was ice cold – the smallest things seemed to make the biggest impression. We even found more of the gooey chocolate chip cookies displayed invitingly on the counter. They disappeared in no time.

I immediately jumped into the discussion. "We lost Mary, Jack, and Lucy. I didn't know them well; they were new divers. They probably panicked in that monster current, maybe ran out of air. I'm sure we'll never know the details. I'm glad the rest of them survived – I expected to hear we were the only ones. And no one suffered a debilitating injury. That's nothing short of miraculous. It could've been so much worse."

Joanne shivered. "Can you imagine floating around in the water all night? Johann and Piper must've been insane with fear."

"Sí, there are many sharks een the water een that area. They have much luck, for sure." Rigo hadn't said much during dinner.

"Are you okay, Rigo? You've been awfully quiet." I touched his hand and he closed his fingers around mine.

"Sí, I no want to say the wrong theeng, so say nothing. And I theenk of mi madre. She worry." He hung his head and added, "I am sorry for bringing you to the new dive place. Eet ees beauteeful but too dangerous. I am sorry for your friends."

Tom interrupted. "We don't blame you, Rigo. You and I have had our differences, but you're a good man and you were invaluable on the island. You saved my ass at least once. If you and Lissy are a 'thing,' you have my blessing as her friend." He held out his hand.

Rigo looked at Tom, looked at me, and clasped Tom's hand in a firm grip. "You are a good man, too, Señor Tom. I am happy that you are only friends to Leesa. What ees thees 'theeng' we might be?" He looked at me and I blushed. Everyone laughed.

"I'll explain it to you sometime, Rigo. Not tonight." I looked at my watch and realized it was almost 10:30. "I'm going to bed. That mattress was too comfortable to ignore any longer. See you in the morning." I waved good-night and headed to my room.

My head had no sooner landed on the cushy pillow than my eyes closed and I drifted into a dreamless sleep.

Hours later, my eyes flew open. *What did I hear?* I lay in the dark, listening, waiting. Eventually, I threw back the covers and pulled on a sweater I found in a drawer. Quietly unlocking and cracking open the door, I heard nothing – no one moved about on the ship. We bobbed gently in the small waves of the lagoon.

Padding to the deck, I glimpsed the crewman on night watch dozing at the helm – I couldn't blame him, considering the quiet stillness surrounding us. At the rail, I surveyed the glimmering scene. Toward the open sea, the moon hung heavy in the night sky and reflected off the silvery water as far as I could see. In the other direction, the peaceful lagoon belied the monsters lurking below the surface; palm trees swayed ever-so-gently in the soft ocean breeze. I could smell the rich earthy aroma of the jungle, slightly tinged with a sweet flowery scent. I tasted salt in the air and pulled the sweater tight around me – the nighttime temperature out here on the water cooler than I remembered when we were snug in our communal shelter.

Staring toward the trees, I pictured BigBoy and Frank asleep in their nests. I smiled sadly, missing them. With no idea what had awakened me, I turned and went back to my cabin, drowsy and convinced nothing was amiss.

I shrugged out of the sweater and snuggled under the covers. As I closed my eyes and relaxed, a faint voice intruded gently on the silence. "Lissssy…" I fell asleep to tiny waves lapping at the boat and the comforting sound of someone calling my name.

Chapter 23

Day 19

<u>Lissy</u>

A niggling thought intruded on my sleep and I woke, thinking, *what?* Lying abed, I recalled getting up in the wee hours and going above deck. Nothing had seemed out of place. What, then, was bothering me this morning? It was still dark, with just a hint of light beginning to chase the night away.

I wanted a last glimpse of the island. Pulling on the sweater, I cracked open the door – a repeat of last night. Strolling up to the deck, I heard no sound of movement and the night watchman was no longer asleep at the helm.

Standing at the rail, I watched the ambient light grow brighter by the moment. I stared hard toward the trees. *Were they up yet? Foraging for fruit? Or still asleep?* Suddenly, I saw movement in the canopy and strained to see. The trees seemed to sway more than the slight morning breeze warranted. There! A figure? An arm? A reddish-blond arm waved back and forth just visible in the faint light, its pale color distinct against the darker green of the leaves. And then I heard it. The same voice that had called to me in the night. "Lissssssssy. Lissssssssy. I love you."

A shiver ran down my spine, gooseflesh pimpled my arms, and my eyes flew wide in amazement. It was BigBoy! I wildly waved my arm back at him, letting him know I heard him and acknowledging his incredible accomplishment. I imagined his face, the pride and satisfaction in his eyes. I wished I could continue to encourage him, to help him become the most amazing orangutan in the world. Tears trickled down my face as I pictured him standing in the tree, tall and powerful, waving at me, loving me enough to find his voice.

"Lissy? What are you waving at?" Tom was up early, too.

"It's BigBoy. He called my name! He said 'I love you.' Listen." We stood together at the rail, silent, listening for a call that never came.

"Are you sure you heard your name?" Tom didn't quite believe that an ape could speak.

"I'm *absolutely positive!* I heard it last night, too," and told him how I'd come up on deck. "BigBoy must've watched the boat all night and seen me come out to the rail. Just before I fell asleep, I heard him call my name. This morning, I saw him in the trees and he waved at me. He called my name twice and said 'I love you,' but when you appeared at my side he stopped."

Afraid I'd draw unwanted attention to the island, Tom reiterated what we'd sworn an oath to protect. "Lissy, you know you can't tell anyone – other than us – what you heard, right? No matter how amazing it is, no one can know."

"I know, Tom. But now that I know BigBoy can speak, I wish I could spend more time with him, help him become even *more* amazing."

"What would be the point, Lissy? Without people on the island to talk to, BigBoy will revert to ape-talk, anyway."

"I know, I know. He was just so special." About then, I heard the engines rumble to life and knew this would be the last time I'd ever see the island – and BigBoy. I waved again but saw no answering signal from the trees.

Tom and I stayed at the rail as the crew weighed anchor. The ship began to swing around and soon faced open water. We moved to the stern and watched the island grow smaller and smaller, a dark, palm tree-studded bit of land in a vast expanse of ocean. Finally, Tom turned and leaned his back against the railing, the better to feel the breeze on his face.

Still staring toward the island, I saw a tiny silhouette lope, ape-like, from the trees onto the beach. It straightened up to its full height and waved one long arm back and forth. I would always be able to envision BigBoy waving goodbye. And in my mind, I would hear him say, "I love you, Lissy!"

GLOSSARY OF TERMS

Air embolism – When a diver breathes compressed air under water (scuba) and bolts to the surface while holding his breath, the compressed air expands and ruptures tiny air sacs in the lungs. Air bubbles enter veins or arteries causing heart attack, stroke, or respiratory failure.

BC (buoyancy compensator) – An inflatable vest worn by scuba divers to maintain neutral buoyancy in the water. Can be inflated manually by blowing into a tube or automatically by pressing a button that allows air from the tank to enter the vest.

NAUI Dive Tables – This chart shows the maximum time a diver can safely stay at any given depth for one or multiple dives without a decompression stop. Divers normally carry a laminated 5" x 7" card clipped somewhere onto their BC.

Octopus (secondary regulator) – a second regulator worn by divers to be used in case the main regulator fails, develops a leak, or for buddy breathing.

SCUBA – **S**elf-**C**ontained **U**nderwater **B**reathing **A**pparatus – a system comprised of a tank and regulator that provides air to a diver to allow him to breathe under water.

Offgas – spending a prescribed amount of time at a shallow depth to allow the body to eliminate nitrogen from the system.

During scuba diving, nitrogen in compressed air accumulates in the body.

The Bends (decompression sickness) – a condition arising from dissolved gases coming out of solution into bubbles inside the body upon ascent. Gases must be eliminated prior to surfacing or bubbles will lodge in the spine and various other locations, causing pain, paralysis, and possible death. Can be avoided by performing slow ascents, adhering to the bottom time posted in the NAUI dive tables, diving with a dive computer that monitors bottom time and decompression stops, and/or performing one or more decompression stops during ascent.

Nitrogen narcosis ("Rapture of the Deep") – Breathing compressed air at depths greater than 130 feet causes symptoms such as lightheadedness, poor judgment, increased anxiety, decreased coordination, hallucinations, coma, and death. Ascending to shallower depths reverses the effects.

AUTHOR'S NOTE

Thank you for reading *STRANDED*. I hope you enjoyed the adventure as much as I did. This book snuck up on me since it actually began as a scuba diving short story. However, like a writer friend of mine often says, "The boys in the basement voiced their opinions" and the tale morphed into something much more than I'd first envisioned. Before I knew it, I had a full-length novel on my hands. Imagine my surprise!

As you've probably surmised, scuba diving is one of my greatest passions and I thoroughly enjoy time spent underwater. Diving can be a very safe sport but the laws of physics cannot be broken without serious consequences.

The book's fierce down-current aside, the beauty and serenity of the undersea world is something that simply cannot be adequately described – it must be experienced to be appreciated.

But whether you're a diver or a non-diver and you enjoyed the underwater portion of the story as well as the deserted-island part, I'd truly appreciate it if you'd take a moment to write a review on Amazon. They are crucial to letting others know if you think it would be worth their time.

If you enjoyed STRANDED, you should also enjoy my novella titled "Saving Serena" – it, too, begins with a diving mishap but has some surprising twists.

You can read the first two chapters here. Enjoy!

SAVING SERENA

1

THE CALM, SUN-DAPPLED WATER surrounding the dive boat suddenly erupted with playful dolphins. The bright, late morning sunlight glinted off their wet bodies and all twelve divers squealed with excited anticipation. Each of us had longed for an opportunity to swim with the intelligent, curious animals, so when the easy-going captain threw up his hands, chuckled at our reaction, and laughingly hollered, "Okay! Go!" we grabbed our fins and leapt back into the water.

The sea closed over my head as I scanned the blue for their sleek, graceful forms, their sonar clicks and whistles seeming to come from all directions. Immediately, though, I knew something was wrong. Kicking fairly hard, I still descended much more rapidly than I should have. I groaned.

As the last diver to climb aboard the boat following our fifty-minute dive this morning, I hadn't shed all of my gear before the dolphins appeared. In my excitement, I had jumped off the boat still wearing mask, snorkel, and fins—and a ten pound weight belt.

Reluctant to send over a hundred dollars-worth of gear to the bottom of the ocean without trying to resolve the problem, I kicked harder, hoping I could reach the boat and grab the lowest ladder rung without releasing the belt. I gulped air and then sank below the surface, kicking madly toward the boat. Frantic kicks sent me back to the surface where I grabbed a quick breath and sank again. I repeated the process over and over and made slow but steady progress.

I was tiring. The combined effort of holding my breath and kicking forcefully enough to move upward and closer to the boat were taking their toll. I determined to make one last-ditch effort to reach the ladder. Then it was adios to the weight belt.

Okay, I was nearly there. I could see the ladder only a few feet ahead and above me. One powerful kick should get me close enough to grab the bottom rung.

As I lunged upward, one arm raised over my head to reach for the ladder, the boat rose lazily on a large swell and dropped heavily into the trough. Unfortunately, my lunge had positioned me directly below the corner of the stern. The metal rung hit my raised arm sharply, snapping the bone cleanly just below the elbow; the boat's impact with my skull drove my body deep below the surface.

Sometime later, my eyes sprang open to see endless deep blue water…above, below, and all around. I clawed and kicked and struggled, trying desperately to make my way to the hopelessly distant surface. As my heart beat a wild rhythm and adrenaline surged through my veins, my uncooperative right arm sent piercing daggers of pain up my shoulder.

I spotted sudden movement to the left and whirled to face it. What type of undersea creature might be approaching? A large turtle? An enormous fish? Or something more menacing? My heart continued its wild tempo as my eyes strained to put a definitive shape to the shadow in the distance, my lungs now screaming for air.

Immobile, exerting as little energy as possible while the form drew near, I was both fascinated and mystified as it assumed a definite female shape. It looked like… It couldn't be… They didn't *really exist,* did they? I wracked my brain in an attempt to recall if I'd ever heard of a documented instance of an encounter with a mermaid. Unless I was hallucinating, I was face-to-face with one of these mythical beings: a mermaid with the face and curvaceous torso of a lovely young woman and the muscular tail of a fish. UN-believable!

Reminiscent of Lady Godiva, her mass of long blonde curls drifted lazily around her body, first hiding, then exposing creamy white skin and full, firm breasts. Her narrow waist flared out at the hips where the skin blended seamlessly into blue-grey, overlapping scales that shimmered in the water. They reflected and magnified the muted ambient light like thousands of tiny mirrors.

Slowly, she swam closer. Mesmerized, I studied every detail of this amazingly graceful creature: high cheekbones, a patrician nose, full lips, and wide blue eyes. Her powerful tail slowly curved, unfurled, and curved again, providing stability and maintaining a vertical position in the water. Radiating curiosity, concern, and uncertainty, her face also expressed warmth and kindness.

Cocking her head slightly to the right, she examined me just as intensely as I scrutinized her. She seemed to understand my dire situation and smiled reassuringly.

Cautiously, I smiled back, almost against my will—and in total disbelief. Miraculously, my lungs no longer strained for air and my body relaxed. Breathing normally, I let out a sigh of relief even though I didn't understand a thing that was happening.

Encouraged by my smile, she floated up and extended her hand. Tentatively, I reached out to gingerly touch her fingers, nearly afraid I grasped for a mirage. At my touch, her smile widened, showing perfect white teeth and her strong fingers clasped mine in friendship. I flinched, shocked to find a tangible hand holding mine.

When her eyes darted past me, I let go and twisted fearfully in the water to see what was approaching from behind. Astonished, I discovered another mermaid stopping some distance away, her wavy black hair floating like long spider webs in the water. Light, café au lait skin, small, perky breasts, and a slim, almost boyish physique suggested a much younger age. The scales of her tail glistened a brilliant green at the hips then blended into a burnished copper at the bottom. Shy and seemingly afraid to draw near, she held back, her dark eyes wide with fascination and trepidation—this creature looked like her, yet did not. She hovered about a dozen feet away, gaping at my mask and snorkel and the neon pink Lycra wetskin encasing me from neck to ankle. The fact that I sported two legs instead of a fish-tail seemed cause for concern.

The blonde mermaid coaxed the brunette into swimming closer and motioned for her to take my other hand. I pointed to my broken right arm and vigorously shook my head, "No!" They understood my injury and the brunette darted off, purpose apparent in every flick of her tail.

When she reappeared a short time later with a ten-inch branch of coral and a length of kelp, she overcame her initial fear and helped the blonde splint my arm, using the strong fibers to secure it. Although they handled the limb carefully, I nearly blacked out from the excruciating pain. When my vision cleared, I could see empathy in their eyes. The blonde then floated in front of me and cautiously backed into my front. The brunette helped me wrap my good arm around the blonde's waist, gently sandwiching the broken limb between our bodies.

Using the remaining long piece of kelp, the brunette lashed us together. Once satisfied I was secure, the blonde swam slowly, jostling my arm as little as possible, and I appreciated her consideration.

Amazed at the power in the mermaid's tail at this slow pace, I could imagine being propelled through the water at astonishing speeds. I wondered at our destination since this had been a most amazing day and I suspected the surprises weren't over yet.

2

WE SAILED OVER sandy bottom, stands of spiky Elkhorn coral, and deep blue water, finally cruising to a halt at the edge of a coral reef. The brunette untied me and I watched the girls glide gracefully down the side of the drop-off to a nearly invisible opening hidden amidst some large boulders and lacy sea fans. Unwilling to be left behind, I followed and saw the young brunette disappear into the fissure. The blonde moved aside, smiled reassuringly, and motioned for me to enter.

Slightly apprehensive, I gently fluttered my fins and floated in through the opening. Narrow at first, the entrance widened as it curved slightly to the right. Once around the corner, the floor dropped away, the ceiling soared high above, and the unbelievable scene took my breath away. We hovered above an enormous cavern inhabited by many mermaids, mermen, and merkids going about apparently normal daily lives. But then, what was *normal* about any of this? I shook my head in an effort to dispel the hallucination but when I looked again, the image remained.

From this vantage point, I observed many couples and families; mermaids and mermen as different from one another as regular people, but all with those incredible, scaly-yet-beautiful, iridescent fish-tails. I noted that the tails came in a variety of colors: silver, gold, copper, green, blue, pink, and nearly everything in between. The mermaids looked strong and muscular while the mermen seemed slimmer and less physically imposing.

I tore my gaze away from the mesmerizing scene when the blonde motioned for me to follow her. I spotted the young brunette peeking around a nearby stone wall. She smiled shyly as we passed and ducked quickly out of sight. The blonde and I cruised along the wall to the floor of the cavern where an older couple relaxed while others served snacks.

As we neared the couple, I noticed a less casual demeanor in those speaking or interacting with this regal, more elderly pair. Heads bowed slightly when approaching or taking leave. No merkids scampered about. Individuals waited on them with obvious respect and reverence. I suspected this couple was held in high regard and possibly even ruled this underwater society.

The blonde stopped about fifteen feet in front of the pair and bowed her head dutifully. I followed suit, figuring it wouldn't do to offend the leaders when I so desperately needed their help. The elderly woman greeted my companion with a smile and apparent affection and I realized I could clearly understand them.

"Maia, who do you bring before us? She is quite visibly not one of our own."

Maia graciously introduced me. "Tinami and Saya, leaders of our sirene, I bring a lost one before you today, injured and in need of help. She is no threat to our people and comes as a friend. I ask for your compassion and wisdom in this matter. I hope to offer this lost one medical attention, food, and temporary lodging."

At their urging, Maia gave a detailed description of how she had found me drifting, injured and panicky.

Saya then addressed me. "Lost one, what name are you known by?"

As I opened my mouth to reply, this most familiar bit of information eluded me and I realized I couldn't recall my name.

Panic and confusion must have shown plainly on my face since Saya kindly intervened. "Don't worry. Often, a blow to the head causes memory lapse and the lump on your forehead indicates that may be the source of your forgetfulness. For now, we'll call you Serena."

Raising my hand to my throbbing head, I smiled gratefully and nodded my thanks as she continued her gentle questions.

"How is it you came to these depths? Humans rarely venture this deep."

I related as many details as I could recall, confirming her suspicion of a blow to the head. Suddenly, I wanted nothing more than a place to lie down, feeling a bit woozy.

Tinami and Saya discussed the situation in low voices.

I caught only a couple phrases: "injuries healed" and "return to the surface." As I awaited their decision, I felt weak from hunger and the stress of the day, my head and arm both throbbed horribly, and I had no idea how I could possibly return to My Life Before Today.

Finally, the royal couple addressed us. "Maia, take Serena to the vacant cubicle we use for occasional guests. She can stay until her injuries heal."

Saya then turned to me. "Serena, our doctor will see you immediately and a meal will be delivered to your room shortly. If there's anything you need, please ask. We don't have many guests and would like to take this opportunity to offer our complete hospitality." She directed one of the servants to fetch the doctor. Relieved, I smiled and bowed my head.

As Tinami and Saya turned to each other and began discussing a different topic, Maia and I slipped away. We swam past numerous family homes to an empty cubicle with an interesting-looking bed and small side table made of rock. She pointed and smiled kindly.

"Lie down and get some rest. The doctor will be here soon." She swam off, leaving me to take her advice.

I eyed the unusual bed and approached it for closer inspection. Comprised of half of a large clam shell, it contained several layers of sea fans atop a deep bed of soft sand. In spite of my situation, it looked inviting.

Lying down slightly eased the throbbing pain and that's where Maia found me a short while later. She gently woke me to introduce a thin, elderly mermaid with a kind smile named Kalani who'd come to address my broken arm while the doctor dealt with a sick child.

First, Kalani pressed her hand to my forehead like Mom used to do. Satisfied my temperature was normal, she then skillfully pried open an oyster shell and scooped the small, still-wriggling creature out into my hand. At my look of disgust, she smiled sympathetically. "It will help ease the pain as I set your broken arm. It'll also soothe your stomach and help you sleep. Please, chew it thoroughly and swallow quickly."

I had no reason not to trust her, so fighting revulsion I popped the little creature into my mouth. Chomping and gnawing on the stringy meat, I nearly gagged at its texture and bitter taste. Thankfully, saliva filled my mouth and helped wash the nasty bitterness off my tongue.

Kalani tenderly examined the contusion on my forehead. "You'll soon have a really ugly bruise here. The doctor should look at it tomorrow. If you develop a stabbing headache, severe dizziness, or impaired vision tonight, please send someone to fetch either the doctor or myself. Would you like someone to sit with you for a while?"

"I'll be fine. In fact, I'm feeling drowsy now. After the kind of day I've had, I doubt I'll have any trouble sleeping."

Convinced the medicinal oyster had taken effect, she deftly set my broken arm with a minimum of fuss or additional pain, finally wrapping it neatly with kelp. Once sure it was exactly right, she smeared a thick, dark, tarry substance over it and said, "This will harden in about fifteen minutes. You need to stay as still as possible until then." She kindly patted my shoulder, a gentle smile crinkling her eyes at the corners, and left Maia and me alone.

Maia stayed until the cast had hardened. A servant delivered a dinner tray as she was preparing to leave and I groaned inwardly at her parting words, wondering what the meal would consist of. "Please eat your dinner. It will help you regain your strength." She left and I turned to examine the repast before me.

In spite of a faint, lingering nausea, I gingerly tasted each item, surprised to find everything very flavorful. I savored the taste of lobster with a side salad of, could it be, kelp? I had no idea what spices they used down here on the ocean floor, but my tongue recognized the familiar tang of salt and pepper, as well as a delicate hint of rosemary and lemon. A small rounded shell containing something resembling a fruit cobbler tempted me to try dessert. A cobbler? Here? I tentatively took a small spoonful and the sweet flavor of unusual berries flooded my mouth. I gobbled the entire bowl, mentally thanking whatever mer-chef had prepared this delectable concoction.

I managed to down every morsel, although eating with my left hand forced me to eat slowly. With a full stomach and Kalani's sleep aid, I immediately dozed off on my sea-fan-and-sand bed and didn't wake until morning.

The lump on my head ached and I assumed I had a huge ugly bruise that would remain for quite a while, however, I suffered no further nausea. My arm still throbbed within the awkward cast, but the initial sharp pain of the break had lessened. In spite of the discomfort, I felt energized, couldn't wait to explore my surroundings and meet some of my neighbors, and hoped Maia would soon appear to show me around.

I impatiently peeked past the rough stone wall of my cubicle and surveyed a hustle-bustle of activity. It took a moment to realize I didn't see any mermaids, only mermen and merkids. As I pondered where the females might be, the young brunette who had helped Maia rescue me the day before appeared at my side, startling me out of my reverie.

"Good morning, Serena. My name is Kiki." She carried breakfast on a thin slice of rectangular stone and placed it on the bedside table. Ducking her head shyly, she said softly, "If you feel up to it, after breakfast I can give you a tour." She blushed and smiled at my eager response.

"Oh, yes, I'd like that!"

Kiki returned shortly after I finished eating the unusual granola ground and shaped into a bar. It seemed like a mixture of grains and nuts with some fruity berries thrown in—similar to the fruit in last night's cobbler.

She waited while I clumsily donned my fins. I wasn't accustomed to putting them on with only one hand, but knew I couldn't swim fast enough without them to keep up with her. We meandered through the enormous cavern, stopping often to chat with inquisitive neighbors. The merkids, especially, were enthralled by my legs and often swam up behind me to touch them with feather-light fingers. When I turned to smile at them, they giggled and darted quickly away, peering out curiously from behind the rock walls.

Recalling Kiki's shyness, I encouraged her to talk about her people. "Why is a group of mer-people called a 'sirene'?"

Blushing again, she related a fascinating tale. "Long ago, unlike today, there were no taboos about mer-people going to the surface. Our ancestors used to play in the surf and enjoy the warmth of the sun." She hung her head and paused for a moment before continuing. "Our lore tells of a group of beautiful young mermaids who lured a ship onto the rocks so they could play with the men, many of whom perished when the ship sank. Frightened and horrified at what they'd done, the mermaids swam into deep water and the remaining humans drowned. Since then, our kind have been called sirens and the name sirene has been adopted to indicate a group of mer-people—like a school of fish or a pod of dolphins."

I frowned, contemplating the tale, and asked another question. "Why am I able to breathe so comfortably?"

"I have heard stories of a few humans who have survived with us as long as they are in close proximity to mer-people. It used to happen more frequently when we were allowed to visit the surface, but from what I understand, it's been over one hundred years since humans have lived with us.

"Maia and I had pushed the limits of where we're allowed to go and were enjoying the warmer water where we found you. And since you are now surrounded by our kind, you are in no danger of drowning."

That explanation made as much sense as anything else I'd experienced recently so I turned my attention to the cavern and its inhabitants. Curious about not seeing any females, I asked, "Where are all the mermaids? I only see mermen and merkids."

As Kiki explained, I enjoyed the musical lilt in her voice. "Mer-people are like the seahorse people. The males have babies and raise the children. The mermaids take care of everyone by going out every morning to hunt for food."

Smiling broadly, she puffed out her pre-adolescent chest and boasted, "Next year, I'll be old enough to hunt with the women." Then she slouched and groused, "But until then, I have to stay with the men and the children. I'm old enough, really I am! What difference does one year make?" Her lower lip pushed out in a pout she murmured, "I feel like a glorified babysitter."

I remembered feeling too old to be a child and too young to be a woman and wanted to help Kiki believe she was doing something important. I peppered her with questions about life in the sirene and she was soon chattering happily in reply. We swam and talked as I absorbed information about this fascinating new world.

Completely engrossed in Kiki's answer to another of my many questions, I abruptly collided with someone exiting the common area. He had been looking the other way and his sharply exhaled "Oomph!" indicated I had hit pretty hard.

I yelped in pain at the impact and he quickly turned to face me. I completely forgot both the pain and the apology that was on my lips. Gazing into the greenest eyes I'd ever seen, I stammered, "Uh, um... Sorry... Wasn't looking... where..." My voice trailed off as my mind went blank.

Long dark lashes framed magnificent green eyes, silver hair with just a hint of curl brushed the back of his neck, and a strong, square jaw hinted at strength and determination. Drawn back to those eyes, I realized he was easily the best-looking man I'd ever seen. And that deep cleft in his chin had me longing to trace it with my tongue.

His murmured, "Excuse me" jolted me back to my senses.

"I'm *so* sorry. I was caught up in what Kiki was saying. Are you alright?"

His dazzling smile showed off full lips and even white teeth, the sexy combination threatening to send me on another mental journey elsewhere. Kiki rescued me again and introduced us. His name was Nathan and he chuckled softly and murmured, "What a beautiful name" when she told him I was called Serena.

With a twinkle in his eyes, he assured me he had survived our collision and then commented on the ugly bruise and the cast on my arm. "Are you in the habit of running into things?" he asked jokingly.

Flustered, I didn't want to launch into an implausible-sounding story so was greatly relieved when Nathan excused himself to go check on a child that began to cry nearby. As he swam away, I couldn't help but notice his muscular physique and the bronze-colored scales that deepened to a glittering black at the tail fin.

Young enough to be oblivious to the effect Nathan had had on me, Kiki launched into a sad story, complete with as many details as she could recall. I listened intently.

"Nathan was older than most mermen when he got married because he studied for a long time with the sirene's doctor. He needed to learn as much as he could before the old merman died. It's really important for every sirene to have its own doctor since we live far enough apart to not overlap when hunting. Finally, Tinami and Saya told Nathan he had to get married. I don't know why."

Kiki shrugged her shoulders and rattled on with her story, not realizing I hung on every detail. "They were only married a little while when Nathan's wife was killed in a hunting accident. It was a shark. And I guess our laws say he has to wait for two years before getting married again. But he doesn't seem to mind. I never see him with any of the mermaids, anyway. And he keeps busy helping with the merkids and taking care of anybody who gets sick. He's lucky since we're pretty healthy."

I tuned out some of her ramblings. *Hmm… That means those green eyes aren't spoken for.*

My head and arm had begun to throb in earnest and after the collision with Nathan I had to constantly drag my errant thoughts back to Kiki's monologue. Since I could no longer concentrate on her tour, I suggested she lead me back to my cubicle. There, I stretched out on the bed where visions of green eyes and silver hair brought a faint smile to my lips. I fell into a deep and restful sleep.

Other Titles by Beverley Scherberger

Saving Serena
http://www.amazon.com/dp/B01KSB3Y4O

Legacy of the Fallen Angel
http://www.amazon.com/dp/B071VZP7FR

The Problem with Men
http://www.amazon.com/dp/B01MQM8RCY

The Accidental Filmmaker
http://www.amazon.com/dp/B073Z4MWBJ

Savage Isle
http://www.amazon.com/dp/B0788BSD5J

.

Made in the USA
Middletown, DE
28 August 2020